# *Dirty* DIX

# *Dirty* DIX

International Bestselling Author

MONICA JAMES

*DIRTY DIX*



Cover Design: Perfect Pear Creative Covers
Cover Models: David Tomasic and Michelle Lancaster
Photographer: Monica James
Formatting: E.M. Tippetts Book Designs

Follow me on:

authormonicajames.com

# OTHER BOOKS BY
# MONICA JAMES

**THE I SURRENDER SERIES**

*I Surrender*

*Surrender to Me*

*Surrendered*

*White*

**SOMETHING LIKE NORMAL SERIES**

*Something like Normal*

*Something like Redemption*

*Something like Love*

**A HARD LOVE ROMANCE**

*Dirty Dix*

*Wicked Dix*

*The Hunt*

**MEMORIES FROM YESTERDAY DUET**

*Forgetting You, Forgetting Me*

*Forgetting You, Remembering Me*

**SINS OF THE HEART DUET**

*Absinthe of the Heart*

*Defiance of the Heart*

**ALL THE PRETTY THINGS TRILOGY**

*Bad Saint*

*Fallen Saint*

*Forever My Saint*

*The Devil's Crown-Part One* (Spin-Off)

*The Devil's Crown-Part Two* (Spin-Off)

**THE MONSTERS WITHIN DUET**

*Bullseye*

*Blowback*

**DELIVER US FROM EVIL TRILOGY**

*Thy Kingdom Come*

*Into Temptation*

*Deliver Us From Evil*

**IN LOVE AND WAR**

*North of the Stars*

*Fall of the Stars*

**STANDALONE**

*Mr. Write*

*Chase the Butterflies*

*Beyond the Roses*

*Someone Else's Shadow*

# One

*Dixon*

"I just…can't…stop…eating…them," says the luscious woman in front of me, inhaling her third Twinkie in one big bite.

I really shouldn't be focusing on anything other than helping her. That's why she's here, after all. But I'm not. And that's because the way her plump, supple mouth gobbles down on that golden sponge has me envisioning that it's my dick she's devouring like it's her last meal, not the damn Twinkie.

Shifting subtly in my leather seat, I tell my cock now is not the time to rear its sinful head as I'm here to help Sharon with her addiction.

According to the ever-resourceful Wikipedia, addiction is "the continued repetition of a behavior despite adverse consequences, or a neurological impairment leading to such behaviors."

So what triggers an addiction? What makes people like

Sharon here completely and utterly addicted to something they can no longer function without? I mean, it sounds ridiculous that we can't stop certain behaviors because we *are* the ones in control of our actions—no one else but ourselves.

So maybe it's a habit. But a habit is done by choice; therefore, we could stop if we wanted to. So, in that case, maybe it's a repressed memory biting at our heels, and we're just using that as an excuse to get high, drunk, STD-ridden, or—in Sharon's case—unable to function without Twinkies.

We all have addictions, whether big or small, in one form or another, and we human beings are complex characters that either deal with it or sweep it under the rug and just don't talk about it. But the people who do want to talk about it, whatever their addiction, come and see me.

My name is Dr. Dixon Mathews, and for five hundred dollars an hour, one can unload their deepest, darkest secrets and leave my office feeling healed and reborn. Most people just want the confirmation that nothing is wrong with them and their abnormal tendencies aren't that abnormal after all. And my patients get that from me. They get the verification from one of New York's top psychiatrists that their need to eat cat hair or masturbate in public is normal.

In just a few sessions, I pledge that my treatment will cure them of their neurotic behavior, and they can blend back into society where citizens are none the wiser that they are walking amongst some batshit-crazy loony tunes.

The reason I can guarantee this is because the majority of people who walk through my doors just want to whine and complain, and once they get whatever the hell off their chests, most see the light and stop with the crazy. The small minority who do have earnest issues, I prescribe the ever-reliable benzodiazepines to treat their insanity, and the world thanks me for creating another pill-popping, asocial zombie.

So call me a bastard, but at thirty-two years of age, I think I'm allowed to be a little jaded and apathetic toward society. You would be too if you had to listen to the same old sob story day in and day out from the spoiled, rich folk who never had to work a hard day in their life. Yet they come to me with pathetic stories of injustice and wrongdoings, totally oblivious to how lucky they really are.

As Sharon is droning on about the woes of her life, I think back to my original question. What triggers addiction? Many trained professionals have stated that the causes of addiction vary considerably, but they are generally caused by a combination of physical, mental, circumstantial, and emotional factors. But me, I know addiction comes down to one simple, primitive concept.

Desire.

Whether we desire success, beauty, food, alcohol, drugs, nicotine, porn, or sex, the result is the same—we all want to experience the euphoria that comes with these factors, and that's *what* we become addicted to. The actual trigger differs from person to person, but in the end, we all just want to be… happy. And in most circumstances, desire leads to pleasure.

People with addictive personalities blow their addiction out to creepy levels, but the majority of us just dabble in our addictions to achieve that happiness, that euphoria because we're human, and we crave the proverbial "happily ever after."

I told you I'm good.

"Dr. Mathews," Sharon says in a small voice. "Shouldn't you

be writing this down?"

Nodding, I refocus my distant eyes on her. "How about you tell me a little more about your father?" I suggest softly, giving her a gentle smile.

And five, four, three, two…one.

Right on cue, I witness Sharon's full bottom lip tremble, and her eyes well with tears.

"There's nothing to say," she states, crossing her arms over her bountiful chest as she bites her lip to stop the tears.

"How would you describe your relationship with him?" I press, casually crossing my legs while attempting to hide my imminent erection as I try not to stare at her tits.

"It's fine." She sniffs, curling in on herself, her bright red hair shrouding her tears.

We all have a trigger, and I've come to learn that the trigger for a lot of women is their nonexistent fathers.

So like I said, call me a bastard because a shitload of daddy issues also means one thing: trying to find the perfect father figure to fill that vacant, loveless void. These women unconsciously seek out their future mate, using their asshole daddies as the blueprint for what they're looking for in a companion. Or in some circumstances…a fuck.

Suddenly, my dick becomes very, very interested in Sharon Witherstone. Yes, we all have a trigger, and just like everyone else, I want to find my happily ever after. And at the moment, my HEA is bending Sharon over my desk and fucking her senseless.

I may be certified in solving other people's problems, but I'm a lost cause. I'm an asshole, and each day I'm losing sight of who I am and who I once was.

I'm not a total prick, however, and I make women just like Sharon Witherstone feel good because sex without emotional ties is so much easier than…feeling.

Placing my notepad onto the armrest, I slowly stand and peer down at Sharon, giving her a smile that I know will disintegrate her underwear in seconds. She raises her eyes, and I can see the confusion flicker behind them. But as her gaze descends down my hardened body, that confusion turns to… desire.

Her entire demeanor changes and out comes daddy's little girl as she shifts in her seat, pushing out her chest daringly. It's really too easy, but I prefer easy as opposed to working hard, putting your heart and soul on the line, only to find out your fiancée is sleeping with your best friend.

So this is much easier.

"Do you love your father?"

"No, I hate him," she confesses in a seductive whisper while biting her lip.

"Oh? Would you be comfortable telling me why?" I take a seat near her on the leather sofa, ensuring our knees are only inches apart.

"Because he loves my stepmother more than me," she replies, her lust-filled stare focusing on my lap as my erection is no doubt poking through my pressed slacks.

"I'm sorry to hear that," I tenderly coo. However, I don't mean a single word. "That must be very hard on you."

"Yes, it is. It is very *hard*." She nods, and I feel a single finger slide deliberately up my thigh toward my crotch.

Opening my legs in welcome, I ask, "Is that what you think triggered your addiction?"

"What can I say, Dr. Mathews? When something delicious is in front of me, I just can't say no," she huskily purrs, her fingers dancing around my straining fly.

"Well, sometimes," I whisper, "it's okay to say yes." I know, I'm going to hell.

And that's all the trigger Ms. Witherstone needs as her head dives into my lap, her fingers fumbling with my zipper.

As her warm, hungry mouth wraps around my red-hot erection, I close my eyes in disgust. I'm disgusted at myself for using someone I have no intention of ever seeing again. But I never said I was the hero of this story or even the good guy.

However, who wants to be good when it feels so *good* being *bad*?

# Two

*Dixon*

Reaching for the jacket off the back of my high-backed leather seat, I try not to recoil when I see my paperwork slightly askew. Memories of Ms. Witherstone's face pressed into my mahogany desktop while I fucked her from behind come flooding back, and I make a quick beeline for the exit before I throw up.

Locking my door, I see that my receptionist, Susanna, is still here.

"Ms. Vale, you should have left hours ago," I reprimand, as it's now seven thirty.

"Oh, that's okay. Leroy is out of town fishing with his buddies, so I don't mind working late," she replies with a nod, her gray hair bobbing with the motion.

Susanna Vale should have retired years ago, but she keeps telling me she's not ready to hang up her hat just yet. Good help is hard to find, so I'm not going to argue with her.

"Well, make sure you note how many extra hours you've worked, and I'll ensure Nancy pays you."

"Oh, Dr. Mathews," she protests with a wave of her wrinkled hand, "don't be silly. Who else is going to make sure you leave at a decent hour?"

I give her a small smile because it's true. On more than one occasion, Susanna has sent me home at an ungodly hour, but I went home to what? I returned to my empty Manhattan condo, which reminded me too much of *her*. Even after twelve months, her presence, her essence, lingers in the walls.

Shaking aside those unwelcome memories, I play it cool, not wanting my nostalgia to show. "If only you were ten years younger," I tease, finishing the sentence with a playful wink.

"Oh, you beast." She shoos me out the door. "Go get something to eat…you skipped lunch."

I blanch at her comment, as my lunch break was occupied with eating—just not food. With that heinous thought in mind, I quickly bid my assistant good night and catch the elevator down to the ground floor. I'm meeting my two best friends, Finch and Hunter, at a local bar around the corner. We were once a foursome, but that was a lifetime ago when I believed in loyalty and love.

"Here he is. Dr. Love has entered the building," shouts Hunter from across the room when I walk in.

His loud, obnoxious voice alerts me to where he sits, but of course I know where to find him because he never leaves the bar.

"Holy fuck balls," he loudly curses, narrowing his eyes. "You totally got laid today." He raises his Budweiser in salute while Finch chuckles.

"How 'bout you shout a little louder? I don't think our neighbors in New Jersey heard." I smack the back of his head playfully.

Taking a seat near Finch, I raise my hand, alerting the pretty blonde behind the bar to my presence. She gives me a small wink while mixing a cocktail.

"So who's the lucky girl?" asks Finch, nudging me in the ribs with a sharp elbow.

"I don't remember." I snag his drink and take an unsatisfying sip. "Ugh, where's the rum?" I cough, nearly gagging on the watered-down Coke.

Finch laughs while twirling his gold wedding band with a smile. "Gotta look after Gabriella in the morning. Heidi has some mothers' club thing, so I'm on baby duty."

I nod because that's what responsible parents do. They don't go out with their single, man-whoring friend, who is looking to get drunk and drown his sorrows in a bottle of Jack jammed between the tits of some blonde barfly. That's what a typical Friday night for me is like, but for Finch, who has been married for two years to the love of his life, Heidi, Friday night consists of one nonalcoholic drink with his best buddies before going home to his hot, loving wife and having amazing, freaky sex.

With that thought in mind, I reach past him and snatch Hunter's beer.

"You look like shit," Hunter states, and as much as I love his honesty, I really am not in the mood.

But he presses, regardless of me clamming up. "It's been a year, man." He holds up a finger just in case I didn't hear him, but I got it, loud and clear.

"I don't want to talk about this," I object with a firm shake of my head and quickly chug the contents of my stolen beer.

"We're just worried about you," Finch joins in, his gray eyes softening when he witnesses my emotional retreat.

"I'm fine," I retort, really needing another drink.

I try to flag down the bartender, but the crowd has suddenly grown, and she's attending to other thirsty patrons.

"Do you want your dick to fall off?" Hunter bluntly demands.

"Excuse me?" I'm unable to wipe the smile from my face, amused by his melodramatics.

"You heard me." He leans forward, his huge body invading Finch's small frame.

"No, Hunter, I do not want my dick to fall off. Get to the point already," I reply, rolling my eyes.

"Well, that's what's gonna happen if you keep boning these random girls."

"I seriously doubt that." I scoff, but Finch nods, obviously agreeing with Hunter.

"Chicks instantly drop their panties the moment you flash those big baby blues their way. It really is too easy, and in turn, you're becoming New York's biggest manwhore," Hunter declares. His bluntness suddenly pisses me off.

"When did you turn into such a pussy?" I bark at him, narrowing my eyes. "I expected it from him…" I gesture with my head toward Finch. "No offense," I add, and he shrugs, not at all offended.

"But you, man," I say to Hunter. "Last I checked, you had no problem screwing random chicks. So quit it with the holier-than-thou crap."

I'm getting pissed off rather quickly, but when I get advice from Hunter, who of all people shouldn't be lecturing me about my hookups, I can't help but lose my cool. I've known these boys for the majority of my life. We did everything together. Therefore, I know the shit we've done, especially Hunter.

Finch, however, has been our voice of reason. He's saved us from many situations that could have turned sour if not for his levelheadedness. But Hunter has always been wild and free.

I love these two morons like brothers. They've seen me at my worst and never once judged me until now.

"What's with the third degree?" I ask, calmed down somewhat.

Finch nervously lowers his eyes, and I still have no fucking clue what's happening.

When Hunter sees my confusion, he clarifies. "We're worried, man. Next week is…you know?"

"No, I don't know. Are you high?" I loosen my navy tie as it's suddenly suffocating me.

Finch's thin lips pull into a tight line, which is never a good sign.

"Spit it out, Finch."

"It's the thirteenth," he replies, finally meeting my eyes.

"Yeah. And?" I question with a baffled shrug.

"Oh, dude." He sighs, and I can hear the pity in his tone. "It would have been your one-year anniver—" He suddenly pauses, not wanting to fill in the blanks.

One year?

Holy shit. One year ago, I would have been married to the love of my life, Lillian Davis. Just thinking her name makes me want to dig my brain out with an ice cream scoop.

If I believed in soul mates, then Lily was mine. We met

three years ago in a line at Starbucks, and it was love at first macchiato. I proposed to her halfway through our relationship because we were happy and ready to take the next step. Well, I was. But I believed she was too until she met my buddy Leo.

Leo also grew up with Hunter, Finch, and me in New Jersey and moved to the Big Smoke with us. But Leo obviously didn't value our friendship the way I did because he fucked Lily behind my back for months.

Lily dumped me six weeks before our wedding because she was in love with Leo. I couldn't accept the words coming from her lips, but her words became crystal clear when she showed me the reason behind her recent weight gain. Not only was she in love with my best friend but she was also having his baby. I knew it wasn't mine because we hadn't had sex in over three months. I know, I know, I should have seen the warning signs, but love is blind and all that crap.

So things couldn't get any clearer after that.

She blamed her infidelity on me, stating she never saw me and I put work first. I *did* put work first, but only so I could pay for the three-carat diamond on her finger and the lavish, upscale Manhattan condo she insisted we buy.

I did all of this for her. And she thanks me by screwing my best friend and bearing his spawn.

So after she left me, I went a little wild.

But this lifestyle is no longer just a phase—it's who I am. I've become addicted to senseless, shameless sexual acts with random women, knowing that, on some level, I'm hoping to replace the face of the one woman who took an ax to my heart and hacked into it, leaving behind a bloodied, broken mess of the man I once was.

But these hookups are slowly losing their appeal, and I'm afraid I'll wake up one day and no longer recognize the person staring back at me in the mirror.

So there you have it, that's my life in a nutshell. I eat, sleep, work, and fuck because that's what I have to do to survive. It's a sad, miserable existence, but it's better than being a love-sick puppy, pining after a woman who doesn't give a damn.

Snapping back into the now, my shields slip into place, and I try my best to appear nonchalant. "Big deal. I'm over it. I'm over *her*."

Finch frowns while Hunter disputes my claim. "No, man, you're not. If you were, then you'd have no problem with me telling you that Leo the Ass and Lily the Whore are getting married next month."

"Jesus, Hunter!" Finch scolds, shaking his head.

"What? If he's over it, me telling him this shouldn't be a problem," Hunter states with a shrug.

Hunter's tactlessness doesn't bother me in the slightest. His statement, however, does.

"She's *marrying* that asshole?" I spit out, disgusted, but more so, I'm hurt.

What does he have that I don't? I swallow down my defeat and repulsion, and need to get the hell outta Dodge before I fucking lose it.

"Dixon," Finch says with nothing but pity in his tone, but I don't want his sympathy.

Wiping my mouth with the back of my hand after finishing my lukewarm, stolen beer, I stand, hoping my friends understand why I need a minute alone.

"I'm going out for a cigarette." I pat down my jacket pockets to find my smokes.

Thankfully, they let it go and don't make a fuss when I push through the massive crowd. As I step outside onto the pavement, I light a Marlboro and take a much-needed drag as I lean back against the brick wall.

I would be a liar if I said I never thought of Lily because I think about her more often than I care to admit. I gave up on the dream of reconciliation long ago, but deep down, I wished her relationship with Leo had failed.

My life is a mess, and the only person I could talk to about this is dead.

My mom passed away six months ago from breast cancer, and the loss destroyed my father. He had a major mental breakdown and now resides at Sunnyfields Hospital. Ironic, isn't it? Dixon Mathews, New York's finest shrink, can't even help his own father.

Automatically taking a drag of my cigarette, I'm lost in the past—a place I'd rather not be. So when I hear the animated voices of a couple to my left, I welcome the distraction.

Turning to see what the commotion is all about, I see a short brunette being manhandled by a meaty jock, who is jerking her a little too roughly by her upper arms. She's fucking tiny, and his huge paws are going to snap her into two.

"Let me go," she scowls, attempting to pull out of his grasp.

I'll give her points for trying, as she looks like she's putting up a pretty good fight. But this asshole has about a hundred pounds on her.

Flicking my smoke into the gutter, I decide to intervene, as it's pretty obvious she's trying to get away. Her anxious green eyes flick in my direction when I approach, and she silently pleads with me to help her.

"How about you let her go," I say firmly, and the wildebeest turns my way with a cocky grin.

"How about you mind your own business, old man," he replies with a deep Southern accent.

*Old man?*

Fuck this little pubescent jerkoff.

"How about you mind your manners? Let the lady go."

"Or what?" he chides, but thankfully he loosens his grip.

"Or I'll call the police because from where I stand, those marks on her arms—" I point at her biceps as he releases them "—are a clear indication that you're a lowlife douchebag who likes to beat up on women to make yourself feel like a man. What's wrong?" I mock. "Trying to act all tough 'cause you want to make up for what you're lacking?" I hold up my pinkie.

The girl giggles, but quickly stifles her outburst with her hand when douchebag turns and glares at her.

"Ah, c'mon, there are pills you can take for your anger, and also, for your little *problem*," I say in a sarcastic whisper as I point at his crotch.

His face blazes a bright red and I can't help but laugh because questioning a dude's manhood always has the desired effect. I can see him mentally sizing me up, and he knows there is no way he can take me on. This guy is big, but he's jacked up on too many steroids, and his ridiculous, air-inflated muscles wouldn't pack a punch.

"So how about you do the world a favor and fuck off? Go work off that anger with some tweezers and a photograph of your mom."

This time, the girl bursts out into fits of laughter, and the sound is utterly magical.

"Fuck you," douchebag snarls. He leaves in a huff when he realizes this is a fight he's bound to lose.

We both watch as he rounds the corner, and when I'm certain he's not coming back, I turn to look at the woman in front of me.

During my tirade, I failed to notice that she is a total babe. She's young, I'm guessing twenty-three, but holy shit, she's beautiful. Large green eyes complement a head of long, brown hair which sits just past her shoulders. Her full lips are the prettiest pink I have ever seen, and when her mouth tips up into a timid smile, I know I'm staring like a creepy old man.

Quickly composing myself, I ask, "Are you okay?" and make a point of looking at her arms.

She wraps her small fingers around her left bicep, as if attempting to hide the red finger marks. "I'm…fi-fine," she stutters unconvincingly, but quickly recovers. "I'm fine. Thanks for the save."

"No problem." I'm mesmerized by the way her straight teeth tug at her lower lip because in no way is she doing this on purpose.

She's not openly flirting with me, or trying to get into my pants, and honestly, it's like a breath of fresh air. She's simply a hot, young, innocent girl with no ulterior motives, and no expectations to where our strange, yet electrifying encounter might lead.

I've forgotten what innocence looks like—how fucking sad is that?

"I'm Madison," she says, extending her hand, and my huge palm dwarfs her tiny one as we shake.

"Dixon," I reply with a genuine smile.

"So do you make it a habit of rescuing damsels in distress?" she says, tongue in cheek as Madison is not that. She can hold her own. I saw that.

"What can I say, it's a hobby of mine," I reply with a casual shrug, and Madison laughs.

"Well, Dixon, thank you again for coming to my rescue." I nod, letting her hand go as I realize I'm still creepily shaking it.

"Anytime. Are you sure you're okay?" I ask as I don't fail to see a small shiver pass through her body.

"Honestly, I'm okay. His bark is worse than his bite."

I notice she doesn't elaborate on who her assailant is. I want to say more, but for once, me, the fancy, sweet-talking shrink, is speechless. And the reason for that is because I have a feeling Madison would see through my bullshit and call me out for the fake I am.

"Maddy? Are you out here?" asks a concerned voice from behind us.

We both turn, and I suddenly have the urge to grab my nuts to protect them when I see a flaming redhead storm our way. She glares at me before focusing on Madison.

"Are you okay?"

Madison nods.

"I'm fine," she replies, giving me a small smile as she extends her hand my way. "This is Dixon."

Her friend looks at me, making it no secret she's sizing me up. "Where did dickhead go?" she asks, totally ignoring me, and I smirk, as I like this girl's spunk.

Madison brushes a tendril of hair behind her ear and frowns. "Oh, he left. Dixon saved the day," she reveals, giving me a shy smile.

Her friend looks at me once again and this time, it doesn't appear she wants to skin me alive. "Well, in that case, it's nice to meet you, Dixon," and she gives me a small wave.

"Likewise," I reply. "And it was nothing. I was just in the right place at the right time."

Or wrong time, as the closer I look at Madison, the more intrigued I become. What is the matter with me?

"Well, regardless, thanks for looking out for my friend."

I give her a small, polite nod, as her protectiveness over Madison reminds me of my friendship with Hunter and Finch. Madison is, without a doubt, someone worth protecting. I mean, look at her.

I can't stop my eyes from darting over to her, and I'm surprised to see her returning my gaze. Her friend must also sense some weird stare off going on between us because she clears her throat, an octave higher than needed.

"Well, we better go back inside. Our friends are probably waiting for us," she explains, breaking my trance-like stupor.

*Dixon, don't be a chump, talk to her.* But what do I say? I haven't properly spoken to a girl in so long; especially not to a girl I actually *wanted* to talk to. I've forgotten how to communicate with the opposite sex—and "faster" or "fuck me harder" doesn't count. So like a wimp, I stand mute and smile.

"Okay, well, it was nice meeting you," Madison says, biting her lip, lingering.

"You too. Stay safe."

I restrain from groaning, as who the hell says "stay safe" other than your parents? I open my mouth, ready to add in a quirky response, but Madison is being dragged toward the entrance by her friend.

She suddenly turns over her shoulder and yells, "I work at The Pony Bar. If you're ever in the neighborhood, come visit."

Before I have time to reply, she's gone.

What the *hell* was that? Madison has left me standing on the pavement, now questioning *my* manhood.

Like a chickenshit, I let the first girl in forever who I actually liked, leave. I need to go back in there and talk to her. I need her to see what a great guy I can be. But that's the problem; I'm not a great guy. This week, I've fucked four different women, and I can't even their names. Or faces. They all blur into one disgusting regret, one I wish I could erase, but can't.

Girls like Madison are too good for the likes of me, and I'm doing her a favor by keeping away. However, tell that to my attentive dick, who became interested in Madison the moment she opened her mouth. Yes, she's fucking gorgeous, but the fact I didn't see her as a conquest is what I find myself most attracted to. I haven't felt that way since…Lily.

All thoughts of Lily come flooding back, and I suddenly remember why I was out here in the first place.

"Hey, handsome," purrs a voice, snapping me back into the here and now.

Raising my eyes, I see the blonde bartender from earlier addressing me, inches from where I stand.

"Hey." I quickly recover when I see her waiting for me to respond.

"I saw you inside." She motions with her head toward the bar while checking me out.

I know I'm not ugly, and if I were a chick, I'd probably want to fuck me, too. I've always been tall, but I stopped growing when I shot up to six foot three. My dark brown hair is short and groomed, and my blue eyes complement my trademark dark stubble; most days, I'm just too lazy to shave.

"Oh, yeah?" I ask, unbelieving at how easy this is.

"Yeah," she confirms with a slow nod, biting her glossy bottom lip. "Can I bum a smoke?"

"Sure." I search through my pockets and offer her one.

As she places the Marlboro between her lips, she waits for me to offer her a light. I try not to recoil when she leers forward, pursing her lips like a fish while I light it. My horny libido tells my stupid brain that this blonde bimbo is exactly what I need to forget all about my encounter with the brown-haired beauty. They are exact opposites, and that's what I need. This is what I do best.

"So sweetheart. How long a break you got?"

She bats her fake eyelashes and smirks. "Fifteen minutes."

Bending down to meet her short frame, I whisper, "I'll make it the best fifteen minutes of your life."

And that's all the miles I have to put in as she flicks her cigarette to the ground with a sly grin. Reaching for the scruff of my shirt collar, she leads me around the corner and I make good on my promise.

It may be the best fifteen minutes of her life, but it's the worst fifteen minutes of mine.

# Three

*Dixon*

Nobody likes Mondays—especially when you've had a shitty weekend. After jacking off in the shower—twice—you'd think my mood would have improved.

My weekend was strange. After hooking up with the blonde on Friday night, I went home alone, which is no surprise, but oddly enough I was kind of disappointed. My number one cardinal rule is never, ever bring anyone home. My home is my sanctuary, it's the one place where I can truly be myself, and I refuse to pollute that purity with my whoring ways. Also, I still see my home as *ours*. Lily is still ingrained into every crevice, and I can't bring myself to taint the happy memories we once shared there.

But Friday night, I found myself wondering what it would be like to actually bring home a chick and fuck her in my bed, as opposed to screwing her up against a brick wall.

I'm a psychiatrist, so I know how the human mind works—

most of the time. My need for comfort was triggered by the lovely Madison. Her innocence sung to me, and I haven't felt that way for a long while. As brief as our encounter was, there was *something* there. Too bad I was too gutless to find out what that *something* was.

I felt fucking disgusting after consorting with the blonde, so for the rest of the weekend, I kept my nose clean and out of random chicks' crotches. It was fairly boring on all accounts, but I feel somewhat unpolluted after my sexual abstinence for two whole days. That's a long time for someone who uses sex as his shield.

"Dr. Mathews, your twelve-thirty appointment is here," Ms. Vale says through the intercom on my phone.

Her singsong voice jars me out of my rut, and I clear my voice before replying, "Send her in."

Pulling up my new patient information sheet on my laptop, I begin entering Ms. Juliet Harte's details into my computer.

*Age: 26*

*Gender: Female*

*Address: 18 Union Square West, New York*

*Problem: Sex Addiction*

*Oh, boy.*

"Dr. Mathews?" asks a soft, velvety voice, which has my dick standing in direct salute.

Raising my eyes from the screen, I see that Ms. Juliet Harte is complete perfection wrapped in pure sin.

Her long blonde hair is wrapped into a twist, and strands fall around her face, drawing attention to her "come fuck me" blue eyes. The sexiest lips I have ever seen are coated in a clear gloss, and images of what those lips could do to me have me subtly rearranging myself in my seat.

My newfound celibacy has just mentally motorboated Juliet's perfect breasts. However, putting my game face on, I give her a small smile and gesture to the leather chair in front of my desk. "Please take a seat."

She nods and saunters over, making sure to straighten out her cream tunic dress before taking a graceful seat.

"Good afternoon, Ms. Harte," I say with a nod, getting the formalities out of the way.

"Good afternoon, Dr. Mathews," she replies, her eyes focusing intently on me.

I see no fear or apprehension behind her poised gaze, and her self-confidence is an absolute turn-on. But I have a job to do.

"So today, we'll mainly be discussing your history. Think of this as 'a getting to know you' session. In order to properly evaluate you, I need you to trust me. In no way will you be judged or condemned for your thoughts. No matter how perverse or wrong your thoughts may be, I need you to be totally honest with me. Do you think you can do that?" I ask with a smile.

Juliet nods. "Yes, I want to get better. I'll do anything it takes."

"Good," I commend. "How about we take a seat on the sofa where we'll both be more comfortable."

Juliet's mouth tips up into a secretive smile, but I ignore it as I reach for my notepad and make my way to the leather recliner. My eyes flick to the clock on my mantel, and I honestly don't know how I'm going to get through an hour session, talking about her sex addiction, without ripping her clothes off.

Clearing my throat, I try not to stare as she takes a seat on the black leather sofa. As she slowly crosses her long legs, images of her black heels digging into my ass while I fuck her up against my office wall assault my brain, and I barely suppress my moan at the erotic vision.

"So what brings you here today, Ms. Harte?"

Juliet shifts in her seat, the leather creaking under her sinful ass as she replies, "I have a problem."

I nod, encouraging her to go on.

"An addiction, I guess you could call it." She pauses, lowering her eyes.

I wait for her to continue, as I will try my hardest to act professional.

As she meets my gaze, she huskily whispers, "I'm addicted… to sex."

Those glorious words coming out of her mouth is what every hot-blooded American male wants to hear, but I appear unaffected as I ask, "How long have you felt this way?"

"For a while now."

"How long roughly?" I press, my pen poised over my notepad.

"For about two years," she discloses, her composure never wavering as I write down her secrets.

"I would like to talk about your personal life, Ms. Harte, would that be okay?"

She nods.

"Did anything happen around that time? Anything that may have caused this behavior change?"

I can see her mulling over my question. "Well, there was this one thing," she states, and I remain impassive, allowing her to continue. "It was the first time I had sex with a girl. Does this mean I'm bisexual? Or gay?" she asks, genuinely curious.

"I don't like to categorize sexuality, Ms. Harte," I reply, pressing the notepad over my looming erection. "How did being with a woman make you feel?"

"I liked it. A lot," she confesses. "There are some things men cannot provide in the bedroom."

"And what's that?"

"Being with a woman, it's soft and familiar. They provide that gentleness and comfort a man doesn't usually offer. The way a woman touches another woman's body, exploring the soft curves and supple planes, it really is beautiful. But being with a man, it's rough and raw. The way a man eats you out, compared to the way a woman does, is completely different. A man wants to devour his meal, while us ladies, we want to take our time and savor the taste," she explains, her pink tongue darting out to wet her bottom lip.

If my erection got any harder, I'd be able to pound nails into the wall. I know I have to steer this conversation into another direction before I show her not all men are barbarians, and we too, like to savor our meals.

"So apart from this event, did anything else happen? How's your family life? Work? Social life?"

Juliet's composure doesn't shift, and she happily answers, "It's all good. I live by myself in an apartment Daddy bought me. He's an investment banker, and well, we're quite well off. My mother passed away when I was seven, so I don't really remember her. Daddy got remarried to Rachel, and Rachel treated me like I was hers. She has two children of her own, and they are both nice people."

"Are they older? Younger? What's your relationship like with them?"

"One older, one younger, and I love…both of them." I don't fail to notice the apprehension in her strained admission.

"What do you do for work?" I question, writing down her stepsiblings as a possible cause for her addiction.

"I work for a law firm. I'm just a file clerk, but I don't really need to work, as Daddy takes care of me."

I nod, feeling a tad disturbed that a twenty-six-year-old woman refers to her father as "Daddy." I write down that a possible cause to her issues could be because she was sexually abused as a child. Most sex addicts describe their parents as being rigid, distant and uncaring. But in Juliet's case, it seems her father was the complete opposite. I make a note to revisit this point later.

"What about your social life? Do you smoke? Drink? Take drugs?"

Juliet smirks, and straightens in her seat. "Yes to all of the above."

Ms. Harte is getting more complex by the minute. "What drugs to do you take? Prescribed or illicit?"

"Mainly illicit," she calmly states. "I like acid, ecstasy and cocaine."

Holy shit, this woman is bad, bad news. But the more she confesses her sins, the more I want her.

"That's quite a cocktail of drugs. When did you start using?"

She ignores my question as she slowly, and purposely, uncrosses her legs. I can clearly see the white triangle of barely-there cloth scarcely covering her pussy, but I remain professional as I don't want to blow this. I know if I give in to my rampant libido, this will be the last time I see Ms. Juliet Harte, and after this introduction, I want more.

"Have you ever fucked while on acid, Dr. Mathews?" She closely gauges my reaction to see how I will respond to her crude question.

"This isn't about me, Ms. Harte, but rather about you, and your feelings. Did you want to tell me how you felt when engaging in a sexual act while high?" I coolly question, cocking an arrogant eyebrow.

I've been in the game for a long, long time, and it's going to take more than a hot piece of ass with a filthy mouth to get me going. She's testing me now, and Ms. Harte is a lot smarter than I gave her credit for. I must watch my back, and dick, with this femme fatale.

"It felt unlike anything I've ever experienced before. My entire skin was on fire, and my senses were so in tune with my body, I anticipated every move my partners made. Every touch, slap, lick, pull, thrust, tickle, everything—it was amplified, tenfold, and nothing has ever felt that good," she says, her pupils dilating, no doubt reliving the memory of her *ménage à trois*, as I didn't fail to note her intentional mention of the word "partners."

"So you enjoy sex?" My over-stimulated brain is begging me to stop with the torture.

She nods, and her eyes dart to my crotch. "Yes, I love it."

"What exactly do you love about it? Besides the physical gratification, that is."

Juliet smirks, before replying, "I love the power."

Images of being cuffed to a bed while I call Ms. Harte "Mistress" flash through my brain, and I realize that this woman could be quite hazardous to one's health.

Ms. Harte is one fucked-up little unit, and I can't wait to find out what makes her tick.

An hour later, I'm sitting in my chair, highly strung, and about ready to come in my pants. Ms. Harte is in the bathroom freshening up, as our session got a little heated and I reduced her almost to tears. I still can't work out whether they were genuine or not, which troubles me. She really is an anomaly, which is a strange, almost-refreshing change, as most women don't keep me guessing. But she does.

"So same time next week?" she asks, exiting the bathroom and jarring me out of my thoughts.

Looking up from my desk, I see that she has applied a bright red shade of lipstick, which stands out against her pale hair. Nodding casually, I pretend to type on my laptop, appearing informal and laid-back.

"Sure, that'll be fine. Please go ahead and schedule your session with Ms. Vale." My curt response is a silent dismissal, and she reads it loud and clear.

"Thank you for today, Dr. Mathews. I feel…better," she says, but I have a sneaking suspicion "better" was not the word she wanted to use.

"See you next week, Ms. Harte," I reply, giving her a small smile.

"Okay, see you then." She firmly nods and I keenly check out her ass as she exits my office.

The moment the door closes, I let out a deep, agonizing

breath and allow my staged composure to slip. That was damn intense, and the unrelenting hard on I'm sporting is proof of how damn tense that really was.

If I were smart, I would tell Susanna to cancel any future appointments Ms. Harte has made and refer her to another doctor. But I never said I was smart. School smart—yes. But sex smart—hell to the fuck, no. I have never met such a sexually aggressive woman before, and I'm man enough to admit that Juliet Harte turns me on *and* scares me, all in the same breath.

I have no idea how to approach this as there is some unseen sexual spark between us. I know that sounds ludicrous, seeing as she is a self-confessed sex addict. But there is something more to her, and I'm intrigued to find out what.

Looking down at my lap, I sigh, as this tenting erection is going nowhere. Deciding to take care of it before my next client, I lock my door and make my way into my personal bathroom. The moment I switch on the light, her perfume assaults my nostrils and I take a moment to bask in her scent. The floral fragrance does nothing to help my predicament and I quickly unsnap the button on my pants, ready to get to work. However, my hand freezes as my eyes fall to the mirror above the basin.

Written in bright red lipstick across my mirror is a phone number—no guessing whose. Underneath sits a perfect imprint of her lipstick-stained kiss marks, taunting me with their blatant sexual innuendo. This is obviously Ms. Harte's way of hinting that I call her, as I've already obtained her contact details via her client form.

Goddammit, I'm screwed.

Surrendering, I unzip my fly, reach into my pants, and find my release within minutes. Who would have thought an innocent, lipstick-stained kiss mark could warrant such an explosive orgasm? But I know there is absolutely nothing innocent about Juliet Harte.

# Four

## Dixon

This week has been an absolute disaster. So when 6p.m. Friday night ticks over, I'm out the door, happily bidding *sayonara* to the week from hell.

I'm meeting with Hunter and his parents, Marie and Ralph, who are in town for the weekend.

Walking into a popular bar and grill, I spot them sitting at a booth in the corner of the room. Hunter gives me a quick wave and I make my way over to them, dodging a lingering server who gives me a sultry smile.

After the fucked-up week of jacking off with zero satisfaction, I've decided to steer clear of all women because at the moment, two women are more than I can handle. I shouldn't even be thinking about Juliet Harte because it's wrong on all counts, the kind of wrong that would send me straight to hell. Yes, I've slept with a few of my clients, which I know is ethically and morally *and* professionally wrong. But they weren't genuine clients; they never really needed my help.

But Juliet, she is someone with genuine issues, and the doctor in me wants to help her. However, the horny male in me wants to help her by screwing her six ways to Sunday.

Pushing these inappropriate thoughts from my mind, I give Marie a double cheek kiss and a warm hug as I approach their booth.

"Hello, Dixon. Oh my, I love your hair," she says, playfully running a hand through my messy locks.

My hair at the moment most likely resembles a bird's nest, as I've been yanking at it in frustration all week.

"Nice to see you, Ralph." I extend my hand.

"You too, son," he replies, shaking it.

We all take our seats and I snatch the menu from Hunter, who bumps me playfully with his shoulder.

"So how was traffic?" I ask, my eyes perusing the menu uselessly, as food will not satisfy my current hunger.

"Ah, it was awful, as usual. It's so much better on our side of the river."

I give Marie a small smile, as I know she'll be forever loyal to New Jersey.

"You look tired, Dixon. Are you unwell?" She reaches across the table and feels my forehead.

Usually, I would shy away from such motherly tendencies, but it's Marie, and I'm used to her babying me.

"Yeah, Dix, you do look a bit off-color. Everything okay?" Hunter teases, looking at my lap. "Is everything where it should be?"

I roll my eyes at his idiocy and ignore him.

"I'm fine, Marie. Work is just crazy at the moment."

"Yeah, lots of crazies out there, that's why," Ralph innocently says, taking a sip of his ice tea.

"Ralph!" Marie scolds, throwing a reprimanding look his way.

"What?" he asks with a shrug.

Her eyes dart my way discreetly, and I know she's subtly attempting to play facial charades, drawing attention to the fact that one of those crazies is my father.

"It's fine, Marie," I insist with a wave of my hand.

I haven't seen my father since the day I admitted him, which was close to four months ago. Seeing my once healthy, vibrant father wither away into a shell of his former self is a sight I can't stand. Call me a bastard, but I would rather remember my dad being happy and well, as opposed to the medicated zombie he most likely resembles nowadays.

Marie must read my expression as she softly says, "I saw your father the other week. He's looking better."

Better? Better than what? Better than the drooling basket case he was when I admitted him? I hate to break it to Marie, but being dead is the only "better" in this scenario.

But I give her a small nod, and try to appear unmoved, as I don't want to hurt her feelings. "That's great. I've been meaning to go see him, but I've just…work has been busy," I conclude unconvincingly.

She smiles. "I understand."

Clearing my throat, I propose, "Maybe you could tell him I said hi? Next time you see him?"

"Of course. I can do that. You know, maybe you could call? I think he'd like that," she softly suggests.

"Yeah, maybe," I reply, not meaning a word.

Thankfully, the server interrupts our awkward conversation and puts an end to me justifying why I'm not a terrible son.

The evening is still young, so we decide to walk down to Central Park.

Ralph and Marie are at a vendor's cart buying pretzels when Hunter pulls me aside and asks, "What's up with you?"

"Care to be a little more specific?" I say, while reading through the emails on my phone.

"You haven't checked out one single girl all night. That brunette server was basically offering her tits as a plate for your steak, and you hardly noticed. What's up, dude? I'm worried. You're not about to do something stupid and become celibate, right?" he asks seriously, and I can't help but chuckle, as Hunter is never one to mince his words.

"You call me a manwhore. And now the thought of me becoming celibate is stupid?"

"Well, I know something is up. So spit it out."

Sighing, I run a hand through my disheveled hair, and I know the only way to shut him up is to tell him the truth. "I met this chick at work. Actually, I met two chicks," I correct.

"You do remember your workplace isn't a brothel, right?"

"Ha, very funny. I met girl number one, Madison, on Friday night," I explain, unable to keep the affection from my voice.

"I thought she was just a random hookup?"

I pull a grossed-out face when I realize he's talking about the blonde. "No, not her. I fucked her to get Madison out of my system."

Hunter grins. "But I'm guessing it didn't work?"

"You guessed right. She was so incredibly…sweet."

"And girl number two?" he asks, folding his arms across his chest.

I sigh. "Girl number two is the complete opposite to Madison. For starters, I met her at work."

"Uh-oh," Hunter butts in, but I hold up my hand, telling him to zip it. Thankfully he complies.

"She's a patient, and before you start with the third degree, I didn't do anything."

Hunter nods, his lips pulled in tight.

"She's trouble, man, I know it, but I can't stop thinking about her. She wrote her fucking number in bright red lipstick across my bathroom mirror," I confess.

"She what?" Hunter says incredulously. "No way!'

"Yes way," I counter because it's very true.

"So what's she seeing you for?" he asks, totally ignoring patient/doctor confidentiality.

"I can't tell you. That's between my patient and me," I reply, half serious.

"Oh, bullshit! If you're thinking about screwing her, then I think that rule is entirely void."

He's right, so I sheepishly reply, "She's addicted to sex."

Hunter's mouth pops open. He shakes his head animatedly and jams his finger into my chest. "You need to stay away from this little sex fiend, Dix. With your man-whoring tendencies, and her out-of-control libido, you'll end up fucking one another to death. Not to mention, she is your patient, *Dr.* Mathews."

"I know, I know. And you're right. But Hunt, I'm intrigued by her."

"You're intrigued by her zeal to fuck anything in sight more like it," he replies with a smirk.

"That's not it. This isn't about sex."

Hunter raises an unconvinced eyebrow.

"Okay, it's a little about sex. But there is something more to her. There is something more to both. I haven't been interested in a chick since..." but I remain mute, not wanting, or needing, to finish that sentence.

Hunter runs a hand down his face and blows out a breath. "Look, bro, this nympho sounds like trouble. Personally, I would refer her to another doctor and forget you ever met her. This will get sticky, and I mean that in every literal sense there is."

I nod, defeated, and also, disappointed. I don't want there to be any truth in what he says, but there is. I need to stop this before things spiral out of control. "You're right. That's what I'll do," I say with a firm nod. "Treating her is not good for either of us."

"'Attaboy," he says, playfully punching me on the arm. "You'll forget you ever met this little sexual deviant in no time."

"Dr. Mathews," a voice says from behind us.

Both Hunter and I turn around and are faced with Juliet Harte. My memories of her have paid her no justice at all, and with the super tight jogging outfit she's currently wearing, I've just made new memories, which I plan on revisiting later tonight.

"Ms. Harte," I reply, hoping I appear calm while I check out her gorgeous breasts in the white crop top she's sporting.

Hunter clears his throat loudly, ruining my ogling, and I sigh. "Hunter, this is Ms. Harte. Ms. Harte, Hunter," I say, waving my hand between the two.

"Please, call me Juliet," she says with a small smile.

"Very well." I nod.

And then, there is silence.

"It's a pleasure to meet you, Juliet," Hunter says, totally saving my ass, as I have no idea what to say to her. "*O Romeo, Romeo,* wherefore art thou, Romeo?" he teases, placing a hand over his heart dramatically.

Juliet giggles, while I shake my head at my friend's stupidity.

The Chihuahua at her feet begins yapping, thankfully cutting through the silence, and Juliet sighs. "I better go. Marcia gets cranky if her walk gets interrupted." The Chihuahua yaps in agreement. "I'll see you Monday?" she says, but it actually sounds more like a question.

"Yes. Monday it is," I reply stiffly.

Juliet looks overjoyed by my response. "Okay, well, it was nice meeting you, Hunter. Awesome name, by the way," she says with a playful wink, before re-inserting her earbuds and taking off into a slow sprint.

Hunter and I eagerly watch, mesmerized by how amazing her ass looks in those tight spandex pants.

Once she's out of sight, Hunter mumbles, "*That's* the nympho?"

"The one and only," I reply with a sigh.

"Change of plans. Fuck finding her another doctor. Send her my way. Make up some excuse as to why she needs to buy stocks."

I don't reply and only shake my head because I know once Monday rolls over, I'm a goner.

As we wait in silence for Marie and Ralph to hurry up and buy their damn pretzels, Hunter lightheartedly mutters, "It's a lot about sex, you lying bastard."

# Five

## *Dixon*

Another uneventful weekend has passed where I stayed indoors and steered clear of all females. Bumping into Juliet on Friday night has thrown me because I can't stop thinking about her. What I told Hunter was true. Yes, I am ridiculously attracted to her, but it's not just the physical attraction. She really *does* intrigue me.

Although I've been lost in my Juliet spell, I haven't forgotten about another woman I found just as intriguing as Juliet. Madison. It's uncanny that I have met two women in the span of a week. I say uncanny because I couldn't even find *one* woman after Lily who remotely sparked my interest, but now I have two.

These two women are opposites, yet I find myself attracted to both. Madison, from the brief minutes spent with her, I could tell she was sweet, innocent, and pure. But Juliet, there's nothing sweet nor innocent about her. They truly represent the stereotypical devil and angel icons.

"Dr. Mathews, Ms. Harte is here to see you. She's a little early. Is it okay to send her in?" Susanna says through the intercom, jolting me from my thoughts.

Taking a deep breath, I push down on the button. "Thank you, Ms. Vale. Please send her in."

Looking at the clock on my laptop, I see that Juliet is fifteen minutes early, and knowing her, there's a reason. I remain seated as the door opens, and in strolls the devil.

Juliet looks out-of-this-world hot, and irony has once again decided to play with my emotions, as she's wearing a bright red dress, totally dressed for her hellish part.

"Ms. Harte," I address her, clearing my throat.

She knows I'm checking her out, but she doesn't shy away—she simply locks my door. Turning around to meet my stunned eyes, she grins, her glossy lips looking good enough to eat.

"Ms. Harte?" I repeat, attempting to sound stern, but I'm so pathetically turned on, my voice betrays my awakening.

"May I call you Dixon?" she calmly says, taking a small step toward me.

"I don't think that would be wise. I'm your doctor," I reply, my eyes briefly dropping to her cleavage.

"I thought about you last night," she confesses with a grin.

I calmly nod, ignoring my rampant libido. "It's not unusual for one to think of their doctor when they start treatment. Therapy evokes new feelings in everyone."

Without pause, she shakes her head and evenly states, "No. I thought of you while touching my pussy."

Holy…shit. I nearly fall out of my seat at her confession. I'm beyond stunned, but more so, I'm incredibly turned on by her sexual aggression.

"I was imagining it was your hand fingering me, coaxing my body to come. I think your fingers could make me come with a single touch," she declares, licking her wet bottom lip as she takes another step toward me.

I really should be backing away from her, demanding she get out of my office, as this is utterly unethical. But if I stood, my hard-on would really make my Good Samaritan act void.

"Ms. Harte."

"I thought I told you to call me Juliet," she purrs with seduction.

"Well, when you're in my office, I think it's best we stick to formalities. Now please, would you be so kind as to unlock my door?" I say, barely holding on to whatever wisdom is animating me right now.

"I may be in your office, *Dr.* Mathews," she replies, "but we're technically off the clock. I mean, my session doesn't start for another thirteen minutes. Couldn't we just be Dixon and Juliet for those thirteen minutes? Not doctor and patient?"

No, we most positively should not be Dixon and Juliet because Dixon wants to violently clear his desk and throw Juliet onto it while he fucks her into next week. But my resolve is slowly slipping away and Juliet can see it.

I want this woman more than I want air itself, but I have a feeling that if I let her in, she'll destroy me. She'll consume every part of my entire being, and I don't want to lose myself that way ever again.

"Dixon," she moans, gliding a hand down her body.

I visibly swallow, my eyes not believing what they're witnessing as her fingers begin lifting the hem of her dress until it bunches mid-thigh. All that creamy, supple skin on display has my dick punching a hole through my pants, but I try my best not to give in.

"Do you want me to show you how much I want you?" she asks, her big blue eyes widening in yearning.

I refuse to reply because yes, fuck yes; I want to see everything she has to offer. So I remain mute, as this is totally Juliet's show.

She saunters over and rounds my desk, while I push back in my chair, leaving room for her small frame to fit between me and the desk. The movement has revealed my tenting erection, and Juliet's eyes smolder with the sight.

"I knew you'd be big. Watch me."

That's definitely not going to be a problem, as I couldn't look away even if I wanted to.

Juliet leans back and presses her ass against the edge of my desk as she slides her dress up until it bunches around her waist. Her tiny black thong barely covers her pussy, and as she slips her fingers inside, I can appreciate the phrase "less is more."

Tiny moans escape her parted lips as she seeks refuge inside herself, and my eyes remain transfixed on the jerking movements her hungry fingers are making as she begins pleasuring herself.

"Hmm…I'm so wet," she pants, and I swallow hard. "Here, let me show you."

Before I can object, Juliet removes her fingers and reaches forward, rubbing her pointer along my bottom lip. A knowing grin spreads across her lips as she watches me struggle with my self-control. My tongue instantly darts out, lapping up what Juliet so kindly offered, and the mere taste is enough to have me salivating in need. It takes all my diminishing willpower not to bury my face between her legs and take over. As much as I want to do that, the vision of watching her touch herself is far more appealing than me helping her along.

Her shallow breaths tell me she's close, and as she unsteadily leans further back, needing to gain deeper access into the cavern of her body, I do the only thing a gentleman can do. I wrap a firm hand around her waist and anchor her so she can really reach her climax with no restrictions. The moment we make contact, she groans in the back of her throat and tosses her head back, her eyes shut tight. She extends one hand behind her, resting it on my desk for extra support, while the other never ceases from the frenzied movement inside her thong. Her hips pump forward violently as she almost attains her goal.

It's nearly too much, and I just about come in my pants like a pubescent teenage boy. But I refuse to look like an inexperienced child and blow my load just by watching Juliet touch herself. I dig deeper into her waist, my fingers betraying how turned on I am by watching this wicked sight before me, and my firm pressure sends Juliet wild. As her frantic rhythm becomes untamed and wild, she unexpectedly falls onto her back, as the hand supporting her slips out from under her.

She's now lying on her back on my desk, her legs dangling over the edge, while her fingers are recklessly coaxing her to come. As her back bows, she lets out a low growl and her body undulates as I watch her explode. It takes every ounce of self-control not to flip her over and make her mine.

I'm not sure how long she lies sprawled out on my desk, breathless and totally spent. But I don't attempt to make a single move because watching this profound creature is akin to discovering a hidden treasure. I take her in, appreciating the way her lissome body comes down from its high, and I know I'm screwed. I'm utterly enchanted by Juliet Harte, and we haven't even fucked.

Juliet turns her head, looking at the clock above the mantel. With a sated sigh, she slowly slips down her dress. I try not to weep, as I preferred her barely clothed. Ever so slowly, she rises to full height, but remains seated, her legs hanging over the edge of my desk. She places one stilettoed foot between my parted legs, and rolls my chair toward her. Of course, I don't hesitate and allow her to draw me closer to her body, curious as to what comes next.

My chest is pressed against her legs, and my eyes are now crotch level. My restraint really is commendable.

"Thank you, Dr. Mathews," she says, and leans forward, placing a single kiss on the corner of my mouth.

Before I can even think of a response, she hops down from my desk and smoothes out her dress before taking a seat on the sofa. I stare, stunned, needing a second to process what the hell just happened. She just called me Dr. Mathews, therefore, does she expect our session to go on like nothing happened?

As she reaches for her bag and pulls out a compact to check her reflection, I know that's exactly what she expects.

I just watched the hottest woman I have ever met come all over my desk, and now I'm expected to play the role of therapist, ignoring the fact my hard-on is about ready to blind anyone who walks through that door.

This is seriously fucked up, and suddenly I realize I think I'm the one in need of therapy.

We never have drinks on a Monday. What with Finch's daddy duties and Hunter's shiatsu, it's fair to say Mondays are usually off-limits, but when Hunter called me and heard the disbelief in my voice after Ms. Harte's session, he called an emergency catch-up, and that's what brings us to now.

If my day wasn't uncomplicated enough, I've organized to meet up at The Pony Bar—Madison's place of employment. Yup, I'm a masochist.

"So how'd it go?" Hunter asks, reaching for his beer, awaiting my bombshell.

"Well…" I commence, lost for words. "Finch, do you want to block your ears?"

Finch holds both hands up, shaking his head bravely. "No, give it to me. It can't be that bad."

If only he knew.

Lowering my voice, I lean forward, and my friends do the same. "She got herself off…on my desk…in my office. And I watched."

Jesus, that sounded dirty. It certainly didn't feel dirty when I watched it happen, but saying it aloud makes it sound like a kinky peepshow.

There is dead silence. I look at my friends, needing them to say something, anything because the silence is killing me.

"Guys?" I say, waiting for one of them to tell me I'm not as perverted as I feel.

Hunter's mouth is hanging open, but a half smile mars his

features, as he's no doubt visualizing the very graphic picture I just painted.

"Finch?" I ask, looking at my best friend, who has paled whiter than a ghost.

"She m-masturbated…on your… desk?" he shrieks, breaking the silence a little louder than anticipated.

"Shh!" I whisper, gesturing with my hand for him to lower his voice.

"I'm sorry," he apologizes with a frown. "But Dix, oh my God, who *is* this woman? Who goes around jerking off on their psychiatrist's desk?"

"Apparently Juliet Harte does," Hunter says with a chuckle.

"Dixon, Gabriella has been in your office. Oh dear Lord, my baby daughter has been subjected to a bordello!" shouts Finch. I groan, as his volume control is nonexistent tonight.

Totally ignoring his melodramatics, Hunter asks with a wink, "So did you, ya know?"

"No, I did not," I reply, reaching for my scotch, failing to mention that she didn't even offer.

"So what happened?"

"Nothing. We had our session…"

"Hold up," Hunter interrupts, brushing his hair from his face, as it's slipped free from his manbun. "You still went through with the session?"

I pathetically nod because the situation is as ridiculous as it sounds.

"You are either the smartest, or stupidest motherfucker alive!" He laughs, slapping his hand on the tabletop.

"He's definitely the smartest. Good on you, Dix," Finch says, nodding his head in encouragement.

"Thanks, man. At least *you're* a good friend." I look pointedly at Hunter.

"Hey, don't be hating on me. I told you to handball her to another doctor. You've got no one to blame but yourself."

I sigh because he's right. It was absolutely ludicrous attempting to act professional. The session was a total disaster, and I should be ashamed of myself for allowing it to ever get that far.

"You're not seeing her next week, are you?" Hunter asks with an incredulous look.

"Well…" I reply, guiltily chugging down my scotch.

"Are you insane?" Finch cries, sitting tall in his seat. "Dixon, this person is a dirty, dirty, slutty slut from the planet 'I'm a big whore who masturbates in offices where babies have been!' You need to never see her again, and you need to buy a new desk!"

I can't help the laugh that rumbles from my chest as Finch is utterly entertaining when riled up. Hunter joins in and Finch runs a hand over his full beard.

"You guys are sick bastards."

And just like that, I instantly feel better.

"I'm going out for a smoke," I say, pushing back my chair.

"Make sure you don't bump into any masturbating fiends on your way out," Hunter playfully chides while I flip him off.

Walking through the packed restaurant, my thoughts drift to Juliet and the predicament I find myself in. The right and smart thing to do would be to tell Ms. Harte I can no longer treat her. But that thought leaves a sour taste in my mouth, and I have no idea why.

My mother was a devout Catholic, and in times of crisis she would tell me to pray to the Lord, and apparently he was supposed to give me some magical answer. I really could do with some answers right about now, so God, if you're listening, how 'bout you cut me some slack and give me a sign. Please?

"Oh, shit!" a voice from beneath me—yes, beneath me—yelps.

I jolt back, part in shock, part in horror, as I blindly walked straight into someone. Now that poor person is sprawled out on the floor on her stomach.

"Are you okay? I'm so sorry, I didn't see you," I say in a rushed breath, quickly dropping to a squat.

"It's okay," she replies, laughing quietly.

As she turns around to face me, my words get caught in my throat. "M-Madison?"

I knew she worked here, that's part of the reason I'm here, but I wasn't expecting to literally bump into her.

"Dixon?" she says, gasping. "What are you doing here?"

"I'm here with friends. We're having drinks. And you did say if I was ever in the neighborhood..." I reply, mesmerized by her stunning green eyes.

"Oh." She sounds surprised that I actually came.

I suddenly realize she's still lying sprawled out on the floor, and like a jerk, I haven't even offered to help her up.

"I'm the one who's sorry. Here, let me help you up." I offer my hand, which she gratefully accepts.

The moment she sits up, I see that her white T-shirt is ruined because when she fell, she was holding a tray of drinks. The drinks have spilled haphazardly across the floor, and I feel like a total ass, as I know those drinks will probably come out of her pay.

"Let me pay for those," I quickly offer, reaching into my

pocket to pull out my wallet.

Madison waves me off. "It's fine, honestly."

"No, I insist," I press, trying to do a mental calculation of how much the drinks would have amounted to.

"It's fine, Dixon," she perseveres kindly, placing a gentle hand on my wrist to halt my movement.

The moment her fingers meet my skin, a zap of *something* singes through my body, and we both pull away, taken aback by the unpredicted response. My eyes unintentionally drop to her soaked chest, and I see a hint of her pink bra peek through the sheer material. She may be a small girl, but damn, she sure is blessed in the boob department.

I quickly clear my throat and raise my eyes, as I'm sure she can see me staring at her.

"I better get back to work," she timidly says, and makes a move to stand.

I move out of her way, and also stand awkwardly, not knowing what to say next.

I've forgotten how short she is, and standing in her black Chucks and black shorts, she looks simply adorable. Her long brown hair has slipped free from a loose ponytail, and with her stained T-shirt, she looks a total mess—but not in a bad way. She looks like a beautiful disaster.

"Well, see ya," she says with a wave, when I don't say anything.

"Oh, yeah, okay, bye." I find myself wanting to ask her what time she gets off, but I don't.

I just watch as she makes her way into the kitchen, leaving me to once again question what the hell *that* was.

# Six

## Dixon

It's Friday, and my week has thankfully remained drama free since Monday. I intend to keep it that way.

Juliet's very public display of self-gratification has definitely been an inspirational vision to accompany my jerking off, but funnily enough, so has Madison's innocent pink bra. I'm attracted to both women, but for entirely different reasons. It's not as simple and clear cut as this, but I'm drawn to Madison's innocence while I'm enticed by Juliet's depravity.

I haven't really figured either of them out yet, but now that I know Madison works Mondays, I intend to pay her a visit and try to get to know her better. As for Juliet, I'm actually a little afraid to get to know her better; I have a feeling the real Juliet Harte would eat me alive for breakfast.

The phone thankfully interrupts my thoughts, and I answer on the third ring.

"Hello, this is Dr. Mathews."

"Dixon, my friend, how are you?" says Chad Turner, who is on the Psychiatry and Behavioral Sciences board.

"Hello, Chad. I'm great, thank you. To what do I owe this pleasure?" I ask, getting straight to the point because this isn't a social call.

Chad chuckles, no doubt appreciating my forwardness, as neither of us are one for small talk. "Dixon, I'm calling because I would like to extend a formal invitation for you to attend our annual Gerald Harriet's Fellowship Award night, which will be held later in the year."

I take a moment to process what he just said, as this is big. I've been trying to get an invite to this prestigious ceremony for years, but I've always missed out.

Without further delay, I reply, "Chad, I would be absolutely honored. Thank you." And I mean every word.

But I can't help but wonder why this year is different.

Chad must be able to read my confusion as he quickly clarifies, "Although you're not in the running for the award this year, your research on neurobiology and addiction hasn't gone unnoticed by the board. You keep it up, and next year, you've got a real good shot at being a strong contender."

It's every doctor's dream to be invited to this event, but the hint of possibly being nominated next year is phenomenal.

Keeping my calm, however, I reply, "Well, I better ensure I keep up the good work. Please send all information to my office, and I'll make sure to RSVP by the date."

"Excellent. I look forward to seeing you there," Chad says happily. "Keep up the good work, Dixon. We're keeping a close eye on you." He hangs up before I have a chance to reply.

Holy shit, this is beyond amazing. Never in my wildest

dreams did I ever imagine that me, Dixon Mathews, the only son of an Italian migrant family, would get this opportunity. I think this calls for a celebration.

Reaching for my phone, an unexpected thought occurs to me. Chad did say they're keeping a close eye on me. And yes, I've mostly kept my nose clean, but this situation with Ms. Harte could certainly turn ugly and taint my career if it ever got out.

What happened earlier in the week would definitely result in my license being revoked for unethical conduct. I've worked hard to maintain the noteworthy position I'm currently in, and I cannot, or rather, I will not allow my cock to fuck up something I've worked too hard to achieve.

With a defeated sigh, I lift the receiver and page Susanna.

"Dr. Mathews?"

"Hello, Ms. Vale. There's a patient I need you to contact."

"Of course. Who might that be?"

Taking a muted breath, I reply, "Ms. Juliet Harte."

"What would you like me to tell her?" Susanna innocently inquires.

Ignoring the pang of regret, I sigh. "Please let her know I can no longer treat her, and pass on Dr. Geo's details."

"Not a problem, Dr. Mathews. Is there anything else you would like me to say?"

There are a thousand things I wish I could say. But this is for the best.

"No, Ms. Vale. Let's leave it at that."

Friday night drinks are what get me through the week, and after today's news, I can't wait to kick back and have a few beers with the boys to celebrate my good fortune.

"If I may, I would like to propose a toast to my good friend, Dr. Dixon Mathews, who may be a womanizing jerk at times—" I roll my eyes, but listen to Hunter's heartfelt speech "—but he's shown great restraint by saying hell no to the foxy nympho to save his career. Some may say he's gone crazy, or maybe even turned a little soft, but I'm proud of him for putting his blue balls in his suitcase, and focusing on what's important."

"Amen!" Finch butts in, raising his glass of Coke.

"Thanks. I think." We clink glasses, and I take a well-deserved sip.

I've told them about my decision to no longer see Juliet, and they were both in agreement that it's for the best.

"So now that the masturbating sexual deviant is outta your life, are you gonna cuddle up to that cute little brunette from the other night?" Hunter asks, waggling his eyebrows.

"Jesus, that's a little rough."

Hunter shrugs. "I call 'em as I see 'em."

"Well, if everyone lived by your rules, whatever do you think they'd call you?" I ask, smiling.

"They'd call me Hunter…the God of fuck."

I chuckle, while Finch rolls his eyes.

"Stop changing the subject, you pussy. So the brunette? What are your plans?" He rubs his hands together mischievously.

After bumping into Madison the other day, the boys have been on my case to go visit her. Both Hunter and Finch commented on some weird "love eyes" I had while looking at her—I honestly have no idea where they come up with this shit. But truthfully, I have been thinking about her, and I do plan on visiting her soon, just not right away.

I don't want to come across as desperate, or come on too strong, so I'll keep my cards close to my chest for now.

Sick of being the lab rat for the evening, I ask with a wink, "So how about you, Hunter? Passing for Chris Hemsworth's brother surely helps with the ladies."

Hunter takes a sip of beer, shaking his head. "He already has a brother, and if the ladies he attracts are any indication of what's headed my way, I'm more than happy to keep flying solo."

I know he's trying to be funny, but the tension around his eyes reveals something is off. I decide to drop it for now, but make a note to ask him later when he's drunk and in a sharing mood.

"So basically, this scrawny little fucker is the only one who's getting laid. How sad is that?" Hunter gags, while I thump Finch on the back.

Finch blushes, and I can't help but laugh. He really is too easy to tease.

After one too many scotches, Finch is begging Hunter and me not to become lion tamers, but the idea is really ingenious, and I can't believe I haven't thought of it sooner.

"You, my man, are too uptight," Hunter slurs, straddling the statue lion, which is standing proud and tall outside the library. "You need to loosen up." He strokes his cheek over the concreted mane, sighing contently.

Everything is so much funnier when you're slightly inebriated, and Hunter and I are getting to the stage where almost *everything* is funny.

"Guys, get off the damn lion!" Finch pleads, while Hunter and I ride the statue proudly.

"Let me ride this big pussy in peace," Hunter playfully retorts, while I lose my balance and fall onto my ass, laughing rowdily.

"Dixon?" a familiar voice asks in shock.

My laughing abruptly dies the moment I hear her, and any hilarity gets caught in my throat as the voice I've been trying so hard to forget addresses me once again.

"Dixon, are you okay?"

Closing my eyes, I count to three before calmly opening them, and I attempt to not keel over when I see the beautiful face of my ex-fiancée. My heart beats against my rib cage frantically, as the organ is beyond elated to see her again. My brain, however, knocks some sense into my whimsical center, and I harden the fuck up.

Standing to full height, I ignore the fact I'm completely drunk and my shirt and tie are askew as I offhandedly reply, "Hi, Lily."

Looking down at my leather shoes, I sigh, as I see I've stepped in pink gum. I look like a total slob, but Lily looks immaculate, as usual.

She's in a tight black dress which stops mid-thigh. Memories of how those long tanned legs wrapped around my neck while I ate her out for what felt like hours assault my brain. However, as my glance falls to her face, I see a silver tiara entangled in her long blonde curls. I can't help but think how out of character a tacky gimmick like this is for her. But then my daft brain registers the fact she's wearing a bright pink sash with the big, glittery words "Bride-to-Be."

The simple phrase may as well have just told me to go fuck myself, and highlight what a failure I am.

Suddenly, I realize the date, and remember it would have been our one-year anniversary this weekend. But instead of mourning, or looking remotely reflective, Lily is out celebrating her bachelorette party, looking absolutely stunning and happy.

She doesn't seem at all bothered that she would have been *my* bride-to-be a year ago. She doesn't even appear to care that this is the first time she's seen me in so many months. She simply doesn't care that she tore out my heart and left me a shell of who I once was. I gave her my all, and it still wasn't good enough.

*I* wasn't good enough. But my best friend was.

However, lifting my head in pride, I snicker, making a point of looking at her sash. "Congratulations. I hope he can provide you everything that I couldn't."

"Dixon, wait!"

"Wait for what?" I spit, hands out wide. "For you to tell me how happy you are?"

"I'm s—"

Before she can finish, I cut her off because if I hear the word "sorry" pass through her deceitful lips, I just may hurl. "Save your excuses for your husband."

"Dixon!" she pleads, reaching out for me.

But I storm down the stairs, ignoring the calls of my best friends. I also ignore the wounded look on my ex-lover's face. But she can go to hell, as I've been wearing that same look since the day she walked out on me.

I simply ignore everything and focus on the only thing that makes a lick of sense.

I shouldn't be here. But this was the first place I thought of running to.

I don't know how to deal with these pent-up feelings. I never have. Other people's feelings, I know how to resolve, but when it comes to me, I just want to forget.

Even for a stolen moment, I just want to forget how much it hurts to love someone who doesn't love you back.

My fist pounding against the door is in sync with my hammering heart, and the moment it opens, the primitive animal comes roaring out of me and I attack.

"Dr. Mathews? Are you okay?" Juliet gasps, taking a step backward, her eyes widening in surprise.

"It's Dixon," I growl and barge into her apartment, kicking the door shut behind me.

We stare at one another, the air sizzling with an intense, electrical current as we engage in the ultimate standoff. Juliet appears confused, but she remains silent, awaiting my next move. Before she has a moment to protest, I pounce on her, smashing my ravenous mouth to hers. She hesitates for a fraction of a second, but then it's game on.

We tackle one another, both demanding dominance over the other, but I willingly submit when she violently unclasps my belt buckle and shoves her hand down my pants, palming my hot erection. I've gone commando, so she goes straight in for the kill and hungrily begins stroking me, her small hand barely wrapping around my straining shaft.

I pump forward, my hips jerking frantically, needing the

friction to be harder and faster, and thank fuck, Juliet complies, her wicked fingers pumping with vigor. I'm about five seconds away from coming in her hand, so I pull away because when I explode, it's going to be inside her.

I push her backward and she stares at me breathlessly, anticipating what happens next.

Reaching for the low neckline of her black lace slip, I rip it down the middle, letting it glide away like melted butter from her hot little body.

I take a moment to appreciate the sight of pure perfection in front of me, and just when I thought my hard-on couldn't get any harder, my dick twitches and painfully demands to break free. The pinkest, perkiest nipples sit erect and swollen, highlighting her flawlessly round, creamy tits. They are more than a handful, and I can't wait to bury my head between those pillows of perfection, and see if they're as soft as they look.

"Spectacular," I say with bated breath.

As she cups both tits and begins plucking her nipples, I can't wait a second longer. Lunging forward, I clasp her bicep and spin her around, smashing her front against the wall. I know I'm being extremely assertive, but my passion is assailing my last tether of rationality, and I need to consume this woman before I explode.

Sliding my hand around her waist, I dip down and slip a finger into her slick, warm wetness, and we both moan at the swift intrusion. Ramming her hips backward, she reaches down and interlaces her hand through mine, inserting a long finger of her own.

We're both steadily fingering her, but this is my show, so I nudge her hand away and insert another finger, stretching her wide. She cries out, taking me deeper, and moans the instant I go in all the way. Her inner muscles clasp around me and I finger her fiercely, showing her no mercy until she comes with a quick, explosive cry. The sound is music to my sex-starved ears, and I yank down my zipper before the final tremor can rock her sated body.

The moment my belt and pants hit the floor, I'm desperately drawing her closer, leading my throbbing dick to her delicious, soaked cunt. But before we do this, I should caution her that things are about to get messy.

"I don't make love. I fuck. I fuck long. And I fuck hard. I'm not here for romance, or to fall in love," I warn, rubbing my tip along her opening. "I don't make empty promises. I'm just here to come. Can you handle that?"

Juliet groans low in her throat, my promises of unrestricted pleasure obviously appealing to her kinky side. "Show me what you've got."

However, my last sense of reason alerts me to the fact I don't fuck without protection. I especially don't fuck someone as promiscuous as Juliet without protection.

She senses my delay and quickly whispers, "I'm clean," and wiggles her ass, begging me to give her what we both want.

Any levelheadedness is lost, and I finally succumb to the lustful Juliet Harte.

With one rough, fluid movement, I thrust forward and impale her, pressing her flat up against the wall. She cries out, but the sound is far from pained.

"Hold on," I breathlessly caution, as I plan for this to get out of control.

She splays out both palms against the wall, and stands on

tippy-toes, angling her body so she can take me in deeper, and harder. Wrapping one hand around her waist, and the other in her long blond hair, I begin pumping my hips ferociously, fucking her so hard her body slams against the wall with every single punishing thrust I deliver. But I can't stop. I'm fucking away my pain, and the harder I push, the further away it seems to fade. I want to fuck it all away, until there's nothing left but this mind-numbing pleasure.

I bunch my fist in her hair and tilt her head to one side, exposing her long neck, her pulse pounding against the heated flesh. I strike down and avidly bite, sucking her floral-scented flesh into my hungry mouth, while she screams out in approval.

Her passion-filled mewls spur me on, and I moan against her throat, my biting and sucking in step with my driving hips. My orgasm is so close, it's bubbling to the surface, so I reach down and begin massaging her swollen clit, my deft fingers never ceasing until she finally comes with a violent, thunderous scream.

One…two…three, and I'm fucking done.

The moment I pull out, jetting my seed all over her back, she slumps down the wall, her trembling legs unable to hold her up because I just fucked her like an animal. A sense of shame and disgust rolls over me, and I open my mouth, ready to apologize for being such a brute. Yes, I did warn her, but that was out of control.

But she surprises me as she turns her head, and with hooded eyes, she pants, "Let's do that again."

# Seven

*Dixon*

I wake the next morning, my body screaming at me for falling asleep at such an awkward angle. One half of me is sprawled out on the sofa, while the other half is on the floor. And I've just come to realize, I'm pantless. The top three buttons of my white shirt are also missing, as they became victim to Juliet's inquisitive fingers.

Memories from last night assault my now-sober brain, and I look down at my lap, the stickiness clinging to my crotch highlighting what a fucking idiot I am.

Between my body collapsing into an exhausted heap after round three, I felt Juliet climb on top of me and fuck the living hell out of me until I forgot my own name. After that, I'm pretty sure I passed out, sticky and spent, and that's where I have remained.

Squinting with one eye closed, I see it's just on 7 a.m. I wonder where Juliet is as I take in my surroundings. The small living room is elegantly decorated, and I take a moment to appreciate the stylish furnishings, as last night, the only thing I was appreciating was Juliet's ass.

I notice my pants are across the room, and Juliet's fluff ball dog is currently using them for her bed. I wearily stand and moan, as my overworked muscles feel like they've been skinned from the bone. Shooing off Marcia or Macy, or whatever its name is, I tuck my crinkled shirt into my pants. I then decide to try to find Juliet because I feel stupid waiting out here.

Not wanting to aimlessly wander around her apartment, I walk down the hallway in hopes the first room will reveal Juliet inside. I sneak a look inside, as I don't want to invade her privacy, which is ridiculous, seeing as I didn't mind violating her privacy last night.

When I see that she's not in there, I decide to take a look in the bathroom. However, that search is also fruitless. Deciding to freshen up, I try to tame my messy hair, but quickly give up and instead use the toilet, splash some water on my face, and gargle with some mouthwash, hoping to look and smell semi-human.

There is another door down the hallway, but I decide to wait it out in the kitchen, as Juliet would have no doubt heard me bashing about, alerting her to the fact I'm awake. However, thirty minutes later, I'm clawing at the walls, desperate for a shower, a couple of Advil, and a cup of coffee. But I feel rude leaving without at least seeing Juliet. After last night, the least I can do is wait, but then a thought hits me. What if she didn't want me to wait? She would have surely left a note if she did, letting me know where she went. But as I scour the counter, I see there is no sign of a note.

Suddenly feeling like a right royal dumbass, I reach for my discarded tie on the back of the sofa, say goodbye to the mutt, and then slam the door shut behind me. I feel like such a chump, sitting around for a woman who obviously doesn't want to be found.

As I push the elevator call button, I ignore the pressing thought that Juliet has just…fucked like a man.

However, in this circumstance, I'm the damn woman, waiting for the man to magically appear after their blatant one-night stand, and not getting that it was just that. This is beyond embarrassing. I should feel relieved, but I'm not.

Bolting out the elevator doors as soon as they slide open, I hang my head, partially as a way to hide my disheveled state, but for the most part because I'm ashamed. This is my first walk of shame, and I'm going to ensure it's my last.

Not looking where I'm going, I charge straight into a wafer-thin frame, but quickly reach out to steady her arms before she tumbles to the ground.

Looking down, I don't know if I should bless, or curse the irony of life as I see Madison's sparkling green eyes shine up at me in amusement.

"We've gotta stop bumping into one another this way." She smiles, tucking a curl of sweaty hair behind her ear.

She looks damp, puffed and perfect. Her tight shorts and crop top reveal way too much milky white skin, and once again I find myself staring at her like a creepy old pervert. What is it about this girl that leaves me tongue-tied?

"What are you doing here?" she asks when I remain silent.

Her innocent question however, has me feeling like an even dirtier old man, but I coolly reply, "Just visiting a friend."

She looks down at my unkempt state, not at all believing my pathetic lie. But she nods, not questioning it. "Oh, cool. I was just coming back from a run. Not that I needed to clarify that." She shuffles her sneaker-clad feet with a small smirk.

I chuckle, and realize she's just as tongue-tied as me.

"What are you doing now?" she asks, biting her lower lip.

"Um, nothing," I reply. "Why?"

"Well, I was just going to head upstairs for a quick shower then head out to grab a bite to eat. Would you like to come?"

Totally ignoring her breakfast invitation, I ask, "You live *here*?" and I point above me.

Madison smiles and nervously nods. "Yes. My stepfather owns the building, and with apartments costing a small fortune in New York, it makes sense to live here."

I whistle. "The entire building? Wow. I'm impressed."

But regardless of how impressed I am, there is no way in *hell* I'm going back upstairs. But I find myself really wanting to accept Madison's invitation.

She must be able to read my dilemma as she quickly says, "You know what, don't worry about it. I can't smell any worse than you do." She bumps into me playfully, laughing at my pallid expression.

Realizing she's joking, I instantly relax and bump her back. "Well, for that comment, you're buying."

We're sitting in the smallest diner known to mankind, and to be honest, I didn't even know it existed. But Madison promised the food was to die for and not to judge its inside by its outer appearance. I try not to read too much into that relevant comment, and rather focus on the fact that this 120-pound girl has enough food in front of her to feed a small starving nation. I have no idea where she puts it.

She senses me watching her and slowly raises her attentive eyes. “What?”

“Nothing,” I reply with a smirk, focusing my attention on sipping my coffee.

“This is why I run every morning,” she explains, adding more salt to her scrambled eggs.

“Every morning? Damn, that’s commitment.”

“I start class at nine, so I’m up early anyway,” she says with a shrug. “I may as well start my day off being healthy because God knows, as it progresses, I’m anything but.” She smirks, picking up her fork and knife, ready to dig into her waffles.

The mention of class has me wondering what she does. “What do you study?” I ask, reaching for the cream cheese.

“I’m at Columbia, studying nursing. Well, I just started a dual degree. Eventually, I would like to end up specializing in midwifery,” she replies, and takes a small bite of her sugary treat.

I’m slightly taken aback, as I really hadn’t given much thought to her occupation. Now that I know what it is, I find myself being even more attracted to her as I know she’s got brains as well as beauty.

“A dual degree? So a Bachelor *and* a Master’s of Science?”

“Yeah,” she replies with a coy nod.

“That’s pretty incredible. A dual degree is a lot to take on. You must be a downright genius, or plain crazy,” I respond with a grin.

Madison laughs, and the sound is absolutely wonderful. "Maybe a bit of both. So how do you know it's a lot of work?"

I usually hate telling people what I do for work, as I get the same old "who's the craziest person you've ever treated?" and "can you prescribe me some Valium?" each and every time. But with Madison, I know she'll probably find what I do remotely interesting as we're in similar fields.

"I'm a psychiatrist," I confess, hoping I don't sound like a stick in the mud. "My specialized field is addiction."

Madison's eyes widen and she stops mid-bite, shaking her head. "Seriously?" she asks with an incredulous look.

I don't know whether I should be insulted or not, and it must show on my face as she quickly backtracks. "Oh my God, I'm so sorry—that sounded so rude. I didn't mean it like 'seriously' I don't believe you. I meant it as 'seriously, holy shit, that's cool!'" she finishes, her eyes still wide. "I'm actually taking a crash course in psych. I figure it'll help if I decide to pursue a different field of nursing down the road. So far however, I suck at it. You must be incredibly smart."

I internally breathe out a sigh of relief. "Well, thank you. Not a lot of people think being a shrink is cool. Or that I'm smart." I smirk. "So I'll take that as a compliment."

Madison nods animatedly. "Hell yes, it's a compliment, *Dr.* Dixon."

I laugh at her comment. "Just Dixon is fine."

"You don't look like a doctor," she randomly professes.

"Once again, thank you?" I phrase it as a question, as I'm not sure what she means by that.

She senses my confusion, and once again quickly clarifies. "I just meant..." Her devilish tongue suddenly darts out to lick away any fallen syrup, while she weighs up her next comment. "I just meant you're so...young."

However, the slight pause has me wondering what she really meant to say. I'd like to think the word she really wanted to use was "hot," but hey, one can dream.

Playing it cool, I run my finger around the rim of my cup and smirk. "Don't let this orderly state fool you," I say, poking fun at my unruly appearance.

Madison laughs, and I don't fail to notice her gaze lingering on my face a little longer than usual. Could it be Madison is just as impressed by me as I am by her?

This could get really, really interesting, or really, really ugly. It'll all depend on how I decide to play it.

"So if you don't mind me asking, how old are you?" I innocently ask, taking a bite of my bagel.

Madison looks to be deep in thought, but she shakes her head as if to clear it. "I'm twenty-three."

I *was* right. However, her young age just confirms what a vile old man I am, as all I'm visualizing is her tight, round, *young* ass and perky, perfect tits in the flesh. My eyes drop to her chest, and I scold myself for being so damn obvious because thus far, I've been a total gentleman.

As sad as this is, I've actually forgotten what it's like to just enjoy the company of the opposite sex without thinking of her naked, or wonder what color underwear she's wearing. But with Madison, that's exactly what's happened. We've been sitting here for—Jesus, I'm not even sure how long—and not once have I thought about sex, or thought about her naked, which for me has got to be some kind of record.

Her company alone was enough stimulation, and I haven't

felt this way since Lily. But just the thought of her ruins my pleasant morning, and I quickly push away my half-eaten bagel.

"You okay?" she asks, and I raise my eyes to meet her gentle concern.

"Yeah, fine," I lie. I feel like a total sook for letting my ex get to me once again.

Wanting to change the subject, I ask, "So I hope you don't mind me asking, but who was the douchebag you were with the other night?"

I really hope my question doesn't freak her out because I need to know.

"Oh, that was Tim."

"He's your boyfriend?" I casually ask, watching her facial expressions.

She surprises me when she laughs. "No way. We went on two dates, and apparently, I'm the love of his life."

"Well, the way he was pawing you, he certainly doesn't know how to treat the love of his life," I utter, only just containing my anger.

Madison nods, and as she lowers her eyes, I know I've struck a nerve. But I let it go and sip my coffee, while Madison demolishes the rest of her meal in silence. After she's done eating, she puts her hands to her flat belly and groans.

"You should have stopped me after my third bite," she says with a smile, the awkwardness from earlier thankfully gone.

"And miss you proclaiming your undying love for French toast? I don't think so," I reply, as I dodge a flying creamer.

As I reach for the bill, Madison playfully slaps her hand over mine. I ignore the instant sparks, and raise my eyebrow, wondering what's triggered her violence.

"I'm paying," she states, and sweet baby Jesus, I nearly rocket off my seat when I see her reach into her crop top.

"What? With your breasts?" I choke out, barely containing my slobber.

Madison bursts into fits of laughter as she produces a twenty. "No, with this." She tosses the note onto the counter.

Oh right, of course—she stores notes in her crop top, and uses her breasts as a purse. Dear Lord. I eye the note, envying it something wicked.

Finally composing myself enough to construct a sentence, I protest. "No, please, I can't let you pay. What kind of cheapskate do you think I am?" I dig into my pants pocket for my wallet, but it's not there. I frantically double-check, but sadly come up empty.

I'm not wearing my jacket, therefore, the only place it could be is…Juliet's. Looks like I'll have to swallow my pride and allow Madison to pay.

"Next time, it's on me," I state—stupidly, for who says there's going to be a next time?

I quickly zip my lips, and try to appear nonchalant as we both silently stand and exit our booth.

"I'd like that," Madison says when we step outside.

"Like what?" I ask, shielding my eyes from the blaring sun.

"For there to be a…next time."

My heart unexpectedly kicks up the pace, and I can't stop the small smile that tugs at my lips. Out here in the huge concrete jungle of New York City, she appears so petite, so tiny, and I literally have to stop myself from reaching out and protecting her from the hustle and bustle of the city that never sleeps. I don't know where this protectiveness has come from, and I stop myself from thinking crazy thoughts because they can't be healthy for either one of us.

I realize Madison is looking at me, waiting for me to comment on her confession, and I quickly put her out of her misery. "Me too."

"Yeah?" she says, the surprise clear in her voice.

"Yeah," I reply with a nod, admiring the way her cheeks turn a soft pink.

I stand staring at her, and she stands staring back at me. The moment is simply perfect, but I suddenly realize she's looking at me because she wants me to stop being a whimsical pussy and ask for her number.

Patting at my empty pockets, I realize I've also left my cell under Juliet's sofa, no doubt. "I don't have my phone on me." Leering forward and pretending to look down her top, I ask, "You wouldn't happen to have anything else hidden in there?"

Madison surprises me by cheekily throwing back, "Wouldn't you like to know?" and winks, while I almost gag on my tongue.

"So what do you suggest we do?"

Madison smiles, and the vision is simply superb. "Well, you know where I work. How 'bout you come in tonight? I start my shift at seven," she casually says.

"Okay, I think I can manage that."

Madison happily nods and then, this is when that awkward situation occurs. You know, where two people who are attracted to one another don't know whether to hug, kiss, shake hands or wave, to bid each other farewell.

I can see that Madison is also torn on what the right protocol here is by the way she's biting her bottom lip, and subtly looking at me to make the first move. But the fact I can still smell Juliet on me has me shying away from hugging her. There's no way I can kiss her for obvious reasons, and shaking hands or waving just feels so detached, like we're strangers. So like an utter moron, I raise my fist and watch as Madison looks at it confused.

I too look at it, cursing my stupidity, but now that I've put it out there, I have no other choice but to follow through before I look like a complete douche.

However, Madison stuns me as she slowly dodges my raised fist, not interested in fist bumping with me, and stands on tippy-toes to kiss my stubbled cheek. The minute she invades my personal space, my body sings, drowning in her vanilla scent.

"I'll catch ya later, Dixon," she says, pulling away way too quickly, and I nod, dropping my fist.

"Bye, Madison," I reply, and watch as the most amazing girl walks away from me, hoping it's not my last image of her.

Thank Christ I somehow managed not to lose my key, and the moment I came home, I had a long shower and fell face-first onto my bed, not even bothering to dress. The only thing that wakes me is a loud, unrelenting knock on my door. Moaning and attempting to clear the fog from my brain, I turn to my right and see that my bedside clock reads 6:27 p.m.

Once the perpetrator makes it clear they're not going away, and their knocking gets louder, I give in and throw on a pair of sweats. I don't even bother with a T-shirt because whoever this person is, they're most definitely not staying.

"What?" I bark as I open the door, but nearly fall flat on my face when I see Juliet standing before me.

It takes me a moment to fire on all four cylinders, but once I do, I coolly question, "What are you doing here?"

Juliet simply grins and holds up my wallet and phone, not needing to explain anything further.

The fact she went through my wallet to find my address feels like a slight invasion of privacy, but I really should be a little more grateful that she made the trip down here. Yet, this feels too personal, too close to home—literally. A woman hasn't set foot inside my home since Lily, but the way Juliet is currently looking at me, she wants to change that.

"So are you going to invite me in? Or am I going to have to blow you in the hallway?"

If not for my acute hearing, I would say I misheard her, but I know there's no mistaking her intentions as her eyes rake down my body, stopping at my ribs and focusing on my tattoo.

"'We are never so defenseless against suffering as when we love,'" she says, reading my Freud-and Lily-inspired tattoo. "Well, well, Dr. Mathews, I would have never thought."

I forgot Juliet never saw me fully unclothed, as due to our animalistic fucking, only the bare essentials were removed and we worked with whatever was left. That thought has me feeling like a complete bastard, so I open the door wider, permitting Juliet into my home.

The moment she steps into my abode, however, every pore in my body demands I kick her out because this feels so wrong. I have no other choice, so I close the exit behind me, feeling like I'm locking my own prison door.

I stand back as Juliet takes in my apartment.

"So" she says, turning around to face me after a minute of

scrutinizing my home.

"So" I parrot, placing my hands into my pockets.

I have nothing I want to say to her because after this morning, I'm a little shocked to see her here. I made peace with the fact I'd probably never see her again. But here she is, standing in front of me, looking deliciously mouth-watering.

"Sorry about this morning, Dixon," she says. "I had somewhere I had to be."

I nod, trying my best to appear unaffected. "Thanks for bringing my things over. You can leave them there." I gesture with my chin toward the kitchen counter.

"You're *mad*?" Juliet says in part shock, part question, as she attempts to contain her surprise.

Am I?

Honestly, I don't know what I feel. I've never had this happen to me before, so I guess my ego is a little bruised.

"To be mad would indicate that I care, Ms. Harte, and to be frank, I do not. Last night was fun, but that's all it was. So the answer to your question is no, I'm not mad," I reply sharply.

Juliet looks taken aback by my curt response, but recovers a second later. "It was more than just *fun*. It's all I've been thinking about all day." She sweeps her hair off her neck, revealing the huge red welt I inflicted with my teeth.

I remain impassive, although I feel like an animal. "Well, I'm glad I've provided you with images you can revisit, as that was the first *and* last time. Last night was a mistake," I firmly state.

"You don't mean that," Juliet counters with a confident smile.

"Yes, I do. It was entirely my fault. I apologize for my

inexcusable behavior. I take all the blame," I say, using my professional voice.

But Juliet won't have a bit of it. "Oh, cut the crap. I was there, I know you enjoyed it. I know you enjoyed fucking me without restraint. You have nothing to apologize for. I wanted it as much as you did. I've wanted *you* from the moment I saw you," she confesses, and this is the first moment I've seen a glimmer of vulnerability in the unbending Juliet. "I still want you. And I know you want me too," she asserts, looking up at me from under her mascara-clad lashes.

Wanting her is not the issue here. It's the fact that I *shouldn't* want her—that's the problem. Juliet is a dangerous woman, and with her, all I can see is that danger escalating into hazardous territory. My brain tells me to throw her out, but my traitorous body is telling me that she's no longer my patient, so what's the harm in two consensual adults giving in to what they both want?

Juliet takes a step toward me, no doubt sensing my retreat, and I don't back away, even though I know I should. She casually unties the sash from around her waist, peeling the brown trench coat from her slender body. The coat pools at her stiletto-clad feet and she takes another step toward me.

"Don't be mad at me. Let me remind you how hot we were together." She runs a red fingernail down my chest.

"Juliet," I protest in a half-assed plea, but the moment she cups my rising erection in her palm, I'm hers.

"You may say no, Dixon, but your body is saying yes," and as she rubs me harder, my treacherous body succumbs.

Before long, she's dropped to her knees in front of me and is pulling down my sweats, my rigid body on full display, betraying how turned I am.

"Do you know how good this felt in me last night?" she says, sliding her hand up and down my length.

"Tell me," I demand, unable to tear my eyes away as she's jerking me off.

"How about I just show you?" she suggests, and the moment she wraps her ruby lips around me, any uncertainties get thrown out the window, and I allow this vixen total control.

Her expert mouth glides down my cock with exact precision, and I can't stop the moan that escapes my lips as I've never been blown this good before. I thrust my hips forward and throw my head backward when I hit the back of her throat. She deep throats me effortlessly.

"That's it, oh fuck. You're so damn good," I pant, trying to rein in my early release. "Deeper, go deeper."

Nothing else matters when she steadies a hand around my waist, her fingers squeezing in sync with her delicious mouth.

The harder she sucks, the faster I pump my hips and before long, I'm fucking her mouth with a desperate speed. The moment I try to pull away, as I'm afraid I'm hurting her, she latches on tighter, reaching down and palming my shaft. The friction of her hand, combined with the speed of her mouth is too much, and I'm seconds away from coming.

She senses my frantic need to explode and holds on tighter, her mouth creating an intense suction around me, and after two cavernous sucks, I'm shamefully done. I pull my hips away, but she licks and strokes with a deep pull and with no other choice, I explode in her mouth while cursing out my release. She milks me until I have nothing left, and only when the last aftershock rocks my body does she let go.

I've just received the best blowjob of my life, in the apartment I once shared with the love of life. The apartment I promised another female would never enter.

Do I feel guilty?

*Hell no.*

# Eight

*Madison*

"Maddy, I hate to say it, but I don't think he's coming," says my best friend, Mary Mitts, as she wipes down table nine.

"You don't know that," I argue, her truthful comment snapping me out of my stare off with the front door. "We never agreed on a time. Maybe something came up and he's on the way. I mean, I did say sometime tonight," I state, making up excuses for why Dixon isn't here.

"Well, technically, it is tomorrow," Mary says, looking at her watch.

"Not helping, Lamb," I reply with a smile, using the nickname I've had for her since we were kids.

"I'm sorry, but what kind of best friend would I be if I wasn't looking out for you? I just don't want to see you get hurt," she says, and I know she's referring to Tim my stalker, who Dixon saved me from the first night we met.

"I know, but Dixon is…"

"Don't you dare say different," Mary warns, wagging her finger at me while I bite back a smile.

"But he is," I quickly rebuke, and duck to avoid getting hit in the face with a coaster.

"No, he isn't. He's a guy, therefore he's a dick," Mary states, but I don't take it to heart, as she's only bitter at the moment because she's going through a tough breakup.

"Lamb, not all men are pigs. He didn't have to jump in and save me from Tim, but he did. He didn't even think twice about it. If that doesn't scream 'non-pig' then I don't know what does."

"Oh please, that's your hormones talking. That man is trouble with a capital T. And not to mention you're like half his age," she adds, fastening her fiery red hair into a tighter ponytail.

I can't help but laugh, as I am so *not* half his age. Early thirties I'd peg him being, but it's not his age I find myself uncharacteristically daydreaming about. His bright blue eyes and messy, chocolate brown hair are another story, however.

"I'll give him another twenty minutes, and if he doesn't show up, then I'll forget I ever met Dr. Dixon," I state, very unconvincingly.

"Ah-ha," Mary retorts, totally not buying my pledge. "Again, I believe that's your hormones talking."

I playfully flip her off while she pokes her tongue out at me before heading off to serve table twelve.

I, however, continue wiping down a spotless table eight with my eyes peeled to the door because I know he'll arrive any minute now.

He has to.

Twenty minutes came and went with no sign of Dixon. It's now 2 a.m., and I'm locking up. I can't wait to go home and forget today ever existed.

I still can't believe he stood me up. I know we didn't have a date per se, but we did kind of have plans. I really thought he *was* different, as there is definitely something there between us. I know he felt it too, and by the not-so-covert glances, I also know he's somewhat attracted to me.

But on the flipside, he did look like he was sneaking out of someone's apartment this morning, and then he wanted me to fist bump him. Maybe I'm just reading into things 'cause God knows, I have limited experience with this kind of stuff.

I've never really had a boyfriend, and Tim doesn't count. We were seeing one another for a month, and after two dates, I knew we wouldn't work. But Tim thought otherwise, and that's the reason he got so mad at me the night Dixon and I met. He pretty much demanded I give him another chance. When I said hell to the fuck no, he suggested I "give it up," as apparently, that's what our nonexistent relationship was missing. When I not so politely declined, he got a little physical, and that's when Dixon saved the day.

Apart from the fact I am in no way attracted to Tim, I don't actually know if I'll ever be ready to "give it up."

I'm good at hiding my emotions and feelings, I always have been. But when Dixon told me he was a psychiatrist, I thought my ruse was up. I almost got up and left, but walking away from the first male I was remotely interested in felt wrong. And besides, I promised myself I would no longer allow my past to weigh me down.

I'm so glad I stayed because for the first time in a long time, I actually enjoyed myself and wasn't constantly looking at my watch, or looking over my shoulder. With Dixon, I felt safe, and I also felt alive.

I switch off the lights and lock up. Living in New York, you just get used to dealing with a trillion locks, and it takes me about two minutes to figure out which key goes into which lock. I'm halfway done when someone taps me on the shoulder, which has me screaming in absolute terror.

"Madison, it's me! Shit, I'm so sorry, I didn't mean to scare you," says a familiar voice. I turn around so fast, I nearly fall flat on my ass.

"Dixon?" I wheeze, my hand poised over my beating heart. "What are you doing here?"

I watch as he averts his beautiful blue eyes and shamefacedly replies, "I said I would drop by. I'm sorry I'm late," he adds.

"Did you run here?" I stupidly ask.

"Well, I would call it a brisk walk," he confesses with a lopsided smirk as he rolls a stone under his sneaker.

The damp hair at his temples reveals he more than just walked, and I try not to bask in the fact that he ran all the way here just to see me. Mentally giving Mary an "I told you so," I turn my back and finish locking up, needing a minute to center my raging nerves.

I can't help but wonder where Dixon has been, as he doesn't appear to be dressed up, and I dare say, he ran here from his house. So what was he doing till 2 a.m.? And more importantly, who was he doing it with? That thought has me envisioning distasteful scenarios and *positions*, but I tell my distrustful mind to quit it with the conspiracy theories for one night.

"Well, I hope you didn't give yourself a stitch," I taunt, wanting to lighten the mood.

Dixon scoffs. "I'll have you know I was a track athlete in high school."

"The operative word being 'was,'" I say as I turn around to face him. "And high school was a lonnng time ago for you."

"Want to put a wager on that?" He smirks, and my God, he is handsome.

"Sure," I reply, crossing my arms over my chest in hopes my beating heart doesn't explode from my rib cage.

"You said you run every morning, well, I challenge you to a race," he smugly declares, raising an eyebrow.

"Name your time and place, Dr. Dixon," I boldly reply.

"Tomorrow. 6 a.m. Central Park. First person to run a mile in the shortest amount of time is the winner."

"Let's make it two miles," I cockily say, but quickly curse my confidence.

Dixon looks impressed. "Very well, two it is. Meet at North Meadow?"

"Sure. What does the winner get?" I ask, my competitive streak shining through.

Dixon taps his chin, deep in thought. "The winner will be treated to a lavish breakfast by the loser."

"Well, you already owe me a breakfast, Doc. And I can't eat two breakfasts in one day."

Dixon chuckles at my self-assurance. "Okay, let's make it

dinner then."

"Dinner it is. I hope you've saved your pennies, 'cause I'm gonna order the lobster," I tease, rubbing my hands together.

"We'll see." He grins, and I'm thankful he appreciates my bad humor.

"Well, on that note, I better go home and get some beauty sleep. Night, Dixon." I search through my bag for my keys.

"Where'd you park? I'll walk you to your car," he quickly offers.

"It's okay. I'm just around the corner."

"Please, I insist," and before I have time to argue, he's leading the way.

With a small smile, I follow, feeling strangely happy that this amazingly hot man wants to walk me to my car—a car that I don't need, but have, thanks to my fears.

We walk in reflective silence as I desperately want to ask him where he was tonight, but it's not really my business. I mean, we just met. We're not even really friends, as I hardly know him, but the thing is, I want to. From the moment I met him, there was something there, but I'm sure a man like Dixon isn't short of female attention, and has *women*, not inexperienced, scarred virgins, to satisfy his needs.

"Everything okay over there?" Dixon asks, disturbing my thoughts.

"Yeah, why?" I ask, suddenly worried my thoughts are transparent.

"You're awfully quiet, which can't be a good sign."

"I was just thinking about where I would like to go for dinner," I tease, hoping to disguise my insecurities as I sound the alarm on my Fiesta. "Well, this is me. I'll see you in a few hours." I fiddle with the strap on my bag, not knowing what to do next.

This is the second time there has been some weird static bouncing between us, and I know he feels it too because he totally just checked out my boobs. But this is not me. I'm not one to feel so comfortable with the opposite sex, or care if they like me or not. But with Dixon, that's exactly how I feel. And I don't understand why.

"Well," he says, clearing his throat. "I'll see you in the morning," and I cringe, hoping he doesn't want me to fist bump him again.

However, he surprises me as he unexpectedly reaches forward and brushes a stray strand of hair off my face. Normally, I would shy away, but in this instance, I find myself wanting to lean into his touch. But I don't.

"Night, Dixon," I whisper.

"Night, Madison."

And with that, he turns his back on me, and only then do I breathe.

# Nine

## Madison

It's now 5:30a.m., and I look like utter shit. Why I agreed to such an early morning run, on a Sunday I might add, is beyond me. But I have a feeling Dixon could ask me just about anything and I would say yes.

I've dressed for comfort, not style, as I intend to run like the wind across that finish line.

Reaching for my water bottle and keys, I lock the door behind me and make my way downstairs. I hit the pavement at a brisk pace, as it always freaks me out being up this early with no one around. But I'm twenty-three and I've decided this is the year I won't allow the skeletons in my closet to haunt me any longer.

For more than half of my life, I've lived with a secret I've never told a single soul, not even my mother, who I love more than life itself. Even though those secrets can never be told, I feel in some sick, twisted way that they've shaped me into the woman I'm determined to become.

Crossing the street, I stop with the nostalgia and focus on finding Dixon. I search the main entrance, but he's nowhere to be found. Maybe he's running late.

Starting my warm-up, I turn my head to the left to stretch out my neck muscles. From the corner of my eye, I see Dixon. Someone who's just about to go for a two-mile run shouldn't look this good, but he does. He's in loose running shorts and a tight white T-shirt, and although it doesn't sound like anything special, on Dixon it looks like he's dressed for runway.

His muscular physique is a lot more obvious now that he's not wearing a suit jacket and pants, and oh my God, as he stretches his arms above his head, his T-shirt rides up, exposing a hardened slab of sculptured abs and toned obliques. My eyes may have deceived me because he's a few feet away, but I'm quite certain I saw a hint of ink tattooed on his side.

The thought has my toes curling, as that image has just made Dr. Dixon a truckload sexier.

Deciding to stop with the drooling, I make my way over to him and will my racing pulse to calm down, as I haven't even started running yet.

"It's not too late to back out, ya know?" I chirp, stopping a few feet away.

"In your dreams," he says with a lopsided smirk. I watch his eyes unexpectedly smolder as he takes in my appearance.

I look like I always do when running. No makeup, my long hair secured in a high ponytail, and my clothes hardly flattering, but there's no denying that he's blatantly checking me out. Maybe he *does* like me.

My insides warm at the idea, but squashing down my

immature fantasies, I quickly say, "So you ready to get your ass whipped?"

Dixon grins and, thankfully, his eyes return to their normal beautiful blue. "Give it your best shot." His cockiness titillates me.

"So what are the rules?" I ask, lunging forward into a hamstring stretch.

Dixon programs his fancy watch. "I'd say the zoo is roughly two miles from here."

I nod in agreement.

"Well, the first person to reach the zoo is the winner. Oh, and we have to run the same route," he adds with a smirk, just in case I thought about taking a shortcut.

"That's it?" I ask, raising a suspicious eyebrow.

"That's it," Dixon confirms with a smile.

He stands by my side and looks over, grinning. "Just a word of warning, I don't like to lose," he confesses as he eyes me up and down.

"Well, isn't that funny, 'cause neither do I. See you on the other side…loser." I take off in a quick sprint, leaving Dixon at our makeshift start line.

I hear him following in quick pursuit, and his chase only has me increasing my speed to an even pace. The first few yards are always the hardest for me, but once I find my rhythm, I can run for miles. I guess you could say I started running to escape my demons, but no matter how hard I ran, they were always biting at my heels.

"Just so you know," Dixon huffs, catching up to me. "I let you have a head start."

We both keep a steady pace, our breaths the only thing

sounding between us, and that's good because if we spoke, I would lose myself in his deep, rough voice. I focus on the way my body feels alive, the blood pumping through my veins and animating my every move.

We jog in silence, side by side for a few minutes, until Dixon pushes forward, taking the lead. I stay back, as I'll save my energy and pull out the big guns on the last half a mile. And besides, back here, I can totally check out Dixon's muscular legs and taut butt. He is a work of art, and I can't help but feel slightly curious to know what that tight butt would feel like in the flesh.

"Tired already?" Dixon teases as he turns around and begins running backward, watching amusingly as I flip him off.

"I'm just being generous. I don't want to show you up too early. That would be kinda embarrassing," I say, puffing.

Dixon laughs and turns back around, thankfully watching where he's going. I decide to catch up to him, as he's gaining a steady lead because I'm lagging behind, distracted by his hot ass.

"So" Dixon pants, his eyes focused ahead. "How long you been running?"

"About nine years," I confess, leaving out why.

"You're quite good," he admits. I turn toward him with a smirk.

"And you're surprised?"

Dixon shakes his head. "Not at all. My mother taught me never to assume anything when it came to women."

I can't stop the laugh that breaks free from my winded chest. "Your mother sounds like a smart lady."

"She was," Dixon says, and I don't fail to pick up on his use of the past tense. "She passed," he explains. "Six months ago, to breast cancer."

"Oh, Dixon. I'm really sorry." I frown, as the thought of losing my mother tears a big hole in my chest.

"Thank you," he says with a sad smile.

"So it's just you and your dad?"

"Um, yeah," he replies with a pause, which confuses me, but I let it slide as I know uncomfortable when I see it.

"How about you?" he innocently asks, not realizing how a simple question such as this is my worst nightmare.

But I casually reply, "What about me?"

"Do you have any siblings?"

"Yeah, I have an older brother. But it's just me and my mom."

"Where's your dad?"

"Oh, um, he left when I was five. I don't really remember him," I disclose, keeping my eyes focused ahead.

"That must've been tough."

"It was okay—my mom is the best. She was my mom *and* my dad. I really am lucky to have her as my mother. We're close," I share, happy to divulge this information about my past.

"She sounds like an amazing lady," Dixon says, and I nod.

"She really is," I reply with sincerity because before my mom remarried, we were doing it tough.

"But I'm sure your big brother looked after his little sister, right?" Dixon randomly says, and I know it's meant to be an innocent question, but the mere mention of my brother has me suddenly losing my footing and I trip, my forehead and wrists breaking the fall.

"Holy shit! Are you okay?" he asks. His voice mingles with the loud ringing in my ears.

I'm pretty sure I'm not okay, but I nod, which has my brain rolling around my head like marbles.

I fell flat on my stomach, and I'm beyond embarrassed to be sprawled out on the ground, so I try to lift myself up, but Dixon quickly warns, "No, no, don't get up too quickly, you've hit your head pretty hard."

"I'm fine," I say, waving him off, as I'm more worried about how I'm going to face him, rather than my injured head.

As I lift myself into a half-sitting position, I see Dixon crouching near me. I watch as his eyes widen, and he gasps, "Fuck, you're bleeding." Before I can protest, he's yanking off his shirt and pressing the amazing-smelling garment to my forehead.

I whine the moment it touches my sore brow, and Dixon flinches, easing the pressure.

"Sorry." He frowns, his intense eyes focused on my temple.

"It's okay," I whisper, mesmerized by being so close to him, and also mesmerized by the fact I'm so close to him while he's topless.

I try my absolute hardest not to stare, but it's extremely hard not to as he's simply stunning.

A totally hair-free, well-defined chest is inches away from my face. As I lower my eyes, I see the only hair visible is the fine dusting of darkened curls painting his navel, which leads into his low-slung shorts. His washboard abs should be illegal, and I won't even touch on his sculptured V-muscle, which has my eyes bulging at its pure perfection.

"Are you sure you're okay?" Dixon kindly asks, and I snap out of my trance.

"Ye-yeah," I stutter, raising my eyes to meet his.

His strong features express nothing but concern, and just when I thought I couldn't fall deeper into obsession with this man, I fall harder than ever before.

I watch as Dixon removes his soiled T-shirt from my brow, his intense eyes examining my wound. "I don't think you'll need stitches, but I dare say you'll have a nasty headache for the next couple of days."

"Nothing a little Advil won't fix," I say with a smile, and attempt to shift so I'm sitting up taller.

Dixon places his hands on my upper arms to help steady me, and I appreciate the support as my head is still spinning.

"So looks like I'm buying," I declare, trying to ignore how my body responds to Dixon's touch.

"Well, you were definitely the winner from where I stood."

"How'd you figure that?" I ask, not quite following.

"Before you so elegantly swan-dived into the asphalt"—I lunge out to playfully smack him on his arm, but he dodges my attack—"I was going to forfeit," he explains.

"You were not, you liar." I chuckle in disbelief.

Dixon grins, placing a hand over his heart, attempting to appear genuine. "Oh, but I was. This old body is obviously no match for your youthful spirit. You won fair and square, Madison."

I'm not buying his story for a second, but he looks too adorable, and I can't argue with him.

"Well, I would still feel wrong, as it kinda feels like I'm cheating. So how about you buy dinner, and I'll buy dessert?" I suggest, hoping he says yes. I'm desperate to draw out any time spent with him.

Dixon appears to mull over my proposal, then with a

lopsided smile, he says, "You drive a hard bargain, but I suppose that's fair."

I barely stop myself from fist pumping in excitement because I'm sure any sudden movement will enrage my impending headache.

"So it's settled then. I'll let you choose the day." I don't want to look too eager and suggest we make good on our agreement tonight.

However, my heart ends up in my throat as Dixon suggests, "How about tomorrow evening?"

Trying not to blind him with my ridiculously excited smile, I nod. "Tomorrow works for me."

Dixon smirks and slowly stands to his full, topless, dominating height. He extends his hand down to me, and I gratefully accept, standing gradually, as I still feel light-headed. As we stand toe-to-toe, my overactive mind invokes images of me pressing myself up against all that tanned, supple skin and getting lost in its soft smoothness. But I shake those thoughts aside, as I feel a little guilty that Dixon is half nude because of me.

A female jogger runs past us, and she makes it more than obvious she's gaping at the naked god in front of her. An unexpected sense of jealousy passes over me, and I try my hardest not to eyeball her because I have no right to.

Dixon seems oblivious and reaches into his pocket, producing a crisp white business card. "Now there are no excuses to run late," he regretfully says, and I know he's referring to last night.

I thankfully accept it, but with nowhere safe to put it, I place it in my sports bra, which is a habit I picked up from running without any pockets. It really isn't a big deal, but as I look up and meet Dixon's heated eyes, it appears he disagrees. He snaps his intense gaze from my chest and meets my eyes.

"Remind me to never ask you to mind my belongings," he says, appearing half serious.

"And why's that?" I ask with a smirk.

"Because I'll no doubt lose a hand," he cheekily replies while I almost gag on my tongue.

Little does he know his hands are always welcome.

# Ten

*Dixon*

So I'm either the smartest or the stupidest motherfucker known to mankind.

I'm betting on the latter.

I've somehow managed to find myself in a predicament where I am interested in two women. A couple of weeks ago, the thought of being interested in *one* woman was comical, but here I am, sitting at my desk, fisting my hair in frustration because I don't know what the hell to do.

After being ridden into next year by Juliet, I fell into an exhausted heap and slept like the dead. The only thing that woke me was a fire engine zipping past at a little past one o'clock in the morning. After my sleep and post-coitus-clogged brain decided to play catch-up, I realized I had stood up Madison as we agreed to meet to exchange numbers and whatnot.

A sense of utter regret passed over me, and before I knew what was happening, I was running toward her work like a bat outta hell.

So the question here is, why? Why did I feel guilty? I mean, I just slept with another woman six hours prior. If I was going to feel guilty about anything, it should be the fact that I still had Juliet's scent all over me when I met up with Madison. But with Juliet, it was just sex—with Madison, it was…more.

The obvious answer here would be to tell Ms. Harte to hit the road and see where things go with Madison. But I can't—sex without strings is so much easier than a relationship. And I have a feeling a relationship with Madison wouldn't be smooth sailing. Call it doctor's intuition, but I think she has some serious baggage buried underneath her sweet smile.

So what do I want? Sex? Or a possible relationship? Because at the moment, I'm currently presented with both options, but I don't know which I want more.

I know this all stems from my damaging breakup with Lily. But I am as much to blame as she is. No, I never forced her to fuck my best friend, but I also never dealt with my emotional scars at the time, and now look what I've turned into—a commitment-phobe.

Massaging my temples, I really am in no state of mind to be counseling anyone today. The wise thing to do would be to take the afternoon off. Just as I'm about to call Ms. Vale and ask her to cancel the rest of my appointments, she buzzes me through the intercom.

"Dr. Mathews," she frantically says, which is very uncharacteristic of her.

"Yes, Ms. Vale?" I quickly reply. "Is everything okay?"

"Dr. Mathews, a patient who doesn't have an appointment insists on seeing you."

I hear Susanna cover the receiver and address whoever is outside, making it quite clear she'll have to make an appointment if she wishes to see me.

"Oh, stop right there! Miss, you can't go in there," Susanna states. Before I know what's happening, my office door flies open, and a hysterical Juliet charges in.

Susanna is chasing after her, her face filled with irritation and concern, but I wave her off, as Juliet looks like hell.

"I'm so sorry, Dr. Mathews! She just barged in here," Susanna apologizes while glaring at a sobbing Juliet.

"It's fine, Ms. Vale. Please shut the door on your way out."

She looks at me, slightly confused, but she does as I ask because she knows I don't mince my words. The moment the door closes, I stand behind my desk, watching Juliet as she weeps uncontrollably. I stand motionless because I don't know what to do.

Professionally, I'm not to hug or canoodle her, as I'm not her friend. I'm not here to cuddle her and tell her everything will be all right. But as her lover, that's exactly what I should be doing. And this is why you do not get involved with your patients.

"Juliet, is everything okay?" I ask, still standing behind my desk, using it as a barrier between us.

"What does it look like? No, everything is not fucking okay!" she cries, her tearstained eyes meeting mine.

Clearing my throat and adjusting my tie, I round my desk and point at the sofa.

"Please, take a seat."

"I'm not here to get fucking psychoanalyzed, Dixon." But she thankfully slumps onto the couch, and her sniffles lessen.

Taking a seat near her, I place my palm on her bare knee. "What's happened? Why are you so upset?"

"No matter how hard I try, I'll never be good enough," she whispers, her lip trembling as she lowers her face.

"Good enough for whom?" I gently ask.

"For…anybody," she replies, and her slight pause has me wondering what she originally wanted to say.

"That's not true," I rebuke. "You just have to believe in yourself, Juliet. I know how messed up that sounds, considering our current circumstances. But any man would be lucky to have your affections."

"You think?" She sniffs, raising her face.

"I know," I confirm. "All these awards on my walls confirm I know what I'm talking about," I add with a small smile, hoping to lighten the mood.

Thankfully, she laughs and reaches into her clutch for a tissue. As she dabs at her eyes, I wonder what brought this on. The doctor in me has long gone, and I'm speaking to her purely as her lover.

"Is there anything I can do?" I ask, reaching forward and brushing aside a strand of blond hair.

"Maybe we could, I don't know, talk?"

This is the first time I've seen her be…vulnerable, and it's a look that suits her.

"Sure, I'd like that." I realize I don't actually know anything about her.

I know how to make her come with my mouth in five quick seconds. And how she likes to be fucked, but I don't actually know *who* she is and what she likes that's non-sex-related. I thought she was happy just being fuck buddies, but that was my screwup, as I should have never assumed—looks like my mother was right once again.

"Do you think we could grab a coffee after work?"

At this moment, the Juliet Harte I thought I knew has just flipped my beliefs onto their ass, and this person sitting before me is a complete stranger. This stranger is one I actually want to get to know better.

"Sure," I reply with a nod. I owe her this.

Juliet takes a deep breath, patting down her hair and face. "I'm really sorry for storming in here like a crazy person. I should have called first."

"It's fine. It happens all the time." I smirk, and she laughs, her beautiful face no longer clogged in tears.

"Okay, well, I'll let you get back to work." She stands, smoothing the crinkles from her dress. "I'll meet you at around seven?"

"Sounds great," I reply, also standing, my hands dug deep into my pockets.

"Great. Well, see you tonight." She throws me completely off guard as she steps forward and hugs me.

It's the first time we've embraced, which is utterly ridiculous and shameful, seeing as I've embraced her insides on more than one occasion. I slowly remove my hands from my pockets, and as I wrap her into my arms, I'm shocked at how fragile and vulnerable she feels. I'm not used to this Juliet, and I have a feeling it'll take some getting used to.

She breaks away after a moment and bids me farewell with a chaste kiss on my cheek. I watch, dumbfounded, as she leaves my office because that woman looked like Juliet, but that person is not the Juliet I thought I knew.

I take a seat behind my desk, still flabbergasted at what just took place. The moment I met Juliet, I knew she'd cause a storm. But where does that leave things with Madison and me?

My cell beeps, alerting me to an awaiting text, and I welcome the distraction. Swiping through my messages, I groan, slapping my palm against my forehead.

Reading the message over, I feel like the world's biggest asshole because the sweet words just taunt me with what I have to do.

***I haven't eaten all day :p***
***See you tonight. Can't wait.***
***Maddy x***

# Eleven

*Madison*

"What do mean 'he can't make it?'" asks Mary from the end of my bed.

I shrug, tossing her my phone so she can see the proof.

As she reads over the message, she curses. "What does he mean 'something came up'? Like what, exactly? The only forgivable excuse here would be that his mother died," she barks, scrunching up her face in obvious disgust that Dixon asked for a "rain check" on our date.

"His mother *is* dead," I reply, sadly putting away the beautiful blue dress I was planning to wear this evening.

"Oh, whatever. This is horseshit!" she cries, jabbing her finger into the phone screen.

"I know, Lamb." I sigh because it really is horseshit.

Over three hours ago, Dixon messaged me, claiming something came up and he wouldn't be able to make our date.

He apologized a number of times, and asked for a rain check. Other than that, he gave me no other reason he couldn't attend or when this alleged rain check was to take place.

I feel so stupid. I can't believe I actually thought a man like Dixon would be interested in a *girl* like me.

"I'm an idiot. Dixon probably doesn't even think of me like that. I mean, look at him and look at me," I say, doing a sweep down my body.

"No, *he's* the idiot. We're going out," Mary angrily states.

She jumps up from my bed, storming over to my closet and rummaging through my garments.

"I don't want to go out." The thought of socializing with anyone sounds like a horrible idea.

"This isn't optional," Mary barks with her head buried in my closet.

"Lamb," I warn, but Mary turns her head, pinning me with a look that screams finality.

"Fine," I huff, throwing my hands in the air, as there really isn't any point in arguing with her.

"You won't regret it," she says with a crooked smile.

Famous last words.

So when Mary said we were going out, I thought we were going out for pizza or to a movie. I didn't realize she meant out, out.

I'm sitting at a table that overlooks a huge dance floor, completely and utterly out of my comfort zone. I watch as Mary bumps and grinds against some pierced rock god without a care in the world. She recently broke up with her high school sweetheart, Corey, and I know under her tough exterior, she's hurting.

The man she trusted, the man she gave her virginity to, turned out to be a lying, cheating jerk, so I really don't blame her for being so bitter. But I like to believe that not all guys think with their dicks.

I mean, yes, Dixon is an ass for totally bailing on me, but not once did I ever feel objectified when in his presence, nor did I ever feel like he was talking to me because he wanted to get into my pants. I felt we had a genuine connection, and maybe he was different from all the other guys I've met.

But I guess I was wrong.

Reaching for my tequila, I decide to drown my sorrows in this sunrise. I don't have class till late tomorrow afternoon.

Just as I begin to feel a buzz, the barstool next to me scrapes along the floor, and I turn to look at who has stolen Mary's seat.

"Hey, is anyone sitting here?" asks the hot, green-eyed stranger beside me.

I nod with a smile. "Actually, yes, there is. You see that crazy redhead on the dance floor?" I point at my best friend, who is currently surrounded by a group of eager suitors.

The hottie beside me nods as he narrows his eyes, looking Mary's way.

"Well, that's who was sitting here," I conclude with a grin.

My stranger gives me a dimpled smile and leans closer to yell into my ear as the music blares over the speakers. "I don't think she'll be back anytime soon," he replies, and I laugh because I think he just may be right.

I don't know if it's the alcohol or the fact I feel a little rejected by Dixon's "rain check," but whatever it is, I extend my hand and smile.

"Hi, I'm Madison."

"Hi, I'm David," my stranger says, and I try not to cringe at the fact his name reminds me of another name that starts with D.

"Nice to meet you, David," I say, quickly recovering from my Dixon depression.

"You too. Can I buy you a drink?" David asks, his long bangs falling into his eyes.

I chug down the rest of my tequila and smile. "Sure."

David laughs, and I instantly feel at ease with him.

"I'll be right back," he says, and I watch as he makes his way through the crowd, impressed with what I see.

Maybe there's hope for me yet. I mean, everything happens for a reason. Maybe I just haven't figured out my reason for meeting Dixon.

# Twelve

*Dixon*

*Two and a half months later*

"Is the garlic minced or chopped?" I mumble to myself as I flip through this wretched cookbook, trying to find the recipe for the confit of salmon with crab crush and dill drizzle.

How can one's life change in the blink of an eye?

One moment, Juliet was my fuck buddy, and in the next, she's my…snuggle buddy?

I really don't know what to call Juliet. She's not really my girlfriend, but she's not really my booty call, either. I haven't slept with anyone other than her for over two months, and the reason for that is because being with Juliet is easy. I don't have to put in the hard yards with her, and she satisfies my every need.

She tells me she hasn't slept with anyone else either, which is a big thing for an ex-sex addict. However, we both agreed it was best she continued therapy for her addiction because once an addict, always an addict. We also agreed I wasn't the best person for the job, as that was all kinds of messed up. I didn't really fancy hearing about how badly she wanted to deep throat her aerobics instructor.

So what are Juliet and I? Honestly, I don't know.

I'm too old to use the word girlfriend, so I don't refer to Juliet as anything other than Juliet—the woman I am currently "sort of" seeing but definitely not dating.

The night we had coffee changed our "situation" dramatically. Juliet and I did the unthinkable: we actually spoke. Of course there was a blow job involved, but after all that, I got to know the real Juliet Harte.

I must admit, I was afraid to know who the enigma was behind the golden cooch, but once I peeled back her layers, I actually liked who I saw. It also didn't hurt that she fucked like a rabbit and kept me sated beyond belief.

That moment of weakness, however, was the last I ever saw. Juliet's back to being guarded and confident, and honestly, I don't know who I prefer more.

Our conversations are occasionally wooden, and our drawn-out silences are becoming more frequent, but who needs conversation when our bodies fill the static?

A major regret is that I felt I chose Juliet over Madison because I haven't spoken to her since I bailed on our date. If Madison and I had met under different circumstances, things could have turned out differently for us. We just met at the wrong time and place because I'm not a total bastard, and I would never play both women that way. And honestly, I could never do to Madison the things I do to Juliet. My need for depravity would soil her innocence because, in the end, my dick won out over my good sense.

Therefore, I like to think it's for the best, and I wish Madison all the luck in finding someone better suited for her. Wherever she is, I hope she's happy and putting her boob purse to good use. That thought still has my dick twitching in interest because although Juliet's rack is spectacular, Madison's was fucking epic.

The burning smell has my thoughts crawling out of Madison's luscious tits to the here and now. "Shit!" I curse because my salmon is starting to resemble a doorstop.

The fact I'm cooking for my non-girlfriend on a Friday night really is appalling, and I know if Hunter were around, he would be sounding the invisible whip. I've turned into a complete and utter pussy. But it's because of the pussy that I'm becoming this domesticated douche.

But Hunter isn't around because, somehow, Friday night has turned into Juliet's and my night. Friday night was usually reserved for the boys, but Juliet has taken precedence over my comrades, and I've tapped out more times than I care to admit.

My rule is slowly becoming nonexistent, as Juliet has slept over a few nights. The best thing about having Juliet here is that memories of Lily, memories I thought I so desperately wanted to hold on to, are now becoming so faint I can barely even remember them. I actually feel like I'm finally moving on and closing that chapter of my life. A chapter I should have closed a long time ago.

So things with Juliet, although not conventional, work. Neither of us has any expectations of where things are headed, which suits me perfectly. But am I happy with this arrangement?

Am I happy being this civilized, monogamous, neutered little bitch?

My phone dings, indicating I have a text, so I reach for it from my marbled countertop while eyeing my salmon and deciding whether it's salvageable.

Distracted by my burned meal, I don't fully understand Juliet's message until I read it twice.

The message is direct, which is fine, as neither of us go for texting.

***Got held up at work.***
***See you this weekend sometime.***

Well, I'll be damned. This is the third Friday night she's been busy, and although I shouldn't really care, I sort of do. I was looking forward to sitting down to a glass of red and dinner and then having dessert in the form of Juliet.

But now that she's not coming, I feel like a chump, sitting at home with a meal I cooked for my ex-fuck buddy. If Hunter were here, he would question my masculinity and loudly express that I don't deserve a dick.

That thought gives me an idea, so I send a text message of my own.

Looking at the sad, shriveled salmon, I reach for the saucepan and toss the contents into the trash, along with the rest of the ingredients I had prepared earlier.

Whistling, while making my way into the bathroom to get ready for the evening, I realize *now*, I'm happy.

"You're a pussy whipped little bitch, Dixon, and you're lucky I'm speaking to you right now. You hear me?" Hunter declares for the umpteenth time as he clutches the scruff of my collar and draws our faces together so we're inches apart.

"Yes, you Neanderthal, I heard you loud and clear. Now either kiss me, or let me finish my damn drink," I tease as I pull out of Hunter's grip.

Finch laughs, looking over the moon we're together once again.

"I really missed you, Dix," he says, sipping his beer.

Finch is on the hard stuff tonight as Heidi is out of town for the weekend. This can really only equate to one thing—trouble.

"I missed you too, man," I reply, slapping him on the back.

"Oh, enough with the touchy-feely crap," Hunter barks, slamming a twenty onto the bar to pay for our drinks. "Let's go see some titties!"

Finch blanches and quickly shakes his head. "No titties for me, thanks. And besides, I'm sure Juliet wouldn't want Dixon going to a strip club."

"Oh, boo-hoo to her!" Hunter cries, passing us a fresh round of drinks. "Last I checked, Dixon was still in possession of his balls, unlike you, Finch." I laugh, although I'm not sure how true that statement really is.

Being out with the boys has made me realize that I'm actually in a "sort of" relationship, without actually knowing I was in one. I don't know how or when it happened, it just did. Although it is in no way normal, Juliet is the closest thing I've had to a girlfriend since Lily. And I don't know how I feel about that.

"Hunter, when you meet the right girl, you'll change your tune." Finch nudges me in the ribs, egging me on to support his claim.

"Oh please, I'm more of a compatible partner for Dixon than Juliet is," Hunter scoffs in disgust. "Once the novelty of Juliet's hungry pussy wears off, Dixon will realize there's plenty of pie out there."

"What in God's name are you talking about?" I ask, almost afraid to hear Hunter's pie analogy.

This is the part where I should be defending Juliet's honor, but for some reason, I can't. Could it be because there's some truth in Hunter's uncouth but accurate statement?

"What happens when you eat the same ole apple pie, day in and day out?" he questions, raising a brow.

"You become a diabetic?" Finch says seriously.

"No, you moron," Hunter scoffs, raising his eyes to the ceiling. "After a while, that apple pie loses its flavor, and before long, you begin to hate apple pie because all the apple pie wants to do is cuddle on the couch and watch reruns of *Friends* while you question when the exact moment was when you handed the apple pie your nuts on a platter."

This is, by far, the most ridiculous analogy, but in a weird, warped way, I totally get what he's saying.

"So once you're done satisfying the apple pie—missionary position, I might add," Hunter says, scrunching up his face, "you begin to think about cherry pie and how much you've missed it. And suddenly, all you can think about is the plump, sugary cherries, and how good they taste compared to the bland, mushy apples, the ones you've been forced to eat for the past two months. Before long, you'll hate apple pie, and you'll move on to cherry pie, totally forgetting apple pie ever existed." He takes a sip of beer, his food-inspired parallel over and done with.

Finch looks to be mulling over what Hunter just said, trying to figure out what the hell it means, while I almost choke on my beer because I'm laughing so hard.

"You're an idiot."

"No, I'm a genius. And tonight, we're going to find you some cherry pie," Hunter adds with a mischievous grin.

I don't know how I feel about that. I mean, I would feel kind of bad screwing some random girl just because Juliet couldn't see me tonight. But it's not like we're exclusive or anything. This "thing" with Juliet has crept up on me and yelled "pussy whipped," and I suddenly don't like it.

Although I'm not interested in eating "cherry pie," I don't see the harm in simply viewing what other pies are on display. Hunter tosses back his beer and hollers when he sees I've made my decision, while Finch looks to have finally understood the analogy.

"Holy shit, Hunter! You're one messed-up bastard," he says in disgust.

Hunter's deep chuckle rumbles low, and he cocks a brow. "You think that's messed up? You really don't wanna know what happens when you eat pecan pie, day in and day out then."

Finch takes the bait, and I bite back my smile.

"What happens?" Finch asks, totally falling for it.

"You become addicted to nuts," Hunter explains with a grin. "And before long, all you can think about is nuts. You've got nuts in your mouth. Nuts on your face. Nuts on your tongue. Nuts at the back of your throat." I burst out laughing, tears filling my eyes.

Finch blanches, finally understanding. He throws him an appalled look while I fist-bump my best friend.

We really are a bunch of nutjobs.

I didn't realize how much I missed these assholes, but now that we three are out hitting the town, I know Fridays are back to being boys' night only.

I've turned my phone off as I'm man enough to admit I have been tempted to check it once or twice. But Hunter's idiotic apple pie analogy had me refusing to yield, so it's just me, Finch, and Hunter—and a thousand-other people crammed into the club.

This club, ironically enough, is called Cherry Pop. It's some new club that just opened up in Manhattan, and the "trendy" trash playing over the speakers really makes me wish they would play some good ole eighties rock ballads.

"Remind me why we're here?" I gripe, looking over at Hunter, who is feasting on the smorgasbord of young flesh in front of him.

"Are you blind?" He scoffs, waving his hand out in front of him, indicating the barely legal girls dancing to this horrible music.

"I'm nowhere near blind enough to touch any of those little girls." I take a swig of my drink and make a pained face. "Good grief, even their scotch is atrocious."

"Oh, lighten up, Mr. Grumpy Pants. Not that long ago, I recall you not having any qualms touching a certain little girl," Hunter says, referring to Madison.

"That was entirely different. First, she wasn't jailbait, and second, she has a lot more sense than to come to a place like this."

"Um, Dixon," Finch says, and I turn to look at him sitting on his stool, his eyes squinting and looking in the direction of the dance floor.

"Yeah?" I reply, wondering what has him so intrigued.

"Isn't *that* your little girl?" he says, pointing in front of him.

"What?" I gasp, my eyes frantically searching the area he's gesturing to. "That's impossible."

Hunter's laughter to my right indicates it's very possible. "Holy shit! Little Miss Cherry Pie has grown up."

I reach out and slap his chest, my eyes never leaving the sight before me because Madison is very much in front of me. Her body, which has always been incredible, looks even better than I remember. She was always on the slender side, but not anymore. It's only been a couple of months, but Jesus, it's like she's taken a crash course in body sculpting, and she's all soft curves and toned, supple flesh.

"And just think, you chose apple pie over *that*," Hunter whispers into my ear.

I would usually retort with a smart-ass comment, but right now, I'm surprised I even remember my own name.

A faster song commences, and Madison excitedly latches onto her redheaded friend. They begin dancing together, laughing as they attempt to keep up with the choppy beat.

Her red tube dress is short and low, and each time she

moves, the dress slips lower and higher. I raise myself off my seat, hoping to get a sneak peek at what she's packing underneath. My raging hormones get doused with a bucket of ice-cold "wake the fuck up!" when an Adonis-looking male wraps his arms around her waist, pressing her back against his hardened front.

The alpha dog in me howls in protest, and I clench the empty glass in my hand, envisioning it's his head I'm squeezing. But by the way Madison is smiling and leaning into his advances, I dare say this ecstatic asshole is her new beau.

But who can blame him? I mean, look at her; she's beautiful.

Her long hair, thanks to the vigorous dancing, looks wild and untamed—perfect freshly fucked hair. The thought, however, has my teeth gnashing together. I don't want to picture her fucking this douchebag in front of me—or any douchebag, for that matter.

Fuck. I need a drink.

"Well, hot damn, I—"

"Zip it, Hunter," I snap as I push back from my stool and make my way toward the bar, totally ignoring his snide remark.

The line is long, and due to my foul mood, I have no desire to wait. If I stay here a minute longer, then I need to get nice and drunk and forget that I ever saw Madison.

I don't fail to see the paradox of my situation. It's the classic case of you want what you can't have. I could have had the sweet, innocent Madison, but instead, I chose the easy, rampant sex fiend, Juliet, who I was sleeping with before I even knew I had a "thing" for Madison.

But after tonight, I'm not so sure I made the right choice, and it's not because I've seen what a goddess Madison is. I always knew she was. Under that fancy makeup and slinky red dress, she's still the clumsy little girl who bought me breakfast and made me smile.

I suppose I'm questioning my decision because I can't help but wonder: Are Juliet and I too alike? The sex is amazing, but when that dies down, and it will die down, will I still want her?

This is what happens when you start a "relationship" with someone who was your patient, who is addicted to sex, who you watched masturbate on your desk and then fucked like a wild animal to get over your lying, cheating ex-fiancée.

This was doomed from the get-go. Why the *hell* did I think otherwise?

"Dixon?"

Internally groaning, I curse whatever gods are looking down on me, laughing at my misfortune.

"Madison?" I say, matching her stunned tone, although mine is completely staged.

As I turn around to look at her, my heart gets stuck in my throat. But I pull my shit together and put my game face on.

"What are you doing here?" she asks, her chest heaving breathlessly after all that energetic dancing.

"Oh, my friends wanted to check the place out," I reply, running a hand through my hair.

She nods, and I don't fail to see her eyes taking in every crevice of my face as we talk. "Oh, cool. Me too. Well, my friends did," she explains, her glossy lips calling out to me.

"Awesome." I clear my throat, as this feels exactly how it used to feel when we first met.

The attraction is undoubtedly still there, but something has changed in Madison. She seems more…confident, more aware of her beauty but not in a conceited way. And I can't help but wonder why the change.

The answer, however, slaps me straight in the face when her beau wraps his meaty hands around her waist, clearly staking his claim. This dude is a giant compared to her, and she looks up to meet his narrowed eyes. Appearing as if she had forgotten where she was, she shakes her head and smiles.

"Dixon, this is David."

David the Giant extends his palm, which I lacklusterly shake.

"Pleasure," I say, my voice dripping with sarcasm.

He returns my unenthused gesture, and I pull back my hand, fighting the urge to wipe it on my jeans. David sizes me up, and warning bells obviously go off in his head as he protectively wraps his arm around Madison's shoulders.

"So how do you know Maddy?" he barks, trying to intimidate me.

This *boy* has a lot to learn if he thinks his playground antics will get a rise out of me.

"Well, Madison was falling all over herself when I was around. Weren't you, *Maddy*?" I sarcastically reply, my eyes never leaving David's.

As his jaw clenches, I internally high-five my wit.

"How's your head?" I ask, reaching forward and brushing away the soft hair from her temple, looking for any scarring evidence from her fall.

I'll be damned; she slowly leans forward into my touch. Her willingness to surrender has the barbarian in me beating my chest in victory. Suck on that, you freakishly ginormous dick.

Thankfully, I'm next to be served, so I end this pleasant

encounter immediately. "Well, it was nice meeting you, Damon," I say, intentionally getting his name wrong.

"It's David," he corrects, his fingers clutching Madison's soft skin.

"Right," I reply dismissively. "Madison." I nod, directing my smug gaze her way, but she looks pissed.

I have no idea what would incite this hostility, and it's too late to find out why as the person in front of me is paying for their drinks.

"It was lovely seeing you again." I lean forward, placing a chaste kiss on her cheek.

The moment her vanilla scent assaults my nostrils, I barely refrain from burying my nose in the crook of her neck.

I pull away calmly, trying my best to appear impassive, but I'm thrown on my ass when she leans forward and purrs into my ear, "You owe me dinner."

My calm demeanor is totally destroyed, but Madison smirks and turns on her heel with the baboon chasing after her.

I stand immobile, transfixed on her tight, curvy ass, totally losing my spot in line, but I don't care, as I just got played at my own game.

Touché, my Cherry Pie, touché.

# Thirteen

## Dixon

I awake from the most vivid dream of Madison sucking my dick. She somehow knew exactly what I liked, and suddenly, I realize what woke me was the fact I am *actually* getting my dick sucked. However, the person on the end of my cock isn't Madison but, rather, Juliet.

Peering down, I see a head of lush blonde hair bobbing up and down between my thighs, and I ignore the fact I wish it was a brunette instead.

Juliet lets me go and seductively raises her face, her lust-filled eyes focusing on mine. "Good morning, babe," she purrs. I cringe, as I *hate* that pet name, but she doesn't seem to care.

"Hi," I reply, my raspy voice raw from too many scotches. "How'd you get in?" She doesn't have a key.

"I have my ways," she huskily replies. I don't even bother questioning how because she lowers her head and picks up where she left off.

Getting blown by Juliet is honestly one of my favorite things in the world. Her mouth, tongue, hands, and throat all work in sync with each other perfectly, and I'm usually done in less than two minutes. But today, she's just not doing it for me. Her mouth is too wet, her tongue is too swirly, her hands are too grabby, and her throat is too deep.

She senses I'm not in the mood and pulls away, her lips wet and plump from sucking like a damn vacuum cleaner.

"What's the matter?" she breathes, brushing her hair off her face.

Looking down into her confused blue eyes, I feel like a total asshole for being so unresponsive because she's trying.

Maybe I just want to fuck.

"Take your clothes off," I demand, sitting up and reaching into my bedside dresser for a condom.

She looks confused as I usually go bareback, but that's only because I'm usually lost in a fuck bubble, and all sense of reason gets lost in my raging hard-on. Nevertheless, she quickly rises and disrobes, yanking off her cashmere sweater and short black skirt. She's boldly standing in a skimpy black strapless bra, matching thong, and red skyscraper heels. I can't deny, she really is beautiful.

"Strip," I command, resting against the headboard, watching her.

She grins, no doubt turned on by the direct order, and reaches around her body, unclasping her bra. It falls to the floor, and my eyes zero in on her heavy, full breasts. Her nipples are pink and incredibly erect, and my mouth waters, begging to suck on both immediately.

"Those too." I point at her underwear.

She licks her glossy lips before turning her back to me and bends at the waist, giving me a full view of her toned ass. She hooks her fingers into the ribboned waistband of her thong and shimmies them down her legs until they too gather at her feet. Slowly rising, she looks at me over her shoulder, her long blond hair veiling her dangerous face.

"Now what, Dr. Mathews?" she asks, tonguing her lower lip.

"Now I'm going to fuck you until you beg me to make you come," I reply, tearing the condom wrapper and getting down to business.

Juliet attempts to turn around, but I stop her.

"Don't move," I scold, and she complies, a shiver passing through her awakened body.

Rising off the bed, I wrap one steady hand around her waist while the other snakes around her front, my fingers brushing over her wet pussy. She moans deep in her throat, and the sound I usually adore strangely does nothing for me. But I continue, dipping a finger into her ravenous cunt and quickly adding another, as one is never enough for the insatiable Juliet.

She rides my hand, her body thrashing wildly when I stroke over her clit with my thumb.

"Fuck me, Dixon," she cries, rubbing her plump ass against my crotch.

"You're a greedy, greedy girl."

I hurriedly remove my fingers while she braces her hands on top of the dresser in front of her and bends at the waist, spreading her legs out wide. Arching her back, she pushes her hips out so her ass is on full display for my perverse pleasure. Bending my knees, I steady her waist with both hands and push into her from behind.

The moment I'm sheathed inside her warmth, my body has a mind of its own, and my hips begin pumping into her with exact precision. I know this won't take long because the harder I push, the louder she moans, which suits me just fine, as we're both here for the same thing. The way she wiggles her ass, I know what she wants, but I'm in no mood for that type of play today.

Placing one hand low on her hip while the other cups her neck, I push down on her nape so her hips rise and I'm able to drive into her at a deeper angle because I can't find my rhythm. I know she's close, but I'm not, and I don't know why. This is one of my favorite positions, but I'm just not with her. I piston my hips and reach up, rubbing over her nipple, which usually gets me going. But today—nothing.

"I'm close," she whimpers, her cheek pressed into the hardwood of my dresser, the contents rattling with each powerful strike I inflict on her softening body.

The moment her inner muscles squeeze my cock, I know she's there, and she comes with a loud scream, her body shuddering around me. Yet I fruitlessly pump and grind into her, my release nowhere in sight.

Juliet is ready for round two, but my home run is nowhere to be found.

"Babe," she moans, her body slumping forward, my forceful movements almost making her one with the dresser.

Why can't I come? My orgasm is tethering so close to the edge, but I just can't get there.

Suddenly, Juliet's locks are replaced with a head of lush, brunette hair, and her small ass is curvier and shapelier. I begin to envision my dick driving into a nameless brunette with large green eyes and plump rosy lips, her cheeks tinted a flushed pink. Her glorious tits bounce uncontrollably as I swathe myself in her warm, innocent body. Now *this* image is one that awakens my body, and I pull out before pushing back in, the sensual feel sending a jolt of pure ecstasy to my toes.

However, unexpectedly, the face is no longer faceless, and as she turns over her shoulder to look at me, I meet the sparkling green eyes of Madison.

Memories of her dancing, and the way her body moved to the music plummet into me, and as I imagine her soft, seductive voice echoing in my ear, I explode with a force so great, I almost collapse with the power of it. My body milks my orgasm, drawing it out until I am panting, gasping, Jesus, about to have a damn heart attack, as I've never come this hard before.

It takes me a full minute to come down and when I do, I meet satisfied blue eyes, instead of the sparking green ones I was envisioning.

"That was…wow," Juliet gasps, her cheek marred with a pattern from the wood grain.

I smile half-heartedly and pull out, as her body suddenly feels cold and amiss. Disposing of my condom, I fall face-first onto my bed and pray sleep overtakes me, burying my shame.

Thankfully, it does.

I wake alone.

Juliet is no doubt long gone, as I made it more than obvious I wasn't in the mood for snuggling.

What the *hell* was that? Not once, not ever, have I had to envision another to get off.

Tossing my blankets off, I reach for my cell and dial the only two people who can explain to me what the fuck is going on.

"You're fucking like a woman."

"Excuse me?" I ask, slightly offended, as I stare at Hunter over my coffee.

"You. Are. Fucking—"

"Yes, I heard you the first time," I say, interrupting him. "But what does that even mean?"

"It means," Hunter explains, waving his fork in my direction, "that you're fucking with your mind, rather than your dick." He finishes the sentence with his silverware pointing at my junk.

"Get the fuck out of here," I cry, but holy shit—he's right.

I've mentioned to both Finch and Hunter on more than one occasion that Juliet fucks like a man. She can fuck anytime, anyplace, just like a man. And I'm usually a hundred percent there with her, but this morning, I could only cross the finish line when it was Madison's face and body I pictured driving into.

"There you go," Hunter says, throwing his hands up in victory.

"That's not possible," I scoff, but it's very possible.

It's a well-known fact that most ladies fuck with their minds, while most men fuck with the head between their legs. It's more of a challenge to stimulate a lady's mind, rather than her G-spot. But if you can do both and you're fucking her body *and* her mind, then you're superman.

Women are, by far, the smarter species. While us men, we are utter morons.

"This is impossible. I mean, I've never had this problem before, and I've slept with some real…" I make a pained face. "But you've seen Juliet. She's beautiful."

"But she's not the one you want to be screwing, obviously," Hunter says around a mouthful of food.

I down my water, suddenly feeling sick.

"How does Juliet make you feel?" Finch asks, chewing on his fruit salad.

"Well, usually, she can make me come in five seconds flat."

"No, that's not what I meant," he says, blanching. "Like afterward. Do you talk? Snuggle?"

"Dude!" Hunter exclaims in disgust.

But Finch ignores him, and continues. "After the act is done, what do you feel?"

I think for a while, and reply honestly. "Nothing."

"Exactly," Finch says. "It's just sex, Dixon. I'm not the professional here…" He looks at me with a smirk. "But do you think Juliet is just filling a…void?"

Hunter snorts, and I eyeball him, as I can only imagine what wiseass comment he's about to say about me filling a void.

"Maybe all these mechanical hookups have started losing their appeal," Finch continues. "And Juliet was the first woman in a long time that was something a little more than just a booty call."

I nod because he's right. From the first moment I met her, I knew she would be trouble. Could it be that subconsciously I *was* trying to fill that void? Was I trying to make something out of nothing? But that doesn't explain Madison.

"I could have filled this so called 'void,'" I say, making quotation marks around the word *void*, "with Madison, but I chose Juliet instead." I'm interested to hear Finch's thoughts.

"Sex is easy, Dix; it's the relationship component that's the hard part. With Madison, it's obviously something more."

"I hardly know her," I pathetically rebuke.

"But from what you do know, you're obviously attracted to her on another level. You must have some kind of…interest in her," he concludes with a nod.

He's right. The few times we have spent together, I found myself enjoying her company, rather than wondering if she likes reverse cowgirl or not.

"And this is what happens when you make your fuck buddy your girlfriend, Dix," Hunter unsympathetically says as he salts his fries.

"She is not my girlfriend," I state for the tenth time.

"She may as well be. You don't sleep with anyone else, and you ditch your friends for her. So she's your girlfriend."

"She's not my girlfriend," I press, restraining myself from flipping him off.

"So is," he childishly chides under his breath.

I choose to ignore him and decide to talk to the adult in our group. "What's it like for you and Heidi? I mean, does she still do it for you?" I ask Finch, who smiles at the mere mention of his wife.

"She is the sexiest woman alive, and I never have a problem making love," he proudly replies while Hunter gags.

"Ugh. Can you not use that word please?"

"What? Love?" Finch questions, puzzled lines furrowing his brow.

"Yes, and please refrain from using the term 'making' before it." Hunter shivers with revulsion.

I can't help but laugh.

"Making love to your beautiful wife is something special," Finch says with a smile. "We please one another. That's what relationships are about. Making the other person happy as well as yourself."

"And this is why Hunter is still single," I tease. He playfully flips me off, but I see a touch of hurt behind his usual mischievous eyes. What's he hiding?

"Sorry to bring this up," Finch says with reservation. "But you were engaged, Dix. I mean, surely when you and Lily were together, you felt some kind of connection?"

The mention of Lily would usually throw me, but today it doesn't at all, and I really take Finch's question onboard.

My "whatever" with Juliet doesn't even compare to what I felt for Lily. I mean, I loved Lily more than life itself. And not once did I ever picture another woman other than her while we were…making…fuck. But with Juliet, I feel like a dick on demand, which is fine, as I suppose she's my cooch on call.

Finch and Hunter are right. I was foolish to think this was anything other than sex.

"You're right." I sigh. Hunter clears his throat. "You're both right," I amend, sarcastically smiling at my friend. Deciding to be honest, I confess, "With Juliet, I feel like a dick on demand."

Sadly, Hunter doesn't appreciate my honesty and bursts into fits of laughter. "Dr. Dixon, the Booty Call MD," he says while mimicking with his hands like he's sign-writing on a billboard.

"Then stop seeing her," Finch says, implying this isn't rocket science. "You know, you're the psychiatrist here. Shouldn't you be the one giving out advice?"

"It's not that simple, Finch," I reply, fisting my hair. "Everything you've learned and applied to others doesn't apply when you're the one who needs the advice. And besides, my forte is addiction, not relationships. I'm a psychiatrist, not a damn relationship guru."

Finch nods. "That's understandable."

"No, you're just a dumbass," Hunter pipes up, pushing his empty plate away from him. "I told you to stay away from her."

"Enough with the third degree. I don't see you happily married to your soul mate."

"That's because I'm not an idiot." Then he quickly corrects, "No offense, Finch."

Finch shakes his head, not at all offended because he's heard it all before.

"Women are trouble, and I plan on living like Hugh Hefner."

"Old, lonely, and addicted to Viagra?" I ask with a smirk.

Hunter throws a bread roll at me, and I dodge its flight path. "No. Rich, surrounded by Playmates, and happy."

Finch and I look at Hunter and chuckle. I suppose one can dream.

"Just call me Hunter Hefner," he jokes, eyeing a blonde server and making bunny ears at her.

"How about I call you Hunter Half-Wit instead?" I suggest, still chuckling.

Hunter crosses his arms across his broad chest as he leans back in his chair. "Okay, Dixon Mathews, Cock on Call. Oh, sorry." He coughs, fist in front of his mouth. "I meant, Doc on

Call."

I can't stop the cackle that bubbles from my throat, and as Finch and Hunter join in with the laughter, I can't believe we're talking about this over brunch.

# Fourteen

*Dixon*

After brunch, I come home and decide to catch up on some paperwork. But I'm soon distracted because I can't stop thinking about what Finch said. *Do* I have feelings for Madison? Surely, that's not possible. If it were, why did I choose Juliet over her? I know it's not that clean-cut and simple, but I could have said no to Juliet the day I was meant to see Madison.

Before this morning, I enjoyed sleeping with Juliet, but now, the thought isn't as appealing as it once was.

I decide to bury my head in the sand and focus on my new research paper.

As I'm drowning in innate behavioral patterns, my phone dings. I reach for it and see it's a text from Juliet.

***I'm deliciously sore from this morning. Thank you x***

I would usually reply with a dirty comment and not-so-hidden innuendo of making her even more sore, but I don't. I don't even reply.

It's nine o'clock on a Saturday night, and I'm home. I'm also alone.

I can't remember the last time this happened because before Juliet, I was chasing tail and about ready to seal the deal. But she's been taking up a big chunk of my Saturday nights, and up until now, I hadn't realized how much so.

I check my cell, and she hasn't texted, but I didn't reply to hers earlier, so the radio silence makes sense.

Goddamn—when did this become so relationship-like?

Sighing, I focus on the idiot box, hoping some mindless TV will occupy me.

Two *Jaws* movies and twelve beers later, I'm craving scotch and porn.

I guess I could jerk off, but the thought has me wondering whose body and face I would use as inspiration.

That's definitely a mood killer, so I reach for my phone and decide to check my emails. However, for some unexplained reason, I go to my contact list instead and stop on the letter M. I really shouldn't be contemplating what I currently am, as it's quite late on a Saturday night/Sunday morning. I'm also semi-drunk and extremely horny. In no way should I text Madison…

says no one ever.

I'm typing out a short message and hitting send before I can talk reason to my impulsive brain. The text is harmless, and I keep it clean as it *is* roughly one o'clock in the morning, and I don't want Madison to think I'm drunk-dialing her for sex.

I stare at my screen for endless minutes, but nothing. Just as I start to curse my reckless move, my screen lights up with a reply from Madison.

***What?*** she asks, in reply to my joke of, "A man walks into a psychiatrist's office wearing nothing but underwear made of Saran Wrap. What does the psychiatrist say?"

I know it's lame, but it's better than the alternative of "What are you wearing?"

**I can clearly see your nuts.**

I cringe at how stupid I sound, but it's an icebreaker. I admit it's a juvenile one, but at least I got her attention with my idiocy. The wait is giving me heartburn, and I toss my phone onto the sofa. But the moment it chimes a second later, I dive for it, eagerly awaiting her reply.

***LOL. My turn...What do you call a nurse who is waiting for someone to call?***

I read the message twice to ensure I haven't misread it, and even though it seems we're no longer joking, I decide to humor her anyway.

**What?**

The wait between replies is killing me, but thankfully, I don't have to wait too long.

***Confused. Why didn't you call?***

Well, this punch line is worse than mine.

I really am an insensitive asshole to think I can just contact her after so many weeks and expect her to laugh and swoon at my lame-ass jokes. I owe her the truth, and I also owe her an apology.

**I'm sorry. I'm a jerk.**

She replies within seconds. ***Yes, you are.***

Her simple reply is a clear indication of her leaving the ball in my court. Pondering what to say, I know this is my moment of glory.

**I was fucking,** but I quickly erase that and settle for, **I was kind of seeing someone.**

My finger hesitates over the send button, but I press it and hold my breath.

Minutes tick by, and I'm just about to text her again when she replies.

***Was?***

I let out a relieved breath, glad her response didn't involve the words, "fuck you, asshat."

**Yes.**

It's too complicated to explain via text without sounding like a sick, sex-crazed maniac. So in this instance, yes will have to suffice.

***Me too.***

**Oh?** I reply quickly.

***Well, seeing as I just saw him tonight.***

No guessing whom.

**Oh, you and Damon?** I reply, not able to type his name without wanting to stab myself in the eyes.

***You know his name is David,*** she replies, calling me out on my bluff.

***And yes,*** she adds a second later.

My teeth clench at the thought of that giganotosaurus touching her, but I remain composed as I write back.

**Congratulations,** I reply, but in reality, I really want to say, "I hope he catches yellow fever and dies."

***Thanks. He's actually my personal trainer.***

I clench my fingers around the phone as I picture David sporting serious wood while watching her work out in her skimpy tight gym clothes. But I decide to play it cool.

**Explains a lot.**

***Was that a compliment or an insult?*** she replies, and I let out a chuckle.

**Definitely a compliment.**

I know, I know, she's in a relationship, but a little harmless flirting won't hurt.

***Wanna elaborate?***

I can just imagine her intuitive mind mulling over what I mean by that comment. But she surely knows she'll never win this mind play with me.

**You can't handle the truth!** I text back, using the classic Jack Nicholson line.

But suddenly, I realize she's probably too young to know that movie, and I quickly tap out a text, not wanting her to think I'm being rude or aggressive or just plain weird.

But before I have a chance to reply, my phone chimes.

***Ooh, I love that movie. Jack Nicholson is a total hottie.***

I read the message three times over, and my dick begins to stir due to the fact she finds someone twice my age "hot." Maybe she likes older men? My dancing libido pipes up in interest, but I swiftly shut it down before I start getting stupid or *stupider* ideas.

Deciding to steer this conversation in a totally different direction, I reply.

**What's your favorite movie?**

I know it's completely lame, but I find myself wanting to actually know what her favorite movie is. I also want to know what Madison's favorite everything is.

***E.T. Yours?***

Wow, she knows who Jack Nicholson *and* E.T. are. And just like that, my lame joke wasn't so lame after all.

Three hours and a bottle of scotch later, I found out what Madison's favorite *everything* was.

We texted until the early hours of the morning, and not

once did I feel bored or want the conversation to end. I wanted to know everything there was to know about her, and by her probing questions, I dare say she felt the same way about me.

She steered clear of the topic of my father when I made it more than obvious he was a matter I was uncomfortable discussing. But there were elements to Madison's past and present (like David the dickhead) that I sensed were also off-limits, and I respected her, just as she did me.

But everything else was open for discussion, and I don't think I've ever known this much about one human being.

Not even Lily.

If I had any doubts as to what I have to do in regard to Juliet and our "situation," tonight cleared up any reservations, as I don't think I've had a conversation with her that's lasted longer than five minutes. I know all the bare essentials that separate us from being total strangers who fuck, but I don't really know her, unlike I now know Madison.

But I don't know how or *what* to tell her. If I end things, it's not like I can pursue Madison because she's seeing Gigantor. Therefore, I'll have to seek out the company of another lady friend, but mindless, faceless fucking has suddenly lost its appeal. I have Juliet, who is more than capable of satisfying all my needs, but can she? After yesterday, has our passion finally burned out? Did our "thing" come with an expiration date all along? I guess there's only one way to find out.

# Fifteen

*Dixon*

I've hit the gym, gone for a run, and it's only nine o'clock on Sunday morning. There's something I've been putting off, but today is the first day since I buried my mother that I've had the balls to pay her a visit.

I park my blue BMW and, taking a deep breath, I look at the gates of the Hillcrest Cemetery. I haven't been back home since the day I admitted my father. Taking yet another deep breath, I look at my pale reflection in the rearview mirror and tell myself to man up.

I walk through the manicured gardens, and the early June weather is bringing out some pretty flowers and plants. But no matter how visually appealing the foliage is, they can't hide the fact there are headstones as far as the eye can see. I can't help but feel a sense of sadness for all these souls that were once alive. Each gravestone represents a person's life, and their life story is chipped away on stone for the world to see what a great person they once were.

I can't help but wonder what my life story will entail. But more importantly, *who* will be the author behind my tale?

Shaking those thoughts aside, I give a polite smile to a woman dressed in black who is clearly mourning her loved one. This place is filled with sadness, but it's also a place for reflection. The living need to weep for the dead, and this is where one can do so.

When I reach my mother's grave, I stop a few feet away, my aviators shielding my approaching tears. I can't step any closer, so this is close enough for now. Dropping to a squat, I stare at the marbled headstone and remember the care taken when I chose it. It had to be perfect for her because she was perfect in life, and I wanted to ensure that followed her into death.

"*Ciao, Mamma*," I say, addressing her as I would if she were alive.

My parents both migrated to the USA in their teens from a small fishing village in Sicily, Italy. When they were barely adults, they met at a factory and married a year later. Two years later, I was born.

My parents didn't have much when they came to America, but they made it work. They worked hard and blended in as best they could, as they didn't speak a lick of English the day they arrived. If the current generation of kids had to rough it like my parents did, they wouldn't survive half a day without their iPads and cell phones.

In a way, back then, things were simpler. You married young, had kids, and provided for your family the best you could. It was hard labor, but family was number one, so you did anything for your loved ones.

If it wasn't for my father and mother working their asses off, I wouldn't be in the position I'm in today. I thank them every day for the sacrifices they made for me.

"I miss you," I whisper, staring at her grave. "I'm sorry it took me so long to visit. But you're in my thoughts every day, and not a moment goes by that I don't wish you were still here." I hesitate before I sadly confess, "I'm sorry for what I did to *Papà*." I hang my head in shame.

If my mother were alive, she would be disgusted by what I did to my father and also how I'm living my life. She'd tell me to marry a nice girl and make her many grandbabies.

As I think about Juliet bearing my children, I realize I can't even picture it because it's too farfetched to even imagine.

"I'm lost," I confess, running a hand through my hair. "I just wish I had more time with you."

I hold onto my tears and sniff back my sorrow because life really is a bitch. When you're younger, you don't appreciate your parents and all that they've done for you. Loving your parents is seen as uncool, and all that matters is your friends, booze, and girls, girls, girls.

But the older you get, you realize that your parents will be there for you when your friends and girlfriends are long gone. Friendship comes and goes, but family is forever.

For today, this is enough. This is more than I expected I could handle.

"*Sogni d'oro*," I say, wishing my mother sweet dreams. "I'll see you soon. I promise," and I stand, feeling like a tiny part of the old Dixon has returned.

Lost in thought while walking to my car, I think back to all the times Juliet and I have spent together that didn't involve sex.

Sadly, all those times can be counted on one hand.

In the words of Shakespeare, "love is merely a madness," and that's because in one corner, I have Juliet, who is a freak in the sack, but boring as batshit out of it. And in the other corner, I have Madison, who I bet would be as interesting *in* the sack as she is out of it, but who is now seeing someone else.

I knew one woman sexually, while I knew the other intellectually, and like a typical male, the pussy won out. Now look how that's ended up.

Unlocking my car, I flip off the sky 'cause karma…can kiss my ass.

The drive back to Manhattan is long and boring, and to top things off, I'm stuck in traffic. Thanks to the wasted time spent in rush hour, my thoughts wander to my father.

Marie said he's better. I highly doubt that, but I decide to find out for myself. Going through my contacts, I find the number which taunts me every time I see it. Telling myself to grow a pair, I hit dial and wait for it to connect through my Bluetooth.

The moment it rings, I drum my fingers on the steering wheel, a sense of dread overtaking me. This is the reason I don't go visit him. This is the reason I don't call. Talking to my father will highlight what a failure I am and confirm that I've let both my parents down.

Just as I'm about to hang up, a friendly voice answers, asking where she can direct my call.

"May I be connected to Pino Di Matteo's room, please?" I

say, waiting a few seconds before speaking.

"Certainly. Putting you through now."

I'm thankful I'm stationary because all I can focus on is the tacky music that separates me from my father. Will he really want to talk to me after all I've done to him?

"Hello?" a female voice says.

"Um, hello," I reply, confused. "I must have the wrong room. I was looking for Pino Di Matteo."

"Yes, this is his room. Hi, I'm Julia, Pino's nurse. I'm looking after him today," she says cheerfully.

"Oh, right. I'm Dixon…Pino's son," I explain because she probably doesn't even know he has a son.

There's a slight pause before she replies, "Oh, what a lovely surprise. Hang on a second." I hear her place down the receiver, her shoes squeaking against the linoleum as she walks across the room.

"Pino," she says, my heart in my throat as she addresses him. "Pino, your son is on the phone. Would you like to talk to him?"

Silence.

"Pino?" she says, pressing once more.

I can't help but smile, as my father always was a stubborn man. Looks like some things never change.

"Hello?" she says into the receiver. "Are you still there?"

"I'm here," I reply, although I know this has all been a mistake.

"I'm going to put you on loudspeaker, okay? That'll make things a little easier," she kindly explains, but I know my dad doesn't want to talk to me. "Okay, you're good to go. I'll give you some privacy." I hear the door shut.

There is complete silence, apart from my father's raspy breaths, waiting for me to speak.

"*Ciao, Papà. Come stai?*" I ask, which is a stupid question, seeing as he's cooped up in a hospital.

But I persevere. "*Mi dispiace per non visitare. Lavoro èstato occupato,*" I say, using the same excuse I gave to Marie for not visiting.

I know he's listening because his breathing has increased. I decide to switch to English, hoping I'll get a response from him.

"Have you been doing any gardening? I remember seeing a beautiful garden out back."

I'm still greeted with silence.

I know my father, and he's not interested in my work or gardening; he wants answers. He wants me to say I'm sorry for abandoning him when he needed me the most. He wants me to explain why I left him.

Clenching the steering wheel, I take a deep breath and say what's been on my mind since the day I left him there. "I'm sorry, *Papà*. I really am. I…I didn't know what else to do. When we lost Mamma, I think she took a piece of us with her. You especially. I know I did you wrong, but I'm asking you to forgive me."

Why won't he talk to me? I can hear him, and I know he can hear me, too. Suddenly, I hear his slippers scuff across the floor. His steps are small and measured, and I can't help but think they're the footsteps of a broken man.

"*Papà?*" I beseech, sitting up straighter in my seat.

It's a plea, a plea for him to talk to me.

His breathing rattles in his chest, his exhalations coming out louder and choppier. The sound has me choking up, and I say the only thing I can that really expresses how I feel.

"*Ti amo.*"

My words of love are greeted with silence, but this time, the silence is because my father has hung up on me.

Closing my eyes in defeat, I numbly end the call and rest my head on the steering wheel. I don't know what I expected. Because if I were him, I would have done the same.

Only when a car horn blares behind me do I raise my head to see that traffic has finally started moving. I put my car into gear and take off, speeding away from demons I must one day face.

That day, however, is not today. And I don't see it happening anytime soon.

I've invited Finch and Hunter over for pizza and beer. Basketball is on, and I can't think of a better way to distract myself from my non-relationship woes. A knock on the door interrupts me from stocking the fridge with beer. I look at my watch and see the boys are early, which is a first.

"Couldn't wait for my boys to kick your ass?" I say as I open the door.

Instead, I'm greeted by Juliet.

"Oh yeah, I can't wait," she purrs, giving me big, innocent eyes.

"What are you doing here?" I abruptly counter instead.

She's visibly taken aback by my curtness, but after this weekend, she's the last person I want to see.

However, she soon recovers from my insolence. "I'm here

to fuck your brains out," she boldly replies, not holding back.

Before, the very vivid picture she just painted would have me tearing her clothes off, but now, it just makes me cringe.

Juliet sees my hesitation and takes a step forward, wrapping her arms around my neck. "What's the matter? You're not happy to see me?" she asks, pouting.

"I just wasn't expecting you," I reply, subtly unchaining her hands from around my neck.

"Well, what a surprise," she replies cockily, her blue eyes glowing with mischief.

Indeed.

We stand silent for a few moments, and Juliet's body language highlights the fact she wants me to invite her in. But the thing is, I don't want to. She looks way too intoxicating in her skinny jeans and peach camisole, and I know she'll end up destroying whatever resolve I have left.

"I'm actually expecting guests," I reveal, feeling a touch guilty, as I've made it more than obvious she's not invited to join us.

"Oh?" She raises a fair brow.

"Yeah, a couple of the guys are coming over to watch the game," I explain with a firm nod.

"Oh," she says once again, brushing back her hair. "Well, I'll leave you to it then."

She gets it. She understands loud and clear that I don't want her socializing with my friends, and she doesn't…care.

Most men would think they've struck gold, but I'm not most men, and I know Juliet doesn't care because she doesn't care about me. For a while, sex without strings was fun, but now? Now, it's just sad.

Is this change of heart because of Madison, who I have a genuine interest in physically *and* emotionally? Or is it because I'm sick of the person I see staring back at me every day? Whatever the reason, I never should have started whatever this is between Juliet and me.

"I'll see you during the week?" Juliet asks, disturbing my thoughts.

"Sure," I reply, as I don't want to share my revelations when my friends are due to turn up on my doorstep at any minute.

Tracing my stubbled jaw with her fingernail, she says, "I'm going shopping for the perfect outfit this week."

I cock a confused eyebrow, and she smiles.

"For the awards night, silly. I'll be the perfect plus-one." She winks. "Speaking of plus-ones…What happens in Boston stays in Boston." She licks her plump lips. "I'd be willing if you were."

I remain stone-faced and nod. "I'll think about it," I reply, casually addressing her suggestion of a threesome.

"Okay. Well, don't think too hard. Just think about me riding your face while you're fucking another girl," she states, while I almost choke. She leans forward and kisses me passionately.

My mouth, the traitorous bastard, kisses her back, and her knowledgeable tongue coaxes my dick to shift to attention. However, I pull away before I lose control.

"I'll talk to you soon, Juliet," I say, my voice wavering.

"Bye, babe." She turns on her booted heel, giving me a clear view of her tight ass as she walks away.

I slam the door shut and lean against it. I forgot I asked Juliet to be my plus-one for the next month's awards ceremony. I was caught in a vulnerable moment as I was fucking her over my desk and the gold invite caught her attention. She asked who I was taking, and the fact I was buried balls deep in her had me asking if she would come. Moments later, she *did* come, and then she agreed to come to the awards night with me. I was planning on going alone, as it's not typically acceptable conduct to bring your fuck buddy to a prestigious event involving your work. But I couldn't exactly tell her that.

Now I'm stuck with no other option but to deal with my fuckup and spend the weekend with Juliet and a possible plus one, if she has her way. I could retract the invite, but honestly, knowing Juliet, she'll just show up anyway.

Frustrated, I push off the door and head into the kitchen to grab a much-needed beer. Tossing back my Budweiser, I reach for another, as I know I'll need it to deal with Hunter, who will smell something is up the moment he enters the room. My cell chimes, and I grab it off the marbled counter. I hope it's not the boys canceling because I really need their advice again.

But the text message is from Madison.

***Did you know that New York cheesecake is the most popular cheesecake in the entire world?***

Smiling, I reply, **No, I did not. Good to see you've been doing your homework. Speaking of, how's the dual degree going?**

***It's going terribly.***

**Why terribly?** I ask, not able to imagine Madison being terrible at anything.

***Because I suck at pharmacology. I'll make a sucky nurse :(***

I chuckle at her wit and text back.

**You will not. It just happens I'm an expert in drugs. Well, prescribing them, not taking them :P**

***You don't say. Would you be willing to offer your expertise? A slice of New York's famous cheesecake is yours if you say yes.***

Before I have time to respond, she adds. ***Pretty please with whipped cream and a cherry on top.***

Madison's begging was enough of a trigger to say yes, but the fact that whipped cream and a cherry is involved has, without a doubt, sealed the deal.

**You drive a hard bargain...but okay.**

***Thank you! Thank you! Would 2mro be ok?***

**Tomorrow would be perfect,** I reply eagerly.

***Great!! Do you remember where I live?***

How could I forget?

Maybe I could suggest she come here. But that doesn't make any sense, as all her books are at her place. I'll just suck it up because it's not like it's a date. I'm helping her study. It's a study date. I'm only offering my expertise and nothing more.

With that thought in mind, I respond.

**Text me the details. I'll be there.**

A loud knocking on my door interrupts my vigil by the phone, and by the obnoxious pounding, I know it's Hunter. Opening the door, I quickly hand him a beer as I want to check my cell. However, the moment he takes one step into my home, he raises a brow. Looking from left to right, he sniffs the air and rotates his finger in a circular motion around the room.

"It smells like sex in here."

A small laugh escapes me.

Looking at me closely, he adds, "But it also smells like…" He takes another sniff. "Cherry pie."

It doesn't surprise me how accurate he can be. I guess these are the perks of knowing someone your entire life.

Closing the door behind him, I say, "Drink that. You're going to need it for what I'm about to tell you."

# Sixteen

*Madison*

"Maddy, why, oh why are you getting messed up with this jerkoff once again?" Mary says, watching in distaste as I try on outfit number five.

"First, I'm not getting messed up with him. He's helping me study, that's all. And second, he's not a jerkoff," I say, defending Dixon's honor.

"Um, yeah, he is," she rebukes, her eyes rising from the magazine she's flicking through. "Do you not remember he stood you up, and *then* he disappeared off the face of this earth for like three months?"

"Only to reappear looking like a damn angel of sin," I softly add, remembering how good Dixon looked in his faded blue jeans and how he filled out his white V-neck tee perfectly.

"Stop that!" Mary throws a pillow at me. "That's your hormones talking. The sensible Maddy would not be allowing this man into her home and heart."

Her accurate comment has me quickly jumping to my own defense. "Lamb, stop being so melodramatic. He's helping me study because he's a doctor. And for the record, he's going nowhere near my heart." I fail to mention he's already wedged his way in there.

"And besides, there's David," I add, taking off my sparkly sweater. "I would never do that to him. I really like him."

We hit it off the first night we met, and before I knew it, we were casually seeing one another a few weeks later.

In the beginning, I knew I was sort of using David to fill the Dixon void, but then I began to actually enjoy his company. He's the perfect gentleman and really is wonderful boyfriend material. But that's the problem—he's too perfect, which I know is crazy.

If I were to really evaluate what the issue is here, the reason I can't one-hundred-percent commit to David is because he's not Dixon.

I met David so soon after Dixon bailed on me, and I guess I was a little hurt he never made good on his rain check. However, I now know the reason he just vanished was because he was seeing someone. Although, it's funny that he never mentioned her or hinted he was in a relationship.

But now that he's back in my life, I don't know what to think or feel. Maybe Mary is right, and it's just my hormones overtaking my good sense.

"Maddy, I love you to death. You're my best friend, but you're living in denial. When that man is involved, you lose all sense of reason, which makes no sense. You've spoken to him like five times."

"I know," I say, turning around to face her. "But the times

we have spoken, they've been, I dunno…" I shrug. "Kind of amazing."

"And they're not with David?" she asks, popping her gum.

"Of course they are. But it's different with Dixon."

"How so?" she questions, crossing her legs and sitting cross-legged on the edge of my bed.

"I just…you know I have skeletons in the closet," I confess, biting my lip.

"Yes, and I wish you'd tell me what. I've known you since we were in diapers. I would never judge you," she says, her voice betraying her hurt.

Mary and I have been inseparable since I was five years old, and we were next-door neighbors. Even when my mom remarried and we moved, Mary and I remained BFFs, and we promised never to allow anything to come between us. So far, we've both stuck to our word.

But my secret isn't just "anything." It's life-changing, and I will do anything to spare Mary that pain.

"I know, Lamb." I sigh, lowering my eyes. "But it's something I just want to forget."

"I wish you'd at least talk to someone. Maybe Dr. Dixon can help," she jokes while I almost choke on my tongue.

"No!" I cry, shaking my head as I meet her warm eyes. "This is something I can never tell him." I hate how vulnerable I sound.

"Whatever it is, I know it's not your fault," she says sympathetically. "But I just know your wicked stepsister is totally to blame."

I swallow down my nausea and reach for my slinky tank. "Ugh, can you not ruin my day by mentioning her? I haven't seen her for two glorious months, and I hope I can push it out to six."

"I don't understand how she can be a product of Sebastian. I mean, he's so nice, and she's…"

"Such a bitch," I mumble, filling in the blanks. "And that's a compliment," I add, reaching for an elastic because my long hair is suddenly pissing me off.

Mary nods and makes a grossed-out face. "I still can't believe she's marrying your brother."

The hair tie goes flying across the room, and I gulp. "Yeah, well, neither can I," I lie because I can so believe it.

"Isn't that like incest or something?" Mary asks, and I shake my head.

"No, they're not related by blood. My mom married Sebastian; therefore, we're related by marriage," I explain, really hoping she drops this, like now.

"So kinda like if Greg married Marcia? God knows it's all about her, so the Marcia analogy suits her perfectly."

"Yes, kinda," I reply, trying my best to remain calm as I hunt through my garments on the floor.

"It's still gross. I mean, Dylan is hot, but he's your brother," Mary says, screwing up her nose.

This conversation is making me so uncomfortable, but I nod anyway. "I know. It really is."

"When are they getting married?" she asks, casually reaching for her bottled water.

"I'm not sure. Their engagement party is a couple of months away. They only just got engaged, so I don't think they'll get married right away. But who knows, it *is* Beth we're talking about. You know she'll do anything for her five minutes of fame," I spit, glaring at the wall, too angry to face Mary in case my expression betrays me.

"Yeah, and poor Sebastian has to foot the bill," Mary says, and I nod. "Do you think—"

I hold up my finger to stop Mary's questioning because I don't want to talk about this any longer.

"What about this?" I ask, holding a knee-length, blue baby-doll dress out in front of me, subtly hinting this conversation has ended.

Mary rests her cheek in her palm as she examines me. "Hmm, it kind of screams 'date.' I mean, it's pretty, but what's wrong with what you have on now?"

Looking down at my ripped blue jeans and black tee, I scrunch up my nose and pinch the hem of my top. "This? Really? It's a little casual, isn't it?"

"Why would that matter? It's not a date, right?" She raises an inquisitive brow.

"Right," I confirm with a half-assed nod. "You're totally right."

However, as I turn to look at my reflection in the mirror, I cringe because my face and hair are one hot mess.

"Yeah, you'll definitely need to redo your hair and makeup."

Turning over my shoulder, I chuckle. "You said it doesn't matter what I wear."

"Yeah I know, but you don't want to totally scare him off. I mean, he might be useful to have around," she explains.

I raise my eyebrow, confused.

"He might have cute friends," she says with a wink.

After washing, straightening, and curling my hair, I've thrown it up into a messy bun as that's the only thing I'm semi-happy with. My makeup is minimal, and the only thing that's "flashy" is my favorite vanilla lip gloss, which plumps up my lips. Mary was right. This most certainly is not a date. I mean, I'm going out with David, for Christ's sake. But it troubles me that I occasionally need to remind myself of that fact.

When the doorbell chimes right at seven o'clock, butterflies suddenly take flight in my belly, but I tell them to cool it because this is *not* a date. Wiping my sweaty palms on my jeans and taking a deep breath, I open the door and am greeted by the *hottest* man on earth.

The first breath I took was in vain, as it hasn't helped calm my nerves whatsoever, so I take another before I pass out from lack of oxygen to the brain.

"Madison," Dixon says in a deep, husky voice that has me loving my own name.

"H-Hi," I stutter, shyly brushing a stray strand of hair behind my ear. "Please come in," I add, opening the door wider and stepping out of the way.

Dixon nods, his lips tipping up into a mischievous, dimpled smile as he takes his first step into my home. I can't help but note how much younger he looks in casual clothing. He's wearing faded blue jeans and a tight black Yankees T-shirt, and even though he looks informal, he still looks damn hot.

When I quickly shut the door behind me, he turns to look

at me over his shoulder and smirks as he points at my framed *From Dusk till Dawn* movie poster. "I love Quentin Tarantino."

"You do?" I ask. He failed to mention that during our texting marathon.

"Oh yeah. I like anything that screws with the mind." He taps his temple.

Of course he does.

"Well good 'cause now I don't feel like a total nerd," I say with a faux sigh.

"Your secret is safe with me," he replies in a conspiratorial tone, and I laugh at his flippant attitude.

"So did you want your dessert now or after?" I ask, still standing with my back against the door. I'm too nervous to move as his gorgeous looks render me useless.

He turns full circle and crosses his arms over his broad chest, a hint of a smile pulling at his supple lips.

"How about we get some studying done first, and then I can pass out into a sugar-induced coma?"

"Good idea." I smirk and push off the door. "I don't really have a desk," I shyly confess and look at where my coffee table was once visible. It's now strewn with books, papers, highlighters, and the occasional candy wrapper.

"That's okay. This is like your little study den. I like it. You should have seen my room when I was studying. I lost two cats in there," he teases.

"Well, now I feel better 'cause at least I know where my cat is."

Dixon laughs, and I realize this is the most casual I've ever seen him. His relaxed attitude calms me down somewhat.

"So shall we?" he suggests, pointing at my sofa.

"Yeah—yes, of course," I counter, mentally giving myself a well-needed slap.

I round the sofa while he does the same, and we both take a seat on opposite ends, our bodies pressed up against the armrests. There's a huge gap between us, seeing as my sofa seats five comfortably.

Wow, this isn't at all awkward. But it's the reality check I needed, as I've probably made Dixon uncomfortable with my excessive staring. With that thought in mind, I kick off my sneakers and reach for my textbook.

Tucking a leg underneath me, I turn to face Dixon and almost forget to breathe when I see he's sporting a pair of thick-rimmed, designer glasses. His incredibly blue eyes are now amplified, and the chic frames give him a sexy professor look.

"Okay, show me whatcha got," he says, and I close my gaping mouth.

"Well, I'm having problems with autonomic pharmacology," I reply, my fingers shaking as I flip open my book to chapter four.

Dixon shifts closer, looking at the open textbook I'm offering him. "This can definitely be a little overwhelming. What don't you understand?"

"All of it," I confess with a smile.

Dixon chuckles, and I ignore how the sound resonates throughout my entire body.

"Well, let's start with the basics. There are four classes of medications. Some medications turn on the sympathetic nervous system. Then some medications turn off the sympathetic nervous system," he explains, holding out his left hand.

Holding up his right hand, he then goes on to say, "There are medications that turn on the parasympathetic nervous system. And then some drugs turn off the parasympathetic nervous system."

"Yeah, but how do you remember which do what?" I ask, reaching for my pen.

"You know the autonomic nervous system is responsible for fight or flight. And rest and digest, right?"

I nod because my autonomic nervous system is running haywire at the moment.

"Well, it's easy. The sympathetic nervous system isn't that sympathetic after all. Just imagine, it's a beautiful, sunny day, and you're taking a hike in the woods when suddenly, a bear..."

Forty-five minutes later, Dixon has managed to explain to me what my lecturer has failed to do all semester.

"Holy shit, that makes perfect sense!" I exclaim, madly writing out critical points as Dixon speaks.

"Of course it does," he cockily scoffs. "Are you telling me you doubted my teaching skills?" he mocks, clutching his chest over his heart.

"Well..." I taunt, giving him a cheeky sideways glance.

"For your lack of belief, you now owe me two pieces of cheesecake," he smugly states, taking off his glasses and rubbing his weary eyes.

"I think I can manage that," I reply, standing up and heading toward the kitchen. However, I stop mid-stride and turn over my shoulder and ask, "So what do you know about adrenergic drugs?"

Three hours later, I know things I didn't even know existed.

After I got over the fact that Dixon was in my house, sitting mere inches away from me, I actually learned stuff. He has turned out to be an incredible teacher, and it doesn't hurt he's pretty incredible to look at.

The way he spoke with excitement on topics he obviously felt passionate about just proved to me that I'm intrigued by all sides of him, which troubles me. I find myself easily slipping and forgetting that I'm in a relationship with David.

"Are you going to eat that?" Dixon asks.

"Huh?" I blurt out, his question disturbing my thoughts as I meet his amused eyes.

"That. Are you going to eat it?" he repeats, pointing at my cheesecake with his fork.

"Oh, no, you can have it," I offer, handing my plate over to him.

He gratefully accepts, and I tell myself to stop staring at his lips as he takes a big bite. I obviously fail, however because Dixon grins.

"I love desserts."

"Me too," I reply, thankful he didn't address my staring issue.

"Yeah, I blame it on growing up with an Italian mother," he replies with a smirk, licking his fork clean.

"Oh, that's right. You mentioned your parents were Italian," I say, remembering our texting conversation where I avoided the topic of my family like the plague. "But Mathews isn't

Italian, is it?" I ask, feeling culturally uneducated. "And neither is Dixon."

Dixon shakes his head, and he leans forward, placing the empty plate on top of a closed textbook. "No, it's actually Di Matteo. But I changed it once I hit college to become a little more Americanized."

I know he must speak Italian because his surname rolls off his tongue, and his accent is very authentic. Holy shit, I have the world's hottest man sitting in my house, eating dessert, and he's literally fluent in the language of love.

"And where did Dixon come from?"

He clears his throat before confessing, "I was named after my father's fishing boat."

I try not to smile. "Oh."

When he sees my reaction, he clarifies. "Well, his boat was actually named *Dixieland*. America was his freedom. A better way of life. So when I was born, my parents mixed a little of their past roots with their present roots."

"I like that it has meaning."

He nods with a smirk. "I guess so. But honestly, I'm just glad they didn't call me Dixie."

I cover my mouth to stifle my laugh.

As I digest everything he just shared, a thought suddenly occurs to me.

*Madison, do not ask him to say something in Italian*, I silently scold.

"So do you know any swear words in Italian?" I ask, totally ignoring my inner voice.

Dixon laughs, the muscles in his thick neck flexing. "Why is that the first question most people ask?"

I lift my shoulders into a playful shrug. "I dunno, you tell me—you're the doctor."

Dixon nods and moves his mouth from side to side, appearing to be in full contemplation of what to say. "You want tame? Or no-holds-barred?"

"Give it to me." I smile.

"*Vaffanculo*."

I have no idea what he just said, and he more than likely just insulted me, but I don't care because that phrase just made me keel over.

"More," I shamelessly demand.

Dixon's lips twitch. "You didn't even ask what I said."

I bashfully smile, as he so knows I'm impressed. "It doesn't matter. I trust you."

And I really do. Dixon looks reflective, but thankfully he doesn't comment on my overshare.

Taking off his glasses, I can see him weighing up on what to say next. "*Sei una bella ragazza con gliocchi belli.*"

Oh…wow.

I'm on the edge of my seat, swooning as Dixon just serenaded me in his native tongue. I know that couldn't be a curse because I'm not totally clueless, and I know the word "*bella*" means beautiful. So did Dixon just call me…beautiful?

My heart begins racing at the possibility, and I whisper, "What did you say?"

The air is charged by an unseen static, and I know I should stop talking, but I can't.

"I thought you said it didn't matter," he says, matching my tone as he inches closer to me while I do the same to him.

"I changed my mind," I reply, my eyes involuntarily

dropping to his mouth.

"I said you're a beautiful girl," he huskily confesses.

"And what else?" I press because I know there's more.

"I also said you have beautiful eyes." He moves another inch closer.

"You think I'm beautiful?" I gasp, not noticing our knees are touching until my leg is on fire.

"Yes," he replies without pause. "You're gorgeous."

"T-Thanks," I stammer as I lean forward, my body wanting to be closer to his.

What am I doing? I need to stop this because this is wrong. But why does it feel so right?

Being with Dixon is effortless, and with him, I'm not afraid or shying away from his touch like I am with others.

"I think you're gorgeous, too." It's out before I can stop myself.

Dixon's eyes widen, and I kick my ass for not putting a lid on my rampant brain. But he doesn't look troubled by my confession; if anything, he looks highly roused by my honesty. I lower my eyes, embarrassed by my frankness, but he gently places two fingers under my chin and raises my face to meet his. I go willingly, and when I meet his heated stare, a gasp escapes me because he looks as if he's about to pounce.

However, he remains absolutely still, and I breathlessly anticipate his next move.

His thumb, which is still grasping my chin, begins a slow, torturous journey of my jaw, and as he sashays the tip back and forth over my skin, my mouth parts, and I lick my lower lip. Dixon hungrily follows the movement, and I squirm when I'm rewarded with a lopsided smirk. I'd give anything to know what he's thinking.

"*Sei un angelo*," he whispers, and the smoldering look in his deep blue eyes hint that his words are of tenderness as he softly lets me go.

"What does that mean?" I breathlessly ask, but he shakes his head, not replying.

I'm completely lost in a Dixon bubble, and suddenly, nothing else exists. I know he feels it too, and as he leans forward, painfully slow, wetting his supple, sinful lips, he only stops when our faces are mere inches apart. My breath leaves me in small, winded gasps, and Dixon smirks, knowing what this intimacy is doing to me.

The electricity passing between us has every nerve ending in my body prickling in awareness. My skin hums in pleasure as Dixon raises his finger and, ever so gently, rubs the back of his knuckle down my cheek and across to my parted lips. He's silently asking for entrance, and damn me, I want him inside.

Opening my mouth wider, Dixon heatedly watches the movement and strokes his finger along the seam of my mouth before finally placing the tip inside. Timidly, I circle the top of his pointer finger with my tongue, and he hisses, which has my insides liquefying.

He watches me slowly tongue him, his eyes blistering, but he never pushes. This is my show as much as it is his, and at this moment, I want to kiss him so bad. I know it's wrong, and I should be pulling away, but I can't. I've felt this way from the moment I met him.

Dixon softly removes his finger from my mouth and slides it down the center of my bottom lip, no doubt sensing my need. And like the true man he is, he boldly bends forward, ready to claim my mouth as his. However, the deathly whistle from *Kill Bill* chimes loudly, interrupting our moment, and I hastily pull back, nearly giving myself whiplash. My cheeks flame in embarrassment and desire, and I clumsily reach for my cell off the coffee table.

"Shit," I curse when I see who's calling me.

Dixon blows out a deep breath as he falls back against the sofa, fisting his hair.

I'm still undecided whether David has the best or worst timing, but I answer the phone on the fifth ring.

"Hey," I say, my shrill voice sounding unlike me.

"Hey, babe, I missed you. Sorry if I interrupted your studying," he replies, his warm voice causing a ball of guilt to subside in my stomach.

"Oh, it's fine," I say, feeling heated, as I know Dixon is listening to every word.

I can't do this with him sitting here because it feels so wrong and dirty. David is happily chatting away, and I slowly stand, turning to look at Dixon, who looks half pissed, half aroused—the look suits him. I raise my pointer finger, indicating I'll only be a minute, and he nods. I excuse myself and duck into my bedroom, taking the first breath since I answered the phone.

"So what do you think?" David asks as I close the door behind me.

"About what?" I counter as I haven't been listening to a word he's said.

"About meeting my parents this weekend. They really want to meet you. And I really want you to meet them."

...Shit.

This is so not good timing. Dixon is in the other room, and

not to mention, I was seconds away from kissing him. Now my kind-of boyfriend has just asked me to meet his parents. Oh God, this is too much. I feel a small bout of anxiety creep over me, and I take a seat on the edge of my bed.

"Um…David, I don't know."

"Why, Maddy? You know I'm crazy about you, and I'm not going anywhere," he softly states.

"I know, and I'm into you, too."

"But?" he prompts.

"But this is a big step."

"I know. But I'm ready to take it with you," he says, his voice displaying nothing but care.

My breath comes out in small pants as I can't take the pressure. *Just say no, Madison,* my inner self screams. *Learn to say no.*

David is sweet and kind, and I'm dating him. Just because the man I'm obsessing over is sitting in my living room doesn't warrant me to be so detached.

"Okay, fine. Early dinner, though," I say, finally caving. "I've got a ton of homework I gotta get through this weekend."

"You got it, babe. Whatever you want," David says excitedly, and I can't help but smile at his enthusiasm. "I'll make all the arrangements. My mom is going to flip. She's really excited to meet you."

"I'm excited to meet your mom, too," I reply, massaging my temple.

I really should go, as Dixon is in the other room, and I'm being extremely rude.

"Maddy?" David questions.

"Yeah?" I reply, not liking his tone.

"Maybe after we're done, you could, I don't know, maybe spend the night? I could help you study," David suggests, and I can hear the apprehension in his voice.

I pause, needing a moment to process his question. David and I have kissed and fooled around a little, but it's been quite tame. He hasn't pushed with the sex stuff, and although I haven't told him about my past, he knows something nasty lies dormant in my memories. However, he respects my need for space and doesn't push.

But meeting his parents and spending the night is too much for me.

I just…can't.

My silence says it all, and David says, "It's okay. I understand. I'm sorry for asking."

The hint of disappointment stabs me in the chest, so I stupidly reply, "I'll think about it. But I'm not making any promises."

"Oh, Maddy," David gushes. "You're the best. I'm so lucky."

His kindness really amazes me and makes me feel like an even bigger bitch for being so insensitive.

"I'm lucky, too. Anyway, I better go. I've got a mountain of homework with my name written all over it."

"Oh, okay, cool. Well, I'll talk to you tomorrow."

"Yeah, sounds good," I reply, picking at a loose thread on my comforter.

"Bye, babe. And I mean it. I'm so lucky to have met you."

I feel like an ass, but this is getting to be too much.

"Thanks, um, bye."

Sighing, I rub my temples and take a moment to center myself before I go back out there. What the hell did I just agree to? I'm so confused, and I hate to admit the reason is sitting in my living room right this second.

Before Dixon re-emerged, I was beginning to open up and could see things with David actually progressing. But now that Dixon's back and almost kissing me, I don't know what to do. Maybe this was a bad idea and I'm kidding myself into thinking we could ever *just* be friends. I don't know what it is about him, but he's the first guy I have ever felt this way about. He's the first guy I can actually think about in a physical way and not freak out.

I just want to be normal, and Dixon makes me feel that way.

Wiping away a stolen tear, I toss my phone onto the dresser and look at my reflection. I look like a complete mess, as my hair is sitting in a lopsided ponytail, and my T-shirt has a cheesecake stain on it from when I missed my mouth. Yet the sophisticated man just beyond my door wanted to kiss me. Why?

Taking a deep breath, I open the door and hope my flushed cheeks don't give me away. Stepping into the living room, I see the sofa is empty, and Dixon is nowhere to be seen. I didn't hear him go into the bathroom, but I do a quick sweep just in case he wanted to stretch his legs. After I've checked my house—twice—I come up empty. Unless he's hiding in my closet, he's gone.

Looking over at my wooden grandfather clock, I see that I was on the phone for twenty minutes.

I should be pissed he left, but I'm actually more pissed at myself for not wrapping things up with David sooner.

Not in the mood to study any longer, I decide to pack up, take a hot shower, and crawl into bed, hoping to dream this day away. However, a loose piece of paper, strewn across my coffee table catches my eye and I bend forward, reaching for it.

In an elegant script are the words: *It means, you're an angel.*

I bite my lip and hold the paper up against my chest, not able to look at his sweet words any longer.

# Seventeen

## *Dixon*

"Good morning, Dr. Mathews," Susanna says as I barge through the door, my rain-soaked coat making a mess on the cream carpet.

"Ms. Vale." I run a hand through my wet locks.

"Oh, you should have called. I would have met you downstairs with an umbrella," she says, quickly standing up and handing me a box of tissues.

"It's June, for Christ's sake! Why is it raining?" I gripe, accepting a few and wiping down my drenched face.

My briefcase is sopping wet and failed as a makeshift umbrella. "When will this blasted construction be over with?" I ask, brushing down the damp lapels of my gray suit jacket.

"It *is* New York. Once this one is finished, another will take its place soon enough," she wisely says.

"You're right. I just wish they'd hurry up so I can park my car in the garage I'm paying thousands for," I snap.

Susanna nods with a smile. "Bad start to the week?"

If this were anyone other than her, I would be telling them to mind their own damn business, but Susanna is practically family.

"You don't want to know the half of it."

"Go. I'll get you a coffee," she says, waving me toward my office.

My morning doesn't get any better, and by midday, I'm convinced I'll murder my next patient. I'm barely refraining from banging my head on the desk when a soft knock sounds on the door.

"Come in," I bellow, giving up on reading over my notes for my next appointment.

"Dr. Mathews, sorry to bother you," Susanna says as she pops her head through my door.

"It's fine. Come in." I motion for her to enter.

"This just arrived," she states. She holds a small, white box in her hand.

"Oh?" I say, raising an eyebrow. "Who's it from?"

"I'm not sure. The courier said there were no sender details recorded."

"How strange," I reply, my curiosity piqued.

"I thought so, too." She walks over to my desk and hands me the package.

Looking at the top and both sides, I still have no idea what could be inside this small box.

"If this is a severed ear, I'll be extremely pissed," I say, and

Susanna laughs.

Unclasping the lid, I open it apprehensively and peer inside while Susanna leans forward so she too can see the box's contents. The moment I see the slice of cheesecake, I know who the sender is.

But why?

"There's an envelope," she says in anticipation, no doubt wondering what the hell is going on.

Reaching for it, I open it. Inside sits the same piece of paper I left for Madison. However, underneath my handwriting are the words: *I saved you a piece—from one angel to another.*

"Dr. Mathews, are you okay?" I remain mute, as the note in front of me has my full attention.

Why did she send this?

Sadly, Madison's walls are paper thin, and I heard the majority of her conversation with David. There's no doubt she's into him. I mean, she said so herself. I just need to forget the fact she nearly kissed me because her actions surely don't match her words.

I couldn't stomach a second longer of listening to her canoodling that love-sick fool, so I left. But I left her a note because I didn't want to just bail yet again. I had no expectations, and yes, I could have chosen something else to write. But I thought this was better than the alternative of, "Your boyfriend is a parasitic dick."

Eyeballing the cheesecake and note, I honestly don't know what to do. I'm drowning in two women who are both toxic to my health for entirely different reasons, but toxic nonetheless.

Slamming the lid shut, I push the box away from me and place the folded letter into my pocket. Kicking the waste bin out from under my desk, I slide the box across my desk and am about to throw it in the trash when Susanna stops me.

"Aren't you going to eat that?" she asks, obviously confused by my distaste toward a harmless piece of cheesecake.

I shake my head. "Nope. Would you like it?" I offer the box her way.

"Are you sure?"

"Knock yourself out," I reply. Susanna happily takes the box from my outstretched palm.

"Are you sure you don't want it?" she questions, and I can't help the dry chuckle that spills from my lips.

"That's the problem, Ms. Vale," I vaguely reply, no longer referring to the dessert.

Susanna looks puzzled by my ambiguous response, but she doesn't push. She takes the box and makes her way toward the door. However, she suddenly stops, and with her hand poised on the handle, she raises the box above her head and says, "Food for thought, Dr. Mathews."

She gently shuts the door behind her, and I sigh because she's absolutely right.

The rest of the week is no better than the start, and come Saturday afternoon, I'm dying for some S&S—scotch and sex.

Juliet has been MIA all week, and after my blow-off last weekend, I really shouldn't be expecting anything less. But having easy, freaky sex on tap for the past three months really spoils a man, and my hormones are in overdrive.

I guess I could call Juliet, but I feel we're both on the same page and realized we're nothing more than fuck buddies who got a little carried away with a Disney HEA.

But now I'm stuck. Do I go out and look for someone to burn some of this pent-up sexual frustration with? Or do I just call Juliet? She ticks all the right boxes sexually, and she's familiar and uncomplicated, but for some unknown reason, I can't seem to make the call.

As I pass a jogger, I know the reason is because of Madison. I can't get that damn image of us almost kissing out of my head, and the more I try to forget it, the more lucid it becomes. I haven't heard a peep from her after she sent the cheesecake, and I've purposely stayed away. I need to clear my head of both women, and to do that, I need to get laid.

Reaching for my cell from my jacket pocket, I quickly dial Hunter, who answers on the second ring.

"S and S?" he asks, and I hum in agreement.

"Let the games begin."

Sadly, Finch hasn't joined us, so it's only Hunter and me, which is never a good combination when we're both horny and drunk. However, I'm the designated driver, so I'm only one of the two, but it's still enough to have me seeing double.

Hunter has dragged me to Cherry Pop, the club where I saw Madison looking like a total goddess on the dance floor.

Although I wish he'd chosen somewhere a little quieter, I can see why he selected this venue. The girls are barely clothed and barely legal, and with the amount of cheap alcohol flowing through their veins, I know this will be an early night.

Hunter seems to also be on the prowl, and our joined bachelorhood must be a magnet because I already have five random phone numbers in my pocket, two of which I have no idea how they ended up in there.

"So what do you feel like? Brunette? Blond? Redhead?" Hunter asks, bowed over the railing, looking at the dancing prey below.

"I'm not sure." I also peer out into the sea of gyrating bodies.

"I'm thinking redhead myself," Hunter says, rubbing his hands together sinisterly.

I chuckle, and when I glance at him, I figure now is a good time to ask what's been bugging him because he's drunk and usually all for the sharing.

"You okay, man?" I ask. "You've been acting weird. Well, weirder," I correct with a smirk. "I'm detecting some hostility when the opposite sex is involved."

Hunter takes a quick sip of his beer, and I know I'm onto something. But he shrugs it off, obviously not wanting to talk about his feelings.

I decide to press. "Want to talk about it?"

"Dude, I'm here to fuck, not to talk. So unless you wanna put out, quit it with the psychobabble. And besides," he adds. "You're drowning in pussy, so you wouldn't understand."

"Understand what?"

"Understand what a lucky son of a bitch you are," he plainly replies.

"Lucky? Please explain how," I say, scratching my head because from where I stand, I'm far from lucky. I'm obsessing over one girl who is totally unattainable while trying to wean myself off another.

Hunter reads my thoughts. "At least you have them coming back for more. What do I get? I'm lucky if I even catch their names. Am I ugly? You'd tell me, right?" he asks, taking a sip of his drink.

So this is what's eating him. Could it be my friend, a bigger manwhore than me, is looking for a steady girlfriend? That's got to be it. The problem is, he's choosing the wrong women. I should know.

"Dude, you're not ugly. If I swung that way, I'd totally fuck you," I say, slapping his shoulder playfully. "So you what, want to settle down?" I ask seriously, wanting to make sure my theory is right.

He shrugs, which in Hunter's language means yes.

"Hunt?" I ask again, determined to get him to speak.

"I dunno, maybe!" he snaps, most likely annoyed with the twenty questions. "I just…why can't I find one I like? Are all women like that? If so, fuck that bullshit. I'll stick to one-nighters," he says, running a hand down his face.

"Maybe the problem is the women you find aren't exactly 'bring home to your mom' kinda material," I suggest, hoping I don't appear judgmental. "And besides, the way you talk, walk, dress, act…Jesus, your entire being doesn't reflect you're looking to settle down."

"Maybe my whoring tendencies are a cry for help?" he quickly suggests, and I don't know whether he's being serious.

Just as I'm about to address his statement, he cuts me off. "Let's just get laid already." He pushes off the railing to look at me.

I know a brush-off when I see one, but I let it slide. He's done talking, but at least I know what's been bugging him.

This conversation, however, will have to be put on hold anyway, as a set of twins is headed our way. And yes, I mean girls, not boobs. And yes, they are identical.

"Punch me," Hunter whispers from the side of his mouth.

"Are you fucking high?" I whisper back, puzzled by his randomness.

"I will be after I fuck twin one or two. Either way, I don't care which it is because I won't be able to tell who's who because they are fucking *twins*," he states, his excitement clearly evident by his shit-eating grin. "This isn't a dream, right? Those two blond bombshells are really headed our way."

I roll my eyes and sip my beer. "Yes, you moron, they are real, and they're headed our way," I reply, watching their fake tits barely wobble as they walk toward us.

"Punch me just in case," he quickly says, but I refrain from the violence as both girls stop beside me.

"Hi, I'm Mandy, and this is Marisa," Mandy says with a smile, her perfect teeth glowing under the fluorescents.

Before I have a chance to reply, Hunter steps forward and takes charge. "Hi, Mandy and Marisa. I'm Hunter, and this ugly bastard is Dixon," he says, hooking his thumb my way.

I sarcastically smile at his charisma and extend my hand. "Nice to meet you ladies."

The way Marisa is eye-fucking me and my hand, I know she would prefer me to put my hand someplace else. She's attractive, but I'm suddenly craving a brunette.

Screaming at my subconscious to shut the hell up, I forget that a certain brunette exists and focus on getting laid.

"So can we buy you girls a drink?" I ask, and both of them nod eagerly.

"We'd like that," they say in unison, giggling.

Hunter looks like he's just died and gone to heaven, and me, I feel like I'm in hell.

Forty-five minutes later, I regret the fact I offered to drive. However, no amount of scotch could ever, *ever* make what the titty twins are proposing okay.

This is the third time Hunter has kicked me in the shin under the table, and if he does it again, I'll take him up on his earlier suggestion and punch the living hell out of him.

Mandy, twin number one, who is older by two minutes, has not so discreetly hinted at us having a good ole fashioned gangbang. Hunter, no surprise, is all for the idea, but me, not so much—hence, the under table violence on his behalf.

Now, I'm no prude, and I have engaged in a threesome or two in my time, but never a foursome with my best friend and two horny sisters. This is gross on all accounts, but more importantly, I'm not interested in seeing Hunter live out his Hugh Hefner dreams with these wannabe bunnies.

"Excuse me, gentlemen," Mandy says, offering a hand to her sister. "We're just going to visit the little girls' room." They both giggle, blowing us kisses before they leave.

The moment they're gone, Hunter quickly reaches over the small table and flicks me in the junk.

"Ow! What the fuck?" I yelp, holding my nuts. "What the hell was that for?"

"Oh, I dunno, I just wanted to check if your balls were still intact and you didn't turn into a giant pussy overnight!" he replies in a huff.

"Jesus, calm down." I chuckle, still protecting my family jewels. "They just referred to the restroom as the little girls' room. Do you not see what's wrong with this picture?" I ask, shuddering.

Hunter does not appreciate my humor, however, and replies, "The only thing that's wrong around here is you being a big pussy. I will not let you ruin this for me," he says, jabbing his finger into my chest. I swat his hand away. "This has been my dream since I found out what boobs and vaginas were capable of," he reveals in all seriousness.

I can't help but laugh at his melodramatics. "It's your dream to catch chlamydia?" I playfully counter, and Hunter goes for another round on my nuts, obviously not seeing the funny side to VD.

"Stop hitting me in the dick," I wheeze.

"What's up with you, Dix? You'd usually be all over this. But now it looks as if these hot, frisky twins have just asked you to donate a kidney. You're not into them?" he questions. I can see the confusion behind his green eyes.

He has every right to be confused. Hell, I'm confused, but this just feels wrong. Juliet's offer of a random threesome didn't sit well with me, and neither does the titty twins' foursome suggestion. It just feels so sleazy and sad. Two thirty-two-year-old men contemplating having a foursome with a couple of horny twins *is* as seedy as it sounds.

"This is what we came here for, right?" Hunter affirms, and I nod.

This is indeed why we're scouting the dark corners, looking for a warm body to help dull the loneliness for a night. But

I'm just not feeling it. Both girls are becoming increasingly unattractive by the minute, and I'm certain that if I were to agree to this little proposition, I would be below par in the sack.

"Listen, I'm not stopping you from living out your Hugh Hefner fantasy, but me, I'm pulling out," I state while Hunter scoffs.

"Yes, you could be pulling out...of Marisa, but you've gone soft. You don't deserve a dick," he says, but his smirk reveals he respects my decision. "Oh well, your loss, more for me," he concludes with a detached shrug. His implication of wanting to settle down just got shot to hell.

Before I have time to reply, the girls return, and Marisa practically ends up in my lap.

"So we were thinking," Mandy says, her freshly painted lips blinding me with their shininess, "you don't really look too keen about the idea of us all playing together."

I try not to scoff at how loosely the term is used.

Hunter looks at me over the table and mouths, "Pussy," but I ignore him and listen to what Mandy has to say.

"But we really like you two, and we still wanted to...play," she concludes with a grin.

I have no idea what "play" means, but my questions are answered when Marisa slides her hand into my lap and softly rubs over my crotch. I jolt in surprise, grabbing onto the edge of the table for support while Marisa looks at me shyly, her hand now firmly affixed to my cock. Hunter raises a confused brow, so I widen my eyes and lower them to my lap. Thankfully, Hunter gets my facial charades and smirks.

"So did you wanna play with me?" Mandy huskily asks Hunter while I'm getting a discreet hand job under the table.

"Abso-fucking-lutely, sweetheart." He quickly stands, wasting no time as he yanks Mandy out of the booth. "Have fun, Dix," he says with a wink. "I'll talk to you tomorrow." Before I can get a word in edgewise, he's dragging Mandy downstairs.

Now that leaves me alone with Marisa and my emerging hard-on. My dick is standing at half mast, but a few more gentle strokes and I'll be at full salute. Her fingers are attentive and slow, and it's exactly what I need.

As a duo, Mandy and Marisa are downright creepy with the whole finishing each other's sentences and wanting to fuck the same men. But as a solo act, Marisa is totally doing it for me.

Closing my eyes and leaning my head back against the seat, I allow her total control, and she takes it by unzipping my jeans and walking her fingers into my crotch. I almost always go commando, and now is no exception, so she's touching my heated flesh the moment she reaches inside. The way her fingers hungrily stroke me and the small hitch to her breath points to the fact she's as turned on as me. Her grip becomes tighter, and as she increases the speed, my sex-starved body sings in relief as my release is waiting in the wings, anticipating the right move to set me off.

However, the here and now comes down around me, and my eyes pop open when I remember where I am. I've come in worse places before, but as glorious as this feels, I really don't want to be caught out ejaculating in a very public place, where a ton of witnesses would be more than willing to recount my depravity to *The New York Times.*

Pulling my hips away slowly, I watch as Marisa turns to look at me, confusion reflected in her aroused blue eyes.

"What's the matter?" she asks, her plump mouth dipping

into a frown.

Leaning forward, I whisper into her ear, "Let's get out of here. When I come, it's going to be inside you. Not in some shitty bar."

I pull back to gauge her reaction, and by her dilated pupils and quickened breaths, I know she's all for the idea. Subtly adjusting myself and zipping up my jeans, I slide out of the booth and offer my hand to help Marisa rise.

I lead the way but don't get very far, as the line to go downstairs is barely moving. Glancing overhead to see what the holdup is, I notice a couple of guys looking over the rail and pointing at something on the dance floor. Out of interest, I casually peer over the ledge, but I suddenly lunge forward to determine if what I'm seeing is actually happening. Marisa's arm is linked through mine so I drag her with me, but I heed no attention to her complaints because I'm about five seconds away from losing my shit.

"What is it, Dixon?" I vaguely hear Marisa ask, but I can't even construct a reply as all my focus is on Madison, who is on the dance floor getting manhandled by Tim.

My feet act before my brain can catch up, and I'm charging forward, pushing anyone or anything that stands in my way out of my line of attack. Thankfully, the sea of people part when they see me headed their way, but when Marisa latches onto my bicep to stop my sprint, I spin on my heel, my anger about ready to explode.

Reaching into my pocket, I pull out the first loose bill I can find and shove it into her hand. "Here, call yourself a cab."

"Dixon!" she cries, but I don't stick around to find out what she has to say.

I charge down the spiral staircase and almost fall down the steps as I take two at a time, my feet moving with unparalleled speed, but I don't care because I need to get to Madison. Elbowing my way through the crowd, I push and shove, not caring who's in my way, and my violence pays off because I get through the horde of people in record time. However, the spot where I last saw Madison is now filled with another couple, and I curse that I've lost her.

Blessing my height, I do a quick scan, and my eyes zero in on Madison walking toward the exit with the ape on her tail. I'm functioning on autopilot and literally pick up anyone who stands in my way, and after many grunts, curses, and slaps, I make it outside. Frantically looking from left to right, I see Madison storming away from Tim, yelling at him to leave her alone.

I take off in a quick march. Before I reach them, I hear Madison yell, "You need to stop following me. I told you I'm not interested in you."

"How do you know you're not interested in me? You won't even give me a chance!" he angrily retorts, lunging forward to grab her.

I see the absolute terror contort her features, and that look sends me wild. Madison's eyes widen when she sees me, which must alert the baboon because he turns quickly, ready to assess the threat. But I'm quicker, and I punch him straight in the jaw.

Madison screams, and Tim stumbles backward, but neither is a deterrent, and I charge forward, ready for strike two. I land a blow on his cheek and then deliver an uppercut to his chin in quick succession, which snaps his head back with a sickening thud.

Tim shakes his head and wobbles on his feet, my punishing blows obviously rattling his tiny brain, but I don't stop. I right hook his face with a powerful swing and he ends up staggering backward, wiping the back of his hand against his bleeding lip.

"Dixon, no!" Madison screams, but I ignore her.

"You again!" he slurs when he sees me, his eyes narrowing in rage.

"I'm back to teach you some manners," I snarl and lunge forward, attempting to knock this son of a bitch down.

He dodges my attack and gets in a lucky jab, connecting with my lip. The metallic taste indicates he's busted my lip open, but the taste just fuels my rage. We both round off, each watching the other like prey, but Tim isn't steady on his feet, and I can see his eye is starting to swell.

"I don't know why you're fighting for her. She doesn't even put out," he spits, his bloodied spittle staining the sidewalk red. "Or maybe she's finally stopped being a cock tease and given it up."

His crudeness feeds my anger, and I'm about to attack, but Madison literally beats me to the punch as she steps between us and socks the asshole in the nose. He staggers backward, no doubt surprised she actually hit him, and he falls to his ass while Madison yelps, clutching her hand against her chest, hissing in pain.

Her safety overtakes my need to kick this guy's ass. "Madison, are you okay?" I ask on a rushed breath, reaching out and touching her shoulder.

However, she surprises me as she shrugs out of my grip, appearing to be angry with me.

As she meets my confused gaze, I can see her eyes are filled with tears, but I have a feeling those tears aren't caused by the pain she's currently experiencing.

"Let me take a look," I gently say.

"I'm okay," she bravely replies, still cradling her wounded hand against her chest.

"Please?" I plead, softly wrapping my fingers around her wrist, coaxing her to let me see.

Thankfully, she complies and lowers her hand, making a pained face at the movement.

"Can you make a fist?" I ask, lightly placing my hand around hers and feeling for any breaks.

She does so but whimpers in pain and tries to pull back. I have a firm grip on her, however, and don't let go. I finish my examination and conclude, "It's not broken, but it's definitely sprained. Let's get you home so you can ice it."

"You're bleeding," she gasps, reaching out and touching my lip with her finger.

Her kind sentiment warms my heart, but I pull out of her touch because I want to get her hand iced before it swells.

"I'm fine. It's just a scratch. Let's just get you home, okay?"

Madison nods. I look over her shoulder at Tim, who is slumped to the floor, too winded to move.

"Nice right hook," I say, wrapping my arm around her shoulder and leading her in the direction of my car.

"Thanks," she replies, trying to appear calm, but her tiny tremors reveal just how shaken up she is.

I bundle her closer into my side, and when she comes willingly, my body sings at the feeling of being needed by her.

As I feel the first sprinkles of rain paint my cheeks, I curse this atrocious weather. However, without warning, the sky suddenly opens up and dumps a torrential downpour in seconds. Madison shrieks while I latch on tighter and quicken our step as we're about to drown.

"How far is it?" Madison yells to be heard over the rain, her face turned into my side.

"Three blocks," I reply, my boots squishing with every step I take.

Madison suddenly places a hand on my bicep and when she squeezes tightly, I stop abruptly, wondering what she's doing. She quickly reaches down and clumsily slips off her heels, dropping about five inches instantly. She looks up at me, looking like a drowned rat, but she smiles and nods, and then we commence a sprint to my car.

By the time we reach my BMW, we are completely saturated, but all I can focus on is getting Madison inside and out of the rain. I practically shove her into the passenger seat when I unlock the door and then make a mad dash for the driver's side, slamming the door shut as I leap in.

The moment the engine purrs to life, I reach down and switch on the heating. I can hear Madison's teeth chattering. I glance over and see her damp clothes sticking to her body.

"Damn this weather," I bark, brushing back my wet hair so I can see the congested road.

Just as I'm about to take off, Madison curses. "Shit."

Looking over, I ask, "What's the matter?"

She curses again and frantically looks around, lifting her ass off the seat and looking beneath her.

"Darn it, I've lost my bag," she says with a small hiccup, and it's only now that I'm not livid and can see relatively clearly that I notice she appears a little glassy-eyed.

"Do you remember when you had it last?" I ask, and she shakes her head, her wet hair sticking to her long neck.

Looking out through the windshield, I see the rain has picked up to biblical proportions, but I unbuckle my seat belt, ready to brace the downpour. However, Madison clutches my forearm, stopping my retreat.

"You can't go out there. It's pouring, and this *is* New York. It's probably already found a new home," she explains, looking out the window.

"But what about your belongings?"

"It's okay. I didn't have much on me. Just my key, some cash, lip balm, and gum," she states, and then she unexpectedly hiccups once again.

She appears mortified and quickly covers her mouth.

"Are you drunk?" I query with a smirk, and Madison lowers her face, embarrassed.

"No, not really. Well, I don't think so," she replies, the heater blowing her matted hair off her face.

"You don't think so?" I ask, confused while buckling my seat belt.

Madison shakes her head and shyly replies, "I'm not a big drinker, so when I do drink, it only takes one or two, and I'm pretty much done for the night."

I turn my blinker on and pull out into traffic, knowing getting home will be a nightmare.

"Ah, a cheap drunk. Every man's dream date," I tease, but zip it when I realize what I just said.

Madison scoffs dryly. "Yeah, well, that's the problem."

"What is?"

"It's the dream date that led me to drink."

"I'm not following," I reply, my eyes focused on the road.

The leather creaks as Madison moves, and I wonder if she's regretting her random disclosure. But she surprises me when she says, "I met David's parents tonight."

"Oh?" I question, but I know damn well she met his parents, as I overheard her phone conversation.

"Yeah," she replies, the heaviness clear in her tone.

"How'd it go?" I attempt to appear casual.

"Great," she responds with a sigh.

"So that's a good thing, right?" I question, my fingers clenching the steering wheel.

"Yeah, I guess. I mean, they were really nice people and very accepting."

"But…?"

"But I dunno. They were too nice and too accepting. Oh my God, what is the matter with me?" she cries, slapping her hands over her face.

I reach out with one arm and uncover her face. "Hey, there's nothing wrong with you. And it's my job to know these things," I say, trying to make light of the situation.

"Yes, there is," she sadly counters with a sniff.

Quickly glancing over, I see tears collecting in her beautiful green eyes. Her sadness breaks my heart, so I decide to set her straight because this self-doubt is painful to watch.

"From where I sit, I don't see anything but perfection." It's out before I can stop myself, and I hope she isn't freaked out by my honesty. I focus on the road, waiting for her reply.

"Thank you, Dixon," she whispers after a minute of silence. "If only that were true."

What is she hiding? We all have a past, but Madison's is one that rules her future. The doctor in me is itching to find out what and dissect her. But the man in me just wants to hold her and tell her everything will be all right. I don't understand why I feel that way, but something inside her makes me want to be a better man.

"Where are we going?" she asks. I shake my head, clearing my thoughts.

Shit, I've ended up driving in the opposite direction from where Madison lives and unintentionally headed into my neighborhood. The rain is still punishing, and my wipers are working overtime, trying to keep up with the heavy shower.

"To my place," I say, then quickly explain before I creep her out. "There's no way I'm leaving you out in the rain with no key to get into your building. I was thinking you could use my phone, as I've left my cell at home, and call someone who may have a spare key. Or, I could drop you off someplace?" I suggest, hoping like hell she doesn't say David's.

There's a slight pause before she nods, and I let out the involuntary breath I was holding.

"I'll call Mary. Although…" She looks at her watch. "She probably won't be home. I was supposed to meet up with her, but—" She halts, chewing on her bottom lip as she tugs at the seat belt nervously.

I wonder what she was going to say, but I don't push. Besides, the way her eyes narrow, I don't think I want to know.

"Thank you for coming to my rescue. Again," she says. "You must think I'm pathetic."

"What?" I gasp, turning into my underground car park. "Why on earth would I think that?"

"Because I'm either falling down, injuring myself, or

getting into fights with my stalker ex when you're around. Or I'm sending you a peace-offering cheesecake and don't hear from you all week," she adds in a whisper.

Pulling into my car space, I turn off the car and swivel to face her as I unbuckle my belt. Her hands are nervously twisting in her lap, and she won't meet my eyes.

"I don't think you're pathetic," I reply firmly.

"Then why haven't I heard from you?" she questions, raising her eyes to meet mine. "I wanted to apologize for being such an inhospitable host, hence the cheesecake. But then I didn't hear from you, so I thought maybe you didn't like cheesecake. Or maybe you just don't like me." She lowers her eyes once again.

This girl is breaking my resolve with her honesty, and I realize it must be the alcohol talking 'cause this is a side to Madison I've never seen. She's usually a little more guarded with her feelings, so I can't help but ask.

"For the record, I do like cheesecake…*and* you. But hypothetically speaking, if I were not to like either, would that matter?"

Madison raises her eyes and bites her lip. "I would say you were mad for not liking cheesecake. I mean, that's just crazy talk," she says with a quiver in her voice.

"And what if I said, hypothetically, of course, that I didn't like you?" I huskily ask, leaning forward a fraction.

She gulps, and my gaze drops to her heaving chest, which is practically transparent through her white silk camisole that is still damp from the rain. The lace imprint of her cream bra can be clearly seen through the wet material, and my mouth salivates at the sight.

"I-I would be…" she stutters, nervously fidgeting. "I would

be terribly upset if you didn't like me, Dixon," she whispers, leaning forward, our breaths mingling as one.

"Why?" I ask, matching her tone as I lean closer, my eyes meeting hers.

I suppress my moan as she licks her full bottom lip, her pink tongue doing unimaginable things to my libido.

"Because…I like…being your friend," she says, which is like a bucket of icy-cold water dousing my heated hormones.

Not allowing my composure to slip, however, I smile. "Well, I like being your friend also."

Madison smiles half-heartedly, and I can't stop myself as I reach forward and softly run my knuckle down her cheek, leaving invisible sparks in its wake. "Let's go inside, you're shivering."

She quickly replies, "I'm not cold."

"You're shaking," I say, watching goose pimples cover her upper body.

"Am I?" she asks, focusing on my mouth.

The dense heat in the car is fogging up the windows and my brain, shrouding us from the outside world. Blind to the universe, it feels like it's only Madison and me, and I can't stop myself as I lean forward, closing the distance between us. A magnetic pull controls my actions, and I'm powerless to stop it. But who am I to fight nature?

Madison's breath gets caught in her throat, and just as I lean in further, mere inches separating our lips, she shakes her head and pulls back quickly, her eyes flighty and wide.

"O-Okay, lead the w-way," she stammers, totally shooting me down.

Taking a deep breath, I nod but hesitate. I suddenly don't

know if going up to my apartment is the best thing to do. And it's not because of my stupid rule.

It's because I don't know how I'll respond to having Madison in my home. All I can think about is how her soft lips would taste as I press her up against my bedroom wall. I really should have thought about this ingenious plan *before* I was sitting in my apartment's underground garage.

Manning up, I pull it together and smile. "Follow me." I exit the car, afraid of what I'm leading us into.

# Eighteen

## *Madison*

"Would you like a towel?" Dixon asks as he tosses his keys onto the marbled countertop.

Looking down at my soiled, very transparent top, I nod. "Yes, please." I shyly cross my arms over my chest.

Dixon smiles. "I won't be a minute. Please make yourself at home." He disappears down the hallway.

The moment he's out of sight, I let out the pent-up breath I was holding and lean over, bracing my hands on my knees and taking five deep breaths. When I feel relatively calm, I stand back up and attempt to process everything.

Tonight has been one of the craziest nights of my life, and I've lived through some crazy shit. It all started with meeting David's parents. I was beyond nervous, but the moment I met Dean and Rhonda, all my nerves were put to rest. Our conversation wasn't forced, and before I knew it, we were bidding one another farewell and promising to catch up soon.

Not once did my thoughts stray to Dixon, and as David glanced at me throughout the evening with nothing but adoration in his eyes, I realized I wasn't being fair to him. While I was barely making an effort, he was trying, so when he asked if I wanted to stay the night at his place, I said yes.

He was beyond excited, and his enthusiasm was contagious because before I knew it, we were making out in my apartment, heading toward my bedroom. We were only supposed to drop by my place so I could grab a change of clothes, but I got caught up in David's hypnotizing eyes and dimpled smile. I was also feeling a touch rejected by Dixon, who I hadn't heard from all week.

I like David. I really do. He's straightforward, and he doesn't mess with my head. Not to mention he's the perfect gentleman with perfect parents. So why did I freak out when we started getting hot and heavy?

It was because being with David is easy, and nothing thus far has been easy in my life. What if he's really too good to be true, and I fall in too deep, letting myself go, and he hurts me? What happens if he finds out the true reason behind my detachment and can't handle the truth?

These thoughts plagued my mind, and before I knew it, he was unzipping my jeans and burying his face where I *never* want anyone to be. He felt me freak out and begged me to tell him what was wrong. But I couldn't. I'm not ready to tell him. I'm not ready to relive the worst night of my life.

But then I did something stupid. I threw him out. I threw him out with no explanation for why I flipped out. And like the true gentleman that he is, he left.

His kind response made me feel even worse, and I called the only person who could make it go away.

Mary.

She was out at Cherry Pop, so I caught a cab and met her there. Even though I didn't want to admit it, I was secretly hoping I would bump into Dixon again. However, my horrible night went from bad to fucking worse.

The club was huge, and it didn't help that half of Manhattan was there. We didn't organize a place to meet, so I went upstairs in hopes I would find her there. Instead, I found Dixon basically getting a lap dance from a blonde barfly, and he didn't seem to mind.

I couldn't get out of there fast enough, and I ended up running down the stairs and directly into Tim.

He was the last person I wanted to see, so I couldn't help but give him a piece of my mind once and for all. I was handling my own just fine, but then out of nowhere, Dixon came throwing down like the fucking Terminator. Memories of the eager, handsy blonde plagued my mind, and I was mad that he was here, saving the day once again because he clearly wasn't thinking about me five minutes ago.

Then before I knew it, Dixon's fragrance and chivalry were screwing with me, and I was being whisked away in the rain.

In the car, Dixon did it to me once again, and I lost all sense of reason and told him things I never intended to say. When he asked me if I wanted to be dropped off anywhere, I couldn't say David's place for obvious reasons. And Mary was probably drunk and on the prowl, as she had finally stopped hating men.

So it made sense to go to his place and call her instead of turning up on her doorstep unannounced, and honestly, I wanted to spend more time with him and ask why he didn't contact me all week. I know I have no right to be mad, but we were moments away from kissing on Monday night, and then I got the cold shoulder all week.

I don't get it. I don't get him. And I don't get my reaction toward him, especially when I'm supposedly dating David.

I need to stay away, but I can't.

"Here you go," Dixon says, snapping me out of my thoughts as he passes me a burgundy towel and his phone.

"Thanks." I unclasp my messy bun and towel off my hair, paying attention to the soaked ends.

"Can I get you a drink? Coffee? Tea? Water?" he asks, rubbing the back of his neck.

"Just water, please," I reply, as my tipsy body needs some H2O.

"Sure thing." He disappears once again.

I'm not sure if it's my imagination, but Dixon appears nervous. I disregard it and dial Mary. As expected, she doesn't answer.

I could call Sebastian, but I don't want to disturb him and my mom at two o'clock in the morning.

Dixon returns moments later with a goblet of water and a bag of peas.

"Did you get ahold of her?" he asks, and I notice he's changed into a navy V-neck tee.

I shake my head. "No. She's not answering. I'll try again."

After ten fruitless phone calls and an abundance of wasted text messages, I give up.

"I'll call a cab," I say with a sigh, and at that precise moment, a thunderclap sounds so loudly, I yelp in terror, dropping my bag of peas to the floor. "I hate storms," I explain, my hand on my chest over my racing heart.

"Well, you can't go back out there then," Dixon says, picking up the peas and placing them against my injured hand.

"So what do you suggest?" I ask, lifting my eyes to meet his, touched by his kindness to tend to my wounds.

"Well…you could stay here," he casually suggests with a shrug, applying firmer pressure to my hand.

"Here?" I gasp, my heart beginning to race once again.

"Sure. I'll sleep on the sofa. No biggie."

"No, I can't do that," I quickly counter because that would be wrong.

"What? Stay here?" he asks, his eyebrows knitting together as he releases my hand.

Yes, I so should not be staying here. But it's getting late, and I'm running out of options.

I've come to a crossroads, and I've decided I want Dixon in my life. Although I'm seeing David, that doesn't mean I can't be Dixon's friend. This is all part of moving on with my life.

So with that affirmation in mind, I clarify, "I can't let you sleep on the sofa." I would feel awful kicking him out of his bed.

"I don't mind," he says with a smirk, crossing his arms over his broad chest.

"Well, I do," I stubbornly argue. "I'll take the couch."

"Don't be ridiculous. You're not sleeping on the sofa."

I'm suddenly struck with a very bold idea. "We're both adults. I mean, we could both sleep in your bed. If you don't mind," I add, not wanting to seem presumptuous.

A smirk tugs at Dixon's lips. "As long as you don't snore, then sure, I don't mind sharing my bed with you."

I laugh, happy he's making jokes. "Not that I'm aware of," I confess.

Dixon nods, and as he slowly scans down my body, my cheeks flush a bright red.

"Would you like a change of clothes and a shower?" he asks after clearing his throat.

Picking at my soaked top, I nod. "Yes, please. Sorry for imposing."

Dixon shakes his head, his damp hair flicking up in deliciously rebellious peaks. "You're no imposition at all."

As Dixon makes his way down the hallway, I realize that I want to ask who the handsy blonde was. But what right do I have? He can see whoever he wants. I mean, we're just friends, right?

# Nineteen

*Dixon*

This is a bad idea on all accounts, yet I can't look away when Madison switches off the bathroom light and enters my room. My Einstein T-shirt looks like a dress on her, and the pajama bottoms are dragging along the floor even though she's rolled them up a number of times. She subconsciously tugs at the loose collar, but it slides off her shoulder, so she gives up with a huff.

"Thanks for lending me your clothes," she says with a small smile.

"No problem."

There's no way I'm having her in my bed in only her underwear, as there will be no hope of me controlling myself.

Madison pads over to the bed and gently pulls back the black comforter and slips underneath. I'm resting against the headboard, trying my best to appear impassive about her being in my bed as I flip through my iPad, looking at God knows what.

She lets out a contented sigh as she settles low, the blankets resting under her chin. She looks way too tempting, snugly wrapped up in my bed, and she also looks like she belongs.

Looking down at her, I realize that my stupid rule is now utterly obsolete because I love having her here in my home, but more so, in my bed.

Clearing my throat, I switch off my device and turn off the light, shrouding my bedroom in almost complete darkness.

My body temperature spikes as I slip under the covers because I don't usually wear anything to bed. But seeing as that was highly inappropriate, I've thrown on a pair of sweats and a tee. Staying dressed is going to be a miracle, however, as my already heated body doesn't need any extra warmth.

"Dixon?" Madison says, her voice the only beacon of light in the dark.

"Yes?"

"Thank you for allowing me to stay over. I like being here. I feel…safe," she professes in a mere whisper.

If that wasn't the sweetest darn thing I've ever heard, then I don't know what is.

"I like you being here too," I declare. "I feel…"

What *do* you feel, Dixon? I question myself. Thinking of the appropriate phrase, I know that only one word is enough.

"Happy," I conclude, not feeling like a total pussy for saying my thoughts aloud.

"And you haven't been before?"

Her simple question strikes a nerve, and I reply honestly. "Not for a long time, no."

And it's true. I may have been sexually satisfied, but I always knew what an egotistical asshole I was, sleeping with endless, faceless women and not giving a damn.

"Well, I'm glad I make you happy because you make me happy too," she confesses, and the strain in her voice reveals just how hard that was for her.

Her petite body wrapped in my huge bed is doing things to my head that I haven't experienced in a very long time. And I don't mean the head between my legs. I think I'm falling and falling hard for Madison. Her innocence, purity, and honesty are like a breath of fresh air, and it's only now I've realized how oxygen-deprived I've been.

As she shuffles closer, her vanilla scent wraps me in a tight bubble, and I can't stop myself as I inch forward, wanting to bask in her fragrance.

"If I snore, wake me up, okay?"

I laugh lightly at her sincerity. "I'm sure you don't. But if by chance you do, I'll just smother you with my pillow." She giggles, the bed jolting with her amusement.

"Okay, deal." There is a pregnant pause before she shyly discloses, "I haven't slept beside anyone before."

"Ever?" I ask, taken aback.

Is this beautiful woman telling me she's a goddamn virgin?

My question is answered when she simply replies, "Never."

That single word is my undoing, and I slowly bend forward, kissing her on the forehead. I linger a little longer than I should, but I can't help it.

"Well, I'll try my best to make it a memorable first time," I say, pulling away slowly.

I hope my admission doesn't freak her out because it could be misconstrued. But in a way, I want her to keep that thought in her mind. We're quiet for a few moments, facing one another in the dark, but I can feel her inquisitive eyes on me, no doubt absorbing what I just said.

"Good night, Madison," I drowsily say, my eyes drifting shut, her gentle breaths lulling me to sleep.

"Dixon?" she whispers.

"Yes."

"You already have," she divulges.

I don't reply because the only way to do so would be smashing my lips to hers. I can't do that for so many reasons, but the one that stands at the forefront is the fact that, once I start, I don't think I'll be able to stop.

And that scares the living hell out of me.

I wake suddenly, a fine sheen of sweat covering my entire body. And it's not because I'm slowly roasting under my sheets. I have a weird feeling that I heard someone outside my front door. Madison is breathing softly beside me, her exhalations deep and relaxed, so she obviously didn't hear a thing.

I still decide to go check it out.

I tiptoe carefully through my room, as the moonlight peeking in from the blinds is my only light source. But I know my apartment like I know the back of my hand and have no problems navigating through it. However, I'm used to things being in certain spots. Madison's discarded shoe is not one of them.

Very ungracefully, I trip and land on both knees as I grab onto the end of the bed to stop my fall. I instantly look up, terrified I've woken Madison from her peaceful slumber. But when she murmurs lightly and rolls onto her side, I know she's still sound asleep. My reaction to protect her was purely innate. I haven't felt that way in so very long, and it's actually nice to care about someone other than myself.

Rising slowly, I focus on the floor to ensure the coast is clear. Thankfully, I make it to the living room without further injury. I stop in the middle of the room and pivot my head toward the door.

Silence.

I could have sworn I heard a noise, but if someone was there, they seem to be gone. Deciding to go back to bed, I turn toward my bedroom but suddenly hear the gentle rustling of someone searching through a bag. I knew it.

Charging to the door as silently as I can, I yank it open to see Juliet outside, looking through her handbag. She stops rummaging through her purse and pulls back, confused, when she sees me in my sweats and tee.

"Nice pajamas," she mocks, her gaze landing on my Yankees top.

She knows I usually wear nothing to bed, and considering I have a serious case of bedhead, I can't exactly say I was bumming around watching TV.

"Why are you here?" I ask, keeping my voice low.

Juliet smiles. "I've come to tuck you in." She takes a step forward, indicating she wants to come in.

That's not going to happen.

I quickly place my arm across the doorjamb, preventing her from entering. She looks at me, raising an eyebrow.

"Who are you hiding in there?" she asks, standing on her

toes to see over my shoulder.

I move to the left to stop her from seeing in. "No one's hiding," I say, trying to appear cool.

"Well, let me in." She attempts to push me out of the way.

I stand my ground, however because there's no way she's setting foot inside this apartment. "I'm tired, Juliet. Can we do this another time?" I say, hoping to stall her.

"Do what, Dixon? I haven't seen you all week. You totally blew me off last time and not in a good way. You owe me," she states, cocking a challenging brow.

I'm afraid to ask, but I question anyway, "Owe you what?"

"You know what," she replies, pursing her lips seductively. "You owe me at least one…" And she holds up a finger. "Two…" She holds up another. "Ten mind-blowing orgasms," she concludes, holding up both hands. "It's time to pay up."

"Now?" I ask, standing rigid so she can't shove past me.

"Yes. Right now." She takes a step closer, her chest almost touching mine.

"Now is not a good time for me," I reply, faking a big yawn. "I'm beat. I don't think I'll be able to deliver one orgasm, let alone ten."

This will hopefully be enough of a deterrent for Juliet because denying her pleasure means she has no reason to be here. But of course she has other ideas.

"Well," she says, pulling back her shoulders. "If you're not going to fuck me, the least you can do is watch."

"Watch what?" I ask, swallowing.

"Watch me fuck myself."

Before I have time to protest, she slides a hand down the front of her skirt and begins pleasuring herself.

"Juliet," I hiss, looking down the hallway, afraid my neighbors will see a masturbating woman outside my door.

"Shh. This won't take long," she says breathlessly, closing her eyes as she bites her lower lip.

I don't care how long she thinks it will take. This display has gone on long enough. But as I watch the way her fingers move frantically underneath her skirt and hear the soft, breathy moans coming from her parted mouth, I know she's close. I also know that if I lend a hand, she'll come even faster and leave me the hell alone.

That fact sickens me, considering I have Madison sound asleep in my bed, but she's the reason I reach forward and stroke the flesh behind Juliet's ear, in step with her demanding rhythm. The move drives her wild because she knows there's more to come.

Gliding up her neck, I wrap my fingers in her hair and yank hard, pulling her head backward. She moans with the forceful movement and steadies herself by placing a hand against my shoulder. I feel disgusting, but the harder I pull, the louder she hums, and the faster this nightmare will end.

"Oh, babe," she pants, her fingers digging into me as her hips buck forward.

The scene before me is highly erotic, but in no way, shape or form am I turned on. All I can think about is Madison lying innocently in my bed, ignorant to the fact that I'm helping my fuck buddy get off.

She's taking longer than usual, and if I know Juliet as well as I think I do, she's doing this on purpose because there's one final thing she wants me to do. Lunging forward, I angrily latch onto her neck and bite over her pulse, sucking her warmed flesh into my mouth.

It's exactly what she wants because, within moments, she comes with a loud, breathless whimper. I let her go and wipe my mouth, revolted when I see her skin red from where I marked her.

If she wasn't still holding me, I would have slammed the door in her face by now. But this will be over in moments, and the worse is over with—well, one can only hope.

Her eyes flutter open, and her smile is sated and relaxed. "See, that wasn't so bad now, was it?" she says, slowly removing the hand from beneath her skirt.

She doesn't give me a chance to reply because with the fingers that were inside her moments ago, she runs her pointer down my lips, leaving a trail of her arousal behind. I won't deny she smells amazing, but I can't help but feel she's done this to mark me, knowing I have someone inside.

"When it's my turn for a sleepover, give me a call." She smirks, confirming my suspicions. "Or if you want to invite me in, we can have one now."

That's not going to happen. Ever.

When she sees my resolve, she shrugs, unaffected that someone else is sleeping in my bed. "Good night, Dr. Mathews. I'll come to collect what's owed to me soon."

Good grief, this woman is insatiable. A quality I once loved.

"Good night, Ms. Harte," I curtly say, thankful when she blows me a kiss and turns on her heel.

I watch as she enters the elevator, not because I'm being a gentleman but rather because I want to ensure she's gone. Waiting a few seconds, I close and lock the door behind me.

Leaning up against the wood grain, I take a deep breath

and instantly smell her on my lips. Quickly wiping away the evidence with the back of my hand, I squash down the urge to go take a shower, as it'll wake Madison and create questions I don't want to answer.

Washing my face in the kitchen sink will have to do. But I'll be sure to scrub every part of me tomorrow. Just for good measure, I use some hand soap and lather up a foamy handful, spreading it all over my face. I want no trace of her on me.

When I'm satisfied I'm Juliet-free, I head back to my bedroom and creep inside. Thankfully Madison is still sleeping soundly, and I slowly pull back the covers, slipping underneath. The moment I smell her unique fragrance, I get hit with a serious case of the guilts.

What I did was appalling, but considering my options, that was the better choice than fucking Juliet in the hall. Juliet is toxic, and that toxicity, which was once my favorite drug, now leaves me numb. I want no more.

# Twenty

## *Dixon*

I'm grateful I wake to an empty bed, and I say grateful because I'm sporting some serious morning wood. Lifting the sheets, I groan because there's no way this boner is going anywhere without a helping hand, and my hands are a poor substitute for the hands I want wrapped around my dick.

"Morning," Madison happily says from the doorway. I quickly drop the sheet.

"Morning," I reply, clearing my throat. "How'd you sleep?" I ask, sitting up and subtly arranging the blankets around my lap. I hope she slept better than me.

"Great," she replies, walking into the bedroom while I run a hand through my messy hair. "Best sleep I've had in ages," she concludes, her eyes fixated on my fingers as I try to gain some order with my mane.

"I'm glad." My gaze drops to the sliver of milky white skin peeking out between her jeans and my T-shirt, which she's tied in a knot, Daisy Duke style.

I quickly raise my eyes, as looking at her supple flesh is so not helping my predicament below the sheets.

"Yup. But we have a problem," she says seriously, sitting on her side of the bed.

*We sure as shit do*, I think, but ask, "We do?"

Madison nods animatedly. "You've run out of coffee."

I can't help but laugh at her dire grievance. She's dead serious. The fact she's hunted through my cupboards doesn't bother me in the slightest. However, the fact I've run out of coffee does.

"So how 'bout you let me buy you a cup to say thank you for letting me crash?" she says with a smile.

I nod. I'm all for the idea of spending any extra time I can with Madison. But I suggest, "How about I buy, seeing as you're penniless?"

Madison smirks. "I have my ways of getting what I want." My eyes widen before they drop to her chest.

She sees my obvious approval and laughs. "Not that, you pervert."

I raise my hands in innocence. "Hey, I'm only human." I witness her cheeks turn a lovely pink.

Deciding to focus on what's important, I ask, "Did you call Mary?"

Madison shakes her head. "No, I didn't want to be rude and use your phone without asking."

"Oh, so you decided to hunt through my cupboards instead?" I playfully tease, and she nods.

"That was a matter of life and death," she states like it's a no-brainer.

"And getting you home isn't?" I ask with interest.

Madison shyly looks at her feet and shrugs. "What can I say? Your bed is way comfier than mine, and besides, is that a memory foam pillow?" she says, finally raising her eyes.

I laugh at her adorability and nod. "Well, you're welcome back anytime," I avow, but pause when I realize how that sounded.

"Dr. Mathews, I just may take you up on that offer. I mean, I've read that studies show that memory foam promotes proper alignment when you sleep. So for science alone, I really should return," she reasons with a smile.

I try not to let my enthusiasm shine through. "Precisely. We're both health professionals, and if we don't look after our bodies, then how are we meant to look after others?" I counter, and Madison nods.

"So it's settled. You must spend another night to really determine if these studies are, in fact, correct," I say, using my professional voice.

Madison giggles. "Yup, it's a price I must pay for the health of my spinal column."

Holy shit, how did this happen? We have just completely fake-reasoned to one another why Madison needs to stay another night in my bed, and it's got nothing to do with my damn pillow, or her spine. The thought of her spending another night doesn't help my current situation, but it's a small price to pay to have Madison in my bed for another night. Here's hoping Juliet doesn't decide on another impromptu visit.

"How about you call Mary and let her know you're alive. I'm not going to lie, she does scare me a little, um…a lot," I confess, and Madison cackles.

"It's okay. She scares everyone."

Thankfully, she stands, and I smile. "I'll just shower. Give me twenty?"

"Okay, see you in twenty," she says and gives me a small wave before she leaves.

I wait a couple of seconds, and when the coast is clear, I throw off the covers, desperate to take control of this raging erection. Just as I'm about to leap out of bed, Madison ducks her head around the doorjamb and asks, "Which remote control is for the TV? You have like, five."

I scramble for the blankets and quickly cover my lap, hoping I appear nonchalant as I reply, "The one with the plastic panel at the bottom."

"Okay, great, thanks," and she disappears as quickly as she appeared.

Taking a deep breath, I decide to try again, but the moment I kick off the covers and attempt to stand, Madison's face reappears in my doorway.

"Is it okay to use your landline?"

Quickly sitting back down and hastily crossing my leg over my tenting erection, I awkwardly attempt to look relaxed by resting my elbow on my thigh and leaning into my palm. "Of course," I reply with a strained smile, drumming my fingers against my cheek.

Madison looks at me strangely, but thankfully, she doesn't address my sudden insanity and nods. "Okay, thanks." And her face vanishes once again.

I wait a full minute, just in case she has any other questions, but when I'm in the clear, I practically jump up and run to the bathroom, locking the door behind me. Letting out a deep breath, I look at my reflection in the mirror, and my rampant hard-on stares back, begging me to put it out of its misery. I feel disgusting doing this with Madison in the next room, but it's either this or I end up dry-humping her leg by lunchtime.

Turning on the shower, I strip down and step into the scorching heat as opposed to the traditional cold one. Whoever said a cold shower is the remedy for a raging libido is a damn fool. I'll take heated water, soap, my hand, and images of Madison's agile body lying next to me any day over hypothermia.

Lathering up some soap, I grip my rock-hard dick and begin the dance we've danced many times before. But this time, my dance partner has two left feet, and I can't seem to find my rhythm. I don't know why. I brace one hand against the tiled wall and try for a different angle, but it's pointless. I'm off when I shouldn't be because there's no doubt that I want to come.

I stroke harder, and yes, it feels fucking amazing, but as I hear Madison laugh, I know the reason I can't cross the finish line is because of her, which is ironic, seeing as she's the cause of my hard-on. But I feel beyond disgusting jerking off with her a few feet away. I mean, what would she think if she knew I was currently beating off, using her as my inspiration?

"What is this woman doing to me?" I sigh, lightly thumping my forehead against the shower wall as I let go of my junk.

Giving up, I wipe an exhausted hand down my face while the other reaches for the faucet and turns the water to cold.

With my teeth chattering and my body shivering, I look down at my semi-flaccid cock and grunt, "I hope you're happy, you damn pussy."

We're on the hunt for coffee, and I'm blindly following Madison, who said she's got it covered. I have no idea what that means, but funnily enough, I trust her. If it were Juliet, however, then I would expect "coffee" to be a code word for an adult superstore, but I know Madison would never be so crude.

Looking at the small *angelo* beside me with nothing but a skip to her step, I realize how at ease I am with her. I know she has a past, but don't we all? Sadly, my past is about to leave me percolated and foaming at the mouth.

We stop in front of a Starbucks, and Madison opens her arms out wide. "Ta-da!"

I cock an eyebrow. "I don't get it."

Madison laughs, screwing up her nose. "Duh, coffee is served. I know the owner, so coffee is on me."

I now understand what she meant by her "having ways." Although, I do prefer my way over hers.

Rubbing the back of my neck, I ask, needing clarification, "Ah, you want to go in here?"

Madison nods, looking at me like I've lost my mind. "Yes. They sell coffee, don't they? What are you waiting for?" She tugs on my arm, while my feet remain firmly rooted to the sidewalk.

Madison jerks forward and almost trips over her feet when I don't budge an inch. Turning to look at me over her shoulder, she raises both eyebrows. "Are you all right? You look like you're about to…cry?" she half teases, but I can hear the concern in her voice.

"Cry?" I scoff, barely containing the edge to my tone. "I just don't like Starbucks. It's too trendy, not to mention their flamboyant, ridiculous names for coffee are downright ludicrous. How about we go to a little cafe up the road where they sell proper coffee and biscotti?" I nod, hoping she comes quietly and willingly.

But of course she does neither.

"How about you tell me what you have against Starbucks?" she says, crossing her arms over her chest stubbornly.

"I don't have anything against them, per se," I reply, clearing my throat.

"So why won't you go inside?" she asks, cocking her head to the side, awaiting my reply.

Goddammit, Madison is as stubborn as she is beautiful. Another quality I like about her. Looking at her hard resolve, I know she won't let this go until I tell her the truth.

"I met my ex…fiancée in a Starbucks, and I guess I associate all Starbucks with her. I'm sure you can guess how this story ends," I confess, feeling utterly ridiculous.

Madison's eyes widen at my sad, pathetic story, but she doesn't throw me a pity party. "Oh, I guess that's as good a reason as any."

I nod, putting my hands in my jeans pockets. "Yeah, I guess," I reply, hating that, as usual, Lily is ruining my day.

But once again, Madison surprises me as she says, "You're right, Starbucks is a little trendy. And besides," she adds, "you had me at biscotti. Lead the way, Dr. Mathews." She smiles, waiting for me to make the first move.

I stand speechless, staring at this mystical creature before me. She really is too good to be true, as I know her Starbucks spiel was entirely for my benefit.

Offering her my hand, she looks at it for a heartbeat but then links her fingers through mine and smiles. "So what flavor biscotti do they have?"

I can't help but laugh at her obvious derailment, but I welcome it. I rattle off the long list of sweets the café Dolci's has available, and Madison listens intently, smacking her lips at the endless options.

As we walk hand in hand on a Sunday morning, I can't help but think how natural this feels. Sadly, I have to remind myself that Madison is currently seeing David the douche nozzle, and this can never extend into anything other than friendship while he's in the picture. I don't like it, but Madison is a big girl and if she chooses to date primates, then I have to respect her decision.

When we arrive at Dolci's, I automatically push open the door for Madison, which is something I haven't done for a very long time.

"Dixon!" Concetta shrieks from behind the counter.

"Good morning, Concetta," I reply with a smile, as the elderly lady hobbles out and gives me a kiss on both cheeks.

"*Dove sei stato?*" she asks, scolding me for being MIA.

"I've been busy with work," I reply in English, as Madison looks completely lost in translation.

"You work too hard," Concetta says with a thick Italian accent. "Look at you. You're too skinny. Here sit, sit. I will make you *frittelle di ricotta* and bring some *pane*."

I laugh as she escorts us over to a booth. "Thank you, but just coffee and those biscotti." I point at the endless display of baked goods. "This is Madison, by the way," I add, and Madison smiles.

"Nice to meet you," she says, and she surprises me as she bends forward, giving Concetta two kisses on the cheek before taking a seat.

When Concetta looks at me approvingly, I know what she's thinking.

"You are a *principessa*," she says, and Madison giggles.

"Thank you. I think."

Concetta cackles, patting my arm. "*Mi piace il suo,*" she says, voicing her approval of Madison before heading over to the coffee machine.

Taking a seat, I look over at Madison, who's looking around the store in awe.

"Wow," she gushes, her eyes widening when she sees the variety of food on display.

Growing up amongst these traditional Italian items, I've completely forgotten how overwhelming all this cultural stuff can be. But when Madison bounces in her seat and claps her hands, I know she's not so much overwhelmed as overjoyed.

"Is that for us?" she asks Concetta, who has a huge tray of sweets in her hands.

"*Si, principessa*," she replies and places the platter on our table.

"Thank you," I say, looking up at Concetta, who I've known since I first moved to Manhattan.

"Anything for you," she replies, and I give her arm a gentle squeeze.

A contented sigh has me turning around to look at Madison, who has slumped back in her seat, happily munching away on a cannoli.

"That's some good shit," she says dreamily, taking another bite.

When her pink tongue darts out to lick up any missed sweetened ricotta on her lips, I barely contain my self-control.

"So," I say, needing an immediate distraction. "I couldn't help but notice you have quite the sweet tooth."

Madison pauses chewing, and I chuckle at her guilt. She swallows quickly. "You got me. I don't eat desserts often, so when I do, I kind of make up for lost time. Sorry," she says, embarrassed.

"You have absolutely nothing to be sorry for," I stress, pushing the platter toward her.

Madison smiles and shyly reaches for a biscotti.

"So why don't you eat dessert?" I ask, stealing a mini fruit tart. "I like that you feel comfortable enough to eat this way around me by the way."

Madison stops chewing, and her cheeks turn a ghastly white.

"That was a compliment," I explain, wondering what I've said that's wrong.

She nods but pushes the plate away from her while I raise my eyebrow, confused.

"Are you okay? Did I say something to upset you? I just meant—"

But she cuts me off. "I know what you meant," she says, lowering her eyes. "Thank you, I just…" She takes a deep breath before continuing. "I was a chubby kid, and well, something, um…it was…" And I see her clam up as she twists a napkin in her hands.

"Hey, hey, it's okay." I reach over the table and place my

palm over hers before she shreds the napkin in half.

Her hand trembles under mine, and I squeeze it lightly. "If ever you want to talk, not psychiatrist to patient but just Dixon and Madison, I'm here, okay?" I say, wanting her to know that I'll never analyze her, or make her feel like a case study.

"Thank you, Dixon," she says with a small sniff, wiping away a tear.

Concetta comes over with our coffees, and I reluctantly release Madison's hand.

"*Grazie*," I say, reaching into my pocket for my wallet to pay, but she waves me off.

"*Non insultarmi, bambino*," she firmly states, and I smirk, as I know better than to fight with a Sicilian.

"Thank you. If you need me for anything, you know where to find me," I say, and she nods.

"You just keep coming back to visit and bring the *principessa* with you, too," she says, looking at Madison, who blushes.

"Deal," I reply, and she bends forward, giving me a kiss on the cheek.

As she shuffles off to serve a customer, Madison asks, "How do you know her? It seems you've known one another for a while."

"I've known Concetta since I moved to Manhattan. This cafe was mine, Hunter, and Finch's savior throughout college. Without her double espressos, I dare say I would have slept through half of my exams."

Madison laughs as she adds sugar to her coffee. "Who are Hunter and Finch?"

"They're my friends. I've known them my whole life, and we moved to New York together for college," I explain. "Finch is happily married to his high school sweetheart, Heidi. They've just had a baby girl."

"And Hunter?" she asks, listening intently.

"Hunter is an acquired taste," I tease, sipping my coffee.

"Well, they both sound awesome."

"They really are," I reply, thinking about how awesome those bastards are. "So what about you?"

"What about me?" she counters quickly, and I notice her hand shaking slightly as she stirs her coffee.

"I know about Mary," I explain. "But what about your family? You mentioned you and your mom were close."

"We are," she replies with a small smile.

I know her family, just like mine, seem to be a touchy subject for her, but I can't help myself as I ask. "And you said you had a brother?" I say, remembering her losing her footing when she mentioned him.

Madison nods, the discomfort obvious in her tense face. As much as I want to know why she's suddenly clammed up, I don't want to know that badly and ruin our day.

"I always wanted a brother," I share, and see Madison's shoulders instantly depress in relief.

"Yeah?"

I nod with a smile.

"Why?"

"So I could blame him for breaking my mother's crystal vase."

She bursts into laughter.

However, thinking about my current predicament, I can't help but confess, "And it would make circumstances a lot easier to deal with."

"What circumstances?" she innocently queries.

"Things with my…dad," I reveal. He made his feelings perfectly clear the other day, so I've given up on a reunion any time soon.

"What do you mean?" She watches me closely, waiting for me to elaborate.

I sigh, deciding to share this one small snippet with her. "If I had a brother, maybe *he* could be the son my father deserves."

Madison's eyes fill with pity, and as she opens her mouth, I dread what she's going to say. But at the last second, it appears she changes her mind. "I think this world can only handle one Dixon Mathews. And besides, I'm sure Hunter and Finch were like brothers, right?"

I grin, grateful for the change of pace. "Yes, they still are. We were neighbors all through school. My poor teachers," I say, shaking my head.

Madison laughs quietly and seems more relaxed now that the topic has shifted away from her family.

"Sounds like Mary and I," she says cheerfully.

"Oh yeah?" I ask, happy she wants to share this piece of information with me.

"Yeah," she replies with a reminiscent smile, as if touching on a memory. "Before my mom married Sebastian, we were dirt poor. We lived in a tiny, one-bedroom apartment, right next door to Mary. Both our moms were single, working two jobs to make ends meet. We were inseparable, and still are."

"So she knows all of your deepest, darkest secrets?" I say jokingly.

Madison frowns, her finger skating around the rim of her cup. "Not all of them."

I give her a small smile, but don't press. She'll tell me when, or if she's ever ready.

My phone chirps, ruining the moment, and I apologize to Madison as I pull it out of my pocket. The sender is someone I was not expecting, considering she got what she wanted from me last night.

***I've got an itch only you can scratch. Are you free tonight?***

Madison must see my face drop as I read Juliet's message because she asks, "Everything okay?"

Slipping my phone back into my pocket, I nod, clearing my throat. "Yeah, fine."

And just like me, she doesn't press; she simply sips her coffee, and gives me a reassuring smile. Both Madison and I have secrets, but every so often some secrets are better left unsaid.

After dropping Madison off at her place, I decide to hit the gym and burn off some of my pent-up sexual energy, and also my smorgasbord of sweets. I texted Hunter and he was keen for a workout, and to brag about his night.

After he's done scarring me with images I so wish I could burn from my hippocampus, he decides to inquire about my night.

"So how was your evening?" he asks, running on the treadmill beside me.

"It was great," I reply, my feet pounding on the belt.

"Oh, yeah? How was Marisa?"

I could try to elude him, but I don't see the point.

"I wouldn't know," I respond breathlessly.

"You wouldn't know? What the fuck are you talking about?" he questions, utterly confused.

When I don't reply and focus on running instead of talking, he grumbles, "You choked, didn't you?"

"Call it whatever you like," I say with a casual shrug. "I call it not catching crabs."

"There was a time in our lives when crabs were cool, Dix," Hunter rebukes, and I blanch.

"There is never, ever, a cool time for VD, Hunt," I say, brushing my sweaty hair off my brow.

"Yeah well, that's what the new, boring Dixon says. But the old, fun Dixon would be down with a medicated crab wash."

"You, my friend, are disgusting," I say, laughing. "And for your information, I didn't choke, I just upgraded."

"Whoa, hold up. What does that mean?" he says, his curiosity piqued.

"Why don't you use that creative mind of yours and figure it out?" I smugly reply, focusing on finishing my two-mile run.

However, one minute I'm running, and the next, I'm almost face planting.

"What the hell?" I bark when Hunter hits the emergency stop button.

"Start talking, Mathews," he demands as I step off the machine and attempt to catch my breath.

"There's not much to tell," I reply, slowly pacing to cool down. "I went home with Madison, instead of the blonde."

"Madison!" Hunter yells in disbelief as he hits the stop button on his own machine. "As in Cherry Pie Madison?"

"Yes," I reply with a smirk, as his nickname for her is quite fitting.

"Holy shit, you dog. Doesn't she have a boyfriend?"

"Yes," I counter, stretching my arms above my head.

"You fucking dog!" he screams excitedly, slapping me on the back.

"It's not like that," I clarify.

"It's exactly like that," Hunter nods. "So how was it? I know you've had a hard-on for her for ages. Did it live up to everything and more?" he asks, rubbing his hands together.

"It's *really* not like that," I say, walking toward the water fountain.

"So what, you're telling me you had like a slumber party or something?" Hunter jokingly says as he follows in hot pursuit.

"Something like that." I shrug and can't help but chuckle at the disgusted look on Hunter's face.

"Sweet baby Jesus! And what, did you braid each other's hair and argue whether Niall or Harry is cuter?"

"Who the hell is Niall?" I ask, pulling away from the water stream and cocking my eyebrow.

When I continue looking at him, afraid for his sanity, he brushes it off. "Never mind. Stop trying to change the subject."

"I'm not trying to change any subject," I reply, wiping runaway water from my lips with the back of my hand as I stand to full height. "And there's only a subject because you keep making it one. Madison and I are friends, and yes, I'm attracted to her. But she has a boyfriend, and I would never screw that up for her because she's the first girl I've met in ages who I actually give two shits about," I say in a huff while Hunter smirks.

"You so braided each other's hair," he counters while I punch him on the arm.

We walk to the change rooms, and the fact Hunter has gone quiet is never a good sign.

"Spit it out." I sigh, knowing he'll explode if he doesn't get whatever is festering in his head out in the open.

"I just…" He pauses, looking stumped. "You're telling me a smokin' hot, gorgeous girl was in your apartment, in your bed, and you did nothing?"

"Yes, that's exactly what I'm telling you," I reply, sitting on the bench and untying my laces.

"Not even a blow job?"

"No."

"Hand job?"

"No."

"Foreplay?"

"No."

"Making out?"

"No."

"Dry-humping?"

"No."

"What about some over-the-clothes touching?"

"No."

"A sensual massage, which led to some kind of skin-on-skin contact, which then led to some kind of penetration?"

"No."

"Dirty pillow talk?"

"No."

"Playing footsie?"

"No."

"What about some peeping Tom action when she was sleeping?"

"No."

"Faked sexsomnia?"

"Fuck, you're one sick man," I say, pulling a sickened face as I reach for my gym bag.

"Anyone would think you're a damn virgin," he states, and his comment reminds me of Madison's confession.

"Speaking of virgins…" I smugly declare while Hunter almost gags on his tongue.

"No? No fucking way," he exclaims, shaking his head, not believing me.

"Yes," I affirm with a nod. "She pretty much told me she was."

"I am actually speechless right now. There are no words to convey how I'm currently feeling," Hunter affirms, appearing to be in utter shock as he slumps down onto the bench seat.

"Good, let's keep it that way," I reply, zipping up my hoodie and shouldering my bag. "I'll catch you later."

"Wait, where's the fire?" he asks, standing up.

"Besides in your pants?" I playfully counter, referring to his sordid night with Mandy and the possible diseases he's caught from sleeping with her.

"Very funny, you tween." He punches me in the arm. "Seriously, though, what's the hurry?"

I failed to mention that Madison will be staying over for another "slumber party." I also excluded the minor detail that Juliet will probably turn up on my doorstep unannounced and quite possibly naked. I didn't reply to her text because I didn't know what to say.

"Man, you really are a masochist," Hunter says with a shake of his head, as he can obviously read my facial expressions. "You're letting a chick, who will in no way put out 'cause she's a damn virgin, and has a boyfriend, sleep in your bed…again. You're the one who needs to see a shrink."

I don't argue with him on that.

"What about the other blonde?" he asks, and I decide to leave out the part about her masturbating on my doorstep.

"I'm pretty sure that's a done deal. I'm out," I reply unaffected because it's true.

"So what now? You become a born-again virgin?"

"I haven't thought that far ahead yet," I answer, looking at my watch. "I've gotta go."

"Dix?" Hunter says as I turn to leave.

"Yeah?"

"I'll leave you with one quote that I live by," he solemnly declares. I'm actually afraid to hear what he has to say, as I know he does not have one alleged life-changing quote.

"Let's hear it then," I say, gesturing with my fingers for him to deliver me his gospel.

"'Why buy the cow…when you can get the milk for free?'" he replies seriously. "You'll thank me one day," he adds with a nod.

Barely containing my laughter, I flip him off and say, "Nice going, Confucius."

Madison is coming over at seven o'clock, and although she said she'll eat at her place, I stopped by the supermarket on the way home and grabbed a few things—mainly of the sugary kind.

I've showered, tidied up, and caught up on some paperwork, and just as I'm about to settle down to watch the news, there is a soft knock on the door. Looking down at my watch, I see that it's only 6:30 p.m. It's a little early for Madison's arrival, so I wonder who it is.

Muting the TV, I walk over to the door. The moment I open it, my brain tells me to shut it again because Juliet is standing before me, looking utterly devious in nothing but a pink silk dress, which could easily pass for lingerie.

"Juliet? I'm sort of in the middle of something," I say, using my arm as a barricade as I rest my hand against the doorframe. This seems to be a trend lately.

"Is that any way to say hello?" Her lips tip up into a sensual smile.

"Hello," I sarcastically retort, and Juliet finally picks up on my irritation at her just turning up, unexpected.

With her eyes narrowed, she asks, "You're not happy to see me?"

Truthfully no, I'm not, and it must show on my face.

"Have I done something wrong, Dixon?" she questions, and I rub the back of my neck, as having this conversation is the last thing I want to do.

But now that she's here, I may as well put us both out of our misery.

"Please, come in." I step backward so she can enter.

She looks at me suspiciously but then nods and saunters in. Shutting the door behind her, I cut to the chase because I'm in no mood to drag this out.

"Look, Juliet, things between us, they've been… interesting, but I think it's best we stop seeing one another."

I lean against the door and cross my arms over my chest, my body language displaying the truth to what I just said. I give her a moment to process my comment.

"You're *serious*?" she scoffs, appearing taken aback.

Her arrogance that I could actually not want her is quite off-putting, and I wonder how I found her self-assurance attractive in the past.

"Yes," I answer firmly, and Juliet looks as if I've slapped her cheek with my curtness.

"I don't know what to say," she replies, visibly stunned.

"There's nothing *to* say. You and I both know what this was. Let's not make something out of nothing," I say, and as harsh as that sounds, it's the truth—the truth I have been avoiding for so long.

"I…" Juliet falters, nervously pulling at the gold necklace around her neck. "I like you, Dixon. And I know you like me, too," she seductively says, stepping toward me.

I've got nowhere to go, but I stand tall.

"Juliet, I liked the sex. I liked the fact I could lose control with you and be someone I thought I wanted to be. But funnily enough, being with you proved to me that that man was a complete jackass."

"You don't mean that," she says with a firm shake of her head.

"Yes, I really do," I reply firmly. "I'm sorry I didn't tell you sooner, but honestly, I didn't think you'd care."

"Of course I care," she cries. "How could you think I don't? I've been fucking you for the past three months!"

I sigh because this is all it comes down to—sex.

"Did you know I was once engaged?" I question, watching the shock pass over Juliet's face.

"No, I did not," she confesses, her composure slipping.

"Did you know that I've loved the Yankees since my father took me to my first game when I was eight years old?"

She lowers her eyes and shakes her head.

"Does that answer your question?" I ask. "But to be fair, there are things about *you* that I should know but don't. And that's because I never asked you. And that's because—"

"You never cared," she finishes for me, completely in step with what I'm saying.

"Juliet—" But she cuts me off.

"Forget it, Dixon. I get it. I don't need you canoodling me or giving me some pep talk. I'm fine. It was fun, but we're done. I get it," she spits, straightening her shoulders and staring me straight in the eye. "Goodbye. It was nice knowing you." She storms forward, cocking her head, silently telling me to move.

I could try to smooth things over, but what would be the point? I have no intention of ever seeing her again, and it wasn't like I ever had feelings for her. So with that thought in mind, I step aside, and she yanks the door open, making sure to slam it shut behind her.

Well, that was a little dramatic, but I never expected

anything less from her.

Letting out a deep breath, I walk to the kitchen, desperate for a much-needed scotch to deal with Hurricane Juliet.

I'm not sorry this has happened; quite frankly, I'm relieved. I know that probably makes me a heartless bastard, but dragging this on for a second longer would make me a *fucking* heartless bastard. I down the contents of my drink, and just as I pour myself another, there's a knock on my door.

Silently cursing, I throw back my scotch, knowing I will probably need another hit. When a knock sounds once again on my door, I groan because if Juliet is standing out there, I just might slam the door shut in her face. Madison will be here any minute, and I really don't want Juliet to be standing in my apartment, half nude, when she arrives.

"What?" I bark, opening the door with force.

"Fuck you, too," Hunter says, looking totally bored as he leans against the doorjamb, glancing at his watch. "What took you so long? Are you baking brownies and listening to Michael Bolton while you get ready for your slumber party?" he says, pushing off the doorframe and shoving past me.

"Hi, Hunter. Please, won't you come inside," I sarcastically quip, shutting the door behind me. "What are you doing here?" I ask, following him as he walks into my kitchen and helps himself to a beer.

"I was bored," he replies with a shrug. "All my friends are supposedly busy, so I thought, what the hell, I'll go annoy my best friend."

"That's a lovely story," I say, "but Madison will be here any minute now. So how 'bout you go annoy Finch?"

"Hell no," Hunter scoffs, taking a sip of beer. "I predict here will be a lot more fun than over at the Millers'. And besides, I wanna meet Cherry Pie."

When I roll my eyes, Hunter faux gasps. "What? Are you ashamed of me?" He bites his knuckle, pretending to cry.

Scoffing at his melodramatics, I press. "Hunt, I'm serious. You gotta go."

"Why?"

"Because you're right, I am ashamed of you," I reply with a grin.

Hunter mockingly laughs at my comment but doesn't take offense as he boosts himself up to sit on my kitchen counter, happily sipping his beer. I know he's not going to leave without some form of bribery, so I rack my brain, wondering what I can use to entice him.

"*Debbie Does Dallas*," I spit out, hoping like hell this works.

It's like dangling a carrot in front of a very horny donkey, and Hunter stops mid-sip, lowering the bottle with a smirk.

"I want the Blu-ray special edition and a stack of old-school Jenna. Please and thank you," he says, waving his beer in my direction, in total understanding of my offer.

"Fine. As soon as you get these, you are leaving, understood?"

"Scout's honor," he says, flipping me off, which is his version of the scout salute.

It's good enough for me, and I race to my bedroom, hoping like hell I find these suckers asap because I haven't watched them in a long time—a small perk of having Juliet on call, but honestly, I would much rather the porn.

Rummaging through my cabinet, I find a stack of Jenna oldies, but for the life of me, I can't find *Debbie Does Dallas*.

Grabbing a stack of discs, I look over at the clock and see that it's 6:50 p.m. Madison will be here any minute, which means I need Hunter gone in seconds. These discs will have to do, but let's face facts, it's porn, and any porn will do.

"I can't find *Debbie*, but will *Riding Miss Daisy* and *Legally Boned* do?" I ask, blindly walking into the kitchen and holding up the discs so I can read the titles off the covers. "Hunt?" I say when he doesn't reply.

I'm completely distracted looking at the picture of the busty blonde on the front cover, and it's only when I hear a throat clearing that I raise my eyes to see what's going on. The moment I see who's standing in front of me, the discs go flying behind my shoulder and into the living area because Madison is standing before me, looking beyond embarrassed, while Hunter is standing beside her, looking beyond amused.

"Madison…Hi. Hello. Good evening," I say with a stiff upper lip, eyeballing a grinning Hunter. "You're early."

Madison nods, her cheeks flustered and blistering a bright red. "Hi, um, yeah. Sorry if I…interrupted," she says, fiddling with her backpack shoulder strap.

Hunter coughs to cover his laugh while I continue glaring at him.

"It's fine. You weren't interrupting anything. Hunter was just collecting his belongings, which he asked me to mind while his house was, er, getting renovated. They are in no way mine, nor have I watched them," I lamely explain, and Hunter coughs louder.

Madison nods but thankfully doesn't address my obvious lie, nor does she go running for the door, afraid to spend the night at a porn fiend's house.

"Here, let me take your bag," I offer and extend my hand so I can take the backpack from her shoulder.

"Thanks," she says, and the moment my fingers brush over her skin, my body hums in exhilaration, thrilled that she's spending the night.

"This is Hunter, by the way," I say, nodding my chin to my friend, who is smiling from ear to ear.

"Oh, *the* Hunter?" she replies with a wink that only I can see.

"The one and only, sweet cheeks," he replies with a confident swagger as he shakes her hand.

Madison laughs while I sigh.

"That wasn't a compliment, you moron," I declare with a grin, and Hunter looks at Madison, who nods, playing along with my ploy.

Hunter's poise falters, and he backtracks. "I'm not sure what he told you, but I can assure you, it's all lies."

Madison looks like she's playfully observing him as she raises an eyebrow and replies, "I don't think so. I think he went light on you, actually."

"Oh yeah?" he rebukes.

"Oh yeah," she confirms with a mischievous smile.

Hunter looks to be totally engaged by her, and I shake my head, leaving them to it, as I have a feeling Madison can handle herself around my friend.

Stepping into the hallway, I quickly gather the pornographic evidence and toss them into a drawer as I enter my bedroom. I place Madison's bag by my bed and take a small breath, as the past twenty minutes have left me winded. The evening has not gone to plan, what with Juliet's impromptu visit and now

Madison thinking I'm some sick porn collector. I can only hope it gets better from here on in.

As I hear Madison laughing in the kitchen, I quickly compose myself and head back out there because she *is* alone with Hunter, and God knows what he'll say unsupervised.

"What did I miss?" I ask, attempting to appear casual.

Hunter looks incredibly proud of himself, while Madison is still chuckling.

"Madison and I share something in common," he says smugly, and I look at Madison for confirmation.

She nods, her hand covering her mouth to contain her laughter.

"This I gotta hear," I say, opening the fridge and grabbing three beers.

Passing Madison one, she accepts with a smile, and Hunter reaches for the other. However, I slap his hand away and shake my head. "I have a feeling I'll be needing this," I clarify, and Hunter seems to weigh up my comment for a second before nodding, obviously agreeing with me. "So what on earth could *you*…" I point my bottle in Hunter's direction. "Have you in common with Madison? I mean—"

But Madison cuts me off, clearing up my puzzlement. "We've both got a nickname for one another," she says happily, taking a sip of beer.

"Oh?" I reply, as this cannot be good.

"Yup. He accidentally called me Cherry Pie." The moment the words leave her lips, I blanch and internally visualize ripping off Hunter's arms and beating him to death with them.

But I remain composed and arch an eyebrow. "Why ever would he do that?" I ask, glowering at Hunter, who laughs.

"Well, he said my top reminded him of cherry pies."

I look down at her tight red tee, checking out her amazing rack along the way, and see the color *is* cherry pie-ish.

"How very observant of him," I sarcastically reply, but I should be thankful he didn't reveal the real reason behind her nickname.

"Yeah, but anyway, I have a little…quirk, I guess you could call it, where I use stupid nicknames for people, too. I've been doing it since I was little, ever since I nicknamed Mary, Lamb."

I nod, as I briefly remember her mentioning this during our texting marathon. We all have our little eccentricities, and this just happens to be Madison's.

I'm afraid to ask what pet name she has given to Hunter, but I bite the bullet. "Let me guess, you've dubbed Hunter, PITA," I say, and Madison raises an eyebrow, confused. "Pain in the ass," I clarify, and she bursts out laughing.

"No," she replies, still chuckling. "Debbie." I almost spit out my beer.

Hunter cackles loudly and shrugs. "Hey, I like it. I'm totally *down* with being Debbie."

"Yeah, you would," Madison and I both reply at the same time, which sets Hunter off.

"Dix, I love this chick. Can we keep her?" He laughs, interlacing his fingers into praying hands, while Madison devilishly joins in with his laughter.

I still can't believe we're talking about porn in code, in my kitchen, with Madison. But I should have known, never underestimate this little…*diavolo.*

# Twenty-One

## *Dixon*

As Madison excuses herself to use the bathroom, Hunter lunges forward and pokes his finger into my chest.

"If you do not have sex with that girl, then I will." I slap his hand away and dodge his pokey pointer before he decides to get another case of the crazies.

"Okay, whatever, *Debbie*," I retort, rolling my eyes.

"Hey, only Maddy gets to call me that. I think she's sweet on me," he teases with a grin.

I can't help but laugh because I think *Hunter* is the one who's sweet on Madison.

After a few episodes of *Dexter* and a dozen beers, Hunter was looking at Madison with stars in his eyes. But I must admit, so was I.

The beers seemed to loosen her up, and as the night progressed, I saw her guard slowly slip and she appeared completely relaxed and at ease. She even laughed at Hunter's ridiculous jokes, which shows just how relaxed she was.

It's now midnight, and by Madison's sleepy yawns and heavy eyes, I know she's a little inebriated and tired, which is a blessing, as I'm hoping the minute her beautiful head hits the pillow, she'll be out like a light. I don't trust myself with her, plain and simple, and after seeing her so laid-back and getting along with Hunter, I'm beginning to like her even more, which is dangerous for us both.

"Dix, I'm going to tell you this once, and once only. You're crazy if you let this one go. I'm actually jealous 'cause I want a Madison of my own," he says, dead serious.

I pull back, stunned, as catching Hunter with his serious face on is a rare occurrence.

"Thank you, Dr. Phil. But I don't have her, so technically, I can't let her go. She has a boyfriend, remember?" I whisper, not wanting Madison to hear us.

"Oh, bullshit! I call her bluff. Not once has she mentioned Dario."

"David," I amend with a grin.

"Whatever," he scoffs. "I see the way she looks at you. She's hot for you, my friend."

"She is not," I say, brushing him off, but I'm actually half hoping that his words hold some truth.

As the night progressed, Madison seemed to edge closer and closer to me until we were sitting so close she casually leaned into me when tucking her bare feet beneath her.

"Don't be a moron," he scolds with a shake of his head. "You're a smart man. You know this one is different. Stop denying it."

"Okay, fine." I sigh, raising my hands to shut him up. "So

what if I do? I can't force her to dump the primate. And besides, it's been so long since I've, I don't know, romanced a girl, I wouldn't even know where to start," I confess.

Hunter suddenly slaps the back of my head and I grunt on impact. "What the hell was that for?" I ask, rubbing the back of my skull.

"*Romanced* a girl? Seriously, what era are you living in? You say that shit to her, and the only person you'll be *romancing* is my grandma," Hunter says, pulling a repulsed face.

"If there's a point to this story, get to it," I say, still rubbing my skull.

"Madison is not just *a* girl. She'll call you out on all your bullshit 'cause she's real. Whatever you're doing is obviously working. She's here now, isn't she?" he questions, waiting for me to answer.

I nod because he's right.

"Don't fuck this one up, man, 'cause she's special. I think I may be a little in love with her," he confesses, waggling his eyebrows, and an unexpected wave of jealousy passes over me. "Ooh, I haven't seen that look in a long, long time. It suits you."

"What are you talking about? What look?" I ask, wanting to know if I'm really that obvious.

"The look of actually giving a shit. You're not a whore, Dixon. Deep down, you're a big, cuddly teddy bear who's had all his stuffing ripped out by some sadistic little bitch. But piece by piece, you're slowly getting put back together again, and you're just waiting for the right girl to give you a big cuddle and make you whole again. Oh, and I'm not talking about only cuddling the good bits." He playfully swoops forward to tickle my stomach. "Who's a big, cuddly teddy? You are. Yes, you are," he coos while I punch him in the nuts.

He wheezes before turning red, and I laugh. "That's payback, you idiot. And by the way, that was the worst analogy ever. Please refrain from giving me a pep talk ever again."

"I take it back," he gasps, holding his junk. "You're a homicidal teddy bear."

"What'd I miss?" Madison raises an eyebrow when she sees Hunter doubled over, still holding his nuts.

"Oh, nothing," I casually reply with a wave of my hand. Madison laughs as she takes a seat near me.

As she leans forward and innocently reaches for her beer, I see Hunter's eyes widen in delight. He's just been rewarded with a tiny glimpse of what she's packing underneath that tight top, and he obviously likes what he's seen. He subtly bites his knuckle while nodding his head, silently voicing his approval while I turn my eyes upward.

"I better get going," he says, getting up and fake yawning to display his staged fatigue.

"Oh?" Madison says, her back instantly straightening, and I notice her poised composure slip.

I have no idea what that's about, but she has brought to my attention the fact that Hunter probably shouldn't be driving. "You can crash here. I mean, you're in no state to drive." I look at the empty beer bottles littering the coffee table.

"As much as I love you, Dix, I'm not sleeping with you," he replies, shaking his head.

I laugh at his idiocy as I stand. "No, you fool, you can sleep on the sofa in here or in the study."

"Thank you for the offer, but I'm not one to impose," he says with a grin, waving me off.

I scoff. "No, not at all."

"Blow me."

"You wish," I quickly counter, and Madison chuckles at our usual banter.

"Cherry Pie, it was a pleasure meeting you," Hunter says, grasping her hand and mischievously kissing the back of it.

"Likewise," she replies, her cheeks stained a bright red.

"Talk tomorrow, Doc." He playfully jabs me in the arm.

"I'll see you out," I say, and we both commence walking to the door.

"Don't be a stranger, Cherry Pie. I'll see you soon," Hunter says over his shoulder while I basically shove him out the door.

"Good night, Hunter."

"Don't fuck this up," he whispers and leaves before I have a chance to reply.

I take a deep breath before shutting the door, and as I turn around, I see Madison clearing the table.

"Hey, leave that. I'll do it in the morning."

But she's insistent and carries a handful of empty bottles into the kitchen, giving me a quick smile. "It's fine. It'll only take a minute."

She suddenly looks incredibly nervous, and I have a feeling that's got to do with the fact that we're alone. I collect the rest of the empty bottles and join her in the kitchen, where she's vigorously wiping down the countertop. I move around her and place the bottles into the recycling, and decide to wait for her to finish before I speak, as she looks to be deep in thought.

However, when she begins washing the empty chip bowls, I know she's not going anywhere for a while. I decide to leave her to it because I know a pensive female when I see one, and like my mother, keeping busy seems to be Madison's escapism.

I quietly exit and head to my en suite to get ready for bed. After I'm done brushing and flossing, I change into a pair of sweats and splash on some Aramis because Madison commented earlier that she likes the scent. The moment I turn the light off in the en suite and step into the bedroom, I hear a stunned gasp. I look up to see Madison's back.

"Madison?" I ask, confused. "Is everything all right?"

She takes a second before she replies, "Um, yes. I'm just, um, being silly." She turns around, the bedside lamp illuminating her flushed cheeks.

I watch the way her eyes timidly swoop down my bare chest, and I now understand her actions—she's shy. I was too busy thinking about what triggered the sudden mood change in her and completely forgot to slip on a tee. However, seeing as I usually sleep nude, she's lucky I remembered the pants.

"Nice ink," she says, her eyes zeroing in on my ribs.

"Thanks," I reply, rubbing over the tattoo.

"'We are never so defenseless against suffering as when we love,'" she says, tilting her head to the side and reading out the cursive text. "That's really beautiful."

"I think you mean pathetic," I correct, and Madison raises an eyebrow, confused by my response.

However, her mouth parts a second later. She understands what I mean. "You got that because of your ex-fiancée?" she asks, and I nod.

"See, pathetic."

I turn toward the dresser and open my drawer to grab a T-shirt, but Madison charges forward and latches onto my bicep. Looking down at her hand, I expect her to remove it, but she doesn't. She loosens her grip but doesn't let go. She takes a step closer while I take one back.

"Tell me what happened," she gently coaxes, but I break free from her hold.

"No," I bluntly reply and instantly feel guilty when I see Madison lower her eyes, wounded by my curt response. "I just don't want to bore you with the pitiful details of my fucked-up relationship because there's not much to tell. I fell in love with someone who I thought loved me back, I proposed, bought her this apartment," I say, spreading my arms out wide. "And in return, she fucked my best friend, got pregnant, got married, and lived happily ever after."

Damn, where the *hell* did that come from? I thought I was over Lily, but obviously, I'm not. And I don't think I will ever make peace with her betrayal.

But looking down at Madison, who has a hand pressed over her mouth, and her honest eyes filled with tears, I know she's the reason for my outburst. Now that Madison is standing before me, looking absolutely at peace in my home and with my friends, I know I want more.

I haven't felt this way in so long, and go figure, the girl I'm attracted to, both inside and out, is unattainable because of a little thing called a boyfriend. But I can't help but think back to what Hunter said. He's right, she hasn't mentioned him all night, and she *is* here, sleeping in my bed, not his.

Madison's words from last night come flooding back, and the reason she's here is because she wants to be. I make her feel safe, and for someone who seems fearful most of the time, it makes sense that she's drawn to a place that gives her a sense of security.

I don't know why she's afraid, but I'll try my hardest to make sure she's never scared again. Whether that's as her friend, or something more, I'll take whatever she wants to give because, right now, I'm her fucking slave.

"I'm going out for a cigarette." I reach for the deck off my dresser and open the balcony doors.

Placing a Marlboro between my lips, I light it and relish in the first much-needed drag. I rest my elbows on the railing and look at the world below, hating how everything looks so simple for everyone while I'm up shit creek without a paddle.

There was always something more, and I was foolish to choose sex over her because that's what I did. I could have had Madison, but I chose the easy way because sex is less complicated than…feeling. But now, all I feel is my resolve slipping whenever I'm around this remarkable woman.

"Dixon?" Madison's voice softly sounds behind me.

Taking a final drag, I butt out my smoke and brush away the nicotine-filled air. "Hey," I reply, but I don't turn around. I just stare at the world spinning below.

"I'm sorry if I upset you. I shouldn't have asked. I know how hard it is talking about something life-changing that's happened in your past," she confesses, and I nod but still don't turn around.

I can hear her bare feet pad across the ground, and when she stands beside me, I feel the regret radiating off her body.

"It's okay." I slowly turn to face her.

Out here in the moonlight, she looks so ethereal and pure. Her long, dark hair catches in the slight breeze, and her signature fragrance once again has my sense of smell salivating in desire. Her large green eyes look apprehensive and scared, and I realize she's worried I'm angry with her.

"It really is okay. I'm not angry with you," I confirm, giving her a small smile.

"Are you sure?" she anxiously questions, biting her lower lip.

"I'm sure." I nod. "Lily is…a touchy subject for me. She's someone I really want to forget, but I know I never will. But in a way, that's good, as it's a reminder of what to avoid in my next partner."

Madison looks deep in thought, but I don't expect her to reply because what can she say—get over it, perhaps?

Just as I suggest we go back inside, Madison surprises me by confessing, "Well, she's a fucking idiot."

I pull back, stunned, as Madison rarely swears, but I smile, appreciating her impassioned response. "It's fine. You live and you learn," I say, which is clichéd but holds some truth.

Madison, however, doesn't agree with the saying. "That's bullshit," she scowls, lightly thumping her fist against the railing.

I'm surprised by her statement and allow her to explain.

"What lesson did you learn from getting your heart ripped out by the one person you loved and trusted the most?" she asks, but I know her comment is not a question but a statement.

I remain quiet because I know there's more to come.

"What lesson did you learn from her betraying you in unspeakable ways?"

Madison's breath begins to catch in her throat, and when a choked sob tries to break free, she puts a hand over her mouth, not wanting to show any vulnerability.

"All you learned is that life is one messed-up, sadistic bitch." A single tear falls down her cheek, betraying the fact that we're no longer talking about me but rather her.

The need to comfort her is overpowering, and I'm powerless to stop it. "Hey, it's okay." I gently rub her arm and watch more tears fall.

It appears now that they've started, they don't seem to want to stop. But that's okay; she can cry a river of tears because I have no intention of moving an inch.

"Let it out," I say, and without thinking, I step forward and embrace her.

She comes willingly, nuzzling into my body, and the moment I comfort her, the soundless sobs begin to rack her fragile frame.

Her tiny fingers dig into my shoulders while she cries into my chest. I'm not sure how long we stand with her clutching at me like I'm her lifeline, but I don't care. She can hold onto me for as long as she likes because each cry seems to lessen her pain.

After a while, her sobs become less frequent until they gradually turn into small sniffles and then heavy breathing. I don't know what's set this off, but it may explain her unusual behavior earlier.

"I'm s-sorry," she stumbles, her voice small and plagued with discarded tears.

"Why on earth are you apologizing?" I ask, my arms still enclosing her.

"For behaving like one of your patients," she replies, attempting to appear lighthearted.

"It's okay. You get the VIP treatment."

Pulling back slightly, she looks up at me, confused.

"I don't usually cuddle my patients," I explain but fail to

mention I have no qualms sleeping with them.

"Oh," she says guiltily, pulling away.

But I hold on tight, not allowing her to move an inch. "But lucky for us, you're not one of my patients," I say, brushing her tears away with my thumb.

"Thank you, Dixon. That's the first time I've cried in a very long time."

"How'd it feel?"

"Good," she replies with a sad smile.

"Well, anytime you need this"—I pat my right shoulder—"it's yours."

It's meant to be a joke, but Madison's eyes widen, and it appears she's only just realized she's been pressing against my bare chest because she quickly pulls out of my arms and blushes as she looks at my body. Her eyes linger on my stomach, and as they briefly drop down to my crotch, my very attentive body jumps to attention, and things begin twitching below the belt. I'm semi-hard by a look alone.

But I stand proud because I want her to know she's elicited this response.

Madison steps forward, and with apprehensive fingers, she reaches out and touches the dip between my collarbones. The moment her trembling fingers make contact with my skin, I hiss in pleasure because her movements are slow and measured. With the tips of her fingers, she then slowly glides down my torso, stopping just above my heart. I never take my eyes off her. I've never experienced something as erotic because I know her exploration of my willing body is probably her first time.

With fumbling fingers, she moves to one pec muscle, her pointer finger lightly circling my nipple, while I barely contain the moan caught in my throat. I watch with heated desire as she bites her lip, her small teeth rolling her ruby flesh backward and forward.

But still, I don't say a word.

She moves across to the other nipple, and as she passes her thumb over it, my dick jumps to attention, and I'm now fully hard. Her eyes drop to my tenting sweats, and instead of seeing fear, I see desire. I almost come in my pants because it's a sight worth coming for.

As much as I want to reach out and touch her, I don't. I remain utterly still and allow her to take control. With delicate apprehension, she slides her fingers down my middle and detours to my ribs, tracing over my tattoo. A single touch has never felt so intimate, and I hum low, about ready to explode.

"I don't think it's pathetic. I think it shows what you did in order to survive." She sweeps her long hair to one side as she bends forward, laying a single kiss on my flank.

Her lips feel like a shot of adrenalin to my starved body, and I shudder under her gentle touch. She lays another kiss, and then another, and another down the length of my tattoo until her lips rest at my waist. Both of her hands are wrapped around my hips, and she's bent low to get full access to my obliques. The sensual sight evokes images of her wrapping her lips around my straining dick and bringing this home. But I won't have her on her knees on this cold, hard floor pleasuring me because all I can think about is seeing her explode because of my hand.

"Come here," I say, my voice hoarse, filled with longing.

Madison slowly rises, standing to full height. We face one another, inches apart, our chests rising and falling as we anticipate what comes next. Madison surprises me, however, as she's the one who makes the first move. She edges forward and places a hand over my racing heart and slowly raises her mouth to mine, our breaths mingling into one.

But before this happens, I need to make sure this is what she wants, and she's not just lost in the moment.

"If you kiss me," I roughly state, my gaze locked with hers. "You can't take it back."

"I don't want to take it back," she whispers, her warm breath caressing my cheeks, her eyes filled with molten desire.

"Good," I growl before swooping forward and devouring her mouth with an impassioned need.

The kiss is frenzied, and we don't start slow. It's a race to determine who can consume the other person first.

I wrap one hand around Madison's waist, and with the other, I fist her long hair, using it as leverage so I can dominate her mouth. She's gasping and moaning, her lithe body writhing against mine, and her jarring movements are rubbing over my dick in the most delicious way possible. She throws both arms around my neck, pulling my mouth down to hers, and the hunger I feel controls my actions as I walk her backward into my room, my lips never leaving hers.

She comes willingly, and the moment the back of her knees hits the edge of the mattress, she falls backward, pulling me down with her. My huge body shadows her tiny frame, and I try to take my full weight off her by resting up on my elbows. She folds her strong legs around me and pulls me down on top of her.

I can't get enough of her and every frenzied kiss I deliver, she kisses me back twice as hard. Her tongue duels with mine, and her desire is like an aphrodisiac within itself. Before long,

I'm tearing at her top, needing to feel her bare skin against mine.

I manage to yank her tee off without parting with her mouth for longer than two seconds, and then I'm back on her, kissing her like I might expire without her lips. Her legs scissor beneath me, and I know she wants a release. I plan on giving her one—and giving it to her good.

As hard as it is, I pull my mouth away from hers, and she takes a much-needed breath, her chest rising and falling so quickly that her juicy, bouncy breasts almost spill free from her black lacy bra. My cock jolts at the sight, and Madison gasps, her eyes widening as I'm pressed against her core.

"Is this okay?" I breathlessly ask, my brain able to see through the lust for a mere moment.

"Yes," she pants, biting her lip. "Keep going."

That's all the response I need, and I kiss the side of her mouth before working my way down her elongated neck, which she tips backward, granting me full access to her delicious-smelling skin. I kiss over her racing pulse, and I can't help but draw her flesh into my mouth and mark her, as I want the world to know I'm the person responsible for the red, passionate wound.

She moans and gasps, and my fuck, those sounds have my dick punching a hole through my pants, demanding to break out and join the party. Her skin pops free, and I kiss lower and lower until I reach the junction of her swelling breasts. I pull back, needing a moment to really appreciate their beauty because they are the *hottest* tits I have ever seen.

"These are fucking amazing," I say, cupping one full mound and then the other.

Madison moans and arches into my touch, my hand barely covering her breasts.

Her bra is black lace, and as her tight pink nipples poke through the see-through material, my mouth waters. When I lower the lace cup, her boob pops free, and I growl low in my throat as the sight is like nothing I've ever seen before.

"Holy shit." I sigh in appreciation. "I knew they were incredible." I reach forward, gently circling her nipple while she shivers. "But tits as perfect as these should be illegal." I bend forward, capturing her nipple into my mouth.

She cries out and wriggles beneath me, encouraging me to continue as she threads her fingers through my hair and pulls hard.

"Oh my God," she whimpers, her head thrashing from side to side.

"You like that, *angelo*?" I ask around her nipple while she groans in response.

I can't help myself, and it's like a boob buffet as I place my hand underneath her heavy breast and suck it into my mouth. Fuck whoever said a handful is more than enough because right now, I'm swimming in tits, and I want more.

I yank down the other cup and brush my thumb over her nipple while tonguing the other something wicked.

"Oh, fuck," she half cries, half yells, her fingers yanking at my hair, her hips rising to meet my raging hard-on, and the movement sends me wild.

Still sucking and laving at her breast, I walk my hand down between us, wanting to feel her muscles clench around my fingers when she comes, calling out my name. I unsnap her button, and the moment I do, I feel her body freeze underneath me. But my brain and body are two separate entities, and I keep going, my need to bury myself within her fueling my every move.

I lower her zipper and am madly trying to seek refuge inside, but her words have me halting instantly. I pull my hand out like I've just been burned.

"No. No. No. No." Madison is repeating over and over, her voice low and guttural, her eyes shut tight, her head moving from side to side.

"Madison?" I ask, pulling away, alarmed by her obvious distress.

She seems to be in a trance, so I instantly get off her and gently touch her shoulder, as I'm concerned she's stuck in an awful memory—a memory I resurfaced because of my greedy hands.

"Madison," I say, louder this time, shaking her shoulder a touch harder, as I'm afraid she'll go into shock.

"Don't touch me!" she cries, her face a deathly white.

I pull my hands away and sit back on my heels. Not touching her seems to calm her down, but her anguished wails reveal she's still lost in the past.

"Madison, it's Dixon. You're safe, *angelo*. No one is going to hurt you. I'm here…shh, I'm here."

My words have the desired effect, and her weeping dies down to small, weakened cries. But I wait and allow her to crawl out of her nightmare because these are her demons, and she needs to be ready to face them on her own.

Her eyes slowly slip open, red and raw from crying, and she looks around the room, frantically taking in her surroundings. She calms down when she sees where she is, which is obviously not where she thought she was.

"Madison?" I ask cautiously, my hands raised, showing I

mean no harm. "Are you okay? What just happened?"

The moment she hears my voice, her terrified eyes meet mine and then drop to her exposed chest. Her once white cheeks are now stained a bright red, and her hands fly up to cover her nakedness.

"Oh God, what have I done?" she whispers, fresh tears filling her eyes.

She jumps up and rearranges herself as she frantically slips on her tee, her eyes darting around the room, looking for her bag. "I'm sorry, I have to go," she says in a rushed breath, but she won't meet my eyes.

"Madison, talk to me," I demand, leaping off the bed and reaching for her arm.

The moment I touch her, however, she recoils so quickly she hits her elbow on the dresser and curses, but that doesn't stop her mad dash toward the door.

"Just leave me alone. Please," she begs, storming into the living room.

But I will not. I need to know what happened because some heavy shit just went down, and I need to know why.

"No, how about you talk to me? Tell me what happened. Tell me what happened to *you*," I add, and Madison looks as if I've slapped her.

"No! I can't," she exclaims, racing through my house with me following closely behind.

She's feet away from the front door, and she's seconds away from walking out of my life. "Please," I plead. "I would never judge you. You can talk to me. You *need* to talk to someone about what just happened."

She spins around so quickly that her hair nearly whips me

in the face from the force. "So you can psychoanalyze me? Or try to fix me? No, thank you. I'm broken, and no amount of talking will ever fix that."

"You don't know that. Just trust me," I press, taking a step toward her.

"No," she barks, lowering her eyes. "I can't. I can never see you again, Dixon. I'm sorry. I never should have let it get this far."

Her words leave me winded, but I try my best to be levelheaded and understanding. "Hey, I was right there with you," I state, her words making no sense. "You certainly didn't feel sorry when you kissed me back."

"It was a mistake," she harshly rebukes, and I flinch.

I know she's scared and probably confused, but I'll be damned if she downplays what just happened in my room.

"You and I both know that's not true," I retort with a heated chuckle.

"I…I have a boyfriend," she pathetically states, clutching at straws, but I see red.

How dare she bring *him* into this because using him as an excuse to hide behind is just cowardly.

"Well, it wasn't your boyfriend's hands all over your willing body five minutes ago, was it?" I challenge with a bite to my tone.

"You bastard," she spits, narrowing her eyes. "This should have never happened."

"Well, too bad, it has happened, so now deal with the consequences."

"No, I take it back," she stubbornly counters, and her bullshit denial infuriates me further.

"I told you," I say, stepping forward and caging her body with mine as I place both hands against the door behind her. "You can't take it back."

"It was a m-mistake," she stutters, her green eyes fearful, her back pressing further into the door.

"So you call what we just did a mistake?" I question, and she unconvincingly nods.

"You and I, we would never work. It was fun, but we're both very different people. We want different things," she says, her words cutting deep as they mirror Lily's parting speech.

"Fun? It was more than just fun, and you know it. Grow up and talk to me like an adult," I say. A touch harsh, but I need her to be honest and tell me what's really going on.

But she's so damn pigheaded. "So you think I'm a child?" she counters, the hurt reflected on her face.

"As of right now, yes, you're behaving like a child," I reply. I don't understand her actions. This isn't the Madison I know. But maybe I don't know the real Madison after all.

"Well, this *child* wishes to leave." Her final words are my undoing. "Like I said, this was a mistake."

I open my mouth to protest, but shut it quickly when she cruelly adds, "*You* are a mistake."

I take a moment to process what's just been said, and although I know she's lying, I refuse to continue this conversation if she won't meet me halfway. "That's bullshit and you know it. The only mistake here is me letting you leave."

I push off the door and step back, my breath leaving me in labored breaths 'cause I'm so pissed off.

If she wants to leave, I'm not going to force her to stay, but once she's gone, she's gone. I don't give second chances, and

I sure as hell don't give them to someone who thinks I'm a mistake.

"Goodbye, Madison," I say, turning my back on her because I can't bear to watch her turn her back on *me*.

"Dixon," she replies with a sigh, but I don't turn around. I simply look around my apartment, wondering when this turned to shit.

"For what it's worth, it's not you, it's me."

"Just leave," I say, not interested in hearing her excuses. Not interested in fighting for someone who doesn't want to be fought for.

"I'm sorry I hurt you." And with those parting words, Madison closes the door on what could have been, but never will.

# Twenty-Two

*Dixon*

*One month later*

Bob.

Bob.

Breathe.

Bob.

Bob.

Gag.

I like getting my dick sucked as much as the next guy, but when it's my fourth blowjob of the week, and I have no idea who each giver is, each suck and lick all tangle into one.

Looking at my smudged reflection in the bathroom mirror, I despise what I see.

Over a month ago, I allowed the only girl I've liked in a very long time to walk away from me because she hurt my damn feelings. What a soft cock. But that's the problem. My not-so-soft cock got me into trouble in the first place, and now I'm back screwing endless women, not giving a damn who or when or why.

My lackluster release comes spilling out of my uninterested dick, and the random brunette at my feet takes it all without missing a drop. My orgasm is the same as the one I had this morning, pointless and hollow. But a man's gotta do what a man's gotta do, and I gotta do every woman in Manhattan because I can't have the one I want.

Wiping her red-painted lips, the chick whose name I've already forgotten looks up at me from under her fake lashes. "My turn," she purrs and stands, boosting herself up on the basin, spreading her legs out wide.

Her short skirt bunches up around her waist, and I can see she's not wearing underwear. Her smooth entrance is slick and glossy, and where most men would be on their knees in a second, pleasuring this wannabe model, I simply rearrange myself and zip up my fly.

"Maybe next time, sweetheart." I'm lying through my teeth.

"What?" she gasps, incredulous that I would leave her high and dry. "You're not going to return the favor?"

When I merely shrug, bored by her melodramatics, she yells, "You pig!"

"Well, that's what happens when you blow a stranger in a public bathroom," I say, adjusting my cuff links.

"You said I was beautiful!" she shouts, her eyes filling with tears.

"You are." I reach forward and pull her dress down, as her cooch is giving me the stink eye. "It's just too bad beauty only gets you so far in this world."

"Huh?" she replies, scrunching up her nose job.

"When you're older, you'll understand beauty is only skin deep. But all this—" I flick my hand at her materialistic getup "—gets you fucked, and not in a good way, by bastards like me." I unlock the bathroom door, avoiding the glares of irritated females who are in desperate need to use the restroom.

Making my way back to our table, Finch and Hunter take one look at me and roll their eyes.

"Again?" Finch asks, raising his eyebrows.

I casually shrug, stealing Harper's beer. "What can I say?"

"You can say you're a dirty manwhore," Hunter pipes up in disgust. "You can keep that," he adds, pointing at his beer. "I have no idea where your mouth has been."

"Not listening," I reply, flipping him off.

"Dix, we're worried," Finch says, and I can't help but compare his comment to the one he said all those months ago.

Same bar. Same night. Same issue. Although this time, it feels a million times worse.

"You've got nothing to worry about," I reply. "I'm fine. Life is peachy. I'll be leaving for Boston tomorrow, and I plan on knocking the socks off all of those bigwigs and making myself known."

"Well, you're certainly doing that here."

Needless to say, Hunter is pissed at me for not being a man and calling Madison. He really took to her, and although I've told him numerous times that it ended before it even began, he's still living in denial.

"Just call her," he exclaims for the twentieth time this hour.

"Why don't you call her?" I suggest but instantly regret it as his face lights up. "It was a joke. You will not be calling her or seeing her at her work, for that matter. All forms of communication are off. Understood?"

When Hunter ignores me, I repeat. "Understood?"

"Yes, loud and clear," he replies unhappily. "I just wish—" But I cut him off by holding up my finger.

"This conversation is over."

Hunter huffs and folds his arms across his chest, but I refuse to give in.

I entertained the notion of maybe contacting Madison within the first few days after she walked out on me, but after those few silent days transpired, I realized her silence was almost deafening, and we were done.

I'm sick of women and their head games. I've had enough to last me a lifetime. So I've decided to go back to what I know and what I'm good at. Work, sleep, and sex.

Work is easy. Sleep is easy. Sex is easy. It's all the stuff in between that gets in the way.

"You looking forward to Boston?" Finch asks, trying to change the subject, and I nod.

"It'll be nice to get away for a few days," I reply. I'm extending my trip out and having a few extra days of R&R.

Thankfully, I'll be going alone, as I haven't heard from Juliet—bar a lacy thong she sent to my office—since the night I told her it was over. At least one good thing came out of that night.

Getting out of NY will do me good because, like the city that never sleeps, neither do I.

I arrive in Boston early the following morning.

The moment I enter my lavish room, I draw the curtains, switch off all forms of technology, and drink myself into oblivion, thanks to the two bottles of scotch I purchased on my drive down here. I plan on staying this way till I pass out, as I'm too exhausted to face the harsh light of day.

Nature calls some time later, so I crawl out of my drunken stupor, unsure of what day or time it is. Quite frankly, I don't give a damn. I have no plans, and the awards ceremony isn't till Saturday evening, which is six days away…I think. On that note, time to face reality because I think I've hibernated enough.

I shower but don't bother to shave. I throw on some jeans and an old tee, and I'm ready to face the world. Firing up my laptop, I groan when I see the three hundred plus emails waiting for me to read. But they can wait. Anything important, Susanna would have attended to anyway.

Checking my stocks and the Yankees score, I switch off my computer, having had enough for the day.

I power up my cell, and when I see it's Monday evening, I can't believe I slept through the entire weekend. But what was the point of staying awake?

My cell dings, indicating I have a text message. I nearly fall out of my seat when I see who the sender is.

***Miss me? ;)*** The message taunts me with its winky emoticon.

I really don't know what to think other than why the hell is

Juliet messaging me?

Honestly, I believed she would have forgotten all about me and moved on to the next chump. So when she texts me once again, I can't help but think that maybe I was wrong.

***I've missed you. All of you.***

No guessing what part she misses the most.

I decide to reply, afraid that if I don't, she'll continue messaging me like nothing happened.

**Hello Juliet. What do you want?**

Not the nicest way to say hello to someone you've slept with, but I'm not in the mood for her formalities.

***I was just wondering what time I should come down for the ceremony.***

I read the message twice because it surely can't say what I think it did. But it does.

Is she insane? When she sends through another text, I know the answer is yes.

***I can't wait to show you my dress...and what's underneath.***

Have I just been transported to the twilight zone without my knowledge? Why on earth does she think she's still coming? I thought the whole "it's been interesting, but I think it's best we stop seeing one another" speech made my intentions clear, but she obviously thinks it was some kind of foreplay.

It's time I set her straight.

**I apologize if there's been some kind of misunderstanding, but I thought I made myself clear. You and I, we're done. Therefore, you turning up to an event, which is highly important to me, is really not appropriate. I do apologize for any confusion.**

This is the nicest possible way I can tell her to back off. I don't have the time or patience to be dealing with this, and quite frankly, I'm insulted that she thinks she can just message me after all this time and believe I would welcome her, dick in hand.

When I don't receive a response for a few minutes, I don't know if I should celebrate or hide. My growling stomach screams at me, demanding I stop being a pussy and go eat. I send a brief text to Hunter, Finch, and Susanna, letting them know I'm alive. I then grab my wallet and room key, and go in search of some food, making sure to leave my cell phone behind.

The moment the glaring sunset hit my light-sensitive corneas, I decided to dine in at the hotel restaurant, as I'm not *that* ready to face the world. I'm also quite certain I still might be a touch intoxicated—but two bottles of scotch over a weekend will do that.

Looking over the menu, I decide to order a feast and make up for lost time because I'm ravenous. After placing my order, I begin flicking through my iPad and decide to take some notes on the paper I'm currently writing. I finally have the time to focus on my research, and I plan on utilizing every second, seeing as I will be amongst fellow comrades who will appreciate my findings.

Lost in the current edition of the *Medical Journal*, I fail to notice someone standing beside me until I hear a throat being cleared. Looking up, I see the blue-eyed server who took my order earlier standing by my table.

"Can I get you another beer?" she asks, looking at my full Budweiser.

"I'm okay for the moment," I reply and notice her looking down at my iPad.

"Are you here for the doctor thingy?" she gushes and points above her head, indicating the ballroom where the event will be held.

"Yes, I am."

"That's really cool," she says, brushing a blond lock of hair behind her ear. "Are you a doctor?"

"Psychiatrist," I reply, slipping off my glasses and reaching for my beer.

"Ooh, so you can read people's minds or something?" she says, and I'm not sure if she's being serious or not, so I chuckle, not wanting to offend her.

"It's one of my many talents."

"I can believe that," she says, her voice dropping low as she does a quick sweep down my body. "What other talents do you have, *Doctor*?"

God, this really is too easy. You'd think I'd be put off on women, considering everything that has happened. But I'm not.

Curling my finger and beckoning her to come closer, she complies and stoops low, cupping her ear when I indicate it's a secret.

"It's probably better if I show you," I say, my voice filled with empty promise.

She giggles and pulls back slightly, but she's still close enough that I can see her pupils dilate in desire. "Maybe you could show me after my shift, then? I get off at ten."

"Oh, you will be getting off at ten, sweetheart," I say with a confident nod. "I'll make sure of it."

Her cheeks instantly flush, and her mouth parts. Yes, I feel like a dirty old man, seeing as she looks no older than twenty-one, but hey, when in Rome—or Boston. She reaches into her apron pocket, pulls out a notepad, and quickly writes something down.

"Here, handsome." She slips me her number across the tabletop. "Make sure you call. I'll be waiting."

I reach for it, but she stops me by placing her palm over mine. "Oh, and by the way," she says, daringly. "You'll be getting off at 10:05." She gives me a coy wink before walking away, leaving me with a clear view of her tight behind.

Watching until she disappears from sight, I fold up her number and place it in my pocket. I really should steer clear of women, seeing as five minutes ago, I had the intention to dedicate all my free time to research. But all work and no play makes Jack a dull boy.

I cringe the moment the phrase enters my mind, as it reminds me of Madison. But a lot of things remind me of her. This past month has been tough, and I'm man enough to admit that I do think about her from time to time. I wonder how she is, what she's doing, *who's* she doing, but more importantly, I wonder if she's thinking about me half as much as I'm thinking about her.

Blowing out a frustrated breath, I tell myself this is the last time I will allow my thoughts to stray to her because the lack of contact is a sure sign she's forgotten about me—just as I should do with her.

"Dixon?" a voice asks, and I look up to see the kind, weathered face of my old college professor Dr. Wellington.

"Dr. Wellington?" I say, unable to keep the surprise from my voice. "Whatever are you doing here?" I ask, standing up and shaking his hand.

"Oh, I'm the guest speaker for the awards ceremony, which is nonsense. I can't imagine what they think an old fool like me would have to say that would be of interest to you young folk," he modestly replies, and I laugh.

"Don't be ridiculous. You taught me everything I know. Without you, I dare say, I would have given up in the first semester."

Dr. Wellington chuckles, which gets caught in his throat, and he coughs while patting his chest. "Well, thank you, I'll take that as a compliment, seeing as I've heard you've made quite a name for yourself, Dr. Mathews."

"Only thanks to you. Please, won't you sit?" I say, gesturing to the booth.

"I better not. I'm here with someone."

"Oh, you Casanova," I say with a playful wink.

Dr. Wellington chuckles once again and shakes his head, his thinning gray hair moving with the movement. "It's not like that at all. I'm old enough to be her grandfather. She's a student of mine."

"I didn't realize you were still teaching," I say, and he nods.

"Yes, only part-time. Just basic psychology," he replies. "This one student has shown great potential, and the facility asked I take her and another student with me, as they see the potential in both pupils. I think they just want me to show her off to all the bigwigs. You know how much Columbia likes to brag about their students when they become a big deal."

I nod because he's right. Colleges love to boast they schooled the next big thing, as it warrants them charging astronomical tuition fees.

"She actually reminds me of you in a way," he says with a playful gleam in his eye.

"What? She's a pain in the ass?" I counter, and Dr. Wellington grins.

"Yes, that too. Well, I best be off. Never leave a beautiful woman waiting."

"So I've heard," I reply, as he's preaching to the choir. "It was lovely seeing you again, Dr. Wellington."

"Please, it's Max. Formalities are only for the classroom, and even then, they are totally unnecessary."

I smirk, pleased his humility is still intact. "I look forward to hearing you speak at the ceremony."

"Thank you, Dixon. If I'm boring you to tears, please feel free to throw a bread roll at me."

"You never could, but yes, I promise."

"Are you staying here for the week?"

"Yes, I am. I needed to get away from the big smoke," I confess. "And I'm also working on a paper on the links between neurobiology and addiction, focusing on the nature versus nurture principle. I needed the downtime to get it finished."

"Oh? How interesting. I would be intrigued to hear your findings," Max says, the scientist in him coming through. "Would you be interested in catching up tomorrow morning? Around eight thirty for breakfast?"

"Sure, that sounds wonderful."

I could really, really do with someone like Max's opinion. Consulting with someone with his expertise and experience could really open up avenues I haven't fully explored. The thought of possibly being a contender for next year's ceremony doesn't seem as farfetched as it once was.

"Splendid. I'll ask Alex and Madison along also, if you don't mind? I'm sure they'll find your research fascinating."

The moment her name passes his lips, I pray and plead that it's another Madison and not *my* Madison. Because if it is her, she no doubt saw me chatting up the server ten minutes ago.

"Is that okay?" he asks when I don't speak.

"Yes, yes, of course, that's fine," I reply, subtly looking around the room.

"Brilliant. Well, tomorrow around eight thirty it is, then," he says, patting my shoulder. "Have a lovely evening." He winks when my overly helpful server arrives with my food.

The moment he turns his back, I frantically scan the room, and when my gaze locks with a familiar pair of stunning green eyes, I don't know whether to cry in relief or just damn cry.

This is bordering on becoming ridiculous. Some may call

our coincidental meetings fate, serendipity bringing two people together. But I call it a curse because every time I see her, it's a constant reminder of what I've lost.

She looks just as I remember her, but a billion times better. She looks intoxicating in a low-cut, flowing dress, which accentuates her amazing body. I don't care that I'm staring because even if I wanted to look away, I couldn't. I'm still mesmerized by her, even though her running and screaming for the hills was a sure sign she doesn't feel the same.

"Doctor?" the server says, snapping me out of my stupor.

Madison cocks a daring brow, and I'm so busted. She so saw me flirting with the blonde, and I suddenly wished I'd stuck to my original thought of focusing on work instead of getting laid.

"Thank you," I reply with a strained smile and take a seat in the booth.

She places my meal on the table and bends low, her loose-fitting tee revealing the tops of a pair of amazing breasts. But it's not her breasts I want. The breasts I want are sitting feet away from me, eyeballing the shit out of me.

"So I'm really looking forward to tonight," she says, placing my bill on the tabletop.

Even though Madison can't hear the exchange, I still squirm in my seat, feeling like a right royal bastard for encouraging this situation in the first place.

"Um, about that," I say with a sigh. "It's not going to happen."

"What?" she replies, taken aback by my honesty.

I could lie, but what would be the point?

"Yes, I'm sorry. I really shouldn't have accepted this in the first place." I reach into my pocket, pulling out the piece of paper with her number on it. "Here," I say, offering it to her.

Thinking this is some kind of game, she says, "Keep it. You might change your mind."

I shake my head. "I won't." And to prove my point, I rip the piece of paper in half and deposit the tattered pieces on the table.

I know my actions are harsh, but it's best to be blunt, and by the server's gaping mouth, my actions have been heard, loud and clear.

"Okay, well, your loss," she defensively says and walks off in a huff.

Sighing, I look down at my meal and push it away, as I've suddenly lost my appetite. The only thing I'm craving is sitting feet away from me, and I don't know what to do. Raising my eyes, I see that Madison is no longer at her table. I'm not sure why I just refused free, easy sex because God knows, I haven't refused it this past month. But seeing Madison has just brought home the fact that I need to kick a habit—her.

# Twenty-Three

## *Madison*

Seeing Dixon after so long was exactly how I predicted it to be—a damn disaster.

My heart sped up the moment I saw him enter the restaurant, looking totally at ease and owning the room with his confidence and poise. However, my heart began racing for an entirely different reason, and that reason was the blonde server who zeroed in on him the moment he entered the room. Jealousy like I've never experienced before hit me so hard I had to excuse myself and take a breather in the bathroom before I did something I regretted, like claw out her eyes.

When I returned, I saw him openly flirt with her and look like a pig in shit when she gave him her number. But why should I care? *I* was the one who ran out on him like an insane person when he did nothing wrong. *I* was also the one who told him I could never see him again without explaining why I had such a sudden change of heart. And *I* was the one who told him *he* was a mistake, which was a total lie.

Honestly, I couldn't tell him why I freaked. It's not something I want to share with anyone, but a small part of me does with Dixon, and that's what scares me the most. Feeling nothing but kindness and tenderness in his touch showed me that maybe, just maybe, I have a second chance at living a normal life.

But then I went and screwed it up.

When I left Dixon's that night, I knew there was something I had to do; I had to tell David it was over. It was unfair to string him along, and I knew he would probably hate me, but I would prefer that than hurt him a second longer.

So for the past month, I have focused on school and have purposely not focused on how I messed things up with Dixon. I know he would never give me another chance, but honestly, I really need to deal with my demons before I go and be intimate with anyone ever again.

However, after being worshipped by Dixon, I don't want to experience that with anyone other than him. The way he touched me was unlike anything I have ever felt. I found a new sense of freedom in my physical liberation with Dixon, but that all went to hell, thanks to my meltdown.

Plain and simple, I'm scared. And I'd rather be scared and push Dixon away than get hurt because with Dixon, that hurt will almost certainly result in tears, heartache, and pain. So staying away is better for everyone.

My apprehension about opening up has me standing in front of my hotel mirror, trying to look enthused for my breakfast date with Dixon, but it's going as expected—terrible. When Dr. Wellington proposed having breakfast with Dixon, I couldn't say no. I was honored he even asked me to attend this event with him in the first place, as I know how prestigious it is.

I just have to suck it up and deal because this is for the best. I can act professional, and I sure as hell can pretend that Dixon never inflamed my body with his gentle mouth and needy hands. Thanks to his flirty encounter with the Barbie Doll, I now have the fuel to douse any nostalgia I may feel because it's obvious he's moved on, and now it's my turn to do the same.

"Everything okay?" Dr. Wellington asks while I nervously fidget with the napkin in my lap.

"Oh, yes, I'm fine," I reply, guiltily meeting his concerned eyes. "I'm just feeling a little off-color."

"Oh, dear, you should have mentioned something earlier. Would you like to go back upstairs?" he kindly suggests, but I shake my head. I'm determined to make it through this one breakfast and prove to myself, and to Dixon, that I've moved on.

But that statement is quickly revoked when I smell the most delicious fragrance known to mankind float through the room. I know in a heartbeat who's wearing that heady scent. It belongs to the owner of that deep, husky voice, which has my entire body spreading out in goose pimples the moment he opens his mouth.

"Good morning," Dixon says, addressing the table while I choke on…air.

Subtly coughing, I hope my asphyxiation passes before I have to face the hottest man on the planet. Thankfully, it does, and I raise my eyes to meet his, but the moment I do, I almost choke once again.

"Good morning, Dixon," Dr. Wellington says, oblivious to my sudden inability to breathe.

"Max," he replies, giving him a small nod, but his eyes never leave mine.

"This is Madison and Alex." Dr. Wellington introduces us, unaware I know Dr. Mathews in a personal way.

That thought has me thinking about someone else who probably also knows Dr. Mathews personally, and that would be the server from last night.

With that vision in mind, I straighten my spine and extend my hand. "Lovely to meet you, Dr. Mathews."

Dixon happily accepts it, and I tell my body to stop somersaulting in excitement the moment our hands touch.

"Pleasure," he replies with a grin, and I try not to stare at the way his checkered shirt highlights his rocky planes and hardened muscles.

He then turns his eyes to Alex, the Russian beauty to my right. "Why hello, Alex," he says, accepting her hand, but delivering a light kiss on the back of her knuckles.

I have no doubt the entire table can hear my teeth grinding at the sight, but I calmly reach for my water and remind myself it's only one breakfast, and then he'll be gone.

When Dixon takes a seat next to me, I try not to stare at his long fingers as he reaches for the menu. Images of those fingers wrapping around my breasts and playing with my nipples suddenly assault my brain, and I clumsily drop my glass, spilling water down the front of my white sundress.

"Shit!" I quietly curse, reaching for my soiled napkin and uselessly wiping down my dress.

"Oh, Madison, are you okay?" Dr. Wellington asks, the concern clear in his voice. "Let me call a server."

My cheeks are flushed, I'm beyond embarrassed, and I need to get away from Dixon's eagle eyes because I can feel him staring at me. "It's fine, Dr. Wellington. I'll just clear it up." Kicking out my chair, I drop to the floor to pick up my glass.

There is really no need for me to be down here, but it gives me a moment to catch my breath before I have to go back up there and face Dixon's smugness.

"Are you going to stay down there all morning?" Dixon asks with a smirk. I raise my eyes to see his baby blues peering down at me as he's leaned across my seat, watching my every move.

I refrain from using an expletive, as his smug expression pisses me off, so I quickly regain my composure and retake my seat without throwing my glass at his face. My cheeks are hot, and I'm a little breathless, but apart from that, I think I'm over my madness.

"Sorry about that," I say, mainly addressing Dr. Wellington, who waves off the apology.

Thankfully, our server arrives and takes our orders, and without thinking, I order the waffles and a side order of French toast.

"In the mood for something sweet this morning, Madison?" Dixon asks, his voice dripping with innuendo.

Turning to meet his arrogant gaze, I boldly nod. "Yes, dinner left a bitter taste in my mouth, so I need something sweet to wash away the taste."

Dixon blanches, knowing full well I'm referring to his rendezvous, and my confidence is lifted when he runs a hand through his hair, suddenly looking mighty uncomfortable.

Dr. Wellington picks up on the hostility and tries to change the subject. "So Dixon, please, enlighten us with your findings."

Dixon takes in my appearance for a final moment before turning to look at Dr. Wellington, appearing unruffled and completely composed. "Well, as you know, addiction is a very complex thing."

I suddenly feel my cheeks begin to heat once again.

"It most definitely is," Dr. Wellington says with a nod. "People lose who they are and what they once were due to some powerful addictions. But the question here is: why do some people become addicts and others, merely appreciators? I mean, I love cotton candy, but I'm not compelled to seek it out on a daily basis, nor do I lose control in limiting my intake. So what's the trigger?"

"Desire," Dixon coolly replies while I shuffle in my seat.

"What about it?" Dr. Wellington asks, and I internally groan because I have a feeling I'm not going to like how this conversation ends.

"Well, most people become addicts because they crave, they desire that high, whether artificial or natural. Is this a classic case of nature versus nurture? Or is it something more? I think it's a lot simpler in some basic circumstances. We all desire pleasure, we want to feel good, and that triggers a neurobiological response, alerting the brain that eating, smoking, taking drugs, or having sex with random strangers feels good," Dixon explains, his voice lowering when he adds in the last point.

I find his thoughts absolutely fascinating, and for a moment, I forget I'm infatuated with the guy and listen to his ingenious beliefs.

"Therefore, we become addicted to that 'high,'" he says, using air quotes. "And the reward that high delivers."

"You're absolutely right," Dr. Wellington affirms, his eyes twinkling in excitement.

"I want my findings to exhibit that, yes, I acknowledge substance abuse, for example, is a disorder, however, simpler 'addictions' are triggered by raw, basic human emotions. The reward itself is what we become addicted to."

I'm lost in Dixon's intelligence, watching the way he uses his hands as explanatory tools, when he turns in his seat to look at me with a sly look in his eye.

"So Madison. You seem like a fairly uncomplicated girl," he smugly says, tongue in cheek, while I narrow my eyes and glare at him, as this is obviously an intentional jab at me. I remain calm and wait for him to finish. "Is there one intrinsic thing you seem to be addicted to?" he asks, raising an eyebrow.

I don't understand what he's trying to achieve by putting me on the spot this way, but I'll be damned if I show weakness.

When I merely shrug, my noncommittal gesture seems to tick Dixon off, and he presses. "C'mon, there's got to be one thing you do that you know is bad for you, but the reward, the stimuli you receive from that one bad action, cancels out all repercussions, and you keep coming back for more."

The table is silent, waiting for me to reply. But when Dixon arrogantly says, "Well, maybe you're a lot more complicated than I originally thought," I lose my cool and let him know the one and only thing I'm addicted to.

"I obviously fall for the wrong men," I spit out, springing out of my chair. "But you know what, Dr. Mathews? The reward is really not worth the pain."

His face softens for a fraction of a second, but it's then replaced with an unkind, callous mask of a man I no longer know.

"If you'll excuse me," I say, on the verge of tears. I quickly dash toward the exit, unable to face him a moment longer.

The second I charge into the empty elevator, a sob escapes me, and I cover my mouth to mute my tears. How could he have been so mean? Yes, we didn't part on the best of terms, but his performance was downright cruel. I would never go out of my way to embarrass him in front of others, especially someone like Dr. Wellington, or flirt with my peer. His actions today have made it perfectly clear he doesn't care. Maybe he never did.

Wiping my eyes, I dejectedly exit the elevator and mope all the way to my room. Slipping off my shoes and soiled dress, I placed the privacy sign on the door and crawl into bed. Here's hoping I don't dream because this time around, my dreams of Dr. Mathews are no longer welcomed.

# Twenty-Four

## *Dixon*

I'm a bastard.

Yes, what I did at breakfast this morning was fairly unorthodox, but kicking the habit means *kicking* the habit. No half-assed attempts at getting Madison out of my life. By the way she looked at me, I know she felt it, too. That invisible, electrical current was once again passing between us, and to rid her from my life, *she* needed to be the one who walked away because I don't think I can be the one who cuts ties.

She made her intentions very clear when she walked out of my apartment and told me to leave her alone. However, I can't help but think about what she said earlier. She said she obviously falls for the wrong men. So inadvertently, she admitted that she's fallen for me.

But if that's the case, then why did she freak out in my apartment? And more importantly, why did she stay away? I have no idea if she's still seeing the jerkoff, I mean, that would be a good reason, but that didn't stop her from returning my kisses. That's why I'm confident that Madison's tainted past is stopping her from moving on. And sadly, no one can fight those demons except Madison herself.

But I can't force her to tell me her secrets or force her to be with me. If I push, I have no doubt Madison will pull away. So what am I supposed to do?

I hate feeling this way, and in times of crisis, I would normally burn off my restlessness by finding a warm body and losing myself in the comfort only a warm body can provide. But I don't want that.

Groaning, I turn off my laptop and decide to hit the gym. It's now ten thirty, and the only chance of getting a wink of sleep is to run until I drop into an exhausted heap.

But no matter how far I run, I know Madison will always be two steps ahead.

It's Friday night, and the majority of guests have arrived for the awards ceremony, which is to take place tomorrow evening. I have kept to myself all week, pretty much barricading myself in my room, and honestly, it's been a nice change focusing on books instead of boobs.

But sadly, my hermit status must be put on hold as all attendees are invited to attend a pre-awards dinner party, and it would be unwise of me not to go.

It's a formal event, so I've dressed smart in a pinstripe monkey suit, but I've slipped on a vest as the heat is atrocious and I have no desire to be sweating into my champagne. As I make my way to the elevator, I bump into Chad Turner, my friend from the Psychiatry and Behavioral Sciences board, and a woman who I'm presuming is his new squeeze, as her enormous rock is blinding me with its brand new sparkle. She also happens to be his junior by about forty years.

"Dixon," Chad happily says, extending his hand. "How lovely to see you. Did you just arrive?"

"No, I actually drove down a few days ago," I explain, pressing the call button and ignoring the predatory eyes of the brunette by Chad's side. "I needed to get out of the city."

"Ah, yes, New York can be rather taxing. Have you enjoyed your stay so far?" he asks as the elevator cart stops on our floor.

As we enter, the brunette makes a point of standing rather close to me, and I make a point of subtly moving away. "Yes, it's been wonderful, although I haven't had much of a chance to sightsee. I've been working on my paper."

"Oh? More research into neurobiology and addiction?" he asks, and I nod. "I love what you have presented thus far; your findings are rather genius. All book work? Or a bit of personal experience?" he asks with a smirk, watching the floors tick by above his head.

"A bit of both," I reply and move back a fraction, as this bold brunette just shifted a touch closer.

"I would love to hear your theories. Are you free tomorrow for a round of golf?" he asks.

"Sure, I would love to," I reply and practically storm out of the elevator when the doors open. "Meet you in the lobby around nine thirty?"

"Yes, that's perfect. Rebecca loves to golf. Don't you, honey?"

"I sure do. I can't wait to see you on the greens," she replies.

She can't be serious.

"Now if you'll excuse me," Chad says. "I have to show this little beauty off to my jealous colleagues."

She giggles, throwing me a flirty wink over her shoulder as we enter the ballroom while I head straight for the bar. After that god-awful experience, I need a scotch to settle me down.

The bartender gives me a small smile as she sneakily slips me a double shot.

I take my drink and decide to work the room because I've already seen half a dozen people I want to talk to. This is what these functions are all about. For people to big-note themselves, for others to boast and brag about the millions of dollars they make, and for people like me to get to the top, using my brain rather than my wallet to succeed.

I've made a name for myself, and for that, I'm proud, but unlike the majority of fossils here, I've done so through hard work and keeping in touch with the newest theories and studies. Yes, I may have fallen off the wagon, but I'm back on it, and I'm determined to win that award next year.

Two hours later, I've worked the room and spoken to everyone I wanted to chat with. My theories were debated by almost every person, but when I explained the facts, nearly all seemed to understand my approach.

Most faces I recognized, but some I didn't, and those were the ones I made sure I got to know. I have made some new allies this evening, and the ones I already had were singing my praises. I may be a failure in my personal life, but career-wise,

I'm fucking nailing it.

Making my way over to the bar, the same bartender from earlier spots me and reaches for the scotch with a smile.

"Make that two," a voice to the left says.

I turn and see Chad's wife or mistress, or whatever the hell she is, standing beside me, a sinister smile marring her ruby red lips. "We weren't formally introduced," she says and extends her hand, her bracelets jingling with the movement. "I'm Rebecca."

Accepting her hand, I shake it lightly. "Nice to meet you, Rebecca. I'm Dixon." I let go of her hand as I'm afraid she'll shove it down the front of her purple dress.

"So Dixon, you wouldn't happen to know what they do for fun around here, would you?" she asks, her finger skirting around the rim of her glass once the bartender places our glasses on the counter.

Trying to remain cool, I smile. "You have looked around, haven't you?" I ask, twirling my pointer. "No fun will be found in a room full of doctors."

She grins, revealing a set of perfect white teeth. "Well, how about you and I go make our own fun?" she suggests, dipping the tip of her finger into the scotch and wetting her lower lip with the liquid.

Jesus H. Christ, no foreplay with this man-eater. She's just gone in for the kill in under sixty seconds. I'm impressed. Too bad she's completely and utterly off-limits.

"Thank you for the very tempting offer," I say, reaching for my glass. "But I'm going to have to decline."

"Excuse me?" she replies in disbelief. "Just in case we're not clear, that was an offer to fuck your brains out. Free of charge."

Free of charge. Is she a hooker? No way would Chad bring

a prostitute to this thing.

Remaining calm, I nod. "Oh, we're clear. But I don't think your husband would appreciate me banging boots with his wife."

Scoffing, she leans in closer, purring into my ear. "He's not my husband…yet. And besides, the old fart will be asleep by eleven. I need a real man to satisfy my needs, not a Viagra-popping grandpa."

Well, Rebecca is not one to sugarcoat, well…anything. She's obviously with Chad for the money, as he's ridiculously loaded. He's also a well-educated, highly intelligent man, but it goes to show that even the smartest of men get lost in the garden of the forbidden coochie.

I don't feel so bad now.

"How 'bout I just blow you then?" she suggests like we're talking sports.

"Again, thank you," I say, stepping away. "But no."

"Are you gay?" she retorts, hand on hip, unbelieving a heterosexual man could turn her down.

With a smug smile, I shake my head. "I'm very much straight, peaches. I just don't want to fuck you. I've been around your kind for far too long, and as of now, I'm detoxing."

"That can't be true. I've been told you were a sure thing," she says, looking annoyed.

Her comment has me stepping in closer, not wanting anyone to overhear what she just said.

"Excuse me? Who told you that?" I ask, horrified.

Rebecca looks around the room, obviously trying to spot the culprit. "Her," she finally says, pointing over my shoulder.

I can't stop myself, and I quickly turn, not caring that I

appear desperate. The moment I see her, I curse myself for not guessing who it was sooner.

"She said that you like to fuck and like to fuck hard," Rebecca states into my ear while I cringe, listening to the words that have come back to bite me in the ass.

"If you'll excuse me," I say, my eyes locked with Juliet's as she gives me a smug wave from across the room while sipping her champagne.

"I'm first in line," Rebecca says, latching onto my arm as I make my escape.

I discreetly pull out of her clutches, not wanting to make a scene. "There *is* no line," I bark, my patience wearing thin. "I don't know what Juliet told you, but I assure you, they're all lies."

"Juliet? She told me her name was Sarah," Rebecca reveals, looking at Juliet and narrowing her eyes. Juliet no doubt gave an alias, as she was hoping to remain undetected as the culprit who has just turned my night to shit.

"See, there you go. If she lied to you about her name, what else did she lie to you about?" I say. Not sticking around to hear her response, I politely push my way through the crowd and storm over to Juliet in record speed.

"Dr. Mathews," she purrs, her lips tipping up into a devious smile.

"Can I have a word?" I snarl under my breath, gripping her bicep.

Thankfully she doesn't object and comes with me as I practically drag her outside and onto the balcony. A few people are smoking out here, but most are too wasted or caught up in conversation to notice me snarling at her, ready to toss her over the railing.

"*What* are you doing here?" I say, the hostility clear in my tone as I release her arm roughly.

"I'm here because you invited me to attend," she replies, smoothing out her gold-colored gown.

"Well, the invitation has been revoked. Now leave," I say from between clenched teeth.

"Babe, what's the matter?" she has the nerve to ask, wrapping a hand around my nape and attempting to draw me close.

I stand my ground and pull away from her because she has clearly lost her mind. "Juliet, I have no idea what game you're playing, but you need to leave immediately. These are my work colleagues. You can't be here, and you most certainly can't be spreading vile rumors."

"Rumors?" Juliet challenges, brushing back her hair. "Rumors would imply a false story. But we both know what you've been up to. I believe what I told your little admirer was indeed fact."

Internally counting to five, I sneer, "What do you want?"

Juliet laughs, and the sound which once made me smile now makes me want to hurl.

"I want things to go back to the way they were. I'm not asking for a commitment, Dixon. I just want you to worship me the way you did before," she reveals, stepping forward and cupping my balls. "I miss you. No one can make me come the way you do."

"Stop it," I scold, stepping out of her hold and looking from left to right to ensure no one saw.

Juliet smirks, and I know she has the power to break me. But what she's proposing, I would rather be exposed for the pervert that I am than be held prisoner by her scheming snatch.

"No," I say firmly.

"Why not? Did you get engaged or something while I was away?"

Her comment inspires me to answer truthfully. "Actually, yes, I met someone," I confess, and Juliet pales.

"Who is she? Your little sleepover buddy?"

"Someone you will never know," I say, taking great pleasure in seeing her seethe.

"I knew it," she says, her red lips dipping into a tight frown. "What's her name? I want to know the name of my conqueror."

"Madison," I reply, unable to stop myself because how I wish it were true.

When Juliet's eyes narrow into mere slits, I almost hold my junk, afraid she's going to take her anger out on my balls.

"Well, good luck to you. All the Madison's I know are boring as batshit," she says with bite. "Maybe I'll book an appointment to see you. We can reminisce about the good old days."

"No," I reply, wishing she'd leave, as her presence here is dangerous.

What if Madison is planning to attend tonight's proceedings with Max? If she saw Juliet and me together, she'd know something was up. I never want to be seen in Juliet's company ever again.

"I must have been absolutely insane to sleep with someone like you," I state, prowling forward, while Juliet pulls back, hurt. "I was happy to leave things amicable, or at least civil, but you turning up here is completely unacceptable."

This is the second time I have actually seen any humanity in Juliet, and I intend to take full advantage of it.

"You were just a fuck, Juliet—one I sincerely regret. So if you have any pride, you'll leave with your head held high and leave me the fuck alone. Do not call me, message me, or turn up unannounced. You got it? We're done."

Her confidence diminishes, and her poise is replaced with fury. "You'll be back, and when you do, you'll be begging for a second chance."

"No, I really won't," I state, shaking my head. "Goodbye, Juliet. I so hope our paths don't ever cross again."

For once, Juliet Harte is speechless, and it's a sight I'll never forget.

# Twenty-Five

## *Dixon*

Golf on a Saturday morning *is* as pretentious as it sounds, but it's my one and only chance to talk to Chad and bond over hitting a small ball into a hole. After last night, however, I don't want to think about any balls going into any holes.

With that thought in mind, I decide to steer clear of Rebecca the man-eater and play the quickest round of golf—ever.

Sadly, my plans for a short game turned to shit when she decided she wanted to learn how to play. Eighteen holes never looked so daunting.

Thankfully, she has gone upstairs to change for lunch and probably fuck the caddy. Her promiscuity, however, has left me alone with Chad. We haven't had a chance to discuss politics, and now that the piranha is gone, it's all business.

We're sitting in the club restaurant, surrounded by rich snobs who have way too much money and time on their hands.

If it weren't for my curiosity and scotch, I would be upstairs watching ESPN.

"So Dixon, I've been thinking about your research."

I casually nod while taking a bite of my club sandwich.

"When you're finished with it, I would be happy to present it to the board on your behalf and maybe sway them into backing your findings. Their support opens up many doors for you. You don't have to only practice, you could teach, and being a recognized, board-endorsed doctor really looks good on the résumé," he says with a wink. "I know you've worked hard to get where you are, but something like this moves you from amateur to pro in months. Next year"—he leans close, cupping his mouth—"it'll be your name they're calling out as the winner of the award."

Chad is the devil, and I want in.

"Thank you, Chad. Your faith in me is something I don't take lightly. This offer is really too much, but I would be a fool to decline. Thank you again," I say, trying to remain composed.

Chad waves me off. "Thank yourself, Dr. Mathews. No one got you here but you alone. You should be proud of yourself."

I smile, as his comment means a lot. "Regardless, I appreciate your support. If I can do anything to return the favor, please let me know."

"I'll hold you to that," he replies with a chuckle as he takes a sip of water.

Sadly, our pleasant conversation is interrupted by Rebecca. "Miss me, boys?" she says, and I nod with a stiff upper lip.

"Always," Chad gushes.

"Muffin, your cell was constantly ringing when I was upstairs. I didn't bring it down here as I knew you boys were probably catching up."

"Oh?" Chad says, scratching his chin. "I wonder who that could be. All my colleagues are either here or know I'm indisposed for the weekend."

"Maybe it's your ex-wife," Rebecca sneers, cocking a daring brow.

"Now, darling," he counters, but Rebecca blows him off by snapping open her compact and applying a coat of lipstick.

Chad sighs and looks to me for help, but I merely shrug, as he's totally alone on this.

"I'd best see who that was," he says after a moment of silence. "I'll be back in a few minutes." Before I can scream, *"Take me with you,"* he's off, leaving me alone with the gold digger.

The moment he's gone, she shifts closer and runs a fingernail down my arm. "So…"

"So," I parrot, moving my arm as I'm surrounded by colleagues.

"Thought about my offer?" she asks, not at all discouraged by my rejection.

"There's nothing to think about. The answer is, and always will be, no."

When she attempts to touch my leg under the table, I grab her wrist and push her hand away. "Stop it, Rebecca. I'm not interested. You are engaged to my friend, someone I respect, and your behavior is completely unacceptable."

"If you don't fuck me, I'll tell Chad you came onto me," she suddenly unveils, and I pull back, stunned.

"You can't be serious?" I shake my head, but I knew she would use this tactic sooner or later.

"I'm very serious," she affirms, her gray eyes widening. "All

I want is one night, and then I'll leave you alone. If not, well, Chad might not be so willing to help you out."

"This is blackmail," I whisper angrily.

"No, this is called a girl getting what she wants. And I want you." She cups my balls, just in case I'm unsure of what she wants from me. "Sarah told me all about you, and I want a taste."

There's no way I can do this. I mean, this is wrong. Yes, I've done some awful things in my time, "Sarah" being the worst, but this is up there with atrocious, unacceptable, heinous acts.

Brushing her hand away, I spit, "Can you be a little more discreet?" I smile as the couple next to us gives me a weird look.

"I always get what I want, and I want you to fuck me."

"What? The caddy wasn't man enough for you?" I bitterly snarl, my patience wearing thin.

Rebecca looks stunned that I clued onto her flirting, but I've been around her kind for far too long. Hell, I am, or *was* her kind.

I'm stuck between a rock and a horny woman, but I will not be blackmailed this way. "The answer is still no," I stubbornly state, while Rebecca frowns.

"You don't really get a say. Fuck me, or get fired. Easy," she replies, looking at her fingernails, bored by this conversation.

"You don't seem to realize if I fuck you, I still get fired. This is a small world, and my actions will come back to haunt me," I say, hoping to appeal to her rational side—if she has one. "Either way, I'm screwed. And I would prefer it to be consensual screwing instead of my hand being forced."

"What are you? A priest?" she barks, scoffing at my plea. "I'm asking you to fuck me, no strings attached, and you're saying no. What, are you saving yourself for someone?" she half-jokingly says. I hate to think how accurate she is.

Before I have time to reply, a pair of arms wrap around my neck and a set of lips kiss my cheek. "Baby, I've missed you."

I turn so quickly, I nearly bump heads with the person standing beside me. But she reads my actions and takes a step backward, just in time.

"Madison?" I choke out, gaping at her, utterly confused. "Um, hi?" I add, which comes out as a question, as I have no idea what's going on.

She reads my confusion and smiles. "Sorry I'm late. Traffic was such a bitch." She pulls up a chair and sits beside me.

"That's okay," I reply, playing along, still baffled by what's happening. "I'm just thankful you're here."

"Me, too," she replies before bending forward, yanking the collar of my polo and smashing her lips to mine.

I freeze, unsure what to do, but as Madison's tongue nudges at my lips, demanding entrance, I open wide and happily comply. We kiss passionately and recklessly, and before long, I'm the one yanking on her nape, drawing her mouth closer to mine. I've missed her taste so much, and kissing her is like coming home.

The little sound she makes as I nip her bottom lip has me regretfully pulling away because if we continue just one more minute of this madness, I'll be clearing the table and throwing her on top of it.

"You look beautiful," I say, my senses on overdrive.

Madison looks down at her short denim shorts, red tank, and Chucks, and smiles. "Thanks. So do you," she lightly replies, pulling a face at my stuffy polo and beige slacks.

I had to wear something presentable on the greens, and in

turn, I look like a complete douche.

I've completely forgotten Rebecca is here until she clears her throat, unhappily. "So this is your girlfriend?" she spits, and I raise my eyebrow at Madison, unsure if she'll feel comfortable with this lie.

Madison, however, answers for me as she leans forward so she can make eye contact with the witch. "I sure am," she says, cuddling into my side.

"Yeah, she sure is," I confirm, kissing her cheek in gratitude. I have no idea why she's playing along with this façade, but I'm grateful that she is.

"Well, that explains a lot," Rebecca smugly says, pleased my rejection was because I was seeing someone and not because I found her unattractive.

However, I have an awful thought. What if Rebecca mentions Juliet? This could get ugly real fast.

Thankfully, Madison fills in the silence. "Thanks for keeping him company."

"The pleasure was all mine," she replies sarcastically, drumming her fingernails on the table.

"Hey, I love your hair color. It really suits you," Madison randomly says, and I'm not sure if she's being serious or not because Rebecca's bi-colored hair resembles a skunk.

But I nod and remain quiet, not understanding the language of women.

"Oh, thank you." Rebecca primps up her mane. "I just got it done for the weekend. I needed something to brighten up my time here."

Madison giggles, cupping a hand over her mouth. "I know exactly what you mean."

I'm staring, my mouth agape, not understanding what is transpiring here. But the fact Rebecca hasn't used the words "fuck me" or "blow job" is a good thing, so I don't question whatever Madison is doing.

"Sorry that took so long," Chad apologizes, returning to the table and taking a seat.

He takes one look at Madison, who is still cuddling into my side, and smiles. "Oh, I didn't realize you were bringing a plus-one, Dixon. I was told she pulled out at the last minute."

I freeze up, as I'm not too sure how Madison will feel, knowing I was originally planning on taking the person I dumped her for, to the event she's now at, saving my ass.

I look over at Rebecca, who smiles at me smugly. Looks like my secret is safe for now.

But Madison doesn't miss a beat as she replies, "You know us women, we like to keep our men guessing." She winks conspiratorially at Rebecca, who happily nods.

"Oh, you got that right." She looks at Chad, giving him a sly little grin.

He melts and gets all love-eyed while I kiss the arch of Madison's neck and whisper, "Thank you."

She subtly nods and surprises me by leaning into my caress.

"I'm Chad, and this is my beautiful fiancée, Rebecca."

"It's a pleasure to meet you both," Madison replies. "Oh my, goddamn, look at your ring. Let me look," she adds, making grabby hands, and Rebecca chuckles as she proudly displays her hand. "That is some ring. It really is beautiful, Rebecca. You're going to make a stunning bride."

Both Chad and Rebecca beam at Madison's comment while I watch the exchange, disbelieving how the tension has fizzled, and I no longer feel the need to protect my nuts. Thanks to Madison, my career is safe for the minute, and so is my dick.

"She sure is," Chad says in agreement. "Well, if you'll excuse us," he adds, and Rebecca looks at him with a smirk.

"Bye, bye," she says, standing up while I try not to vomit because they are so going upstairs to bump wrinkly uglies.

"I'll see you tonight," Chad says while hooking a hand around Rebecca's waist.

"Tonight?" I dreamily ask, lost in Madison's vanilla fragrance.

"Yes, for the ceremony."

"Oh right," I reply, shaking my head and pulling my shit together.

"We can meet in the lobby? Around seven?" he suggests.

Madison has already done too much, what with saving my ass from Rebecca's claws. I surely can't ask her to continue with this charade into the night, can I?

Chad and Rebecca look at me expectantly, and just as I'm about to make up an excuse as to why Madison can't come, she says, "Great, we can't wait."

I turn to look at her quickly, and she nods, a small smile gracing her cherub lips.

"Yes, great; seven it is," I say, my eyes never leaving Madison's.

"Wonderful, we'll see you then." They're both off, Rebecca giggling in the distance.

The moment they disappear, I let out the breath I was holding.

Now that we're alone, Madison appears to regret her decision to come to my rescue. I don't blame her, though, as I was a right royal dick to her.

I feel a purge approaching.

"I'm sorry, Madison," I say, and when she opens her mouth to speak, I place a finger over her lips to silence her. "Just let me finish." She nods, her eyes softening as I remove my finger. "About the other day, I was out of line. I acted like a real asshole, and well…" I state, rubbing the back of my neck. "I'm sorry."

But it's not only the other day I need to apologize for.

"I'm sorry for everything," I add, meaning every single word. "I should have called and made sure you were all right, but I thought you made your feelings quite clear that you never wanted to see me again."

She lowers her eyes as I've obviously struck a nerve, but she still doesn't speak.

"I'm so sorry for hurting you. It was never my intention to make you feel uncomfortable or scared. If I could take back that night, I would."

My confession has struck a nerve, and she looks up, tears pooling in her eyes. "You regret it?" she whispers, her lower lip quivering.

"No," I quickly reply, not wanting her to run away. "I've never regretted a moment spent with you. Especially not that," I add, reaching out and running my knuckles down her cheek.

I don't know where this honesty has come from, but I decide to go with it because it feels so right.

She leans into my touch, and her willingness has the alpha in me beating my chest in pride. "I know you have skeletons in your closet, we all do, but until you can get past whatever is biting at your heels, I think it's for the best that, after this weekend, we don't see one another."

Madison frowns. "Thank you for apologizing. You're right, you were an asshole. I was actually coming down here to give you a piece of my mind. You were awful to me, Dixon," she asserts, making me feel even worse than I already do. "But I was awful to you, too. I also owe you an apology."

"You owe me nothing," I say with a firm shake of my head.

But Madison perseveres. "Yes, I do. You're not a mistake. You never were. I'm sorry for saying something so cruel. But you're right. I do have a terrible past, and I'm trying to work through it. I'm just sorry I couldn't work through it before I met you. But maybe we could still be friends? I mean...I've missed you this past month."

As appealing as that sounds, seeing her, touching her, and being near her proves I can't just be her friend. We were never just friends. After tasting her, I want something more, so being her friend will end up driving me insane.

She can see it written all over my face and nods. "Okay, I get it. Not gonna happen."

"I'm sorry, but we were never just friends. There was always something more. I still want more, but it's either all or nothing. I'm tired of playing games," I say, watching a single tear roll down her cheek. "I should have told you earlier, but honestly, I didn't know I wanted more until you walked out on me. I'm just as messed up as you are," I confess and let out a sarcastic snort.

"I highly doubt that," she replies with a sniff. "I meant what I said. It's not you, it's me."

Unable to help myself, I wrap my hand around her nape and draw our foreheads together. "In this circumstance, I think it's both of us. Maybe in another lifetime, *angelo*?" I say, and Madison gasps, her warm breath tickling my cheeks.

"Maybe," she replies half-heartedly.

"Thank you so much for saving my ass today. I owe you." I pull away and try to lighten the mood.

Madison sniffs with a sad smile. "Consider it paying back my dues. You've saved my ass on more than one occasion, so it's time I start paying you back."

And that answers my question. She's come to my rescue because she feels guilty for what transpired between us. But what she doesn't realize is that I'm the one who's sorry—for everything.

"You owe me nothing," I say once again.

"I know, but I want to do this for you. I could see how uncomfortable you looked, and I couldn't just walk by and not help you. I mean, even though you *were* a complete bastard to me the other morning, I can't hate you. I tried," she admits shyly. "This is the least I can do. I really am sorry, Dixon. I shouldn't have kissed you back. You warned me I couldn't take it back, and I didn't want to, but..."

"I understand," I finish when she doesn't continue. "Maybe in another lifetime," I add, as that seems to fit our situation perfectly.

"Maybe in another lifetime," she sadly repeats with a nod. "So we get through tonight, and I'll be by your side, acting the part of the perfect girlfriend, I promise. And then when the night is over, it's...goodbye?" she questions, her voice quivering.

"Let's just get through the evening first," I reply, not wanting to be the one who makes that call.

"Okay." She nods, wiping her eyes. "Well, I better go find something to wear. I didn't pack too many nice things, so I need all the time I can get to try to pull something presentable together."

As she attempts to stand, I stop her by placing my hand on her forearm. She looks down at our connection, and I know she feels it too.

But ignoring those incessant sparks, I say, "Leave it to me." When Madison raises a confused brow, I smile. "Let me do this for you."

She understands what I mean and nods. "Okay, I'll be waiting in my room. It's two thirty-five."

"Perfect. Meet you in the lobby at seven?" I ask, still disbelieving she's just agreed to be my girlfriend for the night.

"Seven it is," she replies and stands. "See you soon."

"See you soon," I repeat, watching her as she walks away from me.

# Twenty-Six

## *Madison*

After trying to hate Dixon for the past few days and failing, I knew I had to find him and confront him because this feeling in the pit of my stomach was making me ill. I was sick of reprimanding him in my mind, and I knew the only way to get over him was to talk to him face-to-face.

It was easy to fall into the façade of pretending to be his girlfriend because if I wasn't so emotionally screwed up, then I wouldn't have to pretend.

Once I get back to New York, I'm going to confront my demons instead of trying to run away from them. I don't know if this strength comes from meeting Dixon, but whatever it is, I'm just glad I finally have the balls to do what's right. My fear protects my assailant, and I'm sick of them living in the light while I'm confined to the dark.

Once I find my light and if Dixon still wants me, then it'll be our time, but until then, I have to work on becoming the stronger person I've always wanted to become. Or, like he said, maybe it'll be our time in another lifetime.

But first things first, I have to get through tonight.

Dixon was quite vague in what he meant by "leave it to me." I didn't want to argue with him because it seems we both want to make right whatever went wrong between us, and doing little things for one another seems like the first step in doing just that.

When a knock sounds at my door at four o'clock, a burst of excitement charges through me, and I walk to the entrance with a skip in my step. I open it and am greeted by a concierge holding a black garment bag.

"Compliments of Dr. Mathews," he says, passing me the bag.

"Thank you." I reach into my pocket for a tip.

He waves me off. "No, miss, it's fine. It's all been taken care of by Dr. Mathews. Enjoy your evening."

I nod and quickly close the door, excited to rip open the bag and see what's inside. The moment I unzip it, a stunned breath leaves me as I'm looking at the most gorgeous dress I've ever seen in my entire life.

It's a royal-blue silk cocktail gown, and as I carefully remove the garment from the bag, I see the mid-section is a sheer mesh decorated with blue sequins, so my upper torso is not totally bare. The sequined dress is long and fitted, and I can tell when I put it on, it'll pool around the floor elegantly. The neckline is a sweetheart cut and quite low. I have no doubt that's the reason Dixon chose it.

As I cautiously drape the dress on the end of my bed, I check the sizing. He's so attentive to detail, so it doesn't surprise me the dress is a perfect fit. I then go in search of appropriate shoes to wear. Hunting through my luggage, I remember I only brought a black-heeled pair, which I intended to wear with the dress I was planning on wearing this evening. They'll have to do, as I don't have anything else.

When a knock sounds on the door, I wonder who that could be, as I've let Dr. Wellington know I'll be accompanying Dixon tonight. After seeing our showdown, he knew we had history and thought it was a good idea to talk through whatever issues we had.

When I open it, I'm greeted by the same concierge from earlier. "Hello, miss. Once again, this is compliments of Dr. Mathews." He hands me a big paper bag.

I accept, stunned, as I was not expecting yet another gift. And I was definitely not expecting yet another *expensive* gift as, to judge from the name on the bag, it's made by the same designer as the dress.

Once my brain catches up, I quickly reach into my pocket for a tip, but the concierge waves me off. "Dr. Mathews is a very generous man," he says with a smile before tipping his hat and walking away.

I stand speechless, but compose myself enough to shut the door behind me. I place the bag onto the desk and hunt through it to find a shoebox and a smaller, rectangular box. Reaching for the shoebox, I open it up and pull away the white tissue paper to see a pair of silver strappy heels. They are simply beautiful, and although the heel is quite high, I know they'll match the dress perfectly.

I almost forget about the other box because the dress and shoes are really too much, but as I open it up, I have to agree with the concierge, Dr. Mathews is a *very* generous man. The small silver clutch matches the sparkly silver heels perfectly, and these accessories will set off the elegant gown beautifully.

Looking at the clock, I decide to take a shower and get ready. However, yet another knock on the door interrupts my plans, and I open it up, once again clueless as to who is standing on the other side.

"Hello, miss," says the concierge with a smile. "This is for you." He hands me a small bag. "Compliments of—"

"Dr. Mathews," I finish for him while he nods. "This is really too much," I state, taken aback, peering inside the bag.

"He mentioned you would say that. But just in case you were thinking of returning them, Dr. Mathews wanted you to know they are non-refundable," the concierge says with a chuckle.

I can't help but laugh as I ask, "Is this the last of them?" because I really cannot accept anything else. It's just too much.

The concierge smirks. "He also mentioned you would say that, too." He tips his hat before leaving.

"Hey, you didn't answer my question," I say, but he keeps on walking, ignoring me, as no doubt, Dr. Mathews probably predicted I would say that, too.

I close the door behind me, and just like the shoes, I place the bag onto the desk and remove the blue velvet box from inside. I brush my fingers over the soft material before nervously opening it up. The moment I see what's inside, a gasp leaves me, and I cover my mouth with a shaky hand because what I'm looking at is really *way* too much.

A double-chained diamond necklace catches the light, and hanging off the delicate length is a sapphire diamond, which is bordered by tiny diamonds. Above the necklace sits a pair of small sapphire studs, and they too glitter in the light, the way only true diamonds do.

This is truly the most beautiful piece of jewelry I have ever seen, and I quickly reach for my cell and text the one person I swore to never text again.

***This is too much, but thank you. I love it.***

I receive a reply within seconds.

**Nothing but the best for my girl.**

How I wish that were true.

It's now 7:02p.m., and I'm rushing around my room, shoving the essentials into my small clutch. Once I have my lipstick, perfume, ID, cash, and room key crammed inside, I'm ready to go. I have to take measured steps as I make my way into the elevator because these heels are a lot higher than I'm accustomed to wearing. They are so worth it, though, because I feel like Cinderella in her glass slippers.

Pushing the button for the lobby, I take a minute to look into the mirrored wall behind me to make sure I look okay. I've curled my hair and swept it to one side, fastening it with a jeweled clip, my loose curls brushing over my shoulder. My makeup is fairly basic because my outfit, combined with the lavish jewelry, is quite formal enough.

Overall, I like what I see, but my huge pupils and heavy breathing indicate one thing—I'm so nervous.

Once the elevator dings, I take my first careful step toward—I don't know. Nervously smoothing out my gown, I will my racing heartbeat to slow down. I gather whatever courage I can find and round the corner to see my Prince Charming.

The moment our eyes meet, I feel that distinctive, pulsating charge ricochet between us, but I ignore it and try my best not to fall as I walk toward him. He looks absolutely hot in a simple but elegant tuxedo, which has been fitted to his muscular body and impressive height. His hair, which is styled into an orderly mess, complements his light, rugged stubble, and his incredibly blue eyes look electric while scanning down my body.

"I'm certain there was a lot more material when I picked this out," he says when I reach his side, his mischievous gaze lifting to meet mine.

"You've got great taste," I reply with a chuckle, ignoring how delectable he smells as I lean forward and kiss his cheek.

Dixon wraps an arm around my waist and draws me close. "Might I propose you borrow my jacket?"

"Whatever for?" I ask, gasping as he runs his nose lightly down my cheek and into my neck.

"So I'm not forced to gouge out the eyeballs of every male in this place," he teasingly replies, his warm breath causing my skin to break out into tiny goose bumps. "But gouging aside, you look beautiful. Although, anything you wear looks stunning on you."

I flush at his comment and turn into him, nuzzling into his embrace. The innocent action has Dixon growling low in his throat and tightening his hold around my waist.

"There they are," a voice says, which has me pulling back, embarrassed to be caught out in such an intimate pose.

However, Dixon looks anything but embarrassed when I meet his heated stare. He gives me a quick once-over before addressing Chad. "Here we are."

"You look positively stunning, Madison," Chad says, his eyes lingering on my boobs.

I redden and turn to look at Dixon, who shrugs with an, "I told you so," look on his amused face.

"Thank you, Chad," I reply, my bashfulness obvious as I subtly cross my arms over my chest.

"You look…lovely, Rebecca," Dixon says with a pause, and I wonder what he really thinks of Rebecca's outfit, which resembles lingerie.

"Thank you. You look lovely, too," she purrs, cocking out her hip, not concealing the fact she's checking out Dixon.

A wave of jealousy overtakes me, but I smile and hold back my homicidal urges.

"Shall we?" Chad suggests, oblivious to the fact his fiancée is eye-fucking my "boyfriend."

Pretend or not, I see Dixon as mine, and I know tonight will be a lot harder than I originally thought.

"Let's," I say in concurrence with Chad as I loop my arm through Dixon's.

As we make our way toward the ballroom, all I can think about is the way Rebecca looked at Dixon. I played nice with her because I know how girls like her operate. If you stroke their already impossibly huge egos and not come across as a threat, then most times, they are happy to be friends because they have the upper hand. But tonight, since I'm all dressed up and on the arm of Dixon, the man she wants, she sees me as competition.

Well, game on.

Just before we enter, Dixon leans down and kisses the shell of my ear. "Thank you for remembering to wear clothes." I burst out laughing, which is exactly what I needed to calm the nerves.

"Anytime. But it's all thanks to you," I reply, my breath catching in my throat as he lays a single kiss along the arch of my neck. "If it weren't for this dress, I would be nothing special."

Dixon pulls away, a look of horror on his face. "That's not true." Placing a hand on my cheek, he smiles. "You don't know how special you are."

His sweet words have me turning into his hold and nuzzling his hand. "Thank you," I whisper, raising my eyes to meet his.

This shouldn't feel so natural, but it does, and the thought of this being our last night together hurts. But Dixon said it's all or nothing, and my fragile mind can't give him my all until I get back to New York and confront my past.

Dixon must be able to read my thoughts because he says, "Even though you're mine for only one night, I'm going to make it the best night of our lives." He lays a single kiss on my lips before pulling away.

As we enter the lavish ballroom, he looks unruffled, and all other thoughts get put on the back burner as I take in the beautiful sight before me. The room has been transformed into an elaborate affair. The servers are zipping around the room, ensuring all seated guests have full glasses, while others escort patrons to their tables.

A server happily greets us and flicks through his iPad

to see where we are seated. Thankfully, Dixon amended the arrangements, and I'm his plus-one. I can't help but wonder who his plus-one originally was, as Chad mentioned they had pulled out at the last minute. Was it supposed to be the girl he was seeing when we first met? The thought has me shuffling uncomfortably, and Dixon slides his hand down my back, resting it above my ass.

"Are you all right?" he whispers as we begin walking toward our table.

"Fine," I reply, but I'm anything but as I see the head of almost every woman in the room turn to look at Dixon.

Women of every age group are currently checking him out, some a little more discreetly than others, but overall, I have a room full of Rebeccas I now have to fight off.

The server stops at a table near the front, and as Dixon pulls out a seat for me, I know I'm the envy of the room. Ignoring their scowls, I take a seat and shakily reach for my glass of water when Rebecca sits next to Dixon.

I eye the bottles of wine in the middle of the table, wondering if it would be considered rude to make a dive for them and get into the booze early. But looking around the room and seeing the jealous stares of every beautiful woman present, I ignore etiquette and reach for a bottle of red.

"Here, let me," Dixon offers, his fingers overlapping mine, beating me to it.

I pull back, my flesh singeing, but try not to make a big deal over it, and smile.

As I down my entire glass, I can feel Dixon watching me, but I ignore him and distract myself by looking around the room. The people here are powerful and important, and I wonder what they did to get to where they are. I have no doubt some worked hard, but others, I wonder who they slept with or who they stabbed in the back to become the influential players that they are.

Two couples take a seat at our table, and thankfully, the ladies are old enough to be Dixon's grandmothers and smile politely when introductions are made. From what I can see, these people are very high up in rank, and all men, minus Dixon, are on the psychiatric board. But that might soon change because by the way they're zoning in on Dixon, they are very interested in what he has to say.

"So Dixon, Chad tells me you've got some interesting material for us to read over," says Fletcher, the older gentleman with salt and pepper hair.

Dixon coolly smiles, reaching for his wine. "Well, Chad is really too kind. But I would be absolutely honored for you to read over my work and to hear your thoughts."

"You will be amazed," Chad says in confirmation. "His findings are true brilliance, and although a little unorthodox, his reasoning is totally justifiable."

Dixon appears completely unruffled by the table singing his praises, but as he lays a hand on my knee and squeezes lightly, I know he's squirming in his seat in excitement. I look over at him and smile, and he returns the gesture, beaming from ear to ear.

Halfway through our main meal, I'm certain I'm about to gag on my lamb as the hundredth woman for the evening comes to our table to talk to Dixon. This has been going on for the past hour and a half, and up until now, I've tried my best to remain calm, but now I've had enough.

Dixon is either oblivious or blind to their deliberate flirting, but I most certainly am not. Their lingering or unnecessary touches have not gone unnoticed by me, and Rebecca seems like a puppy dog compared to these vultures.

Dixon has introduced me to everyone, but he has failed to mention I'm his "girlfriend," leaving who I am open to interpretation. Rebecca has picked up on this fact and decides now is a good time to address why that is.

"Madison, how long have you and Dixon been together?" she innocently asks, but I know there is nothing innocent about her question.

I shuffle in my seat, my eyes flicking to Dixon, who pauses talking to the bouncy blonde by his side. I bite my lip and realize we really should have worked out a credible story before we went ahead and pretended to be lovers.

"Um…" I reply, appearing as if I'm calculating the time in my head.

But Dixon stills my hands, which are twisting in my lap. "Six months," he replies, turning to look at Rebecca.

"How did you meet?"

Dixon takes a small breath, a smile overtaking his beautiful features. "Some ape was hassling her, so I sent him on his way."

"You mean you scared the living daylights out of him," I add, remembering how frightened Tim looked when confronted by a bad-ass Dixon.

The table chuckles, bar Rebecca, and Dixon grins as he addresses the table. "What can I say; he had his hands on the woman I wanted. From the moment I saw her, I knew there was something special about her. I would do almost anything to get to know her, and once I did, I fell deeper and deeper under her spell."

A breath catches in my throat, but I try to remain composed as Dixon continues.

"But it wasn't smooth sailing; I mean, like a typical male, I screwed things up to astronomical levels." He lightly squeezes my hand as the table laughs in unison. "I know she has her own demons to deal with, but here she is," he says, turning to me, his eyes glowing with pride. "Sitting by my side, supporting me unlike anyone has ever done for me before. She is my angel because every minute spent with her is truly a blessing, and one I never want to end. I'm so lucky to have met you, Madison. You give me the strength to want to be a better man," he says, no longer addressing the table, but only me.

My eyes begin to water, but I bite the inside of my cheek to stop the tears. "I'm the lucky one, Dixon," I say in a mere whisper. "And you already are a better man. You're the only man I want," I add, meaning every single word, and the table coos.

Dixon smiles, and he leans forward, brushing away a runaway tear. "Good, 'cause you're the only woman I want, *angelo*."

We're no longer in a room full of people. It's only Dixon and me, and as he returns my gaze, I realize something I've been trying to avoid for a very long time. I'm falling head over heels for Dr. Mathews. I don't throw the word "love" around loosely, but with Dixon, this feels something like it. The connection between us was instant, and no matter how hard I try to fight it, it only seems to get stronger and stronger.

"Ladies and gentlemen, we have a real treat for you this evening," the emcee announces. "Please welcome to the stage, the brilliant and well-loved genius, Dr. Maxwell Wellington."

At the mention of Dr. Wellington's name, both Dixon and I seem to snap out of our daze, bringing home the fact we're sitting in a room full of people and not alone.

"Thank you for that kind introduction," he says, looking over at the emcee. "I'll make sure to pay you later tonight." The room erupts in laughter.

Once the cackles die down, Dr. Wellington gets serious and puts on his glasses. "So I was asked to talk about my experiences and share with you lovely people my thoughts about psychiatry today. I had an entire speech prepared, and after many rehearsals, I was ready to deliver my 'wisdom' and hope my insight came across as that, and not incoherent babble."

The room once again chuckles. Dr. Wellington owns the room as he continues.

"But something occurred a few days ago and, well, this particular occurrence really opened up a can of worms."

I gulp as Dr. Wellington looks my way with a cheeky grin.

"If easily offended, I suggest you turn away now because my topic is one that may be considered a little taboo."

The room breaks out into tiny whispers, people wondering what this unthinkable topic is all about.

Dr. Wellington gestures with his wrinkled hands for silence and smiles. "I'm going to talk about…women."

Twenty minutes later, Dr. Wellington has the entire room at his mercy and eagerly awaiting his punch line. His speech has touched on the topic of men and women and why after so many years of civilization, we just can't seem to understand how the other half of the species operates.

"It's no secret that men and women are very different. And us scientists, we generally study four primary areas of difference in male and female brains. Now, I could go on and bore you with the details of what each component entails. But if I may, can I kindly ask you to look at the person beside you?"

The room does as he asks.

"Do you see that?" he questions after the room quiets down. "Whether we're male or female, at the end of the day…we're all just human beings."

When Dr. Wellington looks our way, I know that without a doubt, Dixon and I were the inspiration behind his brilliant talk. And Dixon knows it too as he turns to look at me with a mischievous smile on his handsome face.

"So what's the answer to this riddle we call relationships?" Dr. Wellington asks, rubbing his chin in thought.

The room is silent, waiting.

He smiles, his crinkled face turning up in amusement. "Who damn well knows?" he says lightheartedly. "But after fifty years of marriage, I've learned one thing." He pauses, adding to the anticipation. "Life and love aren't about waiting for the storm to pass…they're about learning to dance in the rain.

Thank you."

The room erupts into a thunderous applause, and everyone stands, clapping loudly as Dr. Wellington shuffles down the stairs. He stops by our table and gently pats me on the shoulder. "I feel a storm brewing," he cheekily says, winking at Dixon, who smirks.

The band starts playing, and everyone uses this interlude to visit the restrooms or talk to guests.

"I'm just sneaking out for a smoke," Dixon confesses into my ear. "But shh, don't tell anyone. Half of these guests would have a coronary if they knew."

I laugh and nod, loving the fact that under his smart tie and sophisticated looks, Dr. Mathews is a rebel at heart.

"I'll be back soon," he promises as he stands, placing a light kiss on my cheek.

The moment he walks away, Rebecca takes his seat.

"You two are soooo cute together," she sarcastically quips, not meaning a word.

But I play along. "Thanks."

There is an uncomfortable silence, which I prefer over Rebecca's harassment.

"I bet he's a real stud in the sack."

My cheeks flush, as nothing good can come from this conversation. "Um, yeah, he sure is," I unconvincingly reply as I nervously toy with the pendant around my neck.

"With looks like that, I bet he could get any woman he wanted. You're real lucky he chose you. I mean, you must be dynamite in bed," she casually says, wiggling her eyebrows.

"It's not like that," I pathetically reply. "Yes, the sexual chemistry is off the charts, but there's something more.

Something deeper."

"Oh yeah, I bet there's something deeper," Rebecca crudely adds, and I turn my nose up at her vulgarity.

She takes a moment to look at me, and whatever she sees must reveal the truth. "Holy shit, you're not fucking him, are you? Oh my God." She covers her mouth, attempting to mask her laughter.

Her ridicule over a touchy topic for me has my cheeks reddening further, and I lower my face, ashamed. Why does everything have to be about sex?

"Sweetheart, from one girl to another, men like that ain't gonna stick around if you're not putting out. I mean, look at him, and well, look at you," she cruelly states. "A man like Dixon wants to fuck, not talk, and if you don't give him what he wants, he'll find it elsewhere. Honey, I'm sure you can see many willing participants in this room who would happily cheat on their spouses to tend to his needs. Me included. You wanna keep a man like that? Well, you better give up the goods."

"What are you talking about?" I defensively ask, the walls closing in around me.

"I'm saying you gotta rock his world before someone else does it for you. This innocent, virginal gig is only going to last for so long."

I gasp, stunned she can read me so easily.

"Gosh, don't look so disgusted. Most women would kill to be in your shoes. Sex is power, and that power best be in your hands, not his. If you want to keep him, you'll do *whatever* it takes," she states, but I'm no longer listening to her.

I begin to feel sick, her words stirring up unwanted memories, memories I promised to deal with once I got back to

New York. But hearing Rebecca say the words I know to be true has my past torpedoing into me, and I'm going to hurl.

"Excuse me," I say, standing quickly and making a mad dash through the room.

The moment I reach the restrooms, I crouch over the toilet bowl and heave up the entire contents of my stomach. I vomit until nothing is left, but I continue to purge until I'm gagging on my tears and regret. My loud sobs echo off the bowl, and I thump the cold tiles underneath me, wishing I wasn't so fucked up and vulnerable to my past.

The dizziness kicks in, and I cover my ears, *his* words on a cruel repetitive loop, one I've been trying to silence for thirteen years.

*"You'll do this, Sunny. If you love me, you'll do this."*

# Twenty-Seven

*Dixon*

I have no idea where she is. I've searched this entire hotel for Madison, but she has vanished without a trace. The concierge has checked her room, but she's not in there, and I've tried her cell, but it goes straight to voicemail.

When I returned to the table and saw she was gone, Rebecca said she went to the restroom and would be back soon. However, when twenty minutes went by and she was still gone, I knew something was wrong.

Charging down the corridor, I see a small group of people crowding around a room. Looks of confusion and concern mar their features, and I race toward them, my heart in my throat.

"What's going on?" I bluntly ask an older lady in a lime pantsuit.

"Someone's in there," she replies, pointing at the linen closet. "Some poor girl ran in there and has locked the door. We've tried contacting staff, but they seem too busy to deal with us commoners," she adds, looking down her nose at me.

Of course they are—they're too busy with my drunken colleagues.

"Please, will you let me through?" I ask, pushing my way past the nosy bystanders.

The moment I reach the door, I squat low and place my ear against the door because I can't hear much, thanks to the murmuring crowd. As I listen closer, I hear a tiny sniffle and then some muffled words, and without a doubt, I know that Madison is inside.

"Madison? Are you in there?" I ask, trying to keep my voice soothing and calm.

When she doesn't reply, I ask again, "Madison, it's Dixon. Can you hear me?"

Still nothing.

"Should I call security?" an onlooker asks.

I hold out my hand, shaking my head. "No, I have this. Please, could you all give me a minute?"

Most comply, while others take a step back, still loitering close by, but it'll have to do.

"*Angelo*, it's me. If you can hear me, please give me a sign that you're okay. You don't have to come out. I'm right here with you. I just need to know that you're okay."

The crowd hushes, listening to me reason through a door.

I press my ear against the wood, listening closely, but hear nothing. I have to keep trying because if she doesn't reply, I'm minutes away from breaking down the door. I could call the concierge, but I really want to save her the embarrassment of the entire hotel staff knowing she's locked herself in a linen closet.

My brain churns through the reasons she would lock herself in such a confined space, and only one reason comes to mind.

She's scared.

Something happened during those few minutes while I was gone, and I hate that I wasn't there to protect her. But I'm here now, and I'll do everything in my power to make her feel safe once again.

Thinking back to when I was a child and scared, I employ the only thing that ever made the monsters go away.

I sing the nursery rhyme my mother used to sing to me when I was a child, and each and every time, she made the nightmares go away. I just hope I can do the same for Madison. Just as I'm about to sing verse two, I hear the lock on the door click open, and the crowd around me gasps.

"Please don't crowd around the door. The person inside is very important to me, and when I go in, I don't want her to think she's in some kind of freak show," I say, hoping they get the hint and leave.

I don't wait long enough to see if they listen or not because I slowly open the door and peer inside the darkened room. My eyes take a moment to adjust to the darkness, but once they do, my heart breaks when I see Madison pushed up against the far wall, her knees drawn up to her chest, her feet bare. She's rocking backward and forward, her face pressed up against her knees, and she's humming softly.

"Madison?" I whisper, pushing open the door a fraction farther.

But she continues humming with her face turned away from me.

The only way I'm going to snap her out of her near-catatonic state is by making contact with her, so I slowly crawl inside, shutting the door behind me. I can't see a thing, so I use Madison's humming as my beacon of light.

"Madison, it's Dixon. I'm not going to hurt you. I'm here to help. I'm going to come over there, okay?"

She doesn't reply, but her humming ceases.

I slowly crawl toward her, all the while cooing to her. "It'll be okay. I'm here, and I won't let anyone hurt you."

Reaching out, I gently place my hand on her leg. Her skin is icy cold, and the moment I make contact, she scurries backward but has nowhere to go because of the wall behind her.

I instantly back off, raising my hands in surrender. "Madison, you're safe. We don't have to go anywhere. I'll stay here with you until you're ready to leave. No matter how long that takes, I'll be here. I won't leave you; I promise."

I decide to make myself comfortable and sit, stretching my legs out in front of me. The sliver of light coming in from under the door is the only light source we have, and although it's dim, it's enough for me to see Madison's broken frame as she curls in on herself, not wanting to face the real world.

It goes without saying something awful happened to this beautiful creature, and I have a feeling that something is one heinous, unspeakable betrayal of the worst degree. I grind my teeth at the thought because there are only a handful of things that would evoke a breakdown such as this.

"Oh, *angelo*, what did they do to you?" I whisper, running a hand down my face and slouching in defeat.

"D-Dixon?" Madison stutters, her voice small and hoarse.

"I'm here," I reply, quickly sitting upright.

"I'm sorry," she cries. "I don't know how I ended up in here.

Last I remember, I was in the bathroom, and everything went blank. I'm so sorry."

"Shh, you have nothing to be sorry for. I'm going to come over, okay?"

"Okay."

I crawl over slowly and extend my hand until I touch Madison's knee. I breathe out a sigh of relief when her skin feels a degree warmer. "I'm just going to slip my hands underneath your knees and around your back," I say, not wanting to freak her out with any sudden movements.

"I can walk," she whispers, but I doubt that she can.

"That's okay. Let me be your knight in shining armor for the night," I reply, thankful she sounds semi-coherent.

"You already are." She surprises me as she reaches out and brushes my cheek.

Her actions inflame my heart, but I'll deal with that later because I want to get her out of here. I place my forearm under her knees and scoop her up. She comes willingly as she sags into my body, resting her head against my chest and wrapping her hands around my neck. I slowly stand and secure my hold around her and take our first step toward freedom.

I blindly reach for the door handle, making sure I keep Madison tucked firmly into me. I open the door slowly, my eyes squinting as the harsh light burns my light-sensitive pupils. They adjust within seconds, and when they do, I see a few spectators standing outside, rudely gawking. They thankfully have a good mind to move out of the way. Madison tucks herself closer into my body, hiding her face in my neck, as she is undoubtedly embarrassed by everyone staring at her.

I push my way through, not caring who I bump into, and

quickly make my way toward the elevator.

Stepping inside, I push my floor number, and the cart charges upward, the dull elevator music and Madison's soft breathing the only noises filling the cart.

Looking at our reflections in the mirrored wall, Madison's frail, fragile appearance breaks my heart.

The moment the cart stops at my floor, I step out, holding Madison's frame like a bag of gold. She tightens her grip around my nape and nuzzles into my neck, making a contented sound. My feet pound onto the carpeted floor as I make my way toward my room, and the moment I'm inside, I head straight for the bedroom and switch on the bedside lamp.

With a little maneuvering, I pull back the sheet and gently place Madison down. The moment she feels the soft sheets beneath her, she sighs and lets go of my neck, nuzzling into the pillow. She's still in her gown, but after tonight, there's no way I'm going to undress her, so I gently cover her with the sheet and comforter. She's asleep within seconds.

I stand and watch her sleeping, mourning her broken appearance. The once-radiant, confident woman now looks like a shattered, scared child.

When I'm certain she's sound asleep, I unfasten my tie and slip off my jacket and shoes. I wearily lower myself onto the floor beside her, using the bedside table as my support.

Here I'll stay, keeping my promise, protecting her until she feels safe once again.

# Twenty-Eight

## *Dixon*

I awake, my body screaming at me for sleeping on the floor. I can't remember when I fell asleep, but I do remember Madison was fairly settled when I passed out.

Looking at my watch, I see it's a little past 6 a.m., and Madison is gone. I jump up, my murky brain trying to play catch-up as I frantically search the room for where she could be.

Just as I'm about to charge out the door, I hear the toilet flushing. Madison turns off the light as she exits the bathroom, giving me a small smile when she sees me standing in the middle of the room like a raving lunatic.

"I had to use the bathroom," she explains. Tugging at the hem of my Yankees tee, she says, "I hope you don't mind."

"Not at all."

She smiles and shyly walks over to the bed, slipping under the covers, leaving me standing and staring like a fool.

"I'll be back," I quickly say, heading toward the bathroom and closing the door behind me.

Bracing my hands on the sink, I turn on the water to appear like I'm actually in here for a reason because I need a damn minute to compose myself. I process through the events of last night and know that, although Madison may not be comfortable discussing what happened, I have to at least try to get her to talk about it. From her response to whatever triggered her episode, I think it's safe to assume she's never had therapy to deal with the monsters in her closet—especially since she's hiding in closets to escape her monsters.

Brushing my teeth and washing my face, I think I've exhausted my bathroom stay long enough and quietly close the bathroom door behind me as I exit.

Madison is sitting up, leaning against the headboard, obviously awaiting my arrival. When our eyes meet, she quickly looks away, biting her lip. I give her some time to regroup and hunt through my closet for a tee and a pair of sweats. Stripping off my shirt, I quickly slip on a T-shirt and try my best to put on my sweats without flashing her.

Once I'm dressed, I make my way over to the bed and stand at the end. I remain silent, waiting for Madison to speak.

"I'm sorry, Dixon," she says after a minute of silence. "I'm so sorry I embarrassed you…"

I gesture with my hand for her to stop talking. "You have nothing to be sorry for. And you most definitely did not embarrass me. I was so worried about you," I confess, and she lowers her eyes. "What happened?" I ask, making no attempt to move.

Madison shrugs and tugs at a loose thread on the comforter.

"Did I do something wrong?" I ask, deciding to play twenty questions and hoping one of them will be the right one.

"No!" she cries, her eyes flicking up to meet mine. "No, you did nothing wrong."

"Then what happened?" I ask, imploring her to tell me.

Madison sighs before confessing, "I was talking to Rebecca, and something she said…upset me," she says, but I know talking to Rebecca was just a trigger to a deep-rooted problem.

"You know nothing that comes out of that woman's mouth is credible, right?" I assert, crossing my arms over my chest. I hold my breath and pray that she hasn't spilled the beans about Juliet.

"I know," she replies with a nod. "But it brought up some bad memories," she finally admits. "I obviously haven't dealt with them as well as I thought I had. But last night," she says, her eyes focusing on mine. "The breakdown, the tears, the near-catatonic state…that hasn't happened in a long time."

"So this has happened before?" I gently press, still making no attempt to move. Her freak-out at my apartment was so different compared to this.

"Yes." Her mouth dips into a small frown.

"Would you like to talk about it?"

Madison shakes her head violently.

I knew she would respond this way, but now that I've broached the topic, I can't let it lie. "I promise I won't psychoanalyze you. I just want to help. You need to talk about whatever happened to you, Madison. It's eating away at your existence, and before long, it'll rule who you are."

"I can't," she cries, drawing her knees up toward her to place a barricade between us.

"Yes, you can," I avow with a nod. "I know you can. The Madison I know is a survivor, a fighter, and I think it's time you let go of your fear."

Madison's lip trembles, and she sniffs back her tears. "I can't tell you...everything. I'm not ready. But I want to at least try. I want to be honest with you because you're right; my past *is* ruling my future."

"That's okay. You tell me what you can. That's the first step, which is always the hardest," I say with a small smile.

Madison takes a deep breath and nods. "My dad left us when I was five. It was only me, my mother, and my brother, Dylan. My father was the breadwinner, so when he left us, my mother was forced to work two jobs to support my brother and me. She was never home, but it was no fault of hers. She was trying her best. My brother was nine, and well, he saw himself to be the man of the house. When Mom was at work, Dylan would look after me. I really looked up to him. I mean, he was my hero."

Her use of past tense paints a picture of feelings she no longer feels. But I remain silent, allowing her to continue.

"I started developing early, much earlier than my friends. By the time I was ten, I had boobs as big as kids in the ninth grade. I guess I forgot my brother was a fourteen-year-old kid with raging hormones. I also forgot he had fourteen-year-old friends with raging hormones," she adds. "I was never shy around Dylan and never thought twice about walking around in just a towel after I showered. But why would I? I had been doing so since I was a kid. I was naïve.

"One night, Dylan had his friends over, and they were causing a commotion in his room. So I spied on them and caught them drooling over a booby blonde in a dirty magazine. I didn't really understand what they were so excited about, but I knew if Dylan caught me spying, he would be mad. I quickly went to my room and got ready for bed, and that's when Dylan came to tuck me in."

She pauses and lowers her eyes, and I know what she's about to say is going to tear out my heart.

"I was wearing my favorite Disney Princess nightie, which was two sizes too small, but I didn't care. I loved that nightie because it made me feel like a princess, and I would fantasize that one day my Prince Charming would find me and sweep me off my feet. Dylan tucked me in, and I remember a look of... arousal," she whispers, "pass over his face when he accidentally brushed against my breasts. I didn't think too much of it, but when it happened the next night and the night after that, I knew something...him...touching me was wrong."

I clench my fists by my sides, and internally count to five before I explode. Madison continues, lost in the past as she recounts her gory tale.

"Stuff...went on for three years, and I...hated it. It would always start the same. He would switch off the light, like the darkness would hide his sins. But it never did. I should have told my mom, but I...oh, God," she cries, covering her face with her hands.

I can't stay still a second longer and rush over to her side, scooping her up in my arms. She comes willingly and cries into my neck, her ice-cold body trembling in my embrace.

I don't want to coo at her and tell her it'll be all right because I know her story has only just begun. I allow her to cry and don't push for her to continue as I know tonight's confession was a big one to make. But she pulls out of my embrace, wiping her tearstained eyes.

"There's more," she says, her lower lip wavering.

"You don't have to tell me anything you don't want to," I reply, brushing her matted hair off her face.

"I know, but I want to," she sadly declares, and I nod.

Taking a deep breath, she continues. "I hated my body, and I blamed my mature figure for evoking Dylan's behavior. The bigger girls at school were teased and ridiculed, and no boys liked them, so I thought if I was like them, then maybe Dylan would stop liking me too. I gained about fifteen pounds, pigging out on all the greasy foods and desserts I could stomach without being sick."

The moment she mentions desserts, I now understand why Madison has such a sweet tooth. She used food as a defense mechanism against her incestuous brother. But I have a feeling that was only a short-term solution.

"For a while, it worked. Dylan seemed distracted, and the late-night visits stopped. I thought everything would be okay, and by this stage, Mom had met a wonderful man, and they were engaged to be married. Mom didn't have to work late nights anymore because Sebastian was filthy rich, and he wanted to provide for us. We moved into Sebastian's home a few months later, and Sebastian loved us like his own kids. I saw him as my savior because, once he entered the picture, Dylan left me the hell alone.

"However, things changed on the night of Dylan's eighteenth birthday. We had a party for him at Sebastian's house. It was a great night, and things were slowly returning to normal. After the celebrations were over, I went to bed and left my door unlocked. I'd got into the habit of locking my door, not that it mattered because Dylan would always find a way in. But that night, I felt safe enough and left my door ajar. I was stupid."

We're sitting side by side, and I can't stop myself as I reach out and brush her cheek. "Go on, but only if you want to."

Madison leans into my touch and nods.

"I had just fallen asleep but was awoken by a hand covering my mouth. I tried to scream, but I was trapped under the full weight of my drunken…brother. I tried fighting him off, but he was too strong, and after a while, I gave up," she whispers, a tear sliding down her cheek. "I should have fought harder, but I was just so scared, and I was tired of fighting him. I just wanted him to leave me alone. But that night was different. He was rough, and he wanted…more. His words haunt me till this very day," she shakily confesses. "All he said to me was, 'You'll do this, Sunny. If you love me, you'll do this.' Sunny was his nickname for me. He said I was his sunshine, which is ironic, seeing as I always felt nothing but darkness when I was near him."

I hate to even imagine what she means by "this." I try my hardest not to crowd her and allow her to finish because I know her tale is one she has never told a soul.

"I just…he raped…it hurt so bad. I should have fought harder," she repeats, shaking her head, unable to finish.

"Madison, I'm so sorry." I sigh, rubbing her arm. "This isn't your fault. It's your *brother's*," I spit, unable to say the word without clenching my teeth.

"It is my fault. I shouldn't have encouraged him. I should have told my mom. I should have done a lot of things," she cries, wiping her eyes.

"You were only a kid," I reply, wanting nothing more than

to comfort her but allowing her the space she needs.

"You don't understand. I should have told my mom because, that night, someone saw," she whispers, and I pull back, stunned by her confession.

"Someone saw you and…?" I question but can't bring myself to say the words I want to say.

"Yes," she replies, her eyes filling with new tears.

"Who?" I ask, my rage boiling to the surface.

Madison shakes her head, closing her eyes in defeat. "It was someone who should have saved me because she knew what he was doing the entire time. She saw him taking away my innocence. She heard me calling out for help. But instead of helping me, she closed the door. And the next day, she acted like she didn't witness a thing."

"Who was it?" I ask again, my fists clenched in rage. Deep down, I know who, but I need to hear it from Maddy.

"I can't. I don't want to talk about it anymore."

But I can't let this rest. I need to know who, so I can find both motherfuckers and kill them. "Tell me," I press, lightly gripping her upper arms and beseeching her to tell me.

The moment I touch her, Madison's body freezes up, and she yelps in terror. "Please let me go," she begs, choking on her fear.

I instantly let go when I realize how hard I'm holding her, and she scurries away from me, her back hitting the headboard.

"I'm sorry, Madison," I remorsefully say, hands raised in surrender. "I would never hurt you. I'm just, I—"

"You're what? Disgusted? Shocked? Think that I'm sick?" she barks, her cheeks flushed.

"What?" I ask, aghast. "No. How could you even think

that?"

"Because that's what I think of myself!" she replies angrily.

Her hurt has vanished and is now replaced with rage.

"None of this is your fault," I say again, but she cuts me off, enraged.

"Stop it! It is my fault! I should have screamed. I should have said no. I should have told my mom, but I just couldn't. After Dad left, she was a broken woman. I couldn't tell her, her son was—" she says with a repulsed look. "She worked so hard, sacrificing everything to put food on the table, and when she met Sebastian, it stopped. But still, I should have told her."

Madison covers her face with her hands, and I can see she's teetering close to the edge.

"I'm disgusting, Dixon. I'm dirty and unclean." She begins scratching at her flesh, trying to cut away her pain.

"No, you're not," I press, placing a palm over her hands as her punishing fingernails are drawing blood.

"Yes, I am!" she bellows, shrugging me off her. "How can you look at me? I'm pathetic."

Her self-hate upsets me, and I can't stop myself as I confess, "When I look at you, I see the same Madison I saw the first moment I met you—the kind, vulnerable woman I had to know. But now that I know the *real* you, I realize you're not vulnerable. You're a survivor, and you're strong."

"I'm—" she interrupts, but I cut her off.

"You're the woman I haven't stopped thinking about since we first met, and you're the woman I'm falling for," I conclude, unable to bottle my emotions.

Her mouth pops open, and mine does too, as I was not expecting that last part to slip out. But who am I kidding?

Madison has gotten under my skin from the moment I met her, and no other woman has been able to take her place.

Juliet seems like a distant memory, one which I never want to relive because this right here, this is real. It's gritty, it's raw, and it's hard, but it's everything I want because I want Madison.

"You're what?" she says, disbelief painting her face.

"You heard me," I reply, inching closer. "You've consumed every part of me."

"But I'm damaged goods, Dixon," she says, shaking her head in mistrust.

"You're perfect to me," I reply in a whisper, and I've never been more certain about anything ever before.

A stunned gasp leaves her parted lips, but I remain still. I'm too heated to make a move because the next move I make will be smashing my lips to hers.

"Dixon, I…" she says, her beautiful green eyes focusing on mine. "I…" But she doesn't fill in the blanks.

She merely lowers her face to mine and closes the distance between us. The kiss is soft and chaste, but the moment I feel her warm lips on mine, I lose all control, and nothing else matters but devouring this woman with my last breath.

I kiss her with a deep, desperate longing and feel like an inexperienced school kid as I thrust my tongue into her mouth, wanting to savor every last part of her. She returns my kiss with frantic fervor as she wraps her arms around my neck and draws me so close that not even a wisp of air could pass between us. But I like it. I like that she's showing no restraint, especially after tonight.

That thought has me backing off, however, as she just confessed her deepest, darkest secrets, and I'm pawing at her like she's a dog in heat. But the moment I do, Madison yanks on my hair and presses my face firmly to hers, not letting me go.

"Make me forget," she breathlessly pants against my lips as she pulls away. "I want it to be *your* hands, *your* mouth, *your* body I remember, not his."

How can I say no to a request such as this? But how far can I take this without freaking her out? Will she regret her decision once we're done?

She must be able to read my apprehension because she reaches for my hand and places it against her heaving chest. "Touch me. Please make new memories. Ones I won't be afraid to remember."

The last of my resolve vanishes with her honesty, and I nod, needing to take away her pain.

Wasting no time, I lower my mouth to hers, determined to make it *my* kisses she remembers, and nobody else's. She kisses me back with such fierce intensity, and as much as I try to rein in my hormones, my dick decides that's an awful idea and raises his intrigued head. I don't want to freak her out, and my impending erection will most likely do just that. But she surprises me when she reaches between us and, with gentle, bashful strokes, she lightly rubs over the bulge in my pants. I can't hide my delight at her touching me. I try to suppress my moan, but her inquisitive fingers feel too good, and a low growl slips past my parted lips.

"Does that feel okay?" she questions, the uncertainty apparent in her tone.

"It feels more than just okay," I breathlessly reply. "It feels incredible. You're incredible."

My words seem to spur her on, and her fingers wrap

around my length, softly stroking me up and down through the material of my sweats. As good as this feels, I want to be the giver, not the receiver, so I tenderly still her hand with mine.

"What's the matter?" she asks, her confused eyes opened wide.

"Lie back," I gently order, kissing the tip of her nose.

"W-Why?"

"Because I really, *really* want to go down on you," I honestly reply, while Madison blushes a bright pink hue, "and I want to make this as comfortable for you as I can."

She hesitates for a mere second, but then slowly lowers herself onto the bed, her dark hair contrasting with the white silk sheets. I take her in, not wanting to rush, but the sight of her flushed face, wild hair, heaving chest, and bare, perfect legs has me eagerly swooping forward and capturing her mouth with mine.

Being with Madison this way feels so perfect, and so right, and any other memory pales compared to what is happening between us right now. Her responsive body succumbs to my touch, and that fact has me walking my hand between us, needing to feel her bare skin. I brush over her erect nipple, and Madison groans into my mouth. I slip lower and curse my damn T-shirt for being so long because it takes me an eternity to find her skin. But the moment I do, nothing else matters.

The muscles in her supple thighs quiver under my touch, and as much as I want to savor this moment, I can't stop myself as I slowly slide my fingers over her lace underwear. She hisses, and to my surprise, she opens her legs wider, granting me access to her most personal treasure. The damp material between her legs reveals that Madison is as turned on as I am, and as I continue rubbing her through her underwear, I know she's not too far from coming.

When I break our kiss, she inhales a large gulp of air, my intense kisses starving her of oxygen. Her unsure eyes meet mine, but I don't give her time to rethink her decision. I slip my hand into her underwear and cup her wet, hot pussy. We both moan at the contact, and Madison raises her hips, silently begging me to continue. With our eyes still locked, I slowly insert my finger, her tight inner walls sucking me into the cavern of her warm body. She's incredibly tight, too tight, and I know I've entered a place no man has ever entered before. The thought sickens me because this just confirms what I knew to be true. Madison *is* a virgin, but her brother, he raped and degraded her in the worst possible way. But I push those vile thoughts aside. I won't allow that bastard to ruin this for us.

"Dixon," she moans, throwing her head back and squeezing her eyes shut.

I begin moving within her, my movements measured and paced, as I don't want to hurt her. But when she arches her back and opens her legs wider, I know measured and paced will no longer do. Tiny whimpers escape her parted lips when I work in another finger and stretch her wide. My deep intrusion is a shock to her sensitive tissues, but she doesn't stop me. She begins rotating her hips, finding a comfortable rhythm as I hungrily finger her, her wetness providing all the lubrication I need.

Her clit is swollen and needy, and as I brush my thumb over the bundle of nerves, she cries out, bucking her hips upward.

"You like that?" I hoarsely ask, my fingers moving faster and deeper within her.

"Yes," she gasps, her greedy muscles holding on tightly, not letting me go. "Please don't stop."

"Never, I'm right here with you. Let go," I gently encourage, pushing my fingers in farther and lightly circling her clit with my thumb.

The action sends her wild, and she bows her back, pumping her hips furiously to match the tempo of my punishing fingers.

"Let go, *angelo*, let go," I repeat, as I can feel her release is moments away.

Without delay, her body responds to my command, and she cries out loudly, her orgasm hitting her so hard her entire body shivers from head to toe. The sight is the hottest thing I have ever seen, and still lost in a pleasure bubble, I allow Madison to laze in her gratification for a mere second before I scoot down her body, grab her flimsy underwear, and rip them clean off. Before she has time to protest, I lap at her drenched pussy in one slow, agonizing lick. She yelps in shock, but I'm holding her prisoner until she explodes once again, and this time, it'll be on my tongue.

I bury my face deeper between her legs and simply bask in the heady fragrance of her arousal. Nothing has ever smelled or tasted sweeter, and when she shuffles away, embarrassed by her unconcealed exposure to my mouth and eyes, I latch onto her thigh, throw her other leg over my shoulder, and fasten my mouth to her glorious pussy.

She moans in approval and relaxes her body, slackening under my gentle sucks and licks. She pushes her leg out further, spread out in front of me, her pinkness glistening with her desire. I lick up her entrance and then down, and she cries out when I insert my tongue, twirling it within her writhing body.

"Oh…my…God," she gasps, taking a breath between each word.

Her pleasure spurs me on, and I dive in deeper, sucking, licking, biting, and worshipping her until Madison is shamelessly fucking my face, her body trembling under every demanding stroke I deliver. She's totally exposed, yet it's not enough, so I insert a finger, opening her up so I can gain full access to her heat.

Her tiny whimpers grow louder as I devour her with my tongue and finger, and when she subtly raises her hips, begging me to get her off, I take her clit into my mouth and suck hard. She thrashes about uncontrollably and screams out her release, her second orgasm ripping through her like a forest fire, her flesh scorching my mouth and tongue.

I growl the moment I taste her coming, lapping at her juices, not able to get enough. She writhes and moans, and as I regretfully slow down my licking, she comes down from her orgasmic high with a satiated groan.

I pull away, watching the goddess in front of me take a minute to catch her breath. Her flushed appearance has my dick throbbing in absolute desire. But this was about Madison, not me, and watching her come undone because of my actions was more of a turn-on than actually having sex. I've never wanted to please anyone as much as I have her, and after tasting her, I'm addicted.

Madison's eyes flutter open, her green jewels heavy and lust-laden.

"Hi," I say, unable to keep the smile off my face as I crawl up her body.

"Hi," she replies, her voice husky and hoarse.

I lie beside her, giving her some room because I don't want to crowd her, as I'm unsure how she'll respond to what went down between us. But she surprises me when she fists my collar and yanks me toward her, smashing her lips to mine. I kiss her back with as much enthusiasm, and when I slip in my tongue, she pulls back, covering her mouth with her hand.

"What's the matter?" I ask, puzzled.

With flushed cheeks, she replies, "I can taste…me, on… you," she manages to get out.

"It's wonderful, isn't it?" I reply with a smirk. "I'm not sure how I'll survive without your taste. One sip and I'm already addicted."

Madison lowers her eyes, and I wonder what's going through that pretty little head of hers to sour the mood.

"What's wrong?"

"I-I don't want you to survive without it," she confesses before covering her face with her hands.

With a chuckle, I uncover her face. "Well, neither do I. I'm quite certain I'll perish without it."

I'm trying to lighten the mood because what just happened between us was beautiful.

"So what now?" she asks nervously, turning on her side and leaning into her palm.

"I see there being only one answer."

"And what's that?" she quickly counters, her chest beginning to rise rapidly.

"You let me do *that*, every day from here on forward," I reply, not seeing any point in being indirect.

Madison smirks. "I think I can handle that."

"Yeah?" I ask, brushing a lock of hair off her brow.

"Yeah," she affirms. "Oh, I know this is probably not the best time, but I broke up with David." She shyly bites her lip.

I clench my jaw, his name like a kick to my balls. However, the context in which she's used it has me smiling happily. "Good because if you hadn't broken up with him, I would be forced to do it for you. And I would be doing a lot more than just breaking up with him. I would be breaking his nose as well," I add while Madison playfully rolls her eyes.

"So it's official? We're actually doing this?"

I nod.

She looks to be pondering her next sentence. "Can we take it slow? I mean, tonight was the first time I opened up emotionally…and physically," she adds with a blush.

"We'll take it as slow as you want to go. I'm here with you every step of the way. I promise."

"I'm messed up, Dixon."

"So am I," I confess. I can't erase my past, but I sure as shit can try to make amends. I can try to make amends for my manwhoring ways and also, for being an awful son.

"I can't promise I won't push you away when things get heated or too intense. But I'll try my best. I really want this to work."

"So do I," I reply, never wanting anything more.

"In that case, I give you permission to knock some sense into me if I start acting a little crazy."

"Thank you, but that's not necessary. I have complete faith in you. In us," I affirm with a nod.

"Us," she repeats with a smile. "I like the sound of that."

"Me too," I reply, my persistent erection throbbing when Madison mysteriously blushes.

She reveals the reason behind her blush when she huskily asks, "So now what?"

Rolling on top of her, I smirk when a small intake of breath gets trapped in her throat. My erection, no doubt, is the cause of her breathlessness.

"Now," I state. "I'm going to kiss you." She gasps as I tongue the shell of her ear. "I'm just not going to tell you where," I add, before taking her mouth and holding it prisoner, with no intent of ever letting go.

# Twenty-Nine

## *Dixon*

*One month later*

"And how does that make you feel?" I ask Ms. Stark, subtly glancing at the clock and internally celebrating that her time is almost up.

"I feel…" She pauses, licking her red lips. "I feel in control."

"Why?" I ask, writing a note in her file, her hazel eyes watching my every move.

"Because, Dr. Mathews, when you have a megalomaniac for a husband, being in control is something you don't experience often. I take what I can get, and at the moment, Pedro, the pool boy, is more than happy to give," she replies, her eyes dipping to my lap.

I straighten my back and nod. "Have you spoken to your husband about his controlling… tendencies?" I say, not liking the predatory look she's giving me.

"What would be the point? After twelve years of marriage,

he hasn't changed. I've just come to accept the fact my husband is a control freak, and no amount of talking to him will change anything," she confesses, uncrossing her legs and leaning forward. "What about you, Dr. Mathews? Do you have someone special in your life?"

Clearing my throat, I lean back into my chair and smile. "Ms. Stark, we're here to talk about you, not me."

"I would much rather talk about you," she replies. "I've been seeing you for a couple of months, and I know nothing about you."

"I'm your therapist, and that's all you need to know," I bluntly reply.

"But—" she counters, but I cut her off.

"Your time is up for today. If you'd like to make another appointment, please see Ms. Vale on your way out."

My response lacks tact, but quite frankly, I couldn't give a damn. She's the third woman this week to hit on me, and yes, I would once have encouraged this behavior, but now, it just makes me sick. Thankfully, she gets the message loud and clear and leaves without a single word.

"Hello, Dr. Mathews," Madison says as she ducks her head around my door.

The moment I see her, my shitty morning seems like a distant nightmare. I jump up from my leather chair and eagerly greet her with my lips as I shut the door behind her. Pressing her up against the wood, I devour her mouth, and my body hums in pleasure as she returns my affection just as passionately.

Madison and I have been taking things slow, but I'm grateful they're moving at all. After Boston, we have been seeing one another exclusively, which suits me just fine, as there is no one

I want other than her.

After much persuasion, I convinced Madison to see a psychologist, and although it's early days, I can see a vast improvement in her behavior. I meant what I said—I have complete faith in her, and in us, and no matter what obstacles are thrown our way, I'm ready to fight them.

Madison breathlessly pulls away while I groan low in my throat. I want this woman with every inch of my body, but I won't push. Yes, Madison has made substantial progress, but physically, she's still stuck in the past—a past that involves her asshole brother defiling her in unspeakable ways. I clench my jaw, thinking about what he did to her, but I rein in my temper because that's what supportive boyfriends do.

"So I just came by to say hi," she says, her beautiful smile lighting up the room.

"Well, hello," I reply, nuzzling her neck, her smell driving me wild.

She giggles, turning into my embrace. "What time is your next appointment?"

"Appointment? I have no idea what you're talking about," I playfully reply, drawing on her neck in a long, wet pull.

She gasps under my lips. "Dixon."

I sigh, pulling away with a pout. "Fine, you win. For now," I add with a wink.

She laughs once again, and I smile, loving how carefree she's become. "We still on for tonight?" she nervously asks, and once again, I restrain my seething temper.

"I wouldn't miss it for the world."

Tonight is the engagement party of her stepsister and *brother*. It is also the night I meet her mother, Rachel, and her stepfather, Sebastian. Like I mentioned, we've been taking things slow, but this is a big step for Madison, and I'm going to try my hardest not to make a scene when I meet her brother. Visions of me beating him to death with his own limbs have been playing on a loop in my head since she invited me, but I will do everything in my power to remain calm because I can only imagine how Madison feels.

She hasn't said much about her stepsister, but from what she has shared, it's safe to assume there would be no tears shed if she contracted an incurable disease and dropped dead tomorrow.

I need to be strong for Madison because I don't know how she'll react to seeing Dylan. She mentioned she hasn't seen her brother in over a year, so tonight will test her mental and physical strength. It sure as shit will test mine.

I know she's made progress, but dealing with what that bastard did to her will be an ongoing battle for her. All I can do is provide her the unconditional love and support she deserves, and show her that nothing will *ever* change my feelings toward her.

"Thank you," she says, nervously tugging on her lip. "I don't think I could do this without you."

"Yes, you could," I affirm, brushing her cheek with my thumb. "You're capable of anything you set your mind to."

"Anything?"

I nod. "Anything. I mean, you entrapped me, didn't you?" I say with a laugh when she playfully slaps my shoulder.

"I think the feeling was mutual," she replies with a dimpled smile.

"It was more than mutual," I say, my voice lowering when I

remember the first time we kissed.

"Dixon," she says, her cheeks flushing.

"Madison," I playfully counter, wrapping my arms around her waist and drawing her close. "I'll pick you up at seven?"

"Sounds like a plan," she replies, her breath hitching when I lean forward and kiss her cheek.

"Okay, well, I'll see you then." I unhappily pull away, not wanting to ever let her go.

"Can't wait," she whispers. "I'll see you tonight."

She gives me a quick peck on the lips and leaves me staring at her perfect ass as she exits my office, wondering how a son of a bitch like me ended up with someone as incredible as her.

"Are you sure we can't skip this gathering and have our own gathering at my place?" I ask, nuzzling into Madison's exposed neck as we ride the elevator to the twenty-second floor.

"I…wish." She gasps as I nip her collarbone. "But I've told my mother we're coming, and she really"—she giggles as I tongue her ear—"wants to meet you." I sigh against her neck. "We'll stay for an hour, tops."

"If we must," I reply, pulling away, my eyes dropping to her amazing breasts, which are pushed up to the high heavens in the gorgeous red strapless dress she's wearing.

"We must, although if you keep looking at me like that, I don't know if we'll make it out of this elevator anytime soon," she says, her smoky eyes doing an appraisal of my sharp Armani suit.

Just as I'm about to pounce on her offer, the elevator dings, indicating we have reached our floor. I feel Madison tense up, and my heart breaks at what she's currently going through. My brave girl is taking her first step toward freedom, and I'm with her every step of the way.

"Ready?" I ask, reaching for her hand and interlacing her fingers through mine.

"As ready as I'll ever be," she replies, squeezing my fingers and giving me a nervous smile.

"I promise I won't leave your side," I say, meaning every word.

"Thank you," she replies, and we take our first step toward the unknown.

The foyer of the ballroom where this engagement party is being held is quite stunning. This would have cost Sebastian a small fortune, no doubt, but from what Madison has shared with me about his daughter, Beth doesn't settle for anything but the best. Quite frankly, she sounds like a spoiled little bitch, but I've got bigger fish to fry—like Madison's lowlife, son of a bitch brother.

"Everything okay?" Madison whispers as we make our way toward the entrance.

"Never better," I lie, my jaw clenching.

"Well, do you think I could have my hand back?"

Looking down, I see her fingers squished under my firm grip, and I instantly loosen my hold. "I'm sorry, *angelo*," I say, lifting her fingers and kissing them gently. "I'm taking my promise of never leaving your side a little too literally," I add while she bursts out laughing.

"Madison?"

Madison and I spin around to see a stunning woman in

a navy gown approaching us quickly. Her green eyes, heart-shaped face, and gentle smile give her away. This lady is no doubt Madison's mother.

"Hi, Mom," Madison says, letting go of my hand and rushing over to her.

They tenderly embrace, and I watch, happy that Madison's excitement to see her mom is reciprocated.

"Sweetheart, you look beautiful," her mother says, pulling out of their embrace and holding her at arm's length. "I've missed you so much."

"Mom, it's only been a month," Madison replies, embarrassed.

"A month too long," she counters, affectionately rubbing her arm. "So where is this doctor friend of yours?" she asks, wiggling her eyebrows up and down. "I must meet the man who—"

But Madison cuts her off, her cheeks flushing a bright red. "Dixon," she says, looking over her mom's shoulder.

Her mother turns around, and the moment her eyes fall on me, I see approval.

"Mom, this is Dixon. Dixon, this is my mom, Rachel," Madison says as I step forward.

"It's a pleasure to meet you, Rachel," I say, advancing and kissing both her cheeks.

"Likewise," she replies, her hand fluttering over her heart. "My, my, you failed to mention what a hunk he is," she adds, turning to look at Madison.

"Mom!" Madison says, her cheeks flushing further while I chuckle.

"What?" she innocently counters.

"Let's just go inside before you mortify me any further," Madison replies, tongue in cheek.

"That's my job," she replies, giving her a kiss on the cheek.

Madison playfully rolls her eyes while her mother gives me a small smile. "You kids be good. Don't do anything I wouldn't do."

"Okay, let's leave before my mother says something embarrassing. Oh, wait a second, too late," Madison teasingly says, latching onto my arm and leading me into the ballroom while Rachel stays to talk to guests.

Laughing, I turn to give Rachel a goodbye wave, which she lightheartedly returns.

Once inside, Madison drags me over to the bar. "Please order anything you like. Alcohol will burn away the memory of meeting my mom."

"Oh, c'mon, she's not that bad," I reply with a grin.

When Madison cocks her brow, I laugh again. I order a scotch for myself and a water for Madison, and then it's time to mingle with the hundred-plus guests. Madison introduces me to family members, friends of the family, distant relatives, neighbors, and her childhood doctor, but the guests of honor are nowhere to be seen. I'm not sure if she's evading them on purpose, but as I look around this lavish affair, I see that most people are mingling among themselves, looking to be awaiting their arrival also.

"There she is," gushes a male voice, and I turn to see an older, distinguished gentleman approach us.

"Sebastian," Madison says, her smile lighting up the room.

Madison has told me about Sebastian and how he was more of a father to her than her biological father. I instantly like him, as I see nothing but love radiating from his gray eyes as he sees Madison.

"Hello, Button," he cheerfully says, and she gives him a big hug.

I stand back, allowing her to reconnect with her stepfather, as the reunion looks to be a happy one.

"We've missed you," Sebastian says, rubbing her back.

"Sorry I haven't been around. I've just been busy," she replies into his shoulder, and I hate that I know the reason she hasn't visited them for so long.

"Never mind, you're here now. You look lovely," he says and pulls away, his eyes landing on me.

"Ah, is this the doctor your mother has been raving about?" he asks, while Madison nods.

"Yes," she replies with a nervous grin. "Sebastian, this is Dixon Mathews."

Sebastian smiles and extends his hand, which I happily accept.

"It's a pleasure meeting you, Sebastian. I have heard so much about you," I say, impressed by his strong handshake.

"The pleasure is all mine, Dr. Mathews."

"Please," I say, waving him off. "Call me Dixon."

"Well, Dixon, we hope to see you around our place for dinner very soon. Anyone who can make my little Button smile this way is always welcome in our home."

"Thank you very much. I would be honored," I reply while Madison loops her arm through mine.

"Excellent. Maddy, you nut out the details with your mom, and I'll let everybody know," Sebastian says while Madison freezes up near me. "If you'll excuse me," he says, waving to somebody. "Save a dance for your old man," he adds and walks away to shake hands with Madison's neighbor.

The moment he's gone, Madison sags into me, and I wrap my arms around her. "Are you okay?" I ask, kissing the top of her head.

"No," she replies against my chest. "I was silly to think I could be normal for one night."

"Shh," I reply, pulling her out of my embrace. "You're perfect, and don't you forget it."

She smiles, but it doesn't reach her eyes, which worries me, as I'm unsure how she'll respond when she actually sees the cause of her self-doubt.

"Did you want to leave?" I ask, but Madison shakes her head.

"We can't. I don't want to upset my mom or Sebastian. I'll be okay."

"Just say the word, and we'll split," I reply, running my knuckle down her cheek.

"Thanks for being here," she says, leaning into my embrace.

"There's no place I would rather be."

"Well, well, Mad Maddy has a boyfriend," says a singsong voice to my left.

I turn quickly, instantly disliking this person, as her voice is dripping with sarcasm. I see a petite brunette in a black dress two sizes too small, but she doesn't seem to care that she's showing the entire room her pink bits.

"Hi, Mona," Madison says, her voice wavering while I glare at the trashy bimbo in front of me.

"Who are you?" Mona says, making it more than obvious she's checking me out.

"I'm Madison's boyfriend," I counter sharply. "And who might you be?"

"I'm Juliet's best friend," she replies, pursing her painted lips.

"Who the hell is Juliet?" I bark, as that name resurfaces frightful memories, ones I wish to never revisit.

Mona laughs, covering her mouth in horror. "Your story of being her 'boyfriend' would be a lot more convincing if you actually knew the name of the bride-to-be. How much do you charge?" Mona says, still laughing at her inappropriate joke.

Madison tenses up beside me, and I would be telling this leech to back the fuck off if I could speak, but I can't. A sense of dread passes over me as I replay the last five seconds over and over in my head. There must be tons of Juliets living in New York, I reason with myself. This is pure coincidence.

"I thought you said your stepsister's name was Beth?" I quickly ask Madison, ignoring Mona's chuckles.

"Um, it's just my nickname for her," she replies, nervously tugging at her diamond earring. "My silly quirk strikes again," she adds, attempting to make a joke.

"So her name *is* Juliet?" I press, not in any mood to laugh.

"Yes," Madison replies, puzzled.

*This is just a coincidence. This is just a coincidence*, I repeat to myself, as there is no way I could be *that* unlucky. I mean, what are the odds? Slim to none, I affirm. It's pure coincidence that Juliet lives in the same apartment complex as Madison. Just like it's pure coincidence that Madison's stepsister, Juliet, is a spoiled little bitch.

But just to be sure, I ask, "What is Sebastian's surname?"

Madison scrunches up her nose, confused. "It's—" But

she's cut off by the lights dimming and an emcee addressing the room.

"Ladies and gentlemen, the moment we've all been waiting for. Would you please put your hands together for the bride- and groom-to-be."

The room erupts in claps and whistles, but Madison and I are at a standoff. She doesn't understand my sudden interest in her stepsister. I try my best to smile, but as I frantically turn to look at the happy couple making their grand entrance, Madison answers my question.

"It's Harte," she whispers into my ear while my entire world crumbles around me.

# Thirty

*Dixon*

As I watch Juliet Harte be led into the room by her fiancé, Dylan Roberts, there are two things I am certain of. Number one: Karma is one messed-up, sadistic bitch, and number two: I was sleeping with the enemy.

So many emotions are running through me right now, but all I can do is clap and pretend I have no idea *who* Juliet is, and *what* Dylan is. I can feel Madison's insightful eyes watching me closely, but like the true bastard that I am, my poker face slips into place, and I remain impassive, giving nothing away.

"Do you know her?" she asks loudly to be heard over the crowd.

This is the moment of truth. I could tell Madison that Juliet was the woman I chose over her. I could also tell her what we had was shallow, hollow, and purely based on sex, unlike what I have with her. The truth would hopefully absolve me of my sins because *she's* the one I want to be with. Juliet was a mistake.

One I am now paying dearly for.

Or I could lie.

"No," I reply, shaking my head. "I've never seen her before in my life."

Madison's eyes narrow, and for a second, I think I've been caught. But when Madison smiles and says, "I didn't think you did. I know you're a better judge of character than that," I know I'm off the hook.

But why do I still feel like utter shit?

Before I have time to question my morals, Juliet and Dylan take to the stage, Dylan accepting the microphone off the emcee. Madison's tiny frame begins trembling beside me, and I wrap my arm around her waist, drawing her into my side.

I watch with distaste as Juliet canoodles into Dylan. "Hi, everyone," Dylan says, addressing the room with a carefree smile. "On behalf of my beautiful fiancée and I, I would like to thank each and every one of you for attending this special occasion. As you know, we're here to celebrate our engagement," he says while the crowd claps and cheers. "But tonight, we're also celebrating another milestone."

Madison's tremors continue, and I hug her closer into my side, never wanting to let her go.

"I'll let my bride-to-be be the bearer of the good news," Dylan says, passing the microphone to Juliet.

Juliet beams, and I have never seen her so…happy. Never once did she smile at me the way she's smiling at Dylan, not that I care. But I guess this just brings home the fact she was using me as much as I was using her. I suddenly feel so dirty, and my filth is polluting the innocent girl beside me.

Juliet happily accepts the microphone, basking in the

limelight and loving the attention. Her eyes casually scan the crowd, and just when things couldn't possibly get any worse, Juliet's eyes land on me. I remain expressionless, refusing to give anything away, as I know this is too important to her, and she'll let nothing stand in the way of her happily ever after.

Like the true actress that she is, she raises the microphone to her lips, her eyes never wavering from mine. "I'm pregnant!"

The crowd gasps, but the biggest gasp comes from me when Juliet removes her lace shawl and reveals a small baby bump. Judging from her size, she would be roughly three months. And three months ago, I was fucking her.

Juliet watches my face as the cold, hard truth hits home, and she grins, smugly raising both brows.

"This is sick," Madison spits, twisting out of my embrace.

I panic, afraid she's seen mine and Juliet's exchange. "Let's go," I say, latching onto her hand and weaving through the crowd to reach the exit.

Thankfully, she doesn't fight me, and it seems she wants to escape this suffocating environment as much as I do. The moment we reach the door, a sense of relief overwhelms me, and getting away from this toxic situation is all that matters.

As I yank on her hand and pull her out into the foyer, Madison slows down, her heels digging into the plush carpet. "Wait for a second," she says, attempting to catch her breath. "I just need a minute."

Goddammit, we don't have a minute. If I know Juliet, she'll be out here in seconds, wanting to rub my face in the mess I've made.

"You can rest in the car," I press, lightly pulling her toward the elevators.

When she looks at me, confusion marring her perfect features, I explain, "I hate seeing you this way, Madison. Look at you, you're shaken up." And I gesture with my chin to her shaking hands.

She wrings her hands together and nods. "You're right. I should find my mom, though, and tell her I'm leaving."

Just as I'm about to refuse, a shiver passes down my spine, and the cause of that shiver is the woman who knows too much.

"Leaving so soon?" Juliet purrs, and I close my eyes, cursing the damn day she walked into my office.

Madison sighs, and I open my eyes, ready to face whatever this whore is about to throw my way.

"Yes," Madison replies, and I'm proud of her bravery.

"Aren't you going to introduce me to your friend?" Juliet asks, a wicked smile turning up her lips.

Madison looks up at me, and I nod, silently giving her the courage she needs. "This is my b-boyfriend, Dixon," she says while Juliet raises a brow.

I have no doubt she's mentally calculating how long we've been together, and whether Madison was the cause of me ending our fling. The question is, is she going to tell her?

Juliet tilts her head to one side, and as she sizes me up, I realize my fate is in her hands. I hate that this troublesome little bitch can make or break the best thing that has ever happened to me.

"Boyfriend?" she asks, and I silently plead with her to find whatever compassion she may have, and not ruin my chance at happiness.

"Yes," Madison replies, looping her arm through mine.

"Isn't he…?" Juliet says, leaving the sentence hanging while

I hold my breath.

Madison and I both wait for Juliet to continue, and just when I think she won't, she concludes, "Too old for you?"

Madison scoffs while I let out the pent-up breath I was holding. If that's what she wants to pick at, then so be it.

"He's perfect," Madison counters, challenging Juliet to argue.

Madison is so far from the truth, it's not even funny. As touched as I am that she feels the need to defend my honor, I know this conversation must end before Juliet reveals just how imperfect I really am.

"Shall we go?" I ask Madison, needing this nightmare to end.

Thankfully, she replies, "Sure," her eyes never leaving Juliet's.

"Um, Dixon," Juliet says as we turn to leave.

"Yes?" I reply, my back turned to her, trying my best to remain calm.

"Can I have a word with you?" she asks while Madison spins around to face her.

"Why?" she angrily questions. "You have no business speaking to him."

"It's fine, Madison," I quickly say, slowly turning around and meeting the eyes of Satan herself.

"In private," Juliet adds with a smirk, crossing her arms over her chest.

"Absolutely not!" Madison snarls, storming forward, but I latch onto her bicep to stop her rampage. "Dixon?" she says, the horror painting her face as she looks at me over her shoulder.

"It's fine. Whatever she has to say will never change the

way I feel about you. Go downstairs and wait for me, okay? I promise, I won't be long," I assure her. "Trust me?"

"Of course I do," she whispers, and her honesty touches me in a way I never thought possible.

The thought of losing Madison tears a huge, gaping hole in my chest. Juliet now has the power to decide my fate, and I can only hope she shows me some mercy when she makes her decision.

"I'll wait for you downstairs," Madison unhappily states, her lower lip trembling.

"*Angelo*," I say as she turns to leave.

She spins around to face me, and I can see the hope behind her eyes that I've changed my mind. I wish I could, but I can't. My hands are chained, and Juliet is the holder of the key.

Madison waits for me to say something, anything, but I can't. There are no words to express how sorry I am. So I let my actions speak for me. In two strides, I'm on her, wrapping my arms around her in a near-suffocating embrace and lowering my hungry mouth to hers. She kisses me back with as much enthusiasm, both of us needing to prove a point to Juliet. She may have the upper hand, but what Madison and I have is real, and it'll take a lot more than a scorned bitch like her to break what we have.

I'm the one to break our kiss, and Madison protests, her plump lower lip dipping into an adorable pout.

"Just giving you a taste of what's to come," I whisper, kissing the tip of her nose. "I'll see you soon."

Madison nods, her eyes filled with concern, but she turns and leaves me alone with the Antichrist in heels.

"What do you want?" I hiss the moment Madison enters

the elevator.

"Is that any way to talk to family?" Juliet sarcastically replies.

"You are *not* my family," I sneer, as she doesn't know the first thing about kin.

"Whatever, I don't have time for chitchat." She gives a small wave to an elderly couple as they walk past us, appearing unaffected by this fucked-up situation.

"Then get to the point," I snap, loosening my tie.

"Ooh, you were always so demanding," she says, a wicked smile passing over her sinful lips. "I'm sure you remember. Or does your memory need refreshing?"

She runs a fingernail down my shoulder while I swat her hand away, not caring if anyone sees me. "Do *not* touch me. You want to talk, then talk. I'm running out of time and patience."

"You better be nice to me, Dixon. I mean, we share a secret that only you and I know about." She cups her belly.

"That baby is *not* mine," I whisper, my eyes dropping to her bump in disgust.

"How do you know? Do you need reminding of all the dirty, disgusting ways you fucked me without protection?" she whispers, stepping close while I take a step back. "Maybe if you hadn't been so mean to me when I saw you last, this wouldn't be so awkward. I can't believe that *she* was your sleepover buddy. How sad for you."

"What do you want?" I repeat, not in the mood for games.

"I won't tell anyone about us," she says, which surprises me.

"What's the catch?" I ask, knowing someone like Juliet doesn't do anything unless it benefits her.

"No catch, but I may just call in a favor every now and then."

"What kind of favor?" I ask, clenching my jaw, unsure where this conversation is going.

"I really liked you, Dixon, and what we had was…fun."

"No fucking way," I spit out, disgusted. "I will never touch you *ever* again. Blackmail me all you want, but I will never, ever cheat on Madison, you hear me?"

"We'll see," Juliet chirps. Her confidence, which I once found alluring, is now turning my stomach.

"Why?" I question, stepping forward. "You're getting married, for fuck's sake. Go fuck your husband and leave me the hell alone."

"I love Dylan, I really do, but he's in love with someone else. He always has been, and I need to change that," she confesses, and my mouth drops open in shock.

He's in *love* with her?

"You're sick," I sneer, repulsed I voluntarily stuck my dick in this woman.

"Oh, I know, Dr. Mathews. Remember where we met? I asked for your help, and you helped me by fucking me in every unimaginable way possible. And I liked it."

I lower my eyes, disgusted in myself for ever consorting with this sick, twisted woman.

"What we had was consensual. Why are you making it out to be more than what it really was? It was sex, Juliet. Nothing more. Nothing less."

"You're right, and I was happy to let things be. But the fact you chose that sniveling little bitch over me hurts. I'm always second best. I'm never good enough for anyone, and I'm sick of being runner-up. I'm especially sick of being runner-up to *her*," she spits, angered.

Our conversation in my office all those months ago comes flooding back. It was right before we started doing whatever the hell we did for those two and a half months. Juliet confessed she was never good enough for anyone, and I now know that *anyone* was Dylan.

Juliet's smug voice snaps me out of my thoughts. "I'll make you a deal. I'll keep my fiancé away from your little girlfriend, and you make sure to keep her far away from him, and everyone is happy."

"What are you talking about?" I snarl. Madison told me she hasn't seen Dylan for over a year.

"Oh, didn't you hear? Dylan is moving in with me," she explains. I'm about to be sick.

That parasitic motherfucker living in the same apartment complex as Madison will undo whatever progress she's made. The fact she might bump into him will no doubt scare the living hell out of her. Not to mention the fear he might break into her room, just like he did when they were kids, will send her crazy. She'll be reliving her childhood all over again, and in the end, it'll kill her.

Juliet sees my resolve slipping and smirks. "All you have to do is make yourself available to me when I need you, and we can continue playing happy families."

"Why are you doing this?" I ask, although I know why. It's the reason she came to see me in the first place. This is about power and control.

And as if on cue, she replies, "Because I can. I told you you'd be back and begging for a second chance. Although, to be fair, I never thought you'd be groveling instead of begging."

My face contorts in rage, and she laughs.

"You really didn't think it would be that easy to get rid of me, did you? You're *my* bitch now," she concludes, discreetly reaching forward and grabbing my balls.

"This is blackmail," I wheeze, my nuts held prisoner in Juliet's grip.

"Karma's a bitch, Dr. Mathews."

"I'll tell Madison everything," I threaten because I am no one's bitch.

I will protect Madison at whatever cost. Hell, she can move in with me.

"Go ahead," Juliet says with a careless shrug. "I'm sure the medical board would love to hear all about how you fucked a patient."

My face whitens, and Juliet's mouth widens in surprise. "Ooh, so I'm not the first? Goddamn, you're a bad, bad boy, Dr. Mathews. I'm sure little Miss Goody Two-shoes would love to hear all about your unethical practices."

Juliet has me by the balls, literally, and I have no way out of this. Even if I tell Madison the truth, that doesn't stop Juliet from ratting me out to the board if I don't do what she wants. She's a scorned woman out for revenge, and I have no one to blame but myself.

"Fine," I snarl, taking a step back. My balls protest with the movement. "You win."

Juliet gasps, stunned I would cause myself more pain, but the physical pain pales compared to what this deal is doing to my humanity. "But just so we're clear, I'm *no one's* bitch. You just signed a deal with the devil, sweetheart," I sneer, getting into her face, not caring who's watching. "You better buckle up because it's going to be a bumpy ride."

Juliet's face pales, and I know the hatred I feel for her radiates out of every pore in my body. But I will do whatever it takes to protect Madison, even sell my own soul for her freedom.

"I'll see you around," I sneer, inches from her face. She takes a step back.

I grin because she has no idea who she's messing with.

She quickly recovers when the elderly couple returns, eyeing us suspiciously. "I'll be in touch," she whispers.

"Can't wait." I snicker.

"If you have any pride, you'll leave with your head held high," she smartly says, repeating my parting words to her.

"Fuck you."

"Oh, I plan to," she replies arrogantly.

She throws me a wink over her shoulder before casually sauntering off like she didn't just blackmail me into being her lapdog.

I need to get out of here. I'm seconds away from losing my shit, and before I do anything rash, I need to think. I charge toward the staircase, needing the physical burn of twenty-two flights of stairs to assure me that I'm still human.

What did I just agree to?

I just signed my soul over to Lucifer herself, and I don't know what to do. There is no way I can do what Juliet is proposing. I can't. I can't touch her the way she wants me to because I'm no longer that man. Madison has changed me, and I've never felt so alive. But what other choice do I have?

Juliet has the power to destroy my personal life *and* my career. Even if her claims fall on deaf ears, they'll plant the seed of doubt, and once planted, my reputation will be ruined. This is not a forgiving world we live in, especially when you live amongst rich, judgmental pricks.

At floor fourteen, I realize I'm fucked.

My sordid past has come back to bite me in the ass, and I have no one to blame but myself. I could blame Lily, or my mother's death, for behaving like an immoral whore, but that would be a cop-out, an excuse. I did the things I did because I liked them. If the tables were turned and *I* was the one facing the judgmental chair, I would diagnose myself as being an addict of the worst kind.

I'm addicted to sin.

My body is dripping in perspiration and shaking in rage as I shoulder open the door and frantically search the foyer for Madison. The moment I see her, my heart sinks in regret because I see her leaning against a wall, crying.

Has Juliet had second thoughts and gone ahead and told her what a filthy bastard I really am?

"Madison?" I anxiously call, charging over to her.

She quickly turns my way, and I hold my breath, unsure of what I'll see reflected in her eyes. But I exhale softly when I see only relief and happiness flash across her troubled face.

"Dixon," she cries, meeting me halfway. "Did you take the stairs?" She sniffs, looking at my disheveled state.

"Ah, yes. The elevator was taking too long, and I couldn't wait to see you. Why are you crying, *angelo*?" I ask, brushing a tear away.

She lowers her face, and I raise her chin with my fingertips. "What's wrong?"

"I…I thought you had second thoughts."

"About us?" I ask, horrified.

"Yes," she confesses, a tear spilling down her cheek.

"Why on earth would you think that?" I coo, wiping away her tear.

"Because of Beth," she sadly admits. "She's toxic, Dixon. Everything she touches turns to shit."

"Well, you've got nothing to worry about," I affirm, pulling her into my arms. "She will *never* touch me," I conclude, meaning every word.

"What did she want to talk to you about?" she muffles against my chest.

"It's not important. The only thing that matters is you. It's been a big night. I'll take you home," I say, needing to get as far away from Juliet as possible.

"Can I stay at your place?" she asks nervously.

Normally, I would be overjoyed at her confidence, but now, I just feel undeserving. But how can I say no? "Of course," I reply. "I would like nothing more." Still in my arms, I can't help but ask her, "Why Beth?"

Madison sniffs, wrapping her arms tighter around my waist. "Apparently, her mom named her after Juliet Capulet. The reason for this, according to Juliet, was because she was exceptionally beautiful and would capture the heart of any man. Friend or foe," she adds, and I can't help but snicker at Juliet's arrogance.

"Anyway, Mary and I decided that Macbeth was a better-suited Shakespearean character for her. And when I say Macbeth, I mean Lady Macbeth. Lady Macbeth is ambitious, manipulative, and evil. And she's also in cahoots with the witches. Therefore, Beth stuck, as it's better suited than Juliet."

"I think you've chosen well," I spit. Madison pulls away, looking up at me curiously. I don't elaborate. I do, however, ask her, “What’s my nickname?”

She thinks about it for a moment and smiles. “You’re just Dixon.”

“Really? I don’t get a special name?” I question with a staged frown.

Madison reaches up and lays her palm against my cheek. “Your name is special enough,” she sincerely confesses while my heart shatters.

# Thirty-One

*Dixon*

In life, you're given a choice to do good, or to do evil. And whatever choice you make, impacts your entire future.

If I knew then what I know now, would I have chosen differently?

Looking down at the sleeping angel beside me, I know the answer is yes. I would have done so many things differently. But that's the thing about hindsight: No one has a crystal ball to predict if your decision was the right one to make. You simply have to live with the consequences and deal with the life you've chosen to live.

So choose wisely, my friends because once you've chosen… there's no turning back. So what choice did I make?

There was only ever one choice to make.

My hand was forced and now…it's time to be wicked.

*What greater punishment is there than life when you've lost everything that made it worth living?*

*Romeo and Juliet, William Shakespeare.*

# Acknowledgements

My author family: Elle and Vi—I love you both very much.

My ever-supporting parents. You guys are the best. I am who I am because of you. I love you. RIP Papa. Gone but never forgotten. You're in my heart. Always.

My agent, Kimberly Brower from Brower Literary & Management. Thank you for your patience and thank you for being an amazing human being.

Sommer Stein, you NAILED this cover! Thank you for being so patient and making the process so fun. I'm sorry for annoying you constantly.

My editor, Jenny Sims. What can I say other than I LOVE YOU! Thank you for everything. You go above and beyond for me.

My publicist—Sarah Ferguson from Social Butterfly PR. Thank you for all your help.

Danielle Sanchez from Wildfire Marketing Solutions—You are amazing. I would be lost without you.

To the endless blogs that have supported me since day one—You guys rock my world.

My bookstagrammers—Your creativity astounds me. The effort you go to is just amazing. Thank you for the posts, the teasers, the support, the messages, the love, the EVERYTHING! I see what you do, and I am so, so thankful.

My ARC TEAM—You guys are THE BEST! Thanks for all the support.

My reader group—sending you all a big kiss.

Samantha and Amelia—I love you both so very much.

Michelle, you're my soul mate. I love you always. Thanks for saving me.

David and Michelle, you SLAYED this cover!

My fur babies—mamma loves you so much! Dacca, I know you're hanging with Jaggy, Dina, Ninja, and Papa.

To anyone I have missed, I'm sorry. It wasn't intentional!

Last but certainly not least, I want to thank YOU! Thank you for welcoming me into your hearts and homes. My readers are the BEST readers in this entire universe! Love you all!

# About the Author

Monica James spent her youth devouring the works of Anne Rice, William Shakespeare, and Emily Dickinson.

When she is not writing, Monica is busy running her own business, but she always finds a balance between the two. She enjoys writing honest, heartfelt, and turbulent stories, hoping to leave an imprint on her readers. She draws her inspiration from life.

She is a bestselling author in the U.S.A., Australia, Canada, France, Germany, Israel, and The U.K.

Monica James resides in Melbourne, Australia, with her wonderful family, and menagerie of animals. She is slightly obsessed with cats, chucks, and lip gloss, and secretly wishes she was a ninja on the weekends.

# Connect with Monica James

**Website:** authormonicajames.com

**Instagram:** @authormonicajames

**Facebook:** facebook.com/authormonicajames

**Twitter:** twitter.com/monicajames81

**Goodreads:** goodreads.com/MonicaJames

**TikTok:** @authormonicajames

**BookBub:** bookbub.com/authors/monica-james

**Amazon:** https://amzn.to/2EWZSyS

**Join my Reader Group:** http://bit.ly/2nUaRyi

www.ingramcontent.com/pod-product-compliance
Lightning Source LLC
Chambersburg PA
CBHW070205120726
47909CB00001B/262

* 9 7 8 0 6 4 5 5 0 8 2 1 5 *